Fragile Lives
Mark Dennis

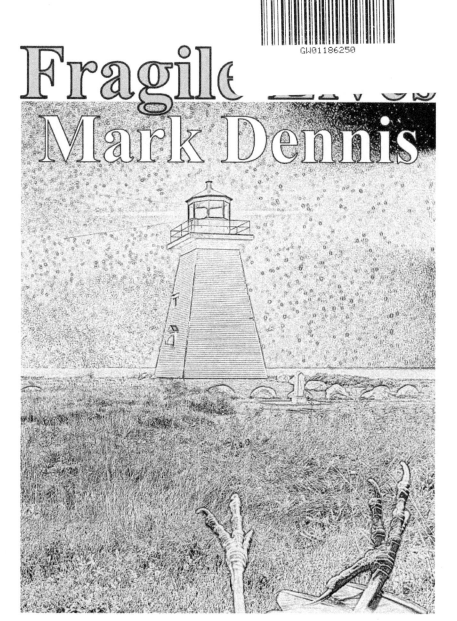

The Sixth Nova Scotia Birder Mystery Novel

Copyright © 2024

Mark Dennis

All rights reserved.

BOOKS IN THIS SERIES

The Frigatebird

Nor'easter

Sea Glass

The Collector

The Final Tick

Fragile Lives

Coming next:

The Chaser

TO...

Sandra

(Dennis) - just to clarify which one!

PREFACE

When I wrote 'The Frigatebird', it was a story based on a simple idea. To understand the idea, you need to read it- but if you're now digging into book six in the Nova Scotia Birder Mystery series, I probably don't need to explain too much to you.

In 'The Frigatebird', stories and people developed, became friends or at least people who I might nod to in a crowd. Then 'Nor'easter' came along and events with major characters moved on apace. We got some back stories as well as some front. New characters were delivered, literally, and the people in the stories became much more solid.

Writing the series as birder mysteries wasn't quite the challenge some people might imagine. As a birder myself, a real one so basically one-dimensional, I knew how to present the bird-side of the story. Too many books in the genre revert to expected cliches for characters, some are just awful. In what I now call 'the Cross series', you get the bird writing presented correctly and the police part near enough, because it really isn't a police procedural.

Book three came along, and in 'Sea Glass' I wanted to be more bird political, and I was. Piping Plovers are a part of the theme, as is the wanton destruction of our planet. By now, my pool of active birders had expanded, and new characters created, possibly and unintentionally, from bits of real people. Nobody in my books is present in real life, but certainly some show the characteristics of, as we birders like to say. Book four, 'The Collector', again went political. Bird collecting is abhorrent to me and all compassionate naturalists. As in all the books I had to think who might be disposable, because an important part of any writing involving crime is to not worry about killing someone, if only in print.

Writing 'The Final Tick' was, perhaps, the hardest book to do. Not only because it has events that affect potential future books, but also because my pool of possible Nova Scotia birds that people could chase and still maintain their enthusiasm for was shrinking fast. As a story I like it, and it carries things nicely into this book.

'Fragile Lives' is a shade darker story than those found in any previous books, although perhaps, 'Nor'easter' might just about match it. Both have troubling content. Lives in both books can turn in the blink of an eye, and they do. In 'Fragile Lives' I try to draw a parallel on how both the life of the main protagonist and that of a migrating bird can change dramatically, it's all down to small decisions. You'll need to read on to see whether I manage to get the point I'm trying to make across or not.

Mark Dennis

Clam Point, NS, April 2024

CHAPTER ONE

Early July 2022

Tiff O'Toole checked her uniform for creases. It looked ok, it usually did, and she knew that she was just trying to fill in the time, rather than think about why she'd been summoned to see Madam. The admin woman wasn't very warm, she didn't smile when Tiff announced her arrival and, when it was time to go in, she got a curt, "She'll see you now, no need to knock".

Tiff approached the door and tried to stand tall. Fighting the instinct to knock and failing, her light tap was almost apologetic. "Tiff, please", came the voice from within.

"Ma'am", said Tiff, almost dropping a curtsey. This was surely her being told that she wasn't going to Kentville after all, or maybe the big boss was going to tell her that she didn't have what it took to be in the police service. Tiff had already decided that she'd fight her corner, if that was the case.

"Take a seat". Carmel Morrell waited until the obviously nervous officer had perched on the very edge of a chair on the other side of the desk. "Tiff, I'm minded to give you a special assignment. I've spoken to your mom, not because she's your mom but because she's an experienced officer who I admire, and she says you're up to it. You can say no, but please indulge me for a moment".

"Ma'am".

"Yes, good. How do you feel about going undercover?"

"A drugs thing? Only I'm not trained, Ma'am". Tiff was a bit taken aback. This was not what she'd expected when summoned to Madam's office, although it was a lot better than some of the scenarios she'd been imagining.

"No, not drugs, I just need you to be a woman who needs a helping hand somewhere", and Carmel went through the Juliette Barker case in fine detail. "You need to look a bit out of it, used, can you do that?"

Tiff considered this, carefully. "I suppose so, you should see me the morning after a few cocktails at Club 98. What would I be doing exactly?"

"Listening, reporting back, moving around the women's refuge system. You only report to me. Nobody else needs to know what you're doing or where you are. The cover for everyone else, bar mom, is that I sent you on secondment for experience, prior to you joining Howey Cross's team in Kentville. Interested?" Tiff looked a lot more enthusiastic as the assignment was explained. This was more like it; this was what she'd joined the police to do.

"Shit, yes. Oops, sorry Ma'am". Tiff looked a bit shamefaced at uttering a swearword in front of the big boss, but Carmel didn't seem to have noticed it.

"Good, is there a boyfriend that might miss you? There was a Michel, I understand".

"Not anymore, Ma'am. Can I ask why I'm not reporting to Staff Sergeant Cross?" This was the thing that worried her. She really didn't want to put her new boss's back up before she'd even joined his team.

"That's for me to deal with, Tiff. Be assured that I will be passing on anything you get, think of it as a two-pronged attack. The official visits will stir up the waters, you, when you can, will keep them spinning. If you do find Barker, and you might, you call it in. Full back up, no being a hero. You won't last long in the force if you can't follow instructions to the letter, understand?"

"Yes, Ma'am, but if you know me, which you seem to, you'll know I'm not stupid. When do I start?"

"You already have. See Janice outside, she's not really as miserable as she appears, she'll give you your first location. The people who run The Mill in Truro know you're coming and are taking you as a personal favour to me to get you into the system. Don't stay there too long, get your story out but don't seem too willing to talk. Watch out for those wanting more than just friendship or offering anything, if a situation looks to be developing, get out. Oh, and in case you were worried, your mom has your cat for the duration. Good luck, Tiff, find us Juliette Barker".

"Yes, Ma'am". Tiff got up and headed for the door, squaring her shoulders as she went. Carmel noticed but decided to say nothing, she'd learn. Next up was to talk to Cross, once he got back from Brazil. The Barker case had been hanging around for too long and it was time they took it in hand, whatever the personal cost might be.

CHAPTER TWO

Mid July 2022

Greg Barnes' phone pinged as eBird delivered another Nova Scotia list needs alert. Like most active birders, and despite him being the person who was head-overseer of eBird in Nova Scotia, Greg had an hourly needs alert set up, in theory so he didn't miss any year birds for his big year. He had a quick look and saw that it was for a Variable Seedeater, ah, another one of those things. For some reason, various eBird users, and some on Facebook, seemed prepared to jump through hoops to go for the least likely species when seeking an ID. Google Lens and the Merlin app had a lot to answer for. Another ping told him it had started, the mini avalanche of comments. He knew that some close to him seemed to think it was his fault that a robin-fondler somewhere kept seeing Black-chinned Hummingbirds, or another person insisted that he was seeing an Ivory-billed Woodpecker. At least it was easy to dismiss such things, but casually sorting the birding dross from the true was always a dangerous exercise, because one day the outlandish report on eBird or Facebook might just be correct.

Tina Peck, President of the Nova Scotia Bird Group, sent out a text. 'I should tell the group that Maisie messaged me again and said the strange bird was still there, she said she'll tell me every day until it goes. She didn't call it a pratincole this time, in fact she just called it 'the bird'. I asked her what she was using, binocs-wise, she only has a pair of compact binocs which she admits are awful, but she's ordered some new ones on-line. We may have new birder in the making here, I think it might be a good idea if someone with time, and living near-ish, went over for a look?' Tina thought she might be wasting her time posting to the informal Nova-Rarity group on Messenger. They all seemed to have dismissed the pratincole as more 'no field guide' silliness and had now moved on to disabusing a claim of a Mountain Chickadee somewhere. Still, it was worth a try, wasn't it?

The silence was deafening.

Howey Cross walked across the parking lot and into the Kentville precinct, looking around. It felt odd to be starting his work week on a Thursday, but 'needs must' when the plane doesn't fly on schedule. Madam had promised and Madam had delivered. Kentville and all it encompassed was his, at least until his Chief of Police, Aldrick Chetwynd's, back had healed and he learned to walk again. That was a little bridge to cross for the future.

In the main office Leah Brown was in early too, waiting for him. As soon as he came through the door she was up and at him straight away, walking with him to his new office and carrying a bundle of files, each desperately needing his attention. "Good morning, Leah. First question, what happened to Gooding?"

"He's recovered from his splinter and gone. Disciplinary pending, he didn't press charges on his wife, so she's fine. Roberts comes next week permanently but she will be in tomorrow for your first joint sergeants' meeting. Darren is in a bit later today, dentist, he can mumble all about it when you see him. Bad news on the Tiff front. Madam decided she needed to see life, raw in tooth and claw, and sent her into the wilderness for a while, multiple short placements to, and I quote, 'get Digby out of her head and her hair'. I gave your sergeants the 10am slot tomorrow unless you decide otherwise. I, figured you'd be up to speed with everything by then. All that's left to say is that the new Emperor has arrived, all hail. Anything you need from me, boss, anything at all, just say. You know I'm only your acting PA until Janet gets back from maternity, right?"

"I do and I'm grateful to you for taking me in hand. I'll try not to be too needy, however, now that I am about to take my throne, I'll need a hundred peeled grapes and a pliant concubine to soothe my furrowed brow. Tell me Leah, do you perhaps have a concubine outfit yourself somewhere?"

"For you, Howey, I'll get straight on to Amazon and order a new one. With my prime account I can be kitted out and attending to your every need by Wednesday, sometime before 8pm, although I hope you're not expecting a virgin". Cross and Leah had what you might call a flirty relationship, it was consensual, and it made them both laugh, much to the embarrassment of Kent Chivers, Leah's not-so-little brother.

"Kent, how's he doing in Yarmouth? He does know it's only a secondment, I definitely want him back here".

"He's enjoying it, but he wonders where you'll fit another sergeant".

"Me too, but I'm sure we'll work something out. I'll take an hour's peace to catch up, then address the ground troops. Is Regis scheduled as I asked?"

"He is and we've set him up a workstation. Darren has taken him out in the field a couple of times, he seems very happy to still be here, lucky too, I'd say. Anyone else would want to be rid of the past".

"Regis has the local knowledge and wants to be involved, it's not all me being philanthropic. I want that knowledge, and, over time and if he stays happy with his role here, I'll get it. Think of it as a symbiotic relationship until it's dissolved at a time of our mutual choosing. Anything else?"

"Not that Darren couldn't deal with, he filled in admirably while you were away. Madam is coming over shortly, so it's 'all hands on deck' time. She seems to like you, Howey, an ally perhaps?"

Cross wasn't answering questions of that nature, not until he knew the answer himself. "Good, I look forward to her arrival, thanks Leah. I'll start the paper backlog once I've got a coffee".

"Luckily, I just brewed a fresh pot Howey. Help yourself".

Cross grinned. He didn't expect anyone to make him a coffee, but if anyone offered, he'd accept. Leah wasn't expected to make anyone coffee either, unless she wanted to, and that was exactly the sort of staff sergeant he wanted to be.

Carmel Morrell was quite subdued when she parked up at Kentville, the case files on her passenger seat had a well-thumbed look about them. It was fair to say that she knew the details off by heart, in fact they'd been stuck in her head for some time now. Checking her look in her mirror, she climbed out of her Jeep and straightened her uniform, by the time she was walking into the police station she'd transformed into 'the big cheese from the RCMP'. "Hello, Leah, how is he?"

"In very good spirits, Ma'am, the break did him good. He even has a bit of a tan giving him a hint of that sexy Latino look, although I've not seen him with his shirt off, yet". Carmel laughed. She knew all about Leah, in fact she knew all about most of the important players in Nova Scotia policing, and the rising stars- it was all a part of her job.

"Any observations?"

"Nothing to report so far, He got straight into the role and is being kept busy. Howey is clearly intent on remodeling the place in his own magnificent image".

Morrell wasn't surprised to hear that things were being reshaped already. Howey Cross was very capable and an advanced project of hers, one that would see him, along with a number of other officers she kept an eye on, ready and able to take the senior reins, when and if she decided to go. Grooming a pool of successors was an important part of the process, if you wanted to maintain continuity. When she got to Cross's office, the door was already open, so she breezed straight in. She knew it was a clever move by Cross, it said 'I won't have you knock and just walk in whatever your rank, so the open door is my invitation to you to enter'.

Without looking up, Cross stopped what he was doing and stood. "Ma'am".

"Carmel now, Howey, no more Ma'am please, sit. You had a good break? I see you've started to reorganise the place, and from what I hear already, I'm not expecting to have people banging on doors telling people we have a monster in our midst. I'd say that was a good start. How do you feel, about taking the seat of power, in control or overwhelmed?"

"Too early to say, Carmel. I'll have to get to grips with not being able to just grab my jacket and follow my nose, but it will come, and I will be involved in cases if I think I can make a difference in the field, otherwise I'll trust my sergeants and they, hopefully, will trust me".

"Glad to hear it. I can't interfere here, unless I must, that's my assurance to you. Pleasantries over then, to business. I know that we are creeping along with the remaining hunter cold cases and that we have several ongoing investigations into various local crimes underway, but there's a case that I want you to look at as a matter of urgency. I know you've had it in the back of your mind since you were called in, back in 2019".

"Juliette Barker?"

"Yes. I've reviewed everything we have multiple times since she vanished and there hasn't been anything solid suggesting that she's still in Nova Scotia, just rumours. Naturally, we all wondered how she could just vanish like that, the truth is you can't without some help. I thought your team might take another look at the women's refuge system, just in case anything was missed last time, I'm sure it was. Did you ever visit Barker's house in Bay Avenue, Annapolis Royal?"

"I didn't, my time on the case only covered the interviews with Barker. I had it in mind to visit the property at the time, to see it for myself and to help my understanding of her, but after she vanished, my involvement ended abruptly, as I'm sure you know. I did listen for news, but none came. There's nothing you've said which is past tense, suggesting that there was nothing to know up to a point, which I presume is recently. Has there been a potential sighting?"

Carmel handed Cross a sheet, a document sparsely populated with names and places. "We've had several potential sightings of women matching Barker's description recently, each were investigated quietly, and a couple seemed to have more grounds than others. Something that did come up but that didn't get connected until recently, was a woman from Annapolis Royal who went missing a short while after Barker fled, she's still missing in fact".

Cross scrolled down the sheet until he saw the name 'Mary Rose'. "Did Barker know her?"

"We don't know for sure, but quite possibly. The right questions weren't asked at the time and the news about Barker was only sketchily reported, deliberately so, I might add. I'd like you to find out if the missing woman did know Barker as part of the reopening of the investigation. I only recently became aware of the missing woman information myself; it seems that the officer investigating didn't see a link, and it just went down as one of many missing persons, you know how it is. Don't worry about the politics of this, Annapolis Royal has undergone a few changes recently, as you'll find out when you or your sergeants go over. The new incumbents there are happy to work with us on this.

"The politics, as you call it Ma'am do worry me, especially here. We're a small force in Kentville, and we're not RCMP. Some are asking how you, as head of the RCMP, are involved?"

"I asked for a favour and Aldrick is an old friend from way back when, you'll like him when he gets back. I understand that the back surgery went well and with physio he'll walk normally, but it will take time. To be honest I'm doing this as much for me as a favour to Aldrick. I want a positive outcome here and that means pulling whatever strings I can lay my hands on to get Barker. Going back to the refuges, there's a lot of them, more than you'd think. Some are just bolt-holes, not registered, some are official and publicly funded in-part, you'll need a starting place".

Cross lifted a sheaf of prepared sheets from a folder and handed them over. Carmel took them, then skimmed through. Cross noticed her linger on one of the locations on page two, he knew which one it would be.

"Good, you're ahead of me then. In the case of The Orchard, will Moira and your sister, Angela, cooperate?"

"I've talked to Moira about this sort of thing before and she's right to hold us to client confidentiality. I do know that her memory will be a factor if I tell her enough about the case, I also know she'll think carefully about helping. My sister has a history of being involved in the refuge network, I'll talk to her too, but she is naturally very protective of people she might have helped. Is my connection to two people who know the system why I'm involved?"

It was a fair question. "No, you're involved because you have a good record, a good team and know something of the issues. It would be rather cynical of me to give you something like this just to exploit your family connections. Whatever people say about me, I try to never be cynical. Calculating, yes, but not cynical".

"I'll speak to Moira tonight; I want her take first".

"Good, because we think The Orchard was used at some point and that Juliette Barker might have called herself Rosemary for a while. I take it the irony of the name she used, if it was her, isn't lost on you?"

"I got it, Rosemary – Mary Rose, she might be teasing us? I guess we'll find out when we catch her. I've never mentioned this to anyone officially before, but in the context of the women's' refuge system, it's relevant. Some time ago I helped a person use the refuge network to escape a toxic family, my sister facilitated things. I only did a bit of driving really. I'd like to think that the system, however it works, will not be affected. It's important that people are there to make a difference". Carmel smiled. The case of the Wilding brothers was one of the things that had put Cross on her radar in the first place, but she wasn't going to say so now nor was she going to reveal how much she knew about his 'just a bit of driving'.

"At least you helped your damsel in distress, many don't. What are you planning for the rest of the cases, specifically tidying up those flapping loose ends in the Coates file?"

"Regarding the two remaining cases of dead hunters that need a resolution, Crystal is obviously up to speed on them so I thought she should be the nominal lead, not that I'm asking for advice or anything. I'll also use her on the Barker case too. Some refuges respond better to a female approach, but I'll be lead on that one".

"Three dead hunter cases, Howey. Sorry, but I'm not happy that we have a solid resolution to Coates' own death yet, notwithstanding the possibilities there. For my part, I'd like something definitive that rules in, or out, any involvement by Thomas Cox. We don't have that at the moment, just supposition".

"I thought we'd done with Cox; I think we might be overthinking unnecessarily there. Dan Bush is the one we need to get after, and we will if we get the chance at him, that's if we can pin him down".

"As a rich American, I can see multiple issues there, political issues. Do what you can where Bush is concerned but keep an open mind about Cox and his involvement is all I'm saying. Now, let's talk about Darren, how will you use him?"

If it had been anyone else from outside the Kentville force asking, he'd tell them it was none of their business who did what, but Carmel was Carmel, and he liked her. "He'll be my second-in-command, he'll run Kentville if I'm out and working a case and he'll be a part of the team on all active cases. He'll also oversee the wildlife crime unit until Tiff arrives from her mysterious deployment".

Morrell ignored the Tiff O'Toole comment. "Make sure you tell him that upfront, don't presume he knows in all the excitement of your new post. I know he's been doing it while you danced the samba on the Copacabana beach, but people still like to be told".

Cross felt it was a given that he'd already told Darren and considered saying so, instead he went for a 'yes, Ma'am'.

Morrell gave Cross a look and laughed. "Sorry, I know it's just force of habit for you, but Ma'am is so not me. It goes without saying that I want to be kept in all loops for everything. If and when you do find Barker, I want to be there when she's interviewed, and I want that shrink of hers there too".

Cross recalled the 2019 case, and the psychiatrist who'd taken Barker as a patient before her arrest and subsequent disappearance. He'd also advised on the best detention option for her, a recommendation that had backfired badly. "I assume that nobody has talked to Watson since Barker vanished? I understand the case priorities in the light of the dead woman, and I'll make sure it happens. Why do you want Watson involved again in particular? I know a very good psychiatrist who I'd be happier working with on this".

"After last time you mean? Watson was right. He might have recommended a low-level detention rather than a high-security unit, but he wasn't the person holding the keys when she went missing. Seriously, Howey, it wasn't his fault. I still want him involved because he's already spoken more to Juliette Barker than any police officer. If anyone has a handle on her, it's him. Think of it as a bone you can toss him for cooperation, he might be glad of the opportunity to help, he might give insights". It made sense, although Cross was generally wary about getting people from outside involved, except for Moira. He found that they tended to build up their role and, ultimately, get in the way. He nodded, and then shuffled his papers, drawing out another memo from the pile.

"I'd like a heads-up on my officers that you've seen fit to deploy elsewhere. Kent and Tiff were going to be used in following up wildlife crime as well as other investigations. I'd appreciate an explanation, Ma'am".

Carmel gave Cross a look that said, 'I know that ma'am was deliberate'. "Kent Chivers needs to expand his range of experience and so I thought the Yarmouth detachment would be good for him, for a while. They have some local problems with fishers, and he has the physical presence that gets respect. O'Toole has only worked in Digby. I expect her to develop nicely, so she's out learning the ways of the world, but she will be here, at some point. Not everyone earned their spurs working the mean street of Halifax".

"I think you mean streets, Carmel".

"I know what I mean, Howey. If you think I'm interfering too much, say so and I'll consider the position, but trust me, my connections in securing placements can only be good for the development of promising young officers. Now, changing the subject, tell me all about Terence Ferry".

Cross wasn't surprised that Carmel knew the name Terence Ferry, she seemed to know about most things. "He's a birder, seems a nice guy. He's originally from Nova Scotia and currently dating Crystal, which is I guess why you asked. I've only met him a few times, once socially at our place when Moira was matchmaking and to my surprise, they seemed to hit it off. Crystal seems happy with him so far, but they're both busy people and it is early days. Is this your motherly instinct kicking in or is there something else, Ma'am?"

"Motherly instinct, me? Why Staff Sergeant Cross you go too far, it will not be borne". Carmel put on her most forbidding stare, but rather spoiled the effect with a suspicious twitching around the mouth, like she was trying hard not to smile. Cross wasn't taken in.

"I've seen Pride and Prejudice too, Carmel, a passable Lady Catherine de Burgh, I'd say".

"I never had you down as a fan of the classics, Howey. I do like my men educated. No 'motherly instinct' here, as you call it, I'm just keeping my active fingers on all pulses and that includes knowing a bit about other halves and the role they play in people's happiness. Crystal is a protégé, as are you. Indulge me, allow me to be interested".

"Why though, Carmel, why me and why Crystal?"

"Because there's been too many Rick Goodings in the service over the years, Howey, and the only way to change that culture is make sure that those on the way up are made of the right stuff. I should have added Darren to that list, but I don't know him that well, yet. Do you?"

"Yes, I'd call him my best friend after Moira. Having said that, I think making sergeant might be the height of his ambition. A good, thorough and intuitive cop, what you see is what you get".

"I think you might underestimate him there. After the Gooding thing, and a few that you don't know about, we need all the good, reliable officers we can muster. Darren is one of them. Where he fits, I don't know yet. Policing in Nova Scotia is complicated but there are moves to make it less so. I can't say anything at the moment, but a report is being commissioned and will be far reaching". Carmel checked her watch and stood up; it was clear that the meeting was over. "One more thing, I meant to ask after Moira. She's been very good for you, you know. There was a time when we thought that you might be lost, but she's put your old spark back. I'd like to meet her, one day. Until next month or my next visit then, whichever comes sooner, Howey", and with that she left.

Cross could tell from the quietening of the hubbub outside, and then the gradual resumption of chatter, that Carmel had left the building. Despite her occupying a very big chair in what was effectively another police force, Carmel Morrell garnered a lot of respect from the rank and file.

Taking her words as direct instructions, Cross called the number he had for Geoffrey Watson, listening to his answerphone. 'I'm in and out of the office until mid-August. If you need to schedule an appointment, please visit my website at WWW...' Cross resisted creating an account as the site requested. Watson was obviously a very busy man, the red crosses on his appointment calendar said so. He opened his own planner, chose a free date and made an appointment. In the comments, he added a brief description of his requirements as requested. The thing pinged a confirmation email. August was fine for now unless he found himself in the area, he still had plenty to do elsewhere.

When Darren knocked and waited, it felt very strange. Although Howey had always been his boss, he'd never acted like it. They'd been a good team for a while and, as close friends, had some idea of how each other ticked. Now there was an office, with a closed door and a new name plate standing between them. It all seemed a bit formal.

"Come in, Darren".

"I thought you might take another day off, what with the delayed flights thing and having to spend hours in a foreign airport. I deliberately kept out of the way at the farm knowing you'd have things to do, still, you're all back now. Can I ask from the get-go, how formal should we be here?"

"You two did a great job of keeping things going on the farm, we really appreciate it. Moira is making plans for a proper catch up soon, so expect an interesting evening with lots of photos. As for our professional situation, naturally I've given my elevation to grand heights due consideration, and I thought I'd call you Darren and you can call me the Exalted One and we'll see how it goes. I was going to take another day off, but Moira said I had to go to work to save the world, so here I am. I've read the activity reports, brought myself up to speed with the hustle and bustle of Kings County and now we need to talk the toot".

"'Toot', oh Exalted One? What is toot?"

"Toot, in one context, means discussing the trivial bits of minutiae that nobody else will tell me, stuff that might even be considered obscure. Sorry, toot comes from my vacation reading, a book by an English author called Robert Rankin, quite eccentric, one of Moira's favourites".

"Toot it is then. Any preference on the toot sequence, or can I just go by my list here and talk that toot you spoke of?"

"Toot away".

For an hour or more they went through the cases, new and old. Laughed a bit, gossiped a bit and even the odd bird was mentioned. Cross had been waiting for the right moment to comment on the birding front. "I'm thinking to step back a bit on the chasing, Darren. I'll have plenty to do here and the farm needs a lot of work now, as you know. I was going to suggest to Moira that we set a hundred-kilometre circle where we go for ticks. Any feasible firsts we go for, perhaps, other than that and we'll play it by ear".

"Right, understandable given the increased workload. So, you've not heard about the pratincole then?"

"A what?" said Cross, grabbing his muted phone.

"No news so far today, Howey, but if it's there, Oriental or Collared, how does that fit in with the newly imposed range limit for chasing?" asked Darren.

Cross opened up eBird and did a species search for a pratincole, until a few minutes ago he'd never even heard of one. It was a very odd-looking bird, it was neither a shorebird nor a tern, despite looking like both at the same time. His phone pinged; it was Moira. 'Pratincole there now, about four hours away, less with flashing lights:)'.

'Weekend if it sticks perhaps, ok. Too busy today'. He didn't get a reply.

"Brave not going for it. You could finish here at four and be there before nine, get the bird and be home by one, two at the latest, we could go together".

"Darren, I've got a ton of things to do, I don't expect to get home until late today. If it stays and we can, we'll go at the weekend and if you try to slip away early for it, I won't be happy. That's the drawback of having a birder boss, I'll know where you've been".

"I know, I expected you to say that, the weekend it is then. To be honest, I'm finding chasing a bit wearing. I might give up too".

"Really?" said Cross, surprised.

"I think so, too busy like you said, the house move and life things, you know how it is. I thought we might go out and grab a beer sometime, have a chat, when you're settled back in". Cross was surprised. Darren and Hinzi were friends and eager farm caretakers, they came over all the time and drank beer or whatever was on offer. He didn't think he and Darren had ever been out for a beer as such but if that was what he wanted to do, why not?

"Sure. As I said, Moira is putting a thing together for the Brazil trip, food and a show she said, I'll let you know when. She might be dressed as a Carnival dancer, just so you know, I'll make sure she's one of the more modestly attired ones. She was going on about body paint, but I think I talked her out of it. Now, can we get on with the brief? I want to talk to you about a case from way back when, have you ever heard of Juliette Barker?"

"Yes, I was told to get up to speed with the case for when you got back. You never mentioned it before, but I remember you slipping off to Annapolis Royal at the time. It was during the Perry case, not long after I'd introduced you to the wonderful world of birding".

"That's right, well, if you've read all we have, here's a bit more", and Cross passed Darren the paper Carmel had given him.

"Interesting. It occurs to me that if we're visiting women's refuges, Crystal needs to be there every time. We might consider ourselves benign, but women who've had to use a refuge, for whatever reason, probably won't. If splitting you and I up when Crystal gets here was bothering you, I'm fine with it. Spread the load and use the tools you have to make a difference. What's our priority though?"

Cross was pleased that Darren had said about splitting them up to accommodate Crystal first. Quite how he was going to keep both sergeants happy had been bothering him in the wee, sleepless, hours he sometimes suffered. "We keep after Bush and the Coates case and, if Madam's moles come up with anything more solid, we'll review. Madam said I have to tell you that you're my second-in-command, you do know that, right?"

"Yes, I thought so, but it's nice to have it confirmed. I'm not sure how it will work when Aldrick gets back, we'll just have to wait and see", said Darren, checking his watch.

"Places to be?"

"Yes, later. I was part-way through detachment activity reviews from when you were away, the brief took longer than I'd expected. I guess that sort of thing's all for you now, I'll send the files over. Are we tooted out for now?"

Darren left and Cross realised that, for the past three weeks, Darren had been running Kentville while he chased parrots and antbirds around the tropical rainforests of Brazil. Had he even thanked him?

Peter Burns, an American birder from New England, had largely shunned the social media side of birding. His six-weeks' vacation, while recovering from illness, had been going well. His wife's extended family had a property near Little Judique and the peace and quiet of the setting, and the very casual birding he'd done, had hastened his recovery to the point where he was out birding more than he'd anticipated being able to. Coming from New England, the countryside around Little Judique was new to him, and he was just enjoying getting to know the local birding spots and seeing what he could find for himself.

"You seem to be in a hurry to finish your breakfast", said Peter's wife, Susie, herself a birder but more laid back in her Californian-roots way. She had hoped, when all the nasty business had been settled, that they might migrate cross-country and well away from the lobster industry, but Peter had the Atlantic in his blood and he was putting up a spirited resistance.

"I thought I'd go for a wander, maybe even to Canso Causeway. I'm ready to spread my wings a bit".

Susie looked concerned. They'd nearly lost him to his illness, they both knew that, but she also knew that he'd be a royal pain if she held him back, so she tried to hide her concern behind the over-large coffee cups which seemed to be the only ones in the whole house.

"I can see what you're thinking, I'll be fine. I have my phone, and this isn't Outer Mongolia, despite what you think about the lack of people here, they're just a bit spread out".

"Ok, but I don't want you hauling that huge lens around, take the little one, be mobile. They texted and said the car would be ready sometime next week, something about a delay in getting a part. I told you buying a British car was dumb. I do like the Range Rover, but when it breaks, it's expensive and time consuming to repair".

Peter smiled, he'd got no intention of hauling the 800mm around, he was surprised that she'd let him pack it for the trip in the first place. Maybe she'd thought the weightlifting aspect involved in carrying it around might be useful for exercise, once he was fit enough. As for the car, it wasn't up for discussion as far as he was concerned.

Susie stood on the porch and watched as he eased the old Ford truck out of the drive. Her uncle had refused to update the family transport to a more modern, and more easily handled, entity; yes, the old Ford was definitely an entity. Her cousins might be more inclined to give it a rethink once they got back from their world tour after having seen how the rest of the world operated. In her opinion the tour was the height of stupidity, given Covid and various travel issues, but they'd taken them to the airport in it and they'd gone anyway. They still had three months to go.

Peter Burns had already identified a new spot that he wanted to check out, it was quite close. He easily found the imaginatively named Shore Road and then just followed his nose, ending up parked by some agricultural fields with a natural depression, in which had formed a large, seasonal pool.

Burns was scanning the pool from the car using just his binocs. He didn't have his spotting scope with him, it had been a choice of either both lenses or the small one and the scope, so he'd gone for the former thinking he might get some nice bird images for his library. He felt his heart flip when a quiet voice said 'hello' right by his ear. A lady had appeared, seemingly from nowhere, he'd not really been paying attention as he intently scanned the pool.

"Hello, er?"

"Maisie. Are you a bird watcher?"

Before him was a woman of about forty, maybe a bit less, quietly dressed. Slim, average height and with long dark hair, there was a slight greyish hint at the temples. She looked worried. "Yes, of a sort. I'm staying in the Fornall's place up the road, I hope I'm not trespassing?"

"No, you're fine here but don't go into the field, the owner can be a bit funny. Have you seen anything unusual here? I'm quite new to all this, just learning".

Burns was a bit surprised that she was asking whether he'd seen anything unusual. Most new birders generally found everything unusual, perhaps it was the generic greeting out here? "No, I don't think so, I only just got here and was scanning. I'm from New England so some of these spots are unfamiliar to me. I thought this one looked promising, although I'm only seeing a few yellowlegs out there at the moment".

"Oh, yes, three Greater and one Lesser, I think, they can look very much alike unless you get them side-by-side. I saw a Least Sandpiper along the edge too, tiny with yellowy legs. Have you seen a brown tern?" Maisie had seemed almost reluctant to ask.

Burns' ears pricked up at that. Did she mean an immature tern, or maybe a Black Tern, how common were they in Nova Scotia? "No, as I say, I just got here. Brown you say, on the back?"

"No, brown, the tail has short streamers, a bit like a swallow and it bounces up and down over the water, it must be after bugs".

"Brown, do you mean like a young Tree Swallow, or more likely a Bank Swallow at this time of year?"

"No, I know the regular swallows, Tree and Barn Swallows nest in the yard, this bird is bigger, a lot bigger. It's been here a week; I can't find it anywhere today though". Maisie had decided not to mention that Merlin was calling it a pratincole to the stranger, 'they' had already told her that it was a mistake by Merlin, 'they' were very firm on that.

"It sounds very interesting, I'd like to see it, where does it go?"

"I don't know, it just comes here sometimes, bounces around a bit and then perches on that lump in the middle. Oh, look, there it is now".

Not really expecting much more than maybe a Spotted Sandpiper, Burns focused his binocs on the mud lump and, sure enough, there was a brown bird sitting on it.

"I can't see much detail with these", said Maisie, waving her compacts around. "I've ordered some better ones but I'm not sure whether to keep it up, bird watching that is. Some people are a bit brusque in the bird group".

Burns was concentrating on the bird while trying to tune Maisie out, he wasn't a great listener when there was a bird to look at. Susie had called it having a lack of multi-tasking skills, something she'd learned to live with over the years. He looked at the stationary bird for a while, it was hard not to call it a brown tern as Maisie had said. He wished he'd packed the scope too, because he really didn't know what he was looking at. The only thing to do was snap it and zoom in the image.

"Here, you take a look at it through my binocs, I'm going to get a photo", he said, handing Maisie his Leica binocs, top of the range and only three months old. She held them as if she'd been given a stick of dynamite. Burns noticed her look of concern. "Take a look then, don't worry about breaking them, they're sturdy. I think you'd need to jump up and down on them in big boots to make an impact".

Maisie laughed, a bit, then raised the binocs to her eyes. "Holy cow!"

Burns leaned on the old Ford's window frame and focused, but his smaller lens wasn't getting a lot of detail. He checked the first three shots of what appeared to be an amorphous lump, still clueless, he switched to rapid fire just before the bird took flight. To all intents and purposes, it was a brown tern. For the next five minutes or so it bounced up and down as Maisie had said it did, although hawked insects was a more accurate description. Then it drifted slowly away, tern-like, towards the ocean and out of sight. He checked the image count on his newly formatted SD card, 220 images. 'I must have at least one decent one in there' he thought.

"That was fantastic, thanks", said Maisie handing the binocs back carefully. "I've ordered some Nikon Monarchs; I hope they're as good as those". Burns decided not to mention the price difference. Nikon Monarchs were alright. but not top-end; still she'd do much better with the Nikons than she had been doing using her glorified opera glasses.

"Any idea what it is?" she asked. Burns knew the question was coming but no, he didn't. He knew his North American birds well enough, but this one didn't seem to fit any of them.

"I think I need to see the photos on my laptop, I can zoom in and see plumage details better. Can I contact you later? I might have an answer for you after I've done a bit of processing".

Maisie found an old receipt in her purse and scribbled down her phone number.

"Thanks, I'll get back to you. I know the bird isn't in my field guide, which one do you use, Sibley, National Geographic?"

Maisie opened her phone and showed him Merlin.

"Ah, right. I've been resisting that, and eBird I'm afraid, I'm very much old school. I like to do my own thing and not be told by an anonymous reviewer what I've seen. Did Merlin suggest anything?"

Wordlessly, Maisie opened up Merlin, changed her loaded bird ID pack to Europe and explored birds, typing in Pratincole. She showed Burns the image.

"Fuck me", Burns exclaimed when he saw the image, then spent the next few minutes apologizing profusely, much to Maisie's amusement.

"From your expressive comment can I take it that you agree then, a Collared Pratincole? Nobody else does".

Burns pulled up an image on the back of his camera and showed her. There was no doubt, the bird was flying and showing a chestnut wing lining, it was the same as the bird shown by Merlin.

"I told them in the bird group, a pratincole I said, but they all said it was impossible, but they've got wings, birds, right?"

Burns laughed. "Yes Maisie, they've got wings. It shouldn't be here though, it's a European bird according to your Merlin. If I send you a photo later, can you put it on Facebook for me?"

"Sure, no problem. It will be nice to show 'them' that what I've been telling them I've been seeing for a week is true".

That evening, the Nova Scotia Bird Group Facebook page received a post from Maisie. "My brown tern today. Collared Pratincole, Shore Road, Little Judique. Photo by Peter Burns", was all she wrote.

There was a lot of continent-wide chatter once the photo went up. People who chased over vast distances were asking most of the questions. Had it been confirmed by local birders, was it still there, can someone eBird it so we have the site? All valid queries. Then a comment came in from Canadian bird tour guide, Roy Simmons, who said he'd be in Nova Scotia later in the year. 'Devil's advocate here, but has Oriental Pratincole been ruled out yet?' Oh my!

On getting a text from Maisie the next morning, telling him about the pratincole possibilities and that 'they' were asking about a flight shot, Peter Burns had to dig in his computer trash box for his only photo of the upperwing anything like in focus. He trimmed and sharpened it before sending it. 'Best I've got, sorry'.

'Good enough, 'they' said it's a Collared. I'm going back on Saturday to see what 'they' look like'.

Burns smiled at the text, 'I just might join you for moral support'.

Thanks to the workload, an accumulation that apparently only a Staff Sergeant could deal with, the day flew by, and it was nearer seven than six when the farmhouse door opened, and Howey walked in. "All hail the Emperor", said Moira as she set the table for two, the terrors had been fed and were abed already, despite their protests. He'd have to wait until the morning before telling them all about his first day in the new job.

"Have you been talking to someone at work by chance?"

"What on earth makes you think that?" said Moira, grinning.

"'All hail the emperor' and you're dressed as a concubine, a very authentic concubine too including the correct number of undergarments".

"I may have chatted with Leah for a while when she called asking about your afternoon drink regime, in case she felt like catering for it. I think the outfit suits me, don't you? I might adopt it for casual wear, supermarket shopping and walks around Miner's Marsh. you'll have to excuse my fingers though, they're red-raw from all the grape peeling".

Cross laughed. "Am I being micro-managed by all the women in my life? Honestly, it's enough to drive a man to drink".

"I was hoping you'd say that; we've got to finish the rest of Brazilian beer before we can start on the new stuff, Speight's from New Zealand, highly recommended".

Howey had been expecting this. They were no sooner back from three weeks in Brazil than Moira was plotting the next big trip. At least with having only a single week of vacation left, it wouldn't be happening until into the following year. For the evening's entertainment, Moira had put together a series of raw videos from the trip, so they sipped beer and laughed again at some of the things they did. "The Lodge, did you make a decision?" asked Howey, knowing that Moira had been torn over whether to give up her part.

"Selling my stake? Yes, I think I will. They can afford it and we'll have plenty of local issues to deal with. It's one less thing to think about, agreed? They did say we'd be welcome anytime though".

"Agreed, and The Orchard?"

"Nothing to know there yet. Why?"

"I was thinking, did The Orchard keep formal records, you know, of the people who stayed there. Not just the made-up names but real names, dates of birth, that sort of thing?"

Moira narrowed her eyes. "Now I'm even more intrigued. I'll ask again, why?"

"I wondered whether we, the police, might elicit the help of whoever manages The Orchard at some future date to help us find people. Missing girls, prosecute offences against, that sort of thing. I'm minded to talk to all of the refuges in Nova Scotia as part of a proactive help scheme, but also for a case. We lose way too many people for it to be healthy. Carmel talked to me about it today, I said I'd talk to you, she asked after you".

"Howey, The Orchard is a refuge from everything, including the jackboot of police oppression, present company excepted. There are records, but I don't have access anymore".

"But you still have a finger in that particular pie. if I asked about a specific person, someone of interest, you'd be able to help?"

"Perhaps, but I'd feel the obligation of confidentiality, you know I would".

"Absolutely, but what if we had a really serious case where some help, any help, would make a real difference to someone and I was to ask without expectation?"

"As I said, I'd consider it, but again, why? Spit it out, what are you after?"

"Some time ago I was called in to a case in Annapolis Royal. I can't talk specific details, but the woman involved, someone who has serious issues, possibly moved silently through the refuge network when she disappeared. We might have a lead on her now; Madam wants me and my team to take a fresh look at the refuge system, amongst other things".

"I see. I'll promise nothing and before saying anything, I think I'd want to know a lot more about this mystery case that you've never mentioned before. You said it was some time ago, was it when we got together? that would be when you worked the Perry case. You had an air of despair at times, and I knew it wasn't just because of the Perry case, sorry, intuition, me being me".

"Yes, it was complicated, serious and the woman involved absconded. For various reasons I've had her in my head for a long time. It was a difficult, sensitive and troubling case, and now it's back in my in-tray".

"Annapolis Royal, unnamed woman goes missing from secure institution, police baffled. I remember the headline, but I don't remember reading any details of any charges or a suggestion of what she might have been up to".

"No, you wouldn't. When she fled it was all closed down very quickly. We, the police, have been looking for her ever since".

"I see, and now Madam wants her best brains and you on the case, correct? If this woman is bright enough to slip away from the police, she'll be someone else entirely by now and changing her place and appearance regularly. That's what I'd do, if I didn't want to be found, be a different person, adopt a new persona. I can see why you'd be advised to tackle the many refuges out there, good luck with that. Changing the subject, the pratincole?"

Howey was surprised to get off so lightly. Normally Moira would lever answers from him, often without him knowing he'd been prompted until he heard himself talk. "Can we not think about it until the weekend? Tomorrow will be another long day".

"Ok, but I warn you, the fruits of your loins will be devastated if we miss it. I showed them the illustrations in the Collins Guide, their excited faces lit up the room. You do know that it will be the only one ever? so if you can carry the vision of their weeping eyes and sad little faces with you for the rest of your days, then so be it".

Cross said nothing. As soon as Moira had said it, the word 'persona' seemed to have lodged in his head on a loop. As a distraction he pressed play, and they watched the videos some more. That night he had trouble sleeping again. Images of Juliette Barker as she'd been when he first saw her kept morphing into different people with different hair and different names.

Moira was right, there was a system out there where a wanted woman could flit about hidden, no questions asked. There was nothing to say that she'd even stayed in Nova Scotia. Now they had the missing woman, Mary Rose, as possibly a link, at least they might have somewhere to start.

CHAPTER THREE

The next morning Cross was surprised to see Crystal in his office when he got in. "With the usual chaos we've come to love about police staffing in Nova Scotia, my desk was cleared when I got back in yesterday afternoon, so now I'm officially yours, do with me as you will, my lord".

"Excellent, we can get busy early then". Cross had deliberately ignored being called 'lord' and entering into any playful banter, he wanted to get on. "Whatever you do, don't mention a pratincole to Darren, he's getting fidgety".

"A pratincole, isn't that some sort of fancy pastry, or is that a profiterole?". Cross told Crystal all about the rare bird in detail and got the looks he expected. Despite having a birder boyfriend, Crystal wasn't very interested in birds and by the time Cross had started telling her the species' plumage in fine detail she'd glazed over, then a thought struck her. "Are you going to see this prantical with Darren?"

"Pratincole, pratincole Crystal, at least get the name right if you're going to mock. Maybe, but not with Darren. Moira is keen to go but I've things to do here and at home, we've been away three weeks, things pile up".

"Didn't Darren and Hinzi do the mucking out while you were away? Bad little stand-in farmers. Is Darren going on his own then? Hinzi doesn't go birdying either, right? Do you think he'd take me?"

"He might, why though? You seemed less than enthusiastic when I was telling you about it just now".

"No, very keen me and besides, I don't know Darren very well and with Terence being away we could bond. I don't think I've ever had a real conversation with Darren, I don't even know whether he likes me or not, he's hard to read. What do you think?"

Cross had to admit that the idea had merit and as it was Crystal who was volunteering her time freely, he smiled on it. He was also quite pleased on a personal level because he was going to have to tell Darren 'no' if he asked whether they could ride up together on Saturday. "Ask him when he gets back in, but first we have a lot to get through. I did Darren yesterday, so I'm doing you today if you're ok with that?"

Crystal smiled, leant back in her chair and slowly opened her legs a touch "Ready, my lord".

"Crystal, behave", laughed Cross before he started to go through the Barker case with her, filling in many blanks. By the time he'd finished, her mood had changed.

"I remember the Barker conversation well. You were worried that your little nutjob proto-girlfriend with a fridge full of her dead boyfriend's sperm might be like Barker, and I said she wasn't. I was right, wasn't I?" There was the merest fraction of a second before Cross answered 'yes'. In normal circumstances, and between regular people, it wouldn't have been noticed, between professional police officers, it was almost a statement to the contrary. "Howey, Moira is eccentric, not nuts. She's different, great, I love her to bits and so do you. No matter what we find with Juliette Barker, don't go seeing any similarities with Moira".

"No, I won't, I just worry. Did I tell you she was on medication for Histrionic Personality Disorder, HPD?"

"Really, are you sure? I've seen people on drugs for HPD before, it makes them very out of it and I've never seen any sign of that in Moira, even after one of her special brownies. You should tell her what's going on in your head, tell her what you're worried about, don't let it fester".

Cross promised that he would, then switched to the Coates case. There wasn't much new to discuss, and he was glad to get away from his fears about Moira. He knew that Crystal was right, but he still worried.

Saturday dawned and something of a record crowd for Nova Scotia was parked along the road skirting the Collared Pratincole pool; all were waiting until it was light enough to check for it properly. Most of the active listers were there, notable absentees being Howey and Moira and a few hardcore types who'd seen it the day before. Rather than get out of the car, birders were swapping texts via their informal Messenger group, set up for managing just such events, and also for spontaneous bitching, something one or two were very good at. From the tenor of the texts so far, people were starting to get impatient.

"Tell me again why you wanted to come with me?" Darren had been wondering whether spending hours in a car with Crystal was a good idea, but she'd asked nicely, how could he say no?

Crystal, who'd been busy finishing off her breakfast, held a finger up to show that an answer was on its way. "I'm at a loose end at the moment. Terence is away and I haven't got anything pressing, so I thought that a civilian day out together might help us bond a bit. I know you and Howey are close, but I'm close to him too. I want us to be a menage-a-trois but without the need for wet wipes".

Darren burst out laughing, Crystal unsettled him a bit. His masculine side naturally appreciated her appearance and personality, not that he fancied her as such. She was right though; they didn't really know each other very well. Aside from her having the distraction of a physique that turned male heads wherever she went, he worried that he was out of her intellectual league too, and that might be a potential block to forming a good working relationship. She was probably right about a trip, getting to know each other better on a one-to-one basis made sense. A twitch was nicely neutral- unless he dipped. "Won't Terence be a bit pissed at you if you see this bird and he doesn't?"

"Perhaps, but I won't lose any beauty sleep over it, not that I need it". Crystal was testing the waters by being a little flirty but in a jokey way, she was looking for a reaction. Just then another two cars arrived, well a car and a truck of sorts, it looked like a refugee from a vintage rally.

A woman got out of the car and started to wander around freely. "What's she doing? We all agreed to sit tight until it was light enough, she might flush it", said Darren, quickly checking his phone for any missed messages, service there was spotty at best. He looked along the line of cars and saw that some of the others were of a similar mind and ready to get out and ask this woman what she was up to, breaking ranks like that. Greg beat everyone to it and moments later Maisie was busy being introduced to people. As word spread, birders were soon abandoning their own cars and lining up to enthusiastically praise her for the find. She seemed a bit perplexed, this was 'them' in the flesh and they weren't so bad after all.

Greg ushered everyone away from the pool, heading for the old truck after deciding it was as good a place as any for the inevitable social to commence, and far enough away to not bother the bird if it turned up. Inside the truck, an older man had sat tight, but Daisy had already told everyone who he was and his part in the pratincole identification. Now people were keen to say hello to him too.

As the group chatted, thankfully in subdued voices, Greg kept an eye on the pool, hoping to be first to spot the bird coming in. Crystal had stayed in the car when Darren went to meet Maisie, she'd not been paying much attention to what was happening, even asking herself why she'd really decided to ride along in the first place, then everyone was suddenly looking in her direction. She was finding it a bit disconcerting, then she noticed a brown bird fluttering by the car, bouncing around before landing not six feet away on a little mud spit. Operating on autopilot, she whipped out her phone and took photos and then a short video, before the bird flew off and away. The crowd were soon dashing back to their own vehicles, many had been unprepared and without binocs, none had their cameras to hand except for Peter Burns who'd been using his, now paired with the big lens, to good effect.

"Wow, did you see it, it landed right next to the car, amazing. Maisie, the finder, let me look through her binocs, they were marginally better than naked eye". Crystal let Darren gush a bit, then played him the video, and did a slideshow of the stills. "Was that it?"

Inside two hours, the pratincole hadn't returned, and a few of the birders had gone off to have a look around elsewhere. Crystal was now very bored, so she decided to walk over and talk to Maisie who was still around and enjoying being the centre of attention for new arrivals.

"You don't look like a birder", said Maisie, matter-of-factly, as Crystal approached.

"I'm not, my boyfriend is though, and so is my colleague, Darren, so I thought I'd come along for the ride. My boyfriend's away at the moment, he's always busy away somewhere and leaving me on my own". It was too much information, but Crystal desperately wanted to chat to someone else. It had been more than a three-hour drive with an anxious Darren, and she needed a less bird-fixated perspective for a while.

"Colleague?" said Peter, who'd been listening in.

"Yes, police, we're with the Kentville detachment. Our boss is a birder too, but he's just come back from Brazil and is too busy to come". Again, more than was necessary had been spewed forth. Maisie said it was very cool to be chatting to a police officer, she didn't meet many, but Burns suddenly seemed keen to be elsewhere. Crystal quickly picked up on it.

"Problem?" she asked.

"No, not with any of the Nova Scotia forces who I'm sure are more attentive than my local bunch back home".

"Bad policing, where would that be, Peter?" It sounded like she was wanting Burns to help her with her enquiries.

"New Hampshire but boring stuff. I got conned, badly, and it did for my health which is why I'm here. My lot didn't do their jobs when I needed them to, so I had to suck it up. Nothing to be done, although if you ever have cause to arrest someone called Dan Bush on his infrequent visits to this part of Nova Scotia, promise you won't be gentle with him".

"You know Dan Bush?" It was Darren who'd heard the name and was getting very interested.

"You know of him? I'm not surprised that his reputation is known even here. He's a nasty piece of work, untrustworthy, intimidatory even, but you don't want to hear my woes, such as they are. There's nothing to be done".

Crystal and Darren looked at each other. "Actually...", said Darren.

Howey Cross sensed the atmosphere when he got back in from feeding the goats, his Saturday treat to himself after nipping in to work for the morning. Phoebe, in particular, had a gaze that Medusa would have been proud of. Moira gave him the same look. "Ok, ok, it's still there, I know. We'll go tomorrow. Actually, I might have to do a bit of work there too, the hunter cold cases. Darren and Crystal have information".

Moira looked surprised. "What's Crystal doing there with Darren?"

"Bonding, winding me up, flirting with Darren to get a reaction, take your pick. Anyway, they've heard of something interesting, and I'd like to check it out for myself. We can do that and the pratincole, good enough?"

"Pratincole and then work, I think you'll find, otherwise we'll have to get counsellors in to go over tick bereavement with the kids". Cross smiled; he knew that she probably didn't really mean it.

It wasn't exactly a stony silence on the way home, but it wasn't very jubilant either. It had been interesting to visit a corner of Nova Scotia that was new to them and, for Howey at least, to talk to Peter Burns. That the pratincole hadn't appeared again, it hadn't been seen since the initial return the previous day, wasn't Howey's fault, but it felt like it.

"I'm really sorry we missed it, but I had so much to do yesterday", he said to those willing to listen.

Moira tried to console him. "We know it's not your fault, it's normal to dip and if it comes back during the week, we'll go over without you. It's just a bit irritating that Crystal got it and we didn't. Don't worry, I'll rationalise it out and we'll all be fine by the end of the year. At least you seem pleased following your cloak-and-dagger conversation with that Peter guy".

"Yes, sorry about that too, nothing like the sinister cases that I routinely shield from you, it's just that I think he might regret his conversation with Darren and Crystal. I have to hope he doesn't die on us before we get the case sorted".

"Nothing to know on the mystery of the disappearing woman, I take it?"

Cross didn't answer, instead he tried to enthuse the kids with the offer of a stop for unsuitable food, but it fell on deaf ears, mostly because they were now both fast asleep. "Stop anyway, I could do with a pee", said Moira, trying hard not to put on a brave face.

The gas station was quiet, but they waved to Frank Conte who seemed reluctant to stop and chat after he'd fueled up. He'd missed the bird too and for Frank that was akin to life and death. Moira put on her smiley face and got back in the van, relieved. "Not to worry, I've seen them before in Spain, so it wasn't a lifer". Without thinking, Howey asked why it hadn't been deleted along with all the Perry-era ticks, which led to a bit of mild bickering. It then went quiet, mostly because Moira was worried. They didn't bicker, they had good-natured banter, but they never, ever bickered. Something unexpected was rocking their boat, it might be her and she didn't know it. Then the phone pinged, it was back!

Without asking, Howey swung back onto the highway and retraced his route. Soon, they were enjoying the pratincole as it resumed insect hunting over the pool, which was obviously slowly drying out. When it flapped off again, Howey introduced his family to the Burns after Susie had been fetched for a look. The kids, as ever, enjoyed being made a fuss over, Howey didn't talk shop and the pratincole had performed beautifully. Even Frank Conte seemed happy.

"Sorry about earlier, guys, not coming over like that", he said. "I was in a funk, I hate missing birds and when it's so special like this one, well, Esther would have loved it all, the bird, the event, everything. Sorry, I'm still struggling to come to terms. You understand?" They did, and they explained to the Burns' how they'd lost the doyen of Nova Scotia birding recently, just as she'd got her final tick.

They said their goodbyes and hit the road; they were going to be late getting home. Strangely, the normal tick euphoria was missing, and Howey could see that something was bothering Moira. He thought it might have been his insensitive question from earlier. She kept fiddling with her phone. "What is it Moira, was it me? I'm sorry".

"No, it was Peter. I noticed a slight droop on his left side as he stood and one eyelid was very slightly lower, did you see it?"

"Not really, I was more interested in chatting birds. Why, what are you thinking?"

"It might be a sign; he might be having another stroke".

Cross fished out Burns' business card from his pocket. "Text him now, tell Susie to get him to hospital as quickly as possible, Antigonish might be nearest, or I think there's one near Port Hawkesbury, at Strait?"

Moira did it straight away, telling them what she thought was happening, nothing came back immediately.

"You see, you still have your superpowers. If you're right, you might have made a real difference to that man, you might have saved his life".

Moira sniffled. Their bickering had hit her quite hard, but Howey saying what he'd said had made her happier than she could say. It meant that things were back to normal in the Cross clan, and they could enjoy the ride home with lots of laughing, some singing and a little bit of cautious banter. Moira wondered whether the bickering had alarmed Howey as much as it had her? If it had, he'd not shown it.

Half an hour from home, a short text told them that Peter Burns was now in intensive care, it was touch and go but they reckoned he might be ok. It was too much for Moira and she cried freely, apologising to everyone for being so silly earlier. Howey looked on, trying hard to not to seem worried, trying to convince himself that this was just one of those things that women do and not a symptom of anything else.

CHAPTER FOUR

Cara Nickerson read the letter from Pennard Cope twice. Such things were always a complication, which is why WildNova had always shied away from accepting them in the past. Thomas Cox had left his house, estate and all his worldly goods to WildNova for use in the protection of wildlife in Nova Scotia. Cope had approximated the estate's value, omitting the contents of the house. It was a substantial sum if fully realised, and welcome in times of high inflation and austerity, but a headache to administer all the same. Cara wasn't a great believer in serendipity, she knew that things only happened because you made it so, which made the call from Staff Sergeant Howey Cross even more poignant as it added a further complication.

"Was Mr. Cox actually a suspect in a crime?" she asked. Cross said not as such, but there were a number of additional issues to resolve and, as he knew that WildNova were now the owners of the property, he was hoping that they'd be able to work something out regarding access.

"I'd like to help but there seems to be no executor for you to deal with, we've had the lot dumped on our lap and don't have people on staff to deal with it at the moment. What I need is a couple of trusted volunteers, reasonably local to the property, who can help us out". Cross asked her to leave it with him, which she was more than happy to do.

Moira listened intently as Howey talked shop. It was unusual for him to furnish her with many details but, although she didn't know Thomas Cox personally, she felt that he was not a stranger. Perhaps it was his link to Esther, being her half-brother, that made it feel different? "I suspect an ulterior motive here, Howey", she said, but hadn't really wanted to.

"I need someone involved who is sensitive to the situation, who can empty the house of Cox's possessions but be aware of anything that we might find interesting, professionally".

"You want me to see if I sense something as we go through all his stuff, but can't say so because the police manual doesn't like that sort of thing, am I right?"

Cross squirmed a bit. Yes, that was exactly what he wanted but he didn't know how to say it without it sounding too odd. "I want people I can trust taking care where it's due. Thomas Cox deserves more than complete strangers going through his most personal possessions and, yes, I want your instincts in there, too. There, I've said it out loud now, will that do?"

"I'll need some help and I'll need clearly defined lines of action, a direct route to a senior officer and carte blanche to just get on with it".

"You're going to dress up as Miss Marple again, aren't you?"

"I might, when my tweed jacket and skirt get back from the dry cleaners".

"Moira, this is quite serious. I wouldn't ask but I need your skills and, in the end, WildNova will get a bunch of cash and we might get something relevant in the cases we're keeping open".

"I'll need my team briefing then, on what to look for, who is involved. Are we talking hidden shooters, forged bank drafts, stolen gold melted down for the African market?"

"You're teasing now. Team, what team?"

"Magowan and Hinzi. She's Cagney, I'm the Lacey one - we're the brassy broads that get the job done, copper", and she raised her skirt to show Howey her lacy frillies.

"For a professional, you're easily distracted you know, but seriously now. I'll ask Hinzi, she's got some spare time before she starts her new job, I'm sure she'd be ok with it. I'll also talk to Cara, leave her to me. I'll take the terrors and resurrect the Bull Pen for the duration. I'll talk to the local auction house for the better-quality stuff. Any wildlife books I'll try to sell through Amazon Marketplace or locally. The rest I'll put where I can but if it's trash, it'll go in a skip or for recycling. It might take a while, but it will be interesting although I was serious about the briefing. If Hinzi agrees, we'll be along to your office for a team meeting where you three professionals can set out what you think you need, agreed?"

Cross wasn't surprised that the idea of Moira doing something mentally challenging appealed, which was another reason why he'd asked. Since they'd got back from Brazil, she'd been mostly buzzing, and he wanted to keep her that way. Her Histrionic Personality Disorder wasn't going to get a foothold again, not on his watch, especially as he'd soon be talking to Geoffrey Watson about an old patient of his who'd supposedly had the same issues. Something he had no intention of mentioning to Moira.

As she opened the door to Thomas Cox's place in Lockhartville, Moira felt that it had a certain charm. The house was old, almost certainly a century home, and all the work Cox had done to it so far was of a high quality. Hinzi seemed quite taken by it too, especially when she went outside and saw that it sat in spacious grounds, most of which had been kept wild.

"About our offer of the stable plot, don't worry if this place appeals more, we'd fully understand", said Moira, correctly reading Hinzi's mind.

"I doubt that we could afford it, Moira, but thanks, I appreciate the flexibility. Let's see what it looks like when we've stripped it bare and see what WildNova expect for it, they'll want fair market value, I wouldn't expect anything less".

Once they'd made a start, it was pretty clear to see that Cox had already started his own clear-out at one time, probably when he first moved over from Ontario. He'd just not got around to taking the boxes to the recycling facility. They inventoried what they took to be of value and placed it all in one room. Then they started on his personal papers. Cox had been a meticulous keeper of documents, all neatly filed and labelled with names and dates. His book notes were well organised but mostly, in Moira's opinion, a bit dry. Anything that suggested it might be case-related was boxed and labelled, ready for Howey and his team to do the real detective work with. Presently, they got to something they'd put off dealing with, a glass case with a rather tatty stuffed bird inside. "Resplendent Quetzal from Central America, an antique by the looks of it although likely not of great value in that condition", said Moira. "You should take a photo for Darren, he'll be interested".

Hinzi took out her phone and took a few shots of the mount from different angles, then sent them to Darren, not telling him what it was. Moira felt uncomfortable near the Quetzal, and she didn't know why, perhaps because it was so badly mounted, or perhaps because it was dead and represented a time when people thought it ok to kill this sort of thing just to have it as an ornament. They were about to take a break for lunch, when Hinzi noticed that Phoebe was quieter than normal. "You ok, Phoebes?".

"Yes, but something bothers me. What's that?"

Moira looked and saw that Phoebe was staring at the Quetzal mount. She'd never seen a stuffed bird before, but Moira sensed that it was more than that. Undoing a set of clips at the back of the case, she opened it up to look inside and felt a sense of dread. Pulling out her phone she called Howey, just as Darren called Hinzi. Suddenly two urgent conversations were taking place. Uncannily, both ended at the same time, Moira and Hinzi looked at each other. "They're on their way".

It was fine out, so they all decamped to the yard while people arrived although the grass was a bit long, and Moira didn't want to be carting ticks around. Instead, they dragged an elderly bench over to the drive, one with a hand-carved message on the back. Moira took a phone shot of the rough engraving, it just said T & B. She wondered when it had been done, clearly in happier times for Thomas Cox and his wife, which was probably why he couldn't bear to leave it behind when he moved.

A van arrived before Howey, Darren and Crystal. Two men got out and started pulling body suits on. "It's a bit late for that", said Moira, but she knew that they were only following procedure. Howey arrived shortly after and apologised for not getting there first. He could see that Phoebe, especially, was a bit disconcerted. "Don't worry", said Moira. "She's not keen on the suits, glasses and masks, she likes to see people's eyes". When Phoebe heard, she gave her mom a look that questioned how old she thought she was.

Inside the house, the case and contents were being looked at before removal. Crystal took a series of photos before they carted it off to the lab, something to look over at leisure before the official ones arrived. "Is it what I think it is?" asked Moira.

"Yes, or at least it's an arrow from somewhere. It looks like the bird was removed from the original perch and the arrow substituted", said Howey. "That bird was there both times we visited but I didn't look closely; Cox was playing with us, or perhaps he didn't care by that point. Are you guys ok to carry on? You've done great so far".

"We're all but done. I have a box of papers to go, case notes on hunter deaths. They might just be copies, but you'll want your people to go through them, just in case. Does Darren have time to walk the grounds with Hinzi?"

"Sure, the forensic people will be off shortly, I'll just get those files".

Moira ushered Hinzi in the direction of her man while she and Crystal chatted. "Is he happier? He seemed to enjoy the trip; I was worried that he might walk".

"You know Howey, he doesn't open up much, at least not to me. Things seem to have improved though. Gooding has gone, Regis is reveling in being a consultant, even though we don't really need him and I'm finding my feet. I'm still shuttling back and forth to Halifax but I'm looking at places and I hope to find something local soon".

"And Terence, how's that?"

Crystal went a bit cool, but perhaps it was only Moira who noticed. "He's ok but I don't see much of him, he has to travel at the moment. He says it's only while he sets something or other up but, still, it can get a bit lonely".

Moira was surprised, She wasn't sure exactly what Terence did and she thought that he and Crystal had been getting on very well. "You don't think this is just hormonal?" she asked.

"Ha, trust you to know my cycle. It might be, I don't know. I think we'd both like to spend some time together, just to see how we are, maybe take a trip somewhere".

"I can give you an address in Brazil, if you're interested".

"No, I'm not quite ready for that yet, although I do now own a pair of compact binoculars, top of the range. I still don't get the birdy thing, but it makes Terence happier, and he's ok with my own little hobby when he's away".

Moira laughed out loud and so did Crystal. "Don't mention that to Howey while he's sat at his desk, he might not be able to stand up for an hour, well half an hour maybe". Crystal and Moira started having the giggles when Howey came back, looking bemused.

"What did I miss? Come on, tell me, I know it's about me. Crystal, I'm your boss, if you don't tell me, it'll go hard on you later". The giggles turned to hysterical laughter, with neither Moira nor Crystal able to speak properly. Eventually, they just waved things away as being the telling of a very funny joke. When Hinzi came back with Darren they were deep in conversation, he didn't look very happy. Howey gave Moira his well-used 'what?' look, but she shook her head, meaning he'd have to wait to find out.

The forensic people had said that they could finish up the sorting, but not to send anything else anywhere until they got back to them, it might take a few days. That suited Moira and Hinzi, so they locked up and went back to the farm.

"Well?" Moira could tell that Hinzi was distracted.

"He's worried about letting you and Howey down over the property, I knew he would be. I told him you'd already said it was ok, but I think it has to come from Howey, and I don't want to build anything up here. Mortgages are hard to come by and this place will be expensive. I'll ask a friend to look it up, she's a realtor in Halifax, she might have a better idea than me".

"I already did that; Going by similar properties on the Multiple Listing Service and taking into account the obvious work that needs doing, I think it could be yours for three-hundred thousand".

"Really, so little, why?"

"To get it done and dusted I think, and like I said, there's a few more repairs needed. I mentioned it to Cara, and she seemed happy with that figure. I expect she can't decide on her own, but it's a ballpark figure to work with. Howey knows something is up, I'll tell him tonight, he'll be fine with it".

"I did wonder when they went off and walked around back. It's a nice place, can they afford it?" Howey said. The kids had been put down for the night and Moira was setting up the machine to play one of her favourite movies.

"If the 'to sell' figure is what I think it is and WildNova are happy with it, then yes. It's going to be a bit complicated though, banks are fussy. I did wonder about buying it myself and then selling it to the Newells, but that would be interfering too much, wouldn't it?"

"Yes, it would. Let things take their course. If they don't get it, they'll still have the option next door and the plot will be sold to them at market value, Darren wouldn't want it any other way".

"No, you're right, we'll let things develop. Can you talk to Darren, tell him he won't be letting us, or mainly you, down if they do get it?"

"I'll do my best", said Howey, although he had no real idea of how to bring it up, other than directly.

"Crystal, I have a bit of a problem and need to talk to Darren about something, I could do with a bit of advice as to how to approach things". Howey knew he was being a bit needy, but he'd still not broached the subject of the house and the plot yet and time was ticking by.

"My advice is to tell him it's not him but it's you and, while you respect him, you don't want to have his baby. Does that help?"

"No, not really, but it being me is an option. It's the housing issue, Hinzi likes Thomas Cox's place and wants to make an offer, WildNova have already indicated that they'll accept it in principle. Darren thinks he'll upset me by buying it, after we said they could buy the plot next to us, the one we own".

"What are we talking, for your plot? I guess that it would take a pre-built type-thing. Straight onto the stable block pad, right?"

"Er, yes, I didn't think you knew about it".

"I do now. My dad owns a company that does pre-builds, I can move quickly because he never says no to his little girl. How much do you want for it, has an offer been made yet?"

"Crystal, are you teasing? Last I heard you were out looking at apartments to rent".

"Not anymore, not if there are better options. I like the idea of roots, rural living, a cop next door to come to my rescue if I need him. Why, are you saying I wouldn't make a good neighbour? I don't believe in closing the curtains".

"Have you been talking to Moira?" and Cross told her all about their old neighbour and the little visual treats she occasionally fed him and how he'd often be out on his deck in all weathers.

Crystal hooted with laughter; it was so Moira. "I can't promise anything like that, but I am interested and ready to move, a cash sale".

Cross wasn't sure how good an idea it was to have Crystal living cheek-by-jowl with him and Moira, but he promised to keep her informed if the Newells offered on Cox's cottage. Crystal countered with a promise to match the Newells' offer for the stable block pad. At least it would mean that, once he knew, Darren wouldn't think that he would be letting him down.

CHAPTER FIVE

Late July 2022

Susie Burns looked drawn, as if she'd not slept for a week, which was probably about right. Darren had volunteered to do the drive to talk to her, in the end it wasn't so bad. She'd taken a room in a hotel near the hospital in Antigonish that Burns had been transferred to, they met in a little restaurant nearby.

"He's not well, sergeant, I don't think it will be good for him to go through it all again, which is why I sent home for these, It's non-negotiable I'm afraid", and she passed over a thick brown envelope. Newell understood and said that they were grateful to get anything. Hopefully, the documents Susie had presented him with would fill in some of the blanks regarding Dan Bush and his underhand activities. Whether they would help in proving his involvement with Kenneth Coates remained to be seen.

"If we have any questions, are you willing to be contacted again, Mrs. Burns?"

"If he walks out, then maybe at some point in the future when he's fit, if not then no. If things go badly, I intend to put it all behind us. Bush is a bastard of the first order. True, what he did was just about legal, but it wasn't moral. Sadly, where we come from, people with a lot of money tend to tread wherever they fancy, and Bush has important friends in high places. Dirty friends who think nothing of doing dirty deeds".

Darren tried not to blurt out 'done cheap'. "If it helps, we're looking to make a case that might see Bush face charges here, serious charges. The more we know about him, the bigger a lever we'll have to pull. Howey Cross sends his best wishes".

"Thank him and thank his wife again. If she'd not noticed things the way she did, we might have lost Peter there and then. I'm sorry to be like this but we need to circle the wagons, I'm sure you understand. If the situation changes, I'll be in touch, otherwise thank you and good luck. Bush is slippery".

Darren texted the news to Howey once he'd got back in the car. As slow-burners went, the two outstanding cold cases had been positively glacial until now. The reply told him that Howey and Crystal were on their way to the Fundy Shores Women's Refuge in Digby. Darren looked at the message for a while, it looked like Crystal's work, Howey must be driving.

The contents of the envelope didn't really add much to the conversation they'd already had with Peter Burns, apart from confirming dates and locations. That Dan Bush had taken Burns' lobster licenses was clear enough, how he'd done it wasn't, but it wasn't their problem either. What shone through was Burns' apparent naivety when dealing with Bush. Darren scribbled a note on the envelope. 'Lobster licenses in New England, redundant, failing industry, not valid in Canada, bargaining chip with Canadian authorities?' Maybe there was a bit more than just legally filching lobster licenses here? It was something to think about. He opened his map app and started a route to a saved location. It was on the way home and a more formal sort of refuge, so he'd probably get a warmer reception than the last place, that was something at least.

'Darren, Moira just told me that you've had an offer on Cox's place accepted. Congratulations, if you need any help with anything you don't even have to ask, you do know that?'

Darren looked at the text for a while before answering, he'd have preferred to have told Howey in person. 'Thanks, I didn't want to say until I saw you. Hinzi was bowled over by the house, you know it's not far away, we still want to tend the farm for you, when you travel. Hinzi was looking at the price of fencing and chickens last night'.

'I'm very pleased for you both, a lovely place and don't worry about the plot here, Crystal wants it, but I wanted to get the ok from you before accepting her offer. Her daddy has a house ready to go, apparently'.

'Right, I see. We've got a full survey going next week but good, say yes to Crystal, I'm pleased for her. If the Cox place is a no-go on a bad survey, we still have options, catch up later'.

'Crystal says thanks and good luck with the survey, just a formality'.

Crystal was obviously still doing the texting and it annoyed Darren that he was annoyed by it. "Right then, coffee and a sausage and egg thing and on to the next place and maybe I'll tell Howey everything, when I think the time is right". Darren realised that he was talking to himself again as he pulled onto the road, heading for 'Never Alone' and whoever he might find there.

CHAPTER SIX

February 1989-Nearly 33 Years Earlier

Mrs. Lester had been quite strict about not going down to the basement, it was, after all, her house and if a guest was going to stay there, then they'd have to follow house rules.

"I was just wanting to help Mrs. Lester, I thought it'd be ok if I did a quick load of washing. I'm lacking smalls, so I was wanting to do a few of my own bits". Melissa had been surprised at how frosty Mrs. Lester had been when she'd tried to use the basement laundry, it was almost a rant. Yes, of course she remembered that the basement was out of bounds, but it was all a bit 'horror story' stuff. What might a grumpy old bat like Mrs. Lester keep down there that was so taboo?

"Leave your stuff in a bag like always, put it by the door but never go down there. I'll do it for you, but don't wait until you run out next time, plan girl, plan ahead", she said sharply, and Mrs. Lester went back to silently peeling potatoes while Melissa sloped off to her room, to her books and their stories of distant places filled with different things, better things.

Mrs. Lester was just Mrs. Lester. No first name had been offered when Melissa had enquired about the vacant room to let after seeing the ad in a local store. *'Clean young person offered lodging, reasonable rates. Contact Mrs. Lester'*. The little store had any number of bits of card festooned over a cork board just inside the door, most had tear-off strips with numbers on, but Mrs. Lester's ad was on a nice piece of card, neatly written in green ink. Melissa charitably thought that perhaps a green pen was all that she'd had to hand, or perhaps she was making a statement about herself, and Melissa started to build a picture of who this Mrs. Lester might really be. The ink suggested that she was mysterious, possibly occult, but that she'd been oppressed into drudgery by controlling parents. The ink was her way of rebelling as a child and she still used it, still found herself saying 'look at me'.

The young woman at the checkout didn't know any more about the room when she'd asked, but she said that Mrs. Lester was ok, well known locally but kept herself to herself. 'Not some crazy psycho with a chainsaw then, well, you do read about them', thought Melissa, and she had to revise her minds-eye image a little. Mrs. Lester then became a dowdy widow with lank hair and a worn look, she'd shuffle about hugging a bag tightly to her chest, inside was a half-finished shawl for a baby she never had. Once on her way to the address, Melissa chided herself for 'romancing' as her sister had called it, but she decided that this time it was just harmless fun, a bit of filling in the blanks with no malice intended, where was the harm?

The interview for the room, such as it was, had been brief. Mrs. Lester had a penetrating stare that she never seemed to turn off, as if she saw through to your very bones. Melissa had a reference from her last place, which was taken and read without any sign of emotion. Melissa had been in her last place for only a year but had decided that now was the time to go more rural. She fancied a new start and the chance to meet some different people. It would also help if she was somewhere far away from a certain man that she really didn't want to get involved with anymore.

The room was ok, but basic. The kitchen was dated, old and in need of thorough renovation. The family room was for family only, which seemed to be just Mrs. Lester. You could go in if you needed to talk to her, but it wasn't anywhere you wanted to be. It was old, as if frozen in time, just like

Mrs. Lester. The front room was where guests could relax, watch the old TV or read one of the even older books. It had a small table and an old sofa with a distressed and patched brown leather cover. There was a lamp that looked like a crafter had attacked it with shells, some of which had made a run for it. There was an old record player that worked, but no records to play on it. A large vase with fresh flowers sat in the window, it changed regularly, one piece of colour in an otherwise monochrome landscape. The flowers didn't fit the mood of the room, not at all, and Melissa thought they must have some great significance Perhaps they were a sign for a long-lost lover to finally find Mrs. Lester and sweep her off her feet. The bathroom was shared and basic. Melissa noticed the lack of a lock on the door immediately, so she took to taking her little transistor radio in with her when she occupied it, just to make a point.

Melissa had decided to take things three months at a time. She wanted to spend time studying but didn't know what she wanted to absorb herself in yet, and so was working through the library in Annapolis Royal, descending on subjects, digesting them then, if they weren't to her taste, casting them aside. Melissa knew that she was hard to please, but she also knew that there was something waiting out there, just for her. It was why she'd originally left home after all, that and her aunt.

Annapolis Royal had the feeling of being a place waiting for people to fill it. The town catered for lots of tourists, mostly day visitors who would walk the old fort, browse the historic gardens, and gorge themselves in local restaurants when the mood took them. It was the sort of place you went home from, which gave it a sense of melancholy when they did. Melissa found that she preferred the quiet weekdays, early in the day when the air was still fresh and tourist cars didn't litter the streets or crawl around the circuit looking for parking. She'd often sit in a cafe watching the drivers doing their never-ending waltz, all the time watching for the cops, whose only duty seemed to be the persecution of any cars daring to go five over.

Just north-east of town was a nice walk along the old railway bed, it was safe and comfortable underfoot. Running off it, an informal path went around a rough area of grass, bushes and trees, it was really just a glorified overflow pond for the local sewage works, a place kept filled by the good people of Annapolis Royal with minimum thought. There was talk of making a more formal trail, with parking, but Melissa thought that the place would lose some of its charm if they did that.

Melissa took great pains to fill in her personal planner. Despite what Mrs. Lester thought, she liked to plan things- unless they were laundry-related. She particularly liked to set herself targets, specify dates, live a random, but ultimately ordered life. She'd even decided that her next place to live would be in the north, Cape Breton, Sydney Mines. It sounded grounded, earthy, remote. She'd written two pages of notes about a place she'd never been to. The woman who had claimed to be her mother, before she'd left her and her sister to their own devices, reckoned Melissa had ants in her pants, but what would she know?

On the March day when it all happened, she'd been doing the rough walk again, watching the ducks, enjoying the sounds and stopping every few hundred metres to listen. Things rustled in the wet grass and sometimes Melissa heard a real racket, but she didn't know what might be making it. It was just something deep in the wet grass, probably a wet grass bird. The house had been dark when she got back, Mrs. Lester was nowhere to be seen. This wasn't unusual, because Mrs. Lester often bustled around the town, shopping, chatting very briefly to a select few, before hurrying home to Bay Avenue, always hurrying, never noticing the beauty of the setting. What was unusual about today was the door to the basement had been left ajar. Although it wasn't ever locked, Mrs. Lester was more than firm about her not being allowed down there. Melissa had been confused about it, but not overly bothered because people were allowed their privacy, secrets even. When she'd previously fallen foul of attempting to go into the basement, not even making the door at the bottom of the stairs, Mrs. Lester had chewed her out badly, piquing Melissa's curiosity. Now the top and bottom doors were open, and Mrs. Lester was definitely out shopping, judging by the lack of her old brown leather bag, Quite a finely crafted thing and something she always took with her when she shopped.

"Hello", called Melissa down the stairs. There was no answer, no noise at all but then she hadn't expected any. Then there was something, what was that? She announced her presence again loudly, just in case. "Hello". She strained to listen, but there was nothing there, nothing at all. Just as she turned to close the door there was a small noise, like a grunt, as if a small and inoffensive animal was snuffling around down there.

'Hello". This time her voice had changed in tone, from being a loud 'hello is anyone there', to a more guarded 'hello, who's there?'

She listened intently, not moving and there it was again, the snuffling, but this time she was absolutely certain that the noise came as a response to her calling. This wasn't right, this didn't make any sense.

Curiosity killed the cat. For some reason that saying popped into her mind, almost as a warning. She shrugged it off. This was Annapolis Royal and just a sour old lady's basement, not the gates of hell. Walking down the stairs in what Melissa liked to think of as her positive manner, she reached the bottom and nervously pushed at the partially open door, it gave a little. Inside was a small room, ill-lit with an old washer and an even older airing rack. There was an ancient sink and a battered table, it was a laundry, nothing more, nothing to fear. The fittings all looked very dated; they were in keeping with the overall neglected quality that the house exuded. It wasn't dirty, it wasn't shabby even, but everything was ready for replacement. Much like Mrs. Lester, thought Melissa, then mentally chastised herself for being so cruel.

Taking in the view slowly, she saw that another room led off from the laundry. It had a substantial bolt on the door, but it wasn't secured, and that door was also ajar. Perhaps this was where Mrs. Lester's dark secret lay? Melissa's eyes were now skipping around the laundry, taking in details, noticing things, clues. She saw a stick leaning against the wall by the door, it was thick, heavy-looking, smooth. It had what appeared to be several dark patches on it, bruises almost. Melissa chose not to examine it too closely in the dull light, it was probably for use in the laundry or something.

The door with the heavy bolt pushed open with no creak. Melissa had been convinced that there would be a creak, the door looked old, strong, there for a purpose. It was a door that said 'creak' in big letters and this door was letting down the genre. Inside, the room had plain, utility colours on the walls and a sturdy table with nothing on it. There was a bed, made up but obviously sat on afterwards, the cover was ruffed up in the middle. In one corner there was a chair and on it a box of what looked like old toys, to the right was a wardrobe, large, mysterious. It was the sort of wardrobe that might lead to an enchanted world if you pushed through the hanging coats and your heart was pure.

Melissa paused, she was narrating her thoughts again, something she tended to do a lot, something that she thought might be an indication of where she should be going career-wise. Perhaps the arts would suit her, certainly something creative because that's who she was. A flimsy door in one wall was wide open and she could see part of what looked like a toilet. It occurred to her that this might be one of those secret apartments that people built, then let out but didn't tell the authorities about, kept a secret so that the property taxes remained unaffected. It was very spartan, so whoever it did house must be up to no good themselves, naughty Mrs. Lester.

The grunt was louder than before and startled her, but before she could react, it went dark, very dark. Strong hands stopped her from screaming, stopped her from doing anything. Whoever had got a hold of her was very strong, much too strong for her, there was no point struggling. Then it occurred to her, surely this must be a mistake or a joke or something. But it wasn't.

It was still dark when she woke up and she found that she could barely move at all. The snuffling was close now, too close, and there was a smell that she couldn't define, or one that her mind refused to even consider. There was movement, pressure. The snuffling was even closer, and she soon felt why. The gag stopping her from screaming was tight, choking almost. Whatever covered her head was blocking out all light and was tied around her neck, but not too tightly, that was something at least. She felt air moving where air shouldn't be, where air wouldn't move normally if she was dressed, but her mind still lied to her. It did it for her own good, for her sanity.

Melissa tried to think about the benches in the botanical gardens where the people they were dedicated to were loved enough to warrant the gesture. She desperately wanted to have a bench there, from someone, one day. A bench for her, with her name on a shiny plate, lovingly engraved. A bench from someone who thought it worthwhile to care enough about her to take the trouble to buy one, buy it and install it and come along on quiet afternoons and remember her. The bench donor would linger, looking at the bench, before slowly walking away, eyes moist at a favourite memory of a special person, her.

There was more grunting happening, then it went quiet for a moment as if the grunter had been disturbed. Her mind's-eye saw a sad creature looking up, hearing something, fearing something. It was noble with a striking profile, handsome even. The peace didn't last long before it all started again, stopping just as suddenly. Melissa sensed a movement then heard a noise, a yelp, as if coming from an animal that had been very bad and was now being punished, beaten, hit time and time again. Each rhythmic yelp got quieter and quieter, until the yelp had gone and only thuds filled her ears. Soft thuds, all she heard was soft thuds, again and again.

The thuds stopped and then it stayed dark, it stayed dark for a long time. Melissa suddenly gasped as if drowning and she knew then that she must have slept again. Now she was awake, and her mind was telling her things, real things that you could only ignore for so long. But her mind was wrong, she knew that; it was unreliable, it hid things from her, important things. She knew that it had been just as wrong every time before, right up until the therapist had cured her, found the problem, the trigger, the root cause. She'd been thirteen at the time.

Things now happened. She was lifted slightly but her arms and legs remained tied to the bed. She'd reasoned that it had to be the bed, based on what she'd seen before it went dark and the shape her body was making. Her mind had been trying to distract her, telling her that this might all be a big misunderstanding, then the moment of truth arrived without warning, and she knew then exactly what had happened to her. Slowly her mind lifted above the bed, and she looked down, looked at her sore wrists and ankles, saw the hood, saw the marks, the bites. She could still feel them being made. Her bloodied body had been in the wars, as her sister would say.

Melissa was shocked to find that she was feeling calm. 'Ok, what now?' She surprised herself, this wasn't what people did in situations like this. They screamed and they clawed, they bit, and they punched. They flailed and swung wildly, they defended their honour, fought for their lives. They didn't think 'what next', but Melissa did, because some of this wasn't unfamiliar, it was just that this time she didn't know who'd been doing these things to her. The light was expected as soon as she felt the hands at whatever was holding the hood on, but when it came it was painful, it burned, seared. It must have only been so uncomfortable for less than a minute, but that was enough. It was like trying to stare down the full sun. When her vision improved, she saw that Mrs. Lester was looking down at her, not with a concerned expression, more looking resigned, even disappointed in her. Mrs. Lester's hands and arms were red to the elbows, her cheeks smeared red too, it looked like she'd inadvertently wiped a red hand across them. Her clothes were darker red, in places stiff-looking, in others, moist. The bright light was reflecting off the damper patches making them shiny. For a moment she just looked down at Melissa, her eyes gave nothing away, not offering any sympathy, not a flicker. The gag stayed in place, along with the ropes binding her.

Most of the room wasn't visible from her position, no matter how Melissa strained to see. The plain walls were still plain, although one seemed to have acquired a row of fine, dark spots. The stick that had been outside was propped up nearby and in view, only the top part. It was wet too, and very red.

There was a muffled noise. Someone was dragging something accompanied by small thuds, then the door shut but the room remained bright, the light stayed on. Melissa forced herself to breathe, it was hard. She wanted to pass out, to go back into a peaceful blackness where none of this was happening. Unconscious she didn't care, unconscious she could go to her safe place, the nice garden with the apple tree that was always covered in blossoms. She could sit there on her own bench, the one with her name on a shiny plate, the one put there just for her.

Melissa could feel that she was drying out, her skin contracting as whatever was on her congealed. It was a long process, the drying, but it was the only thing to think about because anything else was the stuff of pure horror. Melissa concentrated on the drying for the longest time, it was an odd sensation, then the door opened. Mrs. Lester had a bucket and a cloth and was wetting Melissa, everywhere, arms, legs, personal places. Wetting, washing, rinsing the cloth in the bucket at irregular intervals. When Mrs. Lester was satisfied, she stood up and draped a couple of large bath towels around Melissa, tucking them under her, changing her temperature. Up until that point, the temperature hadn't been a factor, but now that she felt warmer it was, and she started to shiver.

Without a word, Mrs. Lester left the room again, the noise of the door closing behind her being amplified to painful proportions. The one single thought that had held Melissa together so far, was that she had some modesty, somewhere. Now she knew that her out-of-body vision wasn't just her coping mechanism kicking-in, it was true. She was totally naked and had been throughout.

Melissa's apple tree was quite old, gnarly, but not that tall. It wasn't a climbing tree because it was quite dense. The blossom on it now was different. It was usually white, a very pure white, virginal even. Now it was red, blood red. Melissa didn't want to sit on her bench under that tree anymore, it didn't feel right.

The bolt slid back over, it was a sound that Melissa hadn't registered individually before, but she did now. Her senses were on full alert, hearing every rustle of clothing or shuffle of feet. She even picked up the sound of a robin singing in the yard, or at least nearby. Mrs. Lester looked at her briefly, coldly, as if deciding what to do with an old appliance that had let her down, then she removed the gag. The air in Melissa's throat was so good that she took a moment to enjoy it. Mrs. Lester was busy with a fresh bucket, cleaning the room, the cloth being rinsed often, the noise of the water as it ran through Mrs. Lester's fingers and back into the bucket impossibly loud.

"What...?"

"I told you not to come down here, girl, I told you and you did anyway and I'm not responsible. I told you and you did anyway". Mrs. Lester had stopped her cleaning and seemed pleased to get something off her chest, something she'd decided had to be said. Melissa felt sorry for Mrs. Lester. She was right, she had told her, she'd made it very clear. It was Melissa's fault again, all of this was Melissa's fault, it always had been, she was a bad girl through and through.

Mrs. Lester's face had changed, she looked resigned. "I've done it now, I should have done it years ago, I know, but I've done it now. I need to think, you be quiet girl, not that anyone can hear you, I know that well enough. You be quiet now; I have to think. Here, drink this", and she produced a child's cup with a bendy straw in it, carefully placing the straw between Melissa's chapped lips. Melissa sucked. The liquid was strawberry flavored and possibly the most fantastic thing that she'd ever tasted. She drained the cup and felt so very grateful to Mrs. Lester, she said so, but Mrs. Lester was unmoved by her thanks and left.

Melissa's mind started to feed her information, slowly, in bite sized pieces, digestible pieces. She laughed to herself at the irony of the words her mind had fed her, bite sized was about right. Melissa listened for the robin again, she liked their song, but the door was shut, and she couldn't hear anything. Soon she tired and, despite trying her best to avoid it, fell asleep and had the dream.

She was hanging by her fingers, gripping an impossibly high branch. She knew that she shouldn't have climbed the apple tree, but now that she had and had slipped, she was going to fall, fall and die. She didn't want to die, but she knew that she would when she couldn't hold on any longer. She felt the warmth go down her legs and into her shoes, it had happened again. She woke with a start, she wasn't alone.

"I've made a decision, you can go".

Melissa was now awake and feeling wet, but Mrs. Lester didn't seem to have noticed and was carrying clean clothes.

"I'm letting you go, understand? You can do what you want. it's time I gave this up too, I should have ended it long ago, I knew it would all come back to haunt me, one day". Mrs. Lester reached over and undid the ropes binding Melissa's hands, then her feet, but Melissa didn't move, she didn't believe that this was real. She didn't want to leave the safety of her warm, wet bed.

"Come on, get up girl, get dressed then take your stuff and go, tell who you want. I'll wait for them to come, it had to happen sometime. I'm ready, I've done right now, made my peace. I'm sorry for you, for this, I truly am, but I told you not to come down, I told you. I won't mention you when they come, not to anyone, I never did before". The confession was a shock, then Melissa suddenly got control, total control with crystal clear clarity of thought. She sat up on the damp mattress and flexed. How long had she been there? Deciding that that was a question for later, she silently got off the bed. Mrs. Lester just sat on the edge of the bed, she had a detached look in her eyes, they were staring at the imprint left by Melissa's now absent body and the recent stains. She was moving only slightly as she breathed, it gave her a slight rocking motion, but you had to look hard to see it.

Melissa dressed quickly as feeling came back to her limbs. Her subconscious told her that she needed to clean up better, but she'd find a way to do that later. First of all, she needed to be dressed, then when she was, the next move would become clearer. 'One fence at a time, girl', her mother's voice said in her head, although she sounded just like Mrs. Lester.

Mrs. Lester looked around slowly just after Melissa had pulled on her top, a hand-knitted jersey and a gift to her from her sister. There was no change in the expression on Mrs. Lester's face as the stick that had been resting silently against the wall described a perfect arc before splitting her forehead. The next blow landed nearby, the third in virtually the same as the first opening it up nicely and spattering the bed. By ten blows it was done. Mrs. Lester keeled forward, landing face-down and losing bits of brain on the soiled sheet.

"Right", said Melissa, pausing with the stick raised and ready to crash it down once again if she needed to. "Right". She lowered the stick and waited. Mrs. Lester uttered a few unformed grunts, but Melissa knew well that the dead made noises for a while, they always did before becoming as silent as the grave. The bolt slid silently into place. It was redundant really because nobody was going anywhere from that room, but it was pushed home anyway because it needed to be, for peace of mind. Melissa climbed the stairs slowly, her legs now less steady than just a few minutes ago. By the top, they gave out and she bounced down two steps on her knees, before grabbing the rail and hauling herself up.

The water in the elderly shower was hot, refreshing, purifying. Melissa dressed in fresh clothes again, bundling up the now messy ones that Mrs. Lester had presented her with, another load ready for the laundry, she'd keep the sheets needing to be washed separately. Standing at the top of the stairs to the basement, she threw them to the bottom. She'd deal with those later too. The doorbell rang, it surprised Melissa because she didn't recall ever hearing it before. After a brief hesitation, she smoothed down her top out of habit and went to answer the door. On the step was a middle-aged lady, almost a Mrs. Lester clone but perhaps fifteen years younger and slightly dumpier. "Are you Melissa?" she asked, cocking her head slightly to one side, a bit like a spaniel that didn't understand a command.

"Yes, why, can I help you?"

"I found this dear, on a bench at the Botanical Gardens. I asked in the store, and they said you were at Mrs. Lester's, is she not here?"

Melissa looked at her planner in confusion. She hadn't realized that it was missing, but there it was, in the clone's hands and now she was asking awkward questions.

"Mrs. Lester? She's gone to stop with her youngest sister Vivienne, in Cumberland County. Yes, I'm Melissa, I'm taking care of the house while she's gone. Vivienne is quite ill. Mrs. Lester is nursing her, but they don't know how long it will be for, it's not looking very good I'm afraid".

"Oh", said the visitor at the unexpected news. "I am sorry, please tell her that Mrs. Rose wished her well. I don't really know her, none of us do, I don't think she ever mentioned a sister. Good that you are around, Melissa, looking after her place like this. We always thought that was what she needed, someone to talk to and help her out, a young and livelier person around the house again".

Melissa was composure personified. "Thank you, I'll tell her Mrs. Rose, that's very thoughtful of you. She is kind of private although, do you know, I think you're right, she has become much chattier since I arrived, and of course I'm only too happy to help out my aunt Muriel at this difficult time".

"Your aunt, Muriel, really? Well, I never. Your mother is Mrs. Lester's sister too, then? Sorry, I'm asking too many questions as usual and I'm sure you have your hands full. I live at the blue house up on the corner, do drop by any time. I'll do us tea, it's so nice to have young people around, and please, tell Mrs. Lester I called, don't forget now".

"I won't and no, you're not asking too much, it must be a surprise to her friends. My father Robert was Muriel's older brother, he died some time ago, just after I was born. My mom is still alive, but she has a new man, and we don't get on, so I left them to it, that's how I came to be in Annapolis Royal. Aunt Muriel knew of my problems and offered space". Melissa knew the story had holes, but she was an expert patcher, and it could be fixed later. Mrs. Rose seemed shocked by the sudden surge of information. "Muriel, her name is Muriel? Well, I never, nobody knew. Thank you dear. I'm sorry to be so nosey, nothing much happens around here, and we could do with some excitement. She handed Melissa her planner and slowly wandered off up the road, audibly talking to herself. Melissa watched her go, shut the door and burst into tears, sliding slowly down until she was sat on her haunches. 'Aunt Muriel and her unknown siblings Vivienne and Robert, what have I done this time?'

The sound of a singing robin outside woke Melissa. She'd fallen asleep on the sofa; her newly returned planner lay on the floor. Retrieving the planner, she looked at her notes in surprise, was she really that cold hearted? In front of her lay a precise plan of what to do now and how to proceed later. It didn't look much like her handwriting, but it must be, it was her planner. She reasoned that the shock of everything had caused her to forget what she'd written, shock did that, or so she'd been told. Melissa patiently read the whole of the plan again, it was actually quite good. If she carried this off, a move north wouldn't be necessary, and then, later and when loose ends had been safely tied up, she could become someone else, somewhere else again.

Mrs. Lister's old Ford Taurus was very roomy. You could sleep in it if you had to, you could certainly lie down full-length with the back seats down, as they handily were. What it didn't have was four-wheel drive, she'd have to be careful where she was going.

It had all been surprisingly easy, apart from getting the old lady up from the basement, which she decided to do in stages in the end. Loading the car might have caused anxiety, but the elderly of Annapolis Royal tended to draw the curtains by seven in the evening and only a few courting couples or kids blowing dope were out and about. The spot she'd selected was soft and easy digging. She was rather glad to ditch the dead cat that was her excuse for the hole if anyone asked, it was getting very high. The M she'd carved lightly on the trunk of a nearby Silver Birch hadn't been her idea, but she'd done it anyway. As Melissa drove home, because it was home now, she ran the events of the past couple of days through her mind. The car screeched to a stop, luckily nobody had been behind her. Where was the boy? Panic started to grip her, but something else took over and she kept driving until a safe pull-in allowed her to regain her composure. Where was the dead boy?

Back at the house, her panic was always there but she pushed it aside as she searched everywhere. At the back of the property, a place she'd never had need to visit, was an old shed in the style of a Dutch Barn. It was padlocked, the lock looked new. If she couldn't find the keys, she'd have to smash the lock off, which would be a shame, it would spoil the shed, but if the boy was in there it would become another problem for her to deal with.

Mrs. Lester's old leather bag was a fine one, hand-made, it exuded quality. Melissa could understand why she was so attached to it, it seemed to have character, it was a possession, now it was her possession and she liked it very much. Inside the bag a variety of compartments held the sort of things an older lady might carry, a compact with a distorted mirror, lipstick in a colour that was probably obsolete and a purse with her driving licence, health card and, oddly, a condom. Melissa looked amazed at the driving license, her name was Muriel, Mrs. Lester's name was Muriel, how had she known that? Resuming her search, at the bottom of the bag and under a nice pair of kid gloves, a bunch of keys gave Melissa what she was looking for. One of the keys was new, shiny and would surely fit the padlock.

The shed relied on natural light to illuminate the interior, but the light had a job on fighting through the grime of the only window, it looked like it had never been cleaned. Melissa fetched a torch from the kitchen and went inside. Sat on a floor of patched concrete was an old chair, on it was a human-shaped parcel, carefully wrapped up as if ready to pop in the mail, it had that smell. Melissa backed the car up to the shed and later went for another drive in the country.

In the kitchen, over coffee, Melissa reviewed the situation. A part of her was telling her to run, but a more sensible, cooler part was telling her that this was now an opportunity if she held her nerve. Wondering about a cookie to go with the coffee, Melissa opened a few cupboards. High at the back of one of them was a tin, a cookie tin, but it wasn't used for cookies. Mrs. Lester clearly didn't much like the idea of banks; in many ways it was, for now, the final piece of the new jigsaw. She had a place to be and money, rather a lot of money, certainly enough to finance her new life until she found a job. This house and this life would do, at least until she'd decided where she was heading next.

Over the next few days, the older lady bush telegraph had been working overtime and various clones called by to say hello, ask after Mrs. Lester and shake their heads sadly as Melissa embroidered the truth, another of her sister's sayings. Fitting in by being Aunt Muriel's niece had required next to no effort, in fact the whole thing had been completely effortless, provided you discounted the energy expended digging a couple of holes. Most days Melissa stayed in and read or walked her favourite trail with its noisy grassbirds. Sometimes she wondered where her ideas came from, wondered whether she really knew a Muriel, Vivienne or Robert, and that was why their names had tripped so readily off her tongue. She couldn't remember anyone of that name though, and she decided that they were probably characters from one of the novels she'd read and forgotten but, the thing was, she rarely forgot anything.

The house had taken the changes in its stride. It seemed to enjoy the energy that Melissa had brought, it almost smiled. True, it made ominous noises, especially in the dark of the night, but Melissa had replaced locks, fitted bolts and turned the place into something of a fortress. The only time it felt unsecure was when she dreamed, of the weight of a body on her, of feeling him, the dead boy, feeling him where he hadn't been invited, and then there was Mrs. Lester looking at her, glass-eyed, as the stick took away her new-found freedom from her secret.

After a few months, Melissa had a new worry. None of her clothes felt very comfortable anymore, too tight. She worried that she was losing her figure and resolved to cut out the cakes, ice cream, candy, comfort food and to walk more, yes, she'd walk more. The house hadn't been physically changed at all either, the same dull walls and tired furnishings, it was starting to bother Melissa. She'd had plans, big plans, but the money wasn't going to last forever and now, on top of the regular bills, she needed some different clothes, at least until she lost all the new fat. She was also feeling sick some mornings, so she called the local practice for an appointment, expecting to be told of a lengthy wait. Now was not the time to fall sick again. Dr. Bond, had already agreed to let her register with the practice, in view of the circumstances, and he made time to fit her in. The next day she was walking into the waiting room looking and feeling confident.

"Are you married, Melissa, I see no rings. Don't get me wrong, I'm not being judgmental, lord knows the world has changed". Doctor Bond was elderly and gave off a learned air. Melissa had hoped he might be more dashing, a bit like Sean Connery, her favourite Bond actor. Instead, he was hunched, crumpled and the glasses clinging to the bridge of his nose looked like antiques. She decided that his look was classic old-school, a real community doctor, she could picture him in the wild west, delivering babies and doling out useless jollop to gullible cowboys.

"No Dr. Bond, why?"

"You're having a baby, and in about five months I'd say. You can do the math if you remember the, er, event". The inflection in Dr. Bond's voice did more than hint at disapproval, but Melissa didn't pick up on it as time slowed. Melissa was good at math, not that this sum needed any more components than Mrs. Lester's obviously fertile son. She quickly rallied and gushed. "Gerry will be so pleased, that's what we thought but, well it had never happened before, and we thought we couldn't. Thank you again Doctor; I can't wait to tell him the good news".

Dr. Bond had been worried, but Melissa's pleasure was his delight, and he was happy to be wrong about her. Soon The Lord would bless us once again with the miracle of life and then welcome Melissa and Gerry into holy matrimony, hopefully.

"I'll go and call him; he works out west. We're hoping to move to a house out there when we can. It's all very exciting, and mother, she'll be so happy, she's always wanted to be a grandmother". Melissa only kept the grin in place until she was out of sight of any surgery windows. Pregnant, shit. It could only be the one time, it had only been the one time, was it only once? She wasn't sure. She needed to think and be creative, so she headed for the little café in town, it was one of her regular spots, they knew her there.

"Penny for them", said Laura, the youngish café proprietor as she welcomed Melissa. Over time she'd become a sort of friend to Melissa, perhaps casual confidant was more like it as Melissa had used her to help build the web of lies that would eventually, and with patience, make the house her own. It had been surprisingly easy so far and would continue to be so unless someone unexpected crawled out of the woodwork.

"Oh, just life things, Laura. I might have to move away; my aunt isn't looking good and I'm not sure we'll see her again. Then there'll be lots of legal things to tie up, wills, that type of thing".

"If she dies, will you sell the house? Property is in big demand here, or maybe you could rent it out. There's an agent here in town that can do that for you, I have her card somewhere. I'll miss you if you leave though, there's not that many younger people around here and you can only talk knitting and how expensive butter is getting for so long. By the way, and I know it's not my place to say so, but I do it as a friend- maybe watch those carbs?" Melissa laughed and went into a routine about how she'd stopped running and working out, but had joined a gym in Digby now, so she'd soon get her shape back. She hadn't even considered renting out, it might be worth doing just that, get someone in, someone handy and make renovation a part of the contract, low rent as compensation. The house might provide a steady income while she sorted out her growing problem and after, well that was a different kettle of fish.

"You know you never talk about guys to me, Melissa, has there ever been a special someone in your life. I know I'm being nosey again, but you won't find a guy around here easily, local boys tend to be earmarked at birth, and if you lean in a different direction, well good luck meeting anyone with similar needs". Melissa quickly processed the confusing conversation, Laura was coming on to her, she'd asked about men and now she'd told her that she was available. Melissa had never even considered that Laura was anything more than a straight local girl. She had to let her down gently.

"I've never mentioned him before, but I've had a long-distance relationship with a man, Gerry, for some years now. We don't get to see each other very often, but I think it's time we spent a bit of quality time together. I'm thinking of going away for a year or more to be with him, if he's ok with it. To tell you the truth I'm a bit worried about asking him".

Laura hid any disappointment she felt well. "If he truly loves you, he'll be delighted you've made a move. Is he stuck somewhere with a job or something?"

"Yes, out west, working for a very needy company, he doesn't get much time off".

"American owned, I bet, they're the worst. They think they can treat people like a stock animal, then discard them when they decide they're of no use, just like some people". Laura was quite animated, and Melissa correctly guessed that she'd been in the same boat at some time, stuck working for a company that only saw dollars on profit sheets, not people. She'd obviously been dumped at one time too. Laura skipped off, promising to come back shortly with the agent's card, she had a newly arrived customer to serve, it was a popular café. Melissa started to feel a bit queasy and made for the bathroom. When she got back to her table, the card was waiting for her, but Laura was still buzzing around busy. Melissa mouthed a 'thank you', paid and slipped out. She was a bit annoyed with herself, if she'd not told her the Gerry tale, Laura might have been an option worth keeping open. Any port in a storm.

The house had become surly recently and had reverted to feeling unloved when you walked in off the street. It was hard to quantify, but it was as if it had a personality, and not always a cheery one. Melissa was quite keen to get away for a while, even if she'd have issues to resolve, difficult issues. She needed thinking time, a space away from the house and its grey thoughts. For any future in Annapolis Royal that she might have, it was better to resolve things well away from the public eye, unless she still had time.

The library was always a place of refuge for Melissa. She was an avid reader, anything from romantic fiction to medical journals. She lapped up new information and had a talent for keeping it all in her head, everything. She had no idea where she got her gift from. Today she was researching, specifically, pregnancy and the termination thereof. She knew that it was a gamble this late, but needs must when the Devil drives. Most of the books she'd accumulated in a pile were about the wonders of pregnancy, not how to stop it without getting the medical community too involved. Nothing she'd read told her what she needed to know. It was no good, she'd have to talk to someone who knew this stuff, unless there was a restricted store of books in the library that you had to ask for.

The librarian was one of those who watched everything, like a vulture deciding which piece of ripe roadkill to descend on first. As if reading Melissa's thoughts, she scowled and nodded towards a metal drawer full of index cards. Melissa smiled what she hoped was a thanks, her mind was screaming 'supercilious bitch'. Whoever had set up the book references had done a good job in obscuring the contents of some of the riskier titles. She smiled when she saw one marked Chatterley, Lady and a large 18 showing that it was not for minors or possibly the under forties. She kept flicking through the cards. Unfortunately, they were filed by author.

"Problem?" said the disapproving voice over her shoulder.

"I'm researching abortion for a paper I'm working on, an advice sheet and I'm anti, if you must know, but I need to know the details, the processes, so I can give the advice as supported by the medical facts, do you see?"

The librarian did and, although she didn't much care for the subject, reached over pulled out a batch of cards from the medical section. She briskly leafed through, selecting two cards and replacing the rest. Then she led Melissa to the front desk, behind which a locked cabinet contained what she wanted. Handing over the books, the librarian grimaced. "Let me know when you're done, we don't want any deadbeats getting a look at these", and she swept off back to her perch.

Melissa returned the look of disgust for the subject and went back to her table. This was better, and Melissa had soon filled in two blank pages of her current planner with notes, the new planner especially bought to cater for what she called 'her future'. Having got what she needed, Melissa returned the books and headed for the Botanical Gardens and her bench of choice. Mary Cummings, for whom the bench had been donated, had been seventy-five when 'the Lord took her to be with the Angles', the plaque said. Melissa always felt inclined to give it a little buff with her sleeve every time she settled in for a think, despite the spelling mistake.

The math told her, as she'd suspected, that she was too late for a regular termination, so this had to be an irregular one. The best solution, one that didn't involve trying to buy chemicals in a small community or crooked bits of wire, involved alcohol and baths, and it would have to do. Afterwards, she'd have to clean up again, but the countryside around Keji was a big place and very accommodating for a girl with a spade.

The liquor store lady gave Melissa a look when she saw the gin in her basket.

"Party, my old school friends are descending on me for three days, city girls. I suggested just a few beers, but they say that gin is all the rage now, so gin it is. I'm not that bothered myself, I prefer the mixer really, but I'll be social, I'm not big city like that bunch". For an off-the-cuff excuse it was pretty good, and the server sympathized and even mentioned twice that returns were possible if the seal wasn't broken. Melissa thanked her and said she'd live in the hope that she'd bring at least two of the bottles back once the crowd had gone.

The house didn't approve of the drink, Melissa could tell. Drawers stuck, it made noises, extra noises, and even let a rodent in that insisted on running right across her path as she walked from the kitchen to the family room one evening. She might even have to get another cat, although they never seemed to last very long. After a week of being less than sober and wrinkly clean much of the time, but with nothing happening, she gave up. Time for plan 'b'.

Tidal Bore rafting looked like it might do the job. Melissa had considered horse riding, a vigorous gallop surely being enough, but she lost her nerve. She wasn't very good with horses and, when she'd visited the stable near Kentville, the pony she was shown and one that they had assured her was usually as docile as a lamb, was downright antsy when she'd tried to pat it. There was no way that she was going to climb on the back of a crazy horse, she only wanted a miscarriage, not a broken back.

Rafting didn't work either.

"I thought you'd be gone by now", said Laura, as she automatically brought coffee and a menu.

Melissa teared up, with practice she'd got very good at it, really good. For the next few minutes, Laura learned all about the other woman, how Gerry was now married with two kids he'd conveniently forgotten to mention on his last trip, and how she was now pregnant from the previous time they'd spent together. Gerry had confessed all when she'd called and said that she was heading over for a year. She'd decided there and then that he wasn't going to know about the pregnancy, about anything in Melissa's life from now on.

Naturally, Laura was a rock. She bought the story without question and soon the women in the town all knew about Melissa's predicament. Laura had been one of the keys to establishing Melissa's place in Mrs. Lester's life, and later how poor Mrs. Lester was now sick herself and never coming back. Everyone in town used the cafe, everyone got to hear the bad news. The months that followed were difficult for Melissa, but Laura turned out to be the best investment that she'd ever made, and several other ladies in the area, especially Mrs. Rose, all made sure that everything went seamlessly well.

"Will you give birth at home or in hospital?" Dr. Bond had become quite attentive. It turned out that his wife was the mainstay of the local Women's Institute and so knew absolutely everything.

"I thought I might go home to BC. My sister has said it's ok, I thought it would be sensible to involve her from the off, but I'll be back. Annapolis Royal is my forever home now".

"I would advise no travel for six-weeks post, is that a problem for your sister?"

"No, she said I can stay as long as I like. She can't have children, her husband left when he found out, so she's very keen to be involved. Do you mind if I call you to check that I'm ok to travel, before I come back? You've been so good to me. I honestly don't know how I'd cope without you".

"Call me anytime, Melissa, you have my private number".

In the months before the birth, and before fatigue had taken hold, Melissa had been through the house from top to bottom, eventually finding what she'd been looking for.

Mrs. Lester had had a child, a boy. She hadn't named the father, but the birth certificate said that the boy would have been twenty-two when she'd taken the room, he'd been called Graham. A wad of prescription receipts that she came across were for tranquilizers and strong ones, she knew of them, they were all for the boy. She'd been raped and impregnated by a crazy boy. The same pile of documents also had another birth certificate, for what had presumably been Mrs. Lester's older sister, who'd also had a child at the same time and around the same date, a girl. From what Melissa had pieced together, the sister, Geraldine, had died and Mrs. Lester had taken her girl in as her own, but there was no further mention of her, nothing. Melissa was puzzled by it all. Where had this girl gone, a girl who would now be a woman of about her own age?

After fixating on the issues for a few days, she decided to occupy her mind and do some decorating, starting with the family room and then the small bedroom upstairs. It was a room that had been in decent condition and was currently being used as a storeroom. It would make a nursery for when she got back and until she decided how she was going to play this. It was all new ground for her, but she'd cope, she always coped.

The first thing to do was to get rid of all the awful pictures that Mrs. Lester had dotted around her house. 'Actually, my house now' she thought, once it goes through the process that she'd influence. Most of the pictures were generic, views of the Annapolis area including what Melissa thought of as 'stock' fort pictures. One was quite interesting, a scene with bright colours, but twee in a basic sort of way. She'd keep that one, she had an idea that she'd seen similar stuff in a gallery in town. Maybe it was by some local artist that Mrs. Lester had bought from directly, possibly out of pity, it might be worth a few dollars now.

As the pictures came down, it was clear that the frames would be ok with a bit of restoration, but the contents of most had to go. That was when she started finding the photos, lots of photos, of a boy and a girl. It was one of those chilling moments, the first time she saw the girl as being older than a child, maybe just about a teen, she looked so like her. Was the resemblance to the missing, mystery girl why Mrs. Lester had given her the room? The boy, though, was odd-looking from early on, his stare intense. It made you uncomfortable, like he could see a part of you that was private, as if he invaded your soul and not just your body.

On a trip to Middleton, Melissa visited a thrift shop, Salvation Army run. She bought some old photo albums, each packed with baseball cards of some sort, common ones presumably, otherwise a collector would have found them and spirited them away. At home, it was home now, she made up two albums charting the boy in one, and the girl in the other. The girl was called Melissa and Melissa then became the girl.

Mrs. Rose was quite surprised when Melissa called round and showed her the girl's photo album. All the information was new, and Mrs. Rose was surprised that Mrs. Lester, Muriel, hadn't mentioned at least some of it when the Women's Institute had run a stall at the town fair, and Mrs. Rose and Mrs. Lester had been given responsibility for it. They'd been serving side-by-side all day, but barely said two words.

"I'm hoping to be able to stay when I get back", said Melissa without being prompted.

"Whatever do you mean?" asked Mrs. Rose. Apart from the BC trip for the birth with family, it had never entered her mind that Melissa would go anywhere else, not now.

"The house. My aunt died last week, died without a will, she said she had one but apparently not. I don't know what to do now. I know I'm the only surviving relative, I have all the documentation, birth and death certificates, that sort of thing. I know that her son, Graham, died at sea. Apparently, he ran away as a late teen and joined the Merchant Navy somewhere. She also told me that they never found his body and I've not found a death certificate yet, if she ever had one for him. Perhaps she did but couldn't bear to keep it".

"A son, what son?"

Mrs. Rose was hooked, and Melissa wove a story intricate enough to be plausible but with enough leeway to be taken either way, the other photo album supported everything if asked. She was playing on her new-found position as the only surviving relative, and a vulnerable one too, what with her circumstances.

Mrs. Rose looked determined. "Can you do something for me, put together what you can, all the legal documents you have. I have a brother who practices law, he does pro bono sometimes, he'll take a look at your situation and advise you. Don't worry, Melissa, you're one of us now, we won't let you down".

It was all going so very well and there was light at the end of the tunnel. Melissa left for BC to do the difficult part. Her sister, Juliette, had said it was ok to come. She hadn't wanted to, but asking Juliette was the only logical thing to do. If nothing else, it gave her some space away from the seat of her immaculate deception to make decisions.

November 1989

"Twins, I wasn't expecting twins!", said a slightly groggy Melissa, spitting out the words accusingly.

"Well twins is what you've got girl, and a healthy pair too, although I'd make sure this one gets plenty to eat for a while, by the looks of her she could do with it", and the midwife held out a pair of pink, wriggling babies for the new mother to see. "Just a few more things to do and then Doctor will call by later, probably tomorrow you can go home. Do you have any names in mind?"

Melissa didn't much care for the woman's tone, no, she hadn't thought of any names, she'd tried very hard to block out the whole thing for as long as possible.

"Thank you, Sheila, I'm sure my sister will be a bit more agreeable once the drugs wear off. Naming the children is a serious thing and not to be taken lightly". The midwife wheeled the babies away as Juliette sat in the only chair available. "She's right you know; I can dig out some family names if you like?"

"No, what to call them will happen organically. Don't worry Juliette, as soon as I can I'm going home. I won't impose on you any longer than I have to".

"Good, you always were headstrong, that's why we never got on. I still don't know why you came here to have your little accidents, or have you suddenly remembered who the father is?"

Melissa bit her tongue. She couldn't say that she'd been raped and hadn't realised that she was pregnant until it was too late because Juliette would ridicule her, she always did. Sometimes Melissa wished she could be more detached, like her sister. "Can I ask you something, it's very important to me?"

Juliette sat tight-lipped, expecting to be asked for money again. "Go on".

"If anything happened to me, anything bad, final, will you promise to take the children?"

Juliette barely paused. "I don't think so".

I have a house, it will be worth your while, I'll write you into my will".

Juliette had heard Melissa's tales before. She was a fantasist, a dreamer, there was no house. "Call me when they say I can fetch you".

In the now quiet room, Melissa could feel the tears tracking down her cheeks. This wasn't supposed to happen. She was supposed to have a life, find a partner, live her dreams. Being a single mother, tied down by two demanding kids wasn't a part of the plan. She needed a new plan.

The door opened and the babies came back. The nurse who brought them was a new face, Melissa had seen lots of new faces in the hospital and had met lots of new mothers, all excited about the future. "Sheila said to tell you that she's been calling the girls Melissa and Juliette after you and your sister for now. Any further thoughts, do you want to wait to speak to the father about it?" This one was a nosey bitch, she sneered when she used the word 'father', knowing full well that Melissa had refused to discuss it. And so, by default, two little girls new to the world were given names, something that would carry for life, however long that life might be and wherever it would take them.

Once home and after a grueling journey by train and bus, Melissa and her 'bundles of joy' were welcomed by every grandmother and clucking spinster of the parish. Details were sought, futures asked about and it seemed that Melissa's life now belonged to other people, two of whom she was responsible for. Little Melissa, as everyone called her, and Juliette thrived on the fuss, although Juliette slept a lot, but this was normal. As the whole story grew, Melissa found more and more that she needed to write whole transcripts of conversations down, she needed the details at hand so that when she was continuing the construction of her life, or reconstruction more like, she'd not get tripped up by a previous lie. It was unlike her, she could normally remember everything with ease, but she'd been having headaches, so now she wrote it all down. It was almost as if she was learning her lines and rehearsing them for some sort of play.

The legal ownership of the house got sorted out, presenting Melissa with more bills that she also got sorted, one way or another. Then her mood and her headaches took a turn for the worse. She thought it might all be linked to post-natal depression, having to care for children had never been a lifegoal for her, so she decided she needed to do something radical, and quick.

Mrs. Rose had been a dear throughout and she regularly looked after the babies at her home while Melissa went about her business, not that she ever said what that business was. When it happened, Melissa said that she was spending the day in Halifax visiting an old friend. She'd told Mrs. Rose that it was an old roommate who she'd always missed once they'd parted. On the evening of her trip, Mrs. Rose was getting quite worried. Melissa wasn't normally late back from wherever it was that she went for a break, but it was now getting late. She'd always found a way to call in the past, if there was a delay. It wasn't a problem taking care of the kids a bit longer, but she instinctively felt that something wasn't right. She picked up the phone and spoke to someone she knew in passing, a police officer who worked in Digby, Constance O'Toole.

"I wouldn't worry just yet, Mary, she's probably broken down or something, do you have a number for her at the place she visited, do you know what sort of car she was driving? I can ask around". Constance was such a good girl, always helpful.

Mrs. Rose decided to make up a bed, just in case Melissa was stuck somewhere and the kids had to stay with her. She fed them and bathed them together. It was odd, the water seemed to confuse them, as if they didn't see it that often. It was true that they weren't the cleanest of kids, but they were just kids and kids got messy. When it came to bedtime story time little Melissa was always the one who seemed to know what was happening, Juliette remained frail and seemed to be dominated by her sister. Dr. Bond had been called in and had assured everyone that Juliette was healthy, just skinny for now.

Mrs. Rose could barely hear the tv, she'd decided to keep the sound down low so as to not wake the kids. They were fast asleep the last time she'd checked, just like the previous seven times, they were very sweet when they slept. The knock on the door was rather loud, and Mrs. Rose realised that she'd dropped off in front of the tv, it happened most nights. When Henry was alive it was different.

"Constance, what's wrong, is Melissa alright?"

Constance and her male colleague from the local station entered the house. He'd obviously decided that Connie could deal with everything because he didn't play a part, in fact he seemed to be trying hard not to appear bored.

"We found Melissa's car, Mrs. Rose, we think there was an accident. The car left the road and crashed into the ocean near Digby. We have people looking for Melissa now. She wasn't in the car, we think she was thrown clear, possibly into the water, I'm sorry".

Mrs. Rose was shocked, Digby, what was she doing near Digby? but she managed to mumble a question about the children.

"Are you ok with them until tomorrow? If so then I'll get Annapolis to send somebody around".

She said she was, and Constance and her silent colleague left. Mrs. Rose tried to remember whether there was a pet at Melissa's house, she'd told her that she'd had cats in the past but not recently, as far as she knew, she'd ask around tomorrow, just in case. After taking one last look at the sleeping children, she made herself a hot drink and sat for a while, it was all too terrible to think about, the poor mites.

The next day some people came. They asked a few questions about next of kin and that sort of thing and Mrs. Rose did her best to fill in the blanks, then they took the children away, it was for the best. Melissa was officially listed as missing, and, after a while, they just stopped looking.

Some months later and in a province far away, the progeny of Melissa began a new life with the only relative available, how long for was open to question.

Over the years, people came and went as the house in Annapolis Royal not so much welcomed the new people renting, as tolerated them. The big ripple that Melissa had caused dissipated and, eventually, she'd all but been forgotten. Mrs. Rose remembered though, and she often passed the house in both sadness and confusion. There's always been something about Melissa and her story that didn't quite add up and it was only after she'd gone that the holes became more visible.

August 2018-Four Years Ago

When Juliette Barker had been told the whole story, of how her real mom had gone missing, presumed drowned, she'd accepted it as plausible, a good reason for being put up for adoption. Then she found out it was all a fabrication; the letter writer knew too much. It never occurred to her to wonder where the letter came from, it was just signed 'a well wisher'. Using the information in the letter, Juliette found the person who'd walked away from her and her sister all those years ago. She called and it wasn't denied, so they'd met, just once. Once was enough.

January 2019

The house in Annapolis Royal was exactly what she wanted, it had been a shock when her mom had finally told her about it, having fed off the income for years. Compensation, she'd reckoned, well deserved in the circumstances. The house appealed strongly to Juliette for reasons she couldn't put her finger on. Phil, her partner, had been pretty easy about it. He'd moaned a bit about the extra travel for work, but he saw the sense in it. A house that was ready-made for them now that the old tenants had gone was too good to turn down. The only possible fly in the ointment would be Juliette's sister, Melissa, and what she might want from it herself.

The house, when she saw it, obviously needed a bit of work, but a succession of tenants had done jobs here and there, not always tastefully, but the whole was basically inhabitable. Moving home wasn't the only big thing to have happened to Juliette recently. She thought that she'd take finding out that the person who called herself mom but hadn't been, badly. She didn't though. Her adoptive mom wasn't very warm as a person which made it easier for her to be indifferent to the news. She clearly didn't know anything about Juliette's real mom, so it was no good asking what she knew would be called 'stupid questions'.

At first all was well, very well and Juliette was less on-edge than she had been at times, Phil was pleased. Then her sister, real, her adoptive mom had said, suffered a mental breakdown when her partner left her for a girl out west. She was being sent to an institution to recover; it was an open-ended stay. Juliette had been very upset when she heard about Melissa, she was the strong one, the elder of the twins by six minutes. Juliette always looked up to Melissa and Melissa always took care of Juliette.

"Well, I'm not taking them", said Juliette's adoptive mom. "It was bad enough with you two hanging around for so long and now I've downsized, I simply don't have room". It was the response Juliette had been expecting, her adoptive mother had always been a reluctant participant in the lives of her children, and now it seemed the same philosophy of life applied to her grandchildren. Now she knew where the indifference came from, even though she still tried hard to think of her as mom. What Juliette couldn't figure was why her adoptive mom had taken them on in the first place, it was a question she never felt brave enough to ask.

"It's not as if they are going to know, is it?" said her mom testily, stating the obvious where the kids were concerned. Julia was shocked, just because they were what some called 'different' didn't mean that they weren't aware, nor that they didn't respond to people, to affection.

"Ok, we'll do it. Unlike you, mom, we do have room in the new house, and we feel a responsibility. If this had been a sick spaniel, you'd have been all over it".

Phil's image on her phone shrugged, as he himself abdicated all responsibility for whatever Juliette would eventually decide. Melissa was in no fit state to sort herself out for this one, they'd said that she would need a lot of peace and quiet to recover. It could be weeks, months even, before she'd be mentally ready to step back into her old life. Juliette understood that, if she agreed now to foster her sister's kids, it might be for the long term.

The social worker who'd been hovering out of the way, a talent most of them quickly acquire for the job, eased back into focus. "We'll be only a phone call away if you need support. I think you'll be a great surrogate mom, Juliette, and Melissa will thank you for it when she's all better, one day. We can sort out all the final paperwork in a few days, my advice is to let the kids say goodbye to mommy then take them straight home. The sooner they get settled the better".

"I still don't see why it all has to be so formal", said Juliette, irritably.

"It's just a legal thing. You might need to make important decisions on theirs and Melissa's behalf. You'll have the legal right to do that now that your mother has abdicated all responsibility".

Juliette took two little hands in hers and led the kids silently to the room where Melissa was only semi-conscious. The kids stood and looked while Juliette did a little speech, the usual stuff. 'Mommy is sick, the doctors will make her all better but first you have to live with Aunt Juliette and Uncle Phil. Think of it as an adventure, be grown up and let mommy get better, then you can be together again'.

The expression on the kids' faces didn't offer any clues as to whether they'd got any of it. They blinked and breathed and that was about it. At least they didn't need nursing themselves, they could use the washroom ok and feed themselves, otherwise they were just empty, vacant.

Melissa made a small noise, probably just an exhalation of air, but the kids had heard it and, although their countenance appeared unchanged, it was.

Juliette turned to go, but there was the slightest resistance before the kids followed. At the back of Juliette's mind, she was feeling envy for the peace that Melissa was enjoying, chemically induced, true, but peace, nevertheless. She knew that ahead was a period of uncertainty, and of all the things about this that pissed her off most, uncertainty was the main player.

The Jeep hummed quietly along, the slightly irritating intermittent rattle that had been developing was behaving itself, for now. The damn thing had been in the shop several times and on each occasion some spotty teenager had driven it around and pronounced that they had to let it get worse because it wasn't making the noise for them. Juliette had even recorded the din on her phone but, when she'd tried to play it for them, nothing came out. The phone hadn't registered anything from start to finish.

The ride home was easy enough and the kids totally silent. They didn't seem to care what was happening around them, it was almost as if it was business as usual.

Phil reached over and patted her leg. "Don't worry, it'll be fine, we're doing the right thing, but you understand that it had to be your choice and not just because it's your sister. I spoke to a friend at work and his eldest, Abigail, is trying to earn a few dollars before going off to college, so we'll not be stuck for a babysitter. He said that she's a very upright girl, yes upright was the term he used. I hope he didn't mean that she's built like a flatpack wardrobe", then he laughed at his own joke.

Juliette felt reassured. A ready-made babysitter was good, the kids would be no trouble and she and Phil could be the couple they once were again, before the trouble came. "I still think I should meet them, Juliette, it seems crazy that we've been together for so long and you still won't take me to meet your mom and sister, even if Melissa is in a stupor".

"I told you, they're both fragile, difficult, they can't handle things like I can, and yet you complain about me. It's not me, I asked them, of course I did, but mom said no, so that's that. It's no good arguing, my mother is a stubborn sort, she doesn't discuss anything once she's decided". She didn't pass on the adopted thing to Phil, now wasn't the time.

Phil seemed to accept it, as he always did, but Juliette suspected that he thought the whole family was crazy, especially her. She almost asked him whether, had he known about her mom and sister beforehand, would they have even got together?

"You know me, anything for a quiet life, whatever they say goes. I'll not make a fuss, it's your family house, I just think it's odd is all". To be fair, he didn't brood, but Juliette couldn't help but think he wasn't being totally honest with her, and a bit of distance developed between them for the rest of the journey. Juliette understood Phil's point of view, but her mother and sister were adults who made their own decisions and not meeting Phil was one of them.

"I can see it's bothering you more than me, but you never met my ex and I've never met any of yours, perhaps we should just think of these people as Exes, it might make it easier".

It was true, she knew that Phil had been in at least one serious relationship before they met, but she really didn't want to know the details. Had he talked about it, she would have struggled to not think of him as being soiled. The only thing she did know was that her Phil had been duped and his ex-girlfriend had had him raising her kids, until he found out that he wasn't the father. Perhaps that was why he was ok with Melissa's kids, maybe he missed those kids and liked the idea of being a father, despite the circumstances?

When they got home, the house appeared to be in a good mood. Juliette had never told anyone about it, but she reckoned that she could sense the mood of the house at any given time. It had been in her family for years, or so she was told, so she felt that she had a natural empathy with it. If there was any friction between her and Phil, or some fool not doing their job, not doing what they were told to do, then the house could be stand-offish. It was hard to explain rationally, and it was probably for the best that she'd never tried to, to anybody.

The kids' room hadn't been redecorated yet, there hadn't been time and Juliette had insisted that she wasn't going to do it alone, so they'd just cleaned out the stuff they thought best not to leave near kids, even what were entirely predictable kids. It was stuff that might get damaged, and Phil had insisted, they had a room in the basement for all that sort of thing, it was almost a family vault. The beds they bought were functional and cheap because they'd been previously enjoyed in a smoke-free home, or so they claimed. The mattresses had been aired and the bedding was new, but all Dollar Shop stock, so not overly expensive. The thing was the kids wouldn't care about any of it. It wasn't as if they would stamp their tiny feet in a temper tantrum, they didn't have tempers, they didn't seem to have emotions.

Juliette put the kids to bed early, they didn't seem tired, but she was, and she wanted to pour a glass of wine and kick back. She might even break out the gummies again, although Phil didn't approve at all, which was ridiculous as it was all legal, now. As she pulled the cover up over each kid, she suddenly had the urge to tell them a story, she was good at stories...

"The end", she said to two indifferent faces. Had they even understood the story after all her effort? She clicked off the lamp as she left, the room was temporarily very dark. The loss of light was enough to make her rush to the slightly open door and the feed of the dull light from the landing, welcoming light, safe light. She slipped downstairs, only to find Phil fast asleep in the chair, really, what was that all about? Glancing at the ornate clock on the mantle, Juliette saw that it was nearly midnight. No, that can't be right, she'd only been twenty minutes with the kids, half-an-hour tops.

Phil stirred, so she accidentally kicked him, lightly.

"There you are, I thought you'd been abducted, then I thought you must be bonding. Very important, you're their mommy now". For some reason Juliette shivered, it was illogical, there was no reason to shiver in a warm house. He was right though, of course she was their mommy. Perhaps that was what had happened, and she'd lost track of the time. She'd been bonding without even knowing it, or consciously intending to. Phil rose and headed off to his room. "See you in the morning", he said. She thought for a moment that he was going to try and kiss her, and she must have flinched involuntarily, because he did a sort of mid-air swerve and was gone. Juliette tried to piece together the evening.

They'd got back around seven, had the kids in bed by eight, then she'd read a story, a four-hour story. How the hell had she done that and not had any idea what the story was, her head started to ache. It was one of her heads coming on, as her mother gleefully reminded her whenever it had happened at home, her old home, her mother's old home.

It was dark when Juliette awoke, but there was a bit of light pushing through the ill-fitting curtains, so she was able to see the table lamp. She reached over and clicked it on, flooding the room with bright, safe light. Being Juliette wasn't always easy, but she was Juliette now and for a while, she had to be more with it, if only for the sake of her new responsibilities.

After a couple of weeks, nothing had changed with the kids. They didn't seem to react to anything, but they knew what you meant and knew when it was time to do something. They ate, they even played but silently and together, never alone. The house had felt different from the off with them in it, less their own, they'd lost something, their space had been invaded. Gradually things improved a little and life, almost normal life, went on.

February 2019

Mrs. Rose walked slowly past the house. To her it had always brooded, but the new tenant seemed happy enough with it, no alarms so far, and she hoped that it would all work out ok. When Melissa had died and the children were taken into care, it was a sad day, but Melissa had left instructions via her will that the house was to be rented out until such time as one of the girls needed it, if that time ever happened. The girls had been fostered together so they were taken care of, then she heard an unsubstantiated rumour that one had died, suddenly. It was all so tragic, if it was true. She contemplated going over to introduce herself to the new people. The woman was blonde, slim, and nicely dressed and she wondered whether there was a partner there somewhere. In the end she didn't say hello, not this time, there was no need to get involved again.

April 2019

Everything had seemed so normal the day it happened, very normal. Phil was chirpy and Juliette had things to do. She was being a domestic goddess, cleaning the house, doing the laundry, shopping later perhaps, just for groceries. She half-considered taking people out for a walk, but it was never Phil's first choice of leisure activity and the kids just walked around like little zombies, so it probably wouldn't happen. She hauled the laundry out of the new tumble drier and into the waiting plastic carrier, which by contrast was old and dropping to bits, the plastic having cracked and fractured after many years of heavy use. It had come with the house, and she'd intended to change it, but hadn't yet. In the room above, she could hear the sound of feet as they pounded around the house, not the kid's feet but Phil's and the dog's, he was probably chasing it from room to room. She wondered whether the dog might stimulate the kids, would she be the one to finally break through?

With a dink, the lights went out. What a time to have an outage! The basement had no windows, so no light found a way in, none at all. It was pitch black. As she tensed up, she thought she heard a very quiet snuffling noise, right on the edge of her hearing.

What with being nervous of the dark, Juliette was always prepared for such an event and easily found the headlamp hanging behind the door, kept there for just such emergencies. Switching it on, the room absorbed the light, almost sucked it greedily from the lamp. A power outage had never happened like that down there before, it was quite odd, unexpected. As she looked around with the headlamp, it almost seemed as if there were places where the light was reluctant to go even though she was looking in that direction.

The lights flashed on again, then off just as quickly, leaving Juliette with an image of the room imprinted on the back of her eyelids. She tried to concentrate on what she thought she'd seen during the moment of illumination, but it faded quickly. Something about the image had bothered her, subconsciously. She looked nervously around the room with the headlamp, but there was nothing there, just the laundry. It was surely her imagination playing up again, the bane of the highly-strung.

The door from the laundry through to the stairs was solid, with a large centre panel. Inside the panel was finished with cheap wallpaper, painted to make the door look better than it was. When they'd first moved in, all the doors in the basement were damaged, literally peppered with holes. The agent had blamed lively kids, but the holes were all the same dimensions, fist sized. Someone had been very angry there at some point and the doors had suffered. As Juliette turned around to go back upstairs, the light from her headlamp briefly illuminated something again, but what? She wasn't sure. Pivoting back quickly to try to get a better look, whatever it was had gone but still the discomfort hung. She hated the uneasiness at something unexplained, an unwelcome impression that was starting to clog up her mind. Telling herself to get a grip, that she was just being silly again, Juliette decided that she'd go upstairs now and join her family in the daylight. She wouldn't panic but move with dignity, quickly, yes, she'd move quickly.

Thirteen steps made up the stairs between the basement door and the one leading to the kitchen. Juliette knew this because she'd counted them. She didn't know why, she wasn't at all superstitious, but she didn't much like it being thirteen steps either. By step three and with both hands carrying the laundry, supported by the elbow of her left arm leaning on the banister, Juliette felt the hairs on her neck rise, she stopped. She felt something brush her leg, or at least thought that she did. It was weird, it couldn't be Sonny, the labrador. He was kept out of the basement; besides, she knew that he was upstairs, she'd heard him moments ago. Then she felt something again and two small children shot past her, taking the steps to the top two at a time. They were perhaps eight-years old or so, slightly built and dressed in rough but modern clothing, two girls. When they reached the top step, they both stopped and looked back at her.

The only sound that Juliette could hear was her heart beating, hammering, louder than any noise she'd ever heard. The normally reliable sounds from upstairs, usually all-pervading when Phil chased the dog around, were completely absent. She breathed heavily and thought that her chest might explode at any minute. The headlamp dimmed in the way they do when the battery is almost done, but she couldn't tear her gaze away. The kids' expressions in the light from the headlamp were melancholy at best, then they both did a slight smile and simply vanished through the curtain covering the door.

Juliette was gasping now, because the curtain that stopped the draft from the basement creeping under the door was still across, and the kids had just run through it, not around it, but through it.

It took a moment or two, but, very slowly, Juliette regained her composure. Taking a deep breath that came out as a cloud in front of her, she ascended the stairs, then she screamed as the lights came back on. Her scream was loud, it was real, delivered from deep within and begging for help, but nobody came. Deciding that she had to get off the stairs, now, she rushed the last few steps and lost her footing at the top, falling a few steps at a time, jarring her left knee badly. The pain from the knee compounded the fear, but Juliette forced herself up again, threw the curtain roughly over and emerged into her safe space, her kitchen.

Nothing was right.

The only available light now came from two low wattage bulbs hanging from the ceiling on ancient wires, they barely lit the area. Thick dust covered the floor and the work surfaces, such as they were. The sink was enamel and rusted, the taps hadn't seen water for years, decades even. This wasn't her kitchen as she knew it.

Normality, I need something normal, she thought, looking down at her washing. It was as she'd expected. The kids' clothes, her partner's socks and their underwear, it was all normal, perfectly normal.

"Are you our new mommy?" said a child's voice behind her.

Slowly Juliette turned to see the two stairway kids standing together perhaps fifteen feet away against a grubby wall.

'Where are their tracks?' her mind asked, but her brain wasn't listening to logic.

"Where am I?" she asked.

"Home", said the slightly taller child, smiling. "Home".

"Juliette, are you ok?"

She knew the voice, it was Phil. Everything had returned to normal, and she was back in her own kitchen, a bright and airy place. The dishwasher rumbled on in the background, the smell of her baking hung in the air, even the burnt smell where some of the cupcakes had caught a bit was welcome.

"Juliette".

"Sorry, what? Sorry".

"You screamed, and then stumbled in through the door, you didn't even draw back the curtain".

She looked at the previously hung curtain lying in a heap on the kitchen floor. The pole had been ripped from the fixing, one part had remained attached to the wall above the door, the other was lying in the middle of the floor, bent and broken.

"Sorry, I stumbled as I came in, my knee, I tweaked it in the dark".

"What dark, the light's been on all the time, why are you wearing a headlamp?"

Juliette felt her forehead, she was still wearing a headlamp, the light was on but flashing red, it did that sometimes.

She waved away the questions. "Sorry, I just need to sit a while, my knee". She wasn't lying, her knee really was killing her.

"Should I call the doctor? What about going to ER?" said Phil concerned.

"No, it'll be fine with rest, just an hour, ok?"

"Ok, but does that mean we're not going out then, date night, remember, we were going to the movies. I'm good with it if you don't want to go but the babysitter will be here soon, we'll have to pay her anyway".

Juliette didn't know what to say, nothing made any sense. Most of all she wanted to be left alone so she could figure out what had happened, it had all been real, so terrifyingly real. Phil was waiting for an answer, his eyes betraying his impatience. "No, we'll still go, just give me ten minutes to put my face on. I can put the knee support on under my jeans, I'll be fine".

Phil did some more fussing, but she knew that it wasn't real, all he wanted was to go out, probably needed to go out. She knew that he got irritated by the kids, their constant presence in his world, intruding. She felt the same way herself, sometimes.

When Juliette emerged from the bedroom, limping slightly, Abigail was already there and looking concerned for Juliette. "Hi Abigail, don't worry, just a little sprain, I'll be fine. Help yourself to anything, you know how the TV works, you've got my cell number, I'll leave it on vibrate, ok?"

"Don't worry Mrs. Barker, you have a good time, nothing will happen. We can watch the kids shows until bedtime, then I've got homework. You'll be back around ten thirty, is that right?"

Juliette agreed that it was, yes, they'd be back about then and did she want anything bringing back, candy, that sort of thing.

"No thanks, watching what I eat, I don't want to be the fat kid in class", and she patted her very flat stomach.

Abigail the babysitter was a nice kid, actually a bit more than a kid. She was seventeen, nearly eighteen, attractive and seemed very stable, apart from her religious beliefs. She was a bit too Christian and Juliette worried about what she might be saying to the kids when they left them with her. In many ways she was too good to be true.

"Ok, see you later Abigail, I hope they behave".

"Don't worry, we'll be fine, enjoy your movie Mrs. Barker. God loves you".

In Juliette's head a voice wanted to scream 'I told you before you sanctimonious bitch, we're not fucking married, I'm not Mrs. anything, we live in sin and you can stuff your god where the sun doesn't shine', but instead she just smiled.

As they pulled away from the drive, Juliette checked the house in the side mirror and everything looked normal, cosy. Since they'd moved into the house, they'd worked hard to make it a home, somewhere comfortable, safe. She didn't feel very safe now though and couldn't understand what had happened to her. It had all seemed so very, very real.

"Are you going to tell me what's bothering you?" asked Phil.

"I don't know myself; it was weird. You say the power stayed on, but it went out in the basement, that's why I had the headlamp on".

"I'll get someone in, check out the breakers and everything, we should have re-wired right through, it's probably a loose connection. You were very shaken up, like you'd seen a ghost".

"No, nothing like that, why would you say that?" said Juliette, sounding rattled.

"Just an expression. Can you put whatever it was that bothered you behind you and just enjoy the movie?"

"Yes, let's be young again for a while, it will do us good".

"You're finding it tough going too, then?"

"Yes, but we expected that, we talked about it, and we did the on-line course on dealing with needy kids. We have to do our best for them, while we can".

"I know", said Phil, and he reached over and gave her leg a pat.

"At least we have Abigail, she's very grounded and she's very good with them", she said.

"They do have names, Juliette, I know it's hard sometimes, but we should call them Tess and Katy all the time. One day soon your sister will be well, then they can go home, and we can be us again. You know we couldn't say no, us and the kids are all Melissa's got, your mom seems to have opted out".

"Yes, you're right, sorry", then Juliette grabbed her seat and yelled for Phil to look out.

Phil was already reacting, they weren't going very fast, they hadn't even left the rough track that led to their house.

"A fox I think, two maybe. I only caught a glimpse".

Juliette smiled weakly. She'd seen well enough what had dashed across the road in front of them, it was all happening again.

"I think we should cancel tonight. I'm worried about Abigail. She's seventeen for fuck's sake, why is she babysitting when she should be out chasing every cute guy in the area?"

"Did you?" asked Phil, casting a sideways glance at her.

"What? No, I'm just saying, she's too good to be true. I bet she's got a boy coming over tonight, they'll be doing a jiggy on our sofa before we know it, I want to go back, it's going to bother me, do you see?"

Phil knew when he 'took Juliette on', as his mom had described the relationship, that she was highly strung, but suggesting that the sweet Abigail might be indulging in some sort of sex session as soon as they'd gone was a bit of a stretch, besides, Abigail wasn't like that. They'd talked and Phil knew that she wasn't unsullied, but she wasn't the type to go wild either.

"Honey, I'm not turning back, I saw you was shook up, I want to know what happened down there. I know it'll come out when you're ready but Abigail, really, she's just a sweet kid".

Juliette felt awful as soon as she'd said what she said, but she needed an excuse to go back, to go down the stairs, to find out what the hell was going on. She desperately needed to know whether it was real or her demons, again.

Juliette's mom talked to her the same way Phil was now, the way she talked to her two dogs, hunting dogs. Her adoptive father had been a hunter before he'd died. Juliette sometimes thought that her mom would have been happy to keep the dogs and find a home for her, a good home if possible, or perhaps she was being optimistic about that and projecting absent emotions onto her mental image of her mom. It was her way of accepting the status quo.

The movie was ok, but Juliette had found it hard to concentrate. The plot was very straightforward, it was a boy meets girl thing of the type that Phil seemed addicted to, maybe he was getting his fix of romance from the screen, or the books he read. It certainly wasn't coming from her at the moment. Abigail was asleep on the sofa when they got back. Juliette glanced at her homework and understood none of it. School had never been her friend despite her passing her exams; she was no good at being a part of a crowd.

"I'll check the kids, you run Abigail home", she said and started to climb the stairs to their room. It was only when she heard the clunk of the car door that she realized that she was alone in the house, the kids didn't count. She peeped through the curtain, seeing Phil holding the door open while Abigail climbed inside. She was rather clumsy, exposing a lot of leg, briefly. Juliette didn't remember her skirt being so short before. Just modern kids and fashion, she presumed.

The kids had been asleep when she went in, when she turned back from the window, they were both sitting bolt upright and staring at her. She almost screamed.

She tried to act normally. "Hey, you two, time for your beauty sleep, come on, lie down. The pretty girl has gone now, it's just me". She hadn't expected a reaction but the kids both smiled at her, then they lay back down and shut their eyes almost machine-like. What had she said?

In the kitchen, Sonny was whining at the door, so she grabbed the leash and walked out into the back yard with him. She'd have to come back in the morning to clean up, she wasn't going to start fishing around for it now. He did the usual sniffing and pulling her around before getting to the reason for being there. As he gave her a hard tug to say, 'all done', she caught something out the corner of her eye, just a movement in the window of her office. Sonny tugged again and she had to concentrate on her balance before looking back, there was nothing there.

The kettle seemed to take an age to boil, and she was about to give up the idea of hot chocolate when the front door went clonk and the kettle reached boiling point simultaneously. "Hot chocolate", she called, but got no answer, Phil might not have heard her. Thinking nothing of it, she poured the water onto the dry powder in their cups. The door went clonk again and Phil walked in. Juliette tried not to look confused. "Er, hot chocolate?"

"Not for me", said Phil. "I thought I'd grab a shower. I'm feeling a bit sweaty, they must turn the heat up in the cinema, didn't you notice?" and he bounded upstairs, taking two at a time. She poured the unwanted drink down the sink, rinsed Phil's cup and climbed the stairs herself.

From her room, she could hear the shower running and Phil humming some tune or other, then it went quiet, and she knew he'd gone to his own room. Sipping the last of her own now tepid chocolate, she scrolled through social media on her pad. It was something she did nightly, tutting at excess, smiling at cute cat images and just generally letting the banality wash over her. Someone she half-knew at the supermarket had posted about a recent local party, there was an album of photos, some sort of birthday bash. She idly clicked through the photos, she didn't know why, and there was the babysitter. She looked very different when she was clearly enjoying herself. The photos wouldn't be up long once someone complained, they were pretty graphic bordering obscene.

Juliette had been right, ten minutes after posting, the whole photo set had gone and with it the evidence that cute little holy roller Abigail was a bit livelier than she let on. Looking at her sleepy-time pills, Juliette made a snap decision. No more pills for a while, maybe it was the pills that were messing with her head again.

The next day after breakfast, the car was loaded and Phil was ready to go, but he was hanging back, checking on Juliette. He had a worried expression, the one he always wore when he thought she was delicate. "I'll be fine, we'll all be fine, it was nothing. I've pushed it out of my mind now, I might even just go for a drive to relax, maybe Keji. I don't want to be a trouble for anyone".

"Ok. Sorry about dropping this on you but they need me there to sort something out in person, seems a phone call isn't the same. I'll be back Friday, late afternoon, I'll call later". Juliette was finding Phil a bit of a pain at the moment, and she hated herself for thinking that but, sometimes…

In the living room, the kids were busy with a soft puzzle. It was a felt thing that you stuck to a board, making colourful montages. It was supposed to stimulate them, but so far all they'd done was make a random mess. In the corner, Sonny the dog was already missing his master, he'd never been the same with Juliette. Phil said that was just how dogs were, leader of the pack first. It didn't help that Juliette was lukewarm towards the animal, she could take or leave dogs, they were too needy and brought back memories of her mom's parental indifference.

The chores were waiting, so she flitted around doing this and that until she felt she deserved a coffee break. The light on the machine meant it needed cleaning, but that could wait, one more cup wasn't going to make a difference. She selected a mocha from the remaining pods. The supply was getting very low, but Phil had insisted that they were not environmentally friendly and that they were going to be buying shade grown beans once the pods had gone. It was probably the right thing to do, the machine was cantankerous and the new machine, the leaflet promising the ideal brew, was still in its box under the stairs awaiting the chance to perform.

Normally Juliette put on some music as she did the chores, nothing demanding, just background that she could pick out the odd word from or sing, quietly, the chorus that had made it a hit. For some reason, this time, she hadn't fired up the CD player. It was another relic at a time when everybody was now happily streaming from Spotify or Amazon. She stopped and listened. It was normally quiet, the kids were almost mutes, but this quiet was deeper. Poking her head around the door frame she saw that that the kids were sitting side-by-side on the sofa staring at Sonny, who was shaking. His tail tucked between his legs.

The room felt a little cool, had she left a window open? She sometimes did. Phil was always going on about security, but they lived in Annapolis Royal and not Chicago for heaven's sake. He could be very anal about it. A glance over at the window confirmed it to be closed, maybe the heating was still turned off? Phil had been cleaning the heat pump filters a few days previously.

"Ok, you two, what's the matter?" Juliette always talked to the kids as adults, it didn't matter, they didn't want to participate, so there was no need to do kiddy talk if you didn't have to. Both kids turned their head to look at her, they were pale, ill? Oh shit. Taking a deep breath, Juliette grabbed the digital thermometer from the drawer in the kitchen and sprinted back to the living room. She put her hand on each forehead and, although there was the usual element of clamminess, they seemed ok. She wasn't taking chances, so she took their temperatures, twice each, they were both perfectly normal.

Sonny suddenly seemed to notice that she was there, and almost jumped right across the room, landing on the sofa next to Juliette and the kids. This was bad, Sonny wasn't allowed on the furniture. They'd had a strange lady come in and trained him, walk to heel, come when called and no climbing on the furniture. Juliette had been very clear on the rules.

"Down, bad, down", she said, but the dog ignored her, instead he sat trembling, his eyes pleading with her, but for what?

The kids were being very still, there was nothing unusual there though, but they were staring, both at the same thing. Juliette hadn't noticed it before, but they were staring at the felt thing on the floor. She looked over, taking in what it said. Her scream could be heard some distance away.

'Are you our mommy' was written in multi-coloured scraps of felt.

The hyperventilating was causing Juliette to feel light-headed, she was desperately trying to calm down, to take control of her breathing. The kids had turned to look at her, watching, impassively, as their stand-in mother took a turn. Slowly it went dark as she almost passed out, pitching forward and landing on the felt message with a thud. It was the dog suddenly howling, yelping, then bolting off the sofa and out the door that dragged her back to the now. Juliette stood up shakily. The kids hadn't moved, but the dog appeared to be intent on digging its way under the back door. She went through and let it out, they had an invisible dog fence, so she was unconcerned. The dog flew out and didn't stop, he just kept going through the invisible fence and away. Juliette rubbed her forehead trying to get things straight in her head, but it was resisting. Making a snap decision, she grabbed her bag, collected the kids and bustled them into the car. She was just going to have to drive around now until she found that stupid dog.

As she left the house, she glanced up at the bedroom window, her bedroom window, not Phil's. She decided that what she thought she'd seen was just a trick of the light. A large Elm opposite might be on its last legs, but the remaining foliage still cast a dappled pattern over the house on sunny days, it had to be that, that she'd seen.

Two hours later and Sonny was nowhere to be found, she'd tried everywhere. She was putting off going home, doing yet another slow circuit of the neighbourhood when her phone went, it was her darling mother.

"What have you done to that poor dog, he's just showed up here, he's in a right state".

Juliette was dumbfounded, her mother lived over the causeway in Granville Ferry. Sonny couldn't possibly have known the way; he'd only been there a handful of times in the car. She'd stopped taking him when her mom just played with the dog rather than have a conversation with her. "I'm out looking for him now, I don't know what's wrong, he wanted to go out and just bolted. I've been out two hours looking, I was about to give up. I'll come get him".

"I don't think so, Phil's away, right? He can stay with me until Phil gets back, you have enough to do with those kids". And the phone went dead. Not for the first time, Juliette truly hated her mother. She hated her for being bossy, for being ignorant and for moving to Annapolis County instead of staying in Dartmouth where she belonged. She hated her for not being her real mother too. When her mother had gleefully told her the news about moving, she'd seriously thought about calling the agent to put the house up for sale there and then, but she couldn't because, as Phil would have no doubt helpfully pointed out when he found out, only half was hers.

The kids in the back looked at her wide-eyed, almost as if they'd been reading her angry thoughts and weren't surprised by what they'd seen. "And you two can shut up", she said, angrily. Juliette sat in the car for an age, her brain was telling her it was nothing, nothing at all, but she was feeling overwhelmed and alone, she needed a break, who could she call?

"I really don't mind, Mrs. Barker", said Abigail as she fed the kids. "I can use the extra money. School is very expensive, and I don't want to not do it justice".

It was a very wholesome approach, from the apparently angelic Abigail. Superficially she was so very squeaky-clean, it was almost painful to watch but Juliette remembered the one photo on Facebook, and what she was doing in it. "If you want a glass of wine, there's a bottle of Tidal Creek in the fridge, you know where the glasses are. I don't mind, at your age I regularly sneaked a beer".

"Oh, no, that's fine thank you, I don't drink, I don't think it would suit me. I like to keep a clear head, be focused, but thank you anyway. I'll just have some pop later. You go and enjoy your visit; a daughter should spend quality time with their mother whenever possible. A loving family is a precious thing".

She was too fucking wholesome by half.

Juliette picked up her bits and pieces, keys, purse, her eBook, there was something on it that she'd been reading. The glance from Abigail was questioning, 'why do you want that if you're seeing your mother?' "Just want to show mom a thing I got; she loves to read too. Ok, I'm going, call me if you need anything, oh, and if anybody drops by to join you, that's fine by me".

"He's away at the moment, the guy I'm seeing, so, no. I'll be taking care of the kids and I have some studying to do when they go to sleep".

As Juliette sat in her car, staring down and not daring looking at any of the windows, she suddenly felt totally ashamed. If there was something going on with the house, she was leaving an innocent kid to deal with it while she ran away to where? Then it occurred to her that she'd never heard Abigail mention a boyfriend before, but now she had. The Facebook images came to mind, she'd as good as told Juliette that she wasn't such a prissy missy after all?

The greeter and seater gave her a look when she asked for a table for one. The restaurant, 'The Ferry' was quite busy and she hadn't booked. She'd not planned to be in Digby that night at all, but the drive had been helpful in calming her down and now she was feeling rather foolish at finding herself dining alone just to get away from the house and the kids.

It took an age to get water, then a menu. The teens serving were rushed off their feet, so Juliette didn't want to be critical, it was all down to the owner and him not hiring enough people, surely. She said as much when a goth-looking girl with rings in her nose and lips took her order. "No, Angelo, he's a nice man, we just can't get people. Too many restaurants in Digby, too few bodies to go around. Why, do you want a job, I can ask?"

Juliette laughed. She'd not done tables for a few years; the idea seemed a bit beneath her now. While waiting for her drink and warming a little to the idea of joining the serving team she thought, why not? It would give me a bit of independence, the chance to meet new people, an opportunity to do something different from working on-line every day. Then she remembered the kids, the commitment, the promise to Melissa, a promise she couldn't break, not that Melissa had been in any fit state to understand what was being said. When the server came back, she had a business card from the owner, and she pointed him out, a nice-looking guy of around her own age. He was busy carrying drinks and chatting to people, a real 'mine host'. "Thanks, I'll think about it".

The meal was ok, tasty, sea food, naturally. The sauce was nice, the fries very crisp and the fish cooked to perfection. She made a mental note to suggest it as a date night venue, it wasn't that far from home and Phil used to like to eat out before the move and the extra travelling. He was eating out and alone every night, probably.

Dessert time came and Juliette caved. They had a banana thing, home-made and it was to die for. She knew she shouldn't, but every mouthful was a few more seconds away from home. As she waited for the bill, the busy owner came over, he asked how the food was, how the service was. He said no tip was necessary because he paid well, it was his policy to look after his people. She liked that; he was clearly a man of principle who knew how to look after people. What she wouldn't give for a genuinely attentive man. "It's nice to see someone leading by example, people don't do that enough these days. Listen to me, I sound like an old maid, I'm not a maid, but you know what I mean. Sorry, I'm gabbling a bit, pressures at home, my lovely meal was a great help".

"I think looking after people is important, I try to be attentive without being overbearing, some bosses make that mistake. My people are happy even though they have to work, but we all have to work so why not make it a better experience if you can. Sorry, I'm gabbling too now, I get like that around attractive people".

Juliette felt a blush start, but Angelo didn't have time to see her discomfort because he'd swept away to deal with another table that seemed to be having a crisis over who ate what and who was paying for it.

All the way home, the escapism of a night out alone was eating away at Juliette. Phil was away working, stopping out, which he said he hated, and here she was playing fast and loose with a guy she didn't know. That might have been fine when she was single but not now. As she turned into the drive, she tried to gauge the mood of the house. It seemed to be ok, if a little edgy. Taking a deep breath, she opened the door and called a greeting, but all was silent. On her neck, the hairs started to rise again. Oh no, the panic was starting. Opening the living room door, she saw that Abigail had dropped off to sleep, like that she looked like a young teen. Her pop glass was half full, her laptop was open beside her, and her skirt had ridden higher, showing off her nice legs. Juliette ignored the legs and tried to peak at the still open laptop, then looked away, not sure what to make of what she'd seen.

Abigail woke with a start, "Mrs. Barker, sorry, I dozed off, is everything good?" She was automatically closing the laptop and packing her work into her bag as she spoke, a nice old leather one that looked very familiar.

"Yes, everything is fine, the kids were good?"

"As gold, they always are with me".

A horn outside broke the moment. "My ride", she said as she got up to go, before pausing.

"Oh, sorry, yes. Here, take a bit extra, we can afford it, I think you're a good cause".

Normally Abigail went through the process of protesting if Juliette tried to give her any extra, but this time she happily accepted the money and was briskly away and through the front door, closing it with a sound thud, the knocker rattling as she did.

The house now seemed normal, the jumbled felt sheet had lost its message and had been placed in the toy-tidy, the room was just a room. Then she recognized the bag she'd seen, the one that Abigail had hastily packed. It was Phil's, a loan from her, why had Abilgail got it and what did the cryptically titled 'case study seven' mean on the page she'd seen? On her rough pad, Abigail's scribble had been barely legible, another little surprise because Juliette had Abigail down for biblical-type script, all sin and damnation.

The house phone rang, and she jumped a mile.

"Just checking in, I called earlier but nobody answered, I assumed you were in the shower or something, everything ok?" Juliette was shocked, why wouldn't Abigail answer the phone. She would, surely? In the background a beat was thumping, Phil was probably in a bar or somewhere, or perhaps the hotel had some event on, a wedding. He'd hate that, hate the noise and the people being drunk, silly. A woman's voice shouted something in the background.

"Yes, I'm fine, sorry I missed you, is everything ok with you?"

"Fine, yes, we've got this bonding thing going on at the moment, bosses' orders so I can't talk for long. I'll call tomorrow when it's quieter, pat Sonny for me, love you".

Before Juliette could respond, Phil was gone, swallowed up by the increasing sound of the jungle drumbeat of whatever was going on. She headed for the kitchen, that bottle of wine she was saving was suddenly very appealing, bonding? She pulled her favourite glass from the back of the cupboard and reached into the fridge for the wine. Next to it was a generic bottle of red, open. She turned it around examining the bottle critically. Interesting, so sweet, no alcohol Abigail did have a slug or two after all.

A dog barking surprised Juliette, she opened the door and Sonny marched in and went straight for his bowl. She watched mesmerised as the dog ate everything put down for him, then drank most of his water. Without acknowledging her, not that she expected much, the dog climbed into its basket and went to sleep.

Juliette rinsed the dog's bowls and replenished them, then went to bed, leaving the bottle of good wine unopened.

May 2019

Juliette always reckoned that a part of the pleasure of working largely from home was that you could decide your own schedule, and, if you wished, could end your breaks when you wanted to and not when peer pressure of management stares made you feel guilty. With her inbox emptied and nothing pending, Juliette sat on her office chair and leafed through a magazine that she'd picked up, just to have something innocuous to read. It was a shiny one with a heavily made-up cover model suggestively biting a strawberry, her equally red lips glistening with juice that was most likely sprayed on and not from the strawberry itself. It was one of those photography tricks they used. Mostly the magazine had self-improvement stuff, the inevitable diets, how to stop one thing or start another, an agony aunt page and a short 'describe' yourself piece linked to an article. It presented it as a 'fun look at how you see yourself or would like others to see you'. Juliette usually skipped past such light-weight things but, this time, she picked up her pen and decided to have a go.

How did she describe herself, petite, slim, regular, generous, other? That was pretty typical of these magazines, missing out bulimic, angular, awkward and obese. She went for 'slim', which was accurate, check.

If she was to describe her personality as if it were a weather forecast, what would she choose? Juliette liked that question; she could see a sharp woman in a meeting being told the usual dross they have to ask but slipping in bits of her own ingenuity while their backs were turned. 'Sunny and fine but with a few cloudy days with the occasional thunderstorm'. Odd how the description seemed to fit her to a T, check.

Was she a caring, compassionate person or did she reserve those feelings for special people? This was an odd one, in the context of the dating app who seemed to be sponsoring the questionnaire. What were they after here? 'Caring and compassionate', check.

Was her ideal partner a true partner or a greater or lesser part of herself? Four questions in and she was having to think hard. This wasn't like any personality quiz thing she'd ever seen before; it was quite searching. She needed some thinking time, so she made another coffee and checked that the kids were still napping. She also looked to see that the dog wasn't chewing anything important. Sonny could be pretty bad if he wanted to be.

Sitting back in the office chair, she readied to continue the test, as she was now thinking of it, writing in 'equal in all things' instead of checking the box provided.

Bang! There was a thud against the window, a bird strike, a big bird by the sound of it. Juliette's mind's eye rewarded the thought with a mental image of Big Bird from tv lying dead below her window, its yellow neck broken, the head grotesquely twisted back on itself. She opened the window and looked down to see a Mourning Dove splayed on the grass, lifeless. She was just about to race down to see whether she could do anything to help it, when a blur passed through her vision and a large tabby cat raced away with the bird in its mouth, the dove's head and wings flopping like dangling pasta on a fork.

Feeling unnerved but assuring herself that she was faultless in the incident, she returned to the magazine.

How far would you go to avenge a slaughtered loved one? What! This was like those psych tests she'd had to do in the past, to prove that she was ok. What was a lowbrow magazine asking such searching questions for? After re-reading it, just to be sure that she was seeing the question correctly, she wrote, 'WHATEVER IT TOOK.

Whose life is more important, yours or your sister's? 'MINE'.

If your partner was unfaithful, would you leave them or exact revenge? 'REVENGE'.

How important is loyalty? 'Paramount'.

What would you like on your gravestone? 'She knew'.

Then, where there appeared to be a blank space, she wrote 'NO, NO, NO'.

There didn't seem to be a way of scoring the thing, so she threw the magazine across the room and went back to her computer.

"Wakey, wakey". The voice was distant then close, then there. It was Phil, she'd dozed off in her chair and was so deep in sleep that she was resisting ever waking up.

"Sorry, I dozed off. What time is it, are you early?"

"Nearly six and no, a little late, actually. The kids seem ok".

Juliette remembered the stupid quiz. "Look at this will you, what sort of thing is this to put in a lighthearted women's magazine? And she recovered the magazine and flicked through to the quiz, roughly forcing it on the bewildered Phil.

He read, frowned, read and frowned some more. "I don't get it", he said, passing it back.

Juliette grabbed the magazine and yanked the pages open until she got to the quiz, none of it made any sense.

How did she describe herself, petite, slim, regular, generous, other? Slim.

How would she describe her personality? 'Sunny, fine but cloudy days with the occasional thunderstorms.'

Was she a caring person? There was nothing written.

Was her ideal partner tall, short, fair, dark? 'Don't know.'

How far would you go to help a loved one? 'Whatever it took.'

Who is more important, the President or parents? 'MINE.'

If your partner was required to work away for long periods, how would you cope? 'REVENGE.'

How important is stability in a relationship? 'Paramount.'

What would you like on your birthday cake? 'She knew.'

"It's all changed, that isn't what it asked, it's twisted my answers".

Phil looked worried but tried to hide it, going into what he thought of as his 'soothing' mode. Juliette recognized it straight away. She thought of it as his condescending mode, something quite different from what he intended.

"I'm not a child", she snapped. "I know what I saw, why do you think I wrote what I wrote?"

Phil knew that he wasn't going to get anywhere and so took the magazine away and left her to it. Often Juliette would think things through, perform a mental 're-set', then act as if nothing had happened. It was her tried and tested way of getting around the bumps in life.

When she went downstairs, the kids had been fed and were sat in the living room watching something on tv that was supposed to entertain them. Amorphous blobs of some sort seemed to be bouncing into each other while making an undefined noise, it really was shit.

"Sorry about that earlier, I was a bit stressed, work mostly. I must have misread the thing, not concentrating".

"Don't worry about it. Look, I arranged for you to see someone, he helps people. Someone at work recommended him and he has offices near here. Please say you'll go and chat to him, please". Phil was almost pleading, and she knew it would be churlish to say no, plus it would keep him off her back.

"Ok, sure, I'll go. I meant to ask, my old leather bag, what happened to it?"

"Oh that, I gave it away, a deserving cause and it was just an old bag, Abigail has it. Money is tight for her, and she was admiring it one day, so I decided to give it to her in a fit of generosity".

"Admiring, I thought it was kept in your room?"

"Yes, that's right. She was talking about things she had to buy for college, and I mentioned the bag. Once she'd seen it, she was keen to have it at any price. It seems they're trendy now, who knew? Me, trendy".

Juliette tried to process, the bag was hers, had always been hers but now it wasn't, otherwise it was a good answer, not avoiding detail, she was satisfied, and he was right, it was only a bag. "When do I see this guy, it is a guy, right?"

"Yes, Geoffrey, tomorrow. Here's his card with directions on the back. Go with an open mind. If you think it's a waste of time then fine, but say you'll give it a fair go, for me, for us".

"I said I would now don't nag. I'll start supper if you're ready".

"Sure, give me an hour, just got to pop out, client stuff, just an hour, ok?"

"Sure".

After the basement incident, Juliette had been reluctant to go back down there and do the laundry, but she'd slowly convinced herself that the moment had passed, whatever it was, and that she needed to move on. In Phil's room his washing basket was half-full, hers too, and the kids barely had anything clean left, so she could do a single wash. She combined the laundry into one large basket, then carried it down the stairs.

The laundry had no atmosphere at all, and she felt fine but, for peace of mind, she wedged the door open so any natural light from upstairs would shine if the power went out again, unlikely though that might be. As she heaved the clothes into the washer, she caught sight of a smudge of red on Phil's boxers. She scratched at it and was surprised to find it looked like lipstick. She looked close at her discoloured finger, then ran a finger from her other hand lightly across her own mouth, they were identical. 'Idiot!', but how? Certainly not recently.

When Phil got back, he was full of beans. She liked that, it meant he was pleased to see her. He said he was just going to take a shower, then shouted down asking what had happened to his laundry. She called back that it was in the washer. He sounded annoyed at that, but she had no idea why.

"Honey, you can't just wash everything together you know".

"I know, I'm not stupid, I checked everything, thoroughly".

"Ok, good".

Juliette now felt very angry, in a few moments her good mood had slipped away. The most annoying thing wasn't Phil questioning her competence with the washing, but her illogical response to his reasonable question. Sometimes she hated herself for it.

Juliette had expected the room to be more business-like, austere even as the previous ones she'd visited had all been, but it was obviously a lived-in office. The consulting couch was a simple office chair of the sort people buy when a place folds and their stuff gets sold off to the highest cash bidder. On the wall behind the desk was the diploma, it said that Geoffrey Watson was qualified to practice psychiatry with a photo below it. He looked more suitable to be a practicing accountant.

"Juliette, please, try to relax, just because you're seeing a shrink, doesn't mean you're nuts", he said in a disarmingly casual way. An opening gambit clearly designed to put his patients at ease, no matter how wound-up they felt.

Ever since childhood Juliette had built pictures in her head, images taken from the visual clues before her, evidence of a life. Watson, she reckoned, was probably single, not very fit looking so likely a couch potato. He had slight stubble, so not the meticulously groomed type and not the fussy type. She liked her picture of him, he was, she decided, comfortable like an old armchair and no threat.

"Sorry about the mess. My wife usually helps out, but she's got her feet up after just having our second, a boy. I gave her time off for good behaviour, although she seems to have spent it moaning about plumbers. Our water system broke down and it's taken three weeks just to get a plumber to call back. We're all washing in buckets, ridiculous. At least when my knee is fit, I can get back to the gym and use their showers, sitting all day is doing me no good", he said, and he patted his girth.

It was a lot of unnecessary information, but Juliette figured they were still in the 'relaxing the patient' phase of the appointment. This wasn't her first visit to what they'd called 'a professional'. She was surprised at how wrong she'd been about Watson though and, in view of recent information, adjusted her mental image accordingly. She knew that she'd remember every last detail.

"Sorry, you're paying big bucks for me to listen to you, not me banging on about my little domestic trivialities. You saw a ghost". It wasn't a question; it was a statement.

Juliette was shocked by the sudden plunge into the subject, into the sea of her instability. Not insanity, nobody had said insanity yet, but she reckoned that it wasn't too far down the line.

"I saw something, something I can't explain, yes", she said, defensively.

Watson seemed to her to be doing five things at once. She knew that it was distraction technique, she'd looked it up. Get the patient to think you're not paying that much attention, then zoom in on the important bits.

"Go on, try and explain it to me. Leave out no details, tell me anything you remember, everything. I want to share the experience with you. I'm not here to judge, no matter what you think or have read on the Internet about the work I do". Watson appeared to be a mind reader but then that was his job, the diploma said so. Why should she be surprised by his performance? It was what his customers expected.

Juliette began with the tedious, mundane parts. The laundry, the chores, everything but the stairs, everything but what had happened on the stairs.

"Ok, you skipped around the houses a little there. I want to know what happened to you that was different from the laundry and yada, yada. In your own time, I don't mind, my clock is running, tick-tock, tick-tock, ker-ching".

Watson had been quite blunt, as if Juliette was wasting his time but that it didn't matter. He'd almost been like Phil, disbelieving, detached, not at all interested in her awful fright, or her.

"I had an experience I can't explain. I felt, then saw, two small children. They came from nowhere and passed me on the stairs from the basement to the kitchen".

"Age?"

"Eight maybe, yes about eight, both of them", she said, anticipating the next question.

Watson looked down at his pad. Juliette was disappointed, it wasn't a leather-bound tome containing the details of each patient, the information entered in fabulously scripted handwriting and a testament to good schooling, self-control and a level of inspirational precision. It was just a jotter, a cheap, Dollar Shop jotter.

The composite of Watson she now had in mind told her that this was a waste of time and money, and that she should never have listened to Phil in the first place. It didn't matter how highly recommended this guy was, he came across as an amateurish jerk.

"Twins, did they look alike, what were they wearing?"

Juliette was shocked, he believed her, or at least seemed to. Maybe he wasn't such a jerk after all? Her head was now spinning, she had too many thoughts going on in there, nothing had punctuation, nothing stood alone, it was all a jumble.

"Does that help? it's not that unusual you know".

Juliette realized that she'd pushed her fingers into her ears, trying to stop the noise, trying to make everything stop spinning. It had worked, her head felt clearer. "Sorry, force of habit, from childhood".

"Really, what started you doing it, why do you still do it?"

Juliette had never been asked that before, even Phil had never mentioned it and her mom had just said it was another one of the little quirks she'd brought with her, one of many. She was never slow to tell people about her adopted daughter Juliette's little quirks.

"I was a bad sleeper, any noise kept me awake, so I used to put my fingers in my ears a while and it seemed to help. Now I do it when I just want a bit of quiet, a bit of peace, just for a few moments". She looked at Watson who had scribbled throughout. Would she be able to read those notes when they'd done?

"We all have little mechanisms like that, I see the sense in it, Juliette. Don't worry, I'm not judging you. Do it anytime you need to if it helps, sometimes our conversations might touch a nerve, bring back a memory you've long buried. If you put your fingers in your ears, I'll stop until you tell me you're ok, deal?"

Juliette found that she was warming to this Geoffrey Watson guy. Geoff, maybe she could call him Geoff, Geoffrey was so formal, Geoff was friendly, almost intimate. Two kids he said, so he was fertile, active.

"Let's just go back to the incident, can we? Two kids, eight or so, on the stairs. You were going to tell me whether you thought that they were twins and what they were wearing".

"Yes, sorry, not twins, I don't think so, maybe not even related, they looked different, I don't remember any familial traits common to both. One, the shorter one looked a little simple, sorry I don't mean to be cruel but simple, yes".

"Is that something you look for in kids, familial traits, as if belonging to the same parents?"

What an odd question, surely everybody, when they see people, wonders who they're related to?

"No, not especially", she lied. "You'll appreciate that I was startled, shocked, not really thinking keenly".

"Do you read, write, do word puzzles, crosswords?"

"Yes, all of them, I like to keep my mind exercised. I read that problem solving is good for your mental health, so I take my brain for a stroll whenever I can".

"Yes, it is, although it depends on the problem you're trying to crack. Take me for example, I've been trying to solve a Rubik's Cube for twenty years now, I haven't yet, I don't know what that says about me", laughed Watson. "These kids then, describe them in more detail".

"Two girls, dressed in fairly modern but rough clothing, like hand-me-downs, shabby. They looked real but insubstantial".

"And what did they do, on the stairs?"

"They ran past, I felt them brush me. At first, I thought that it must be the dog. They ran past me going upstairs, they stopped on the top step, then ran through a closed curtain".

"Was it your curtain".

Juliette didn't understand the question at first, of course it was her curtain, she was in her own fucking house! "Juliette?" She closed her eyes, just for a moment, and saw the curtain in her head. No, it wasn't their curtain, it hadn't occurred to her before that it might not be. How had this Geoff guy known that?

"No, now I think about it, no, it wasn't my curtain. I didn't recognize it".

"Ok, describe it, tell me in detail about the different curtain".

It seemed such a trivial to be asked, surely the key to this was the kids, why was she seeing kids? The curtain was just a curtain, peripheral. She looked at Geoff, he was waiting patiently. Juliette closed her eyes again and remembered. "It was pale, dirty white, there was a hole, top left, a small hole but no light came through, but I could see a scrap of material from the hole, dangling. It was like it had been cut deliberately".

"They went through the curtain you say. Did the curtain part or did they just pass through it, did you follow?" he said, checking another pad he had and one that she'd missed. It was more a folder with notes in it, different pages, loose. She couldn't quite see what was on them, but they were typed.

"Yes, I went through when I got to the top. No, they didn't open it, they just went though. It never even moved when they did".

"What was it like, in the kitchen?"

Juliette felt a bit of panic rising. She didn't remember mentioning the kitchen, her brain was busy replaying the recent conversation, her description of events. She was very sure she'd not mentioned the kitchen to anyone.

"Kitchen?"

"Yes, you said just now", and he read from his notes. "'I had an experience, I felt, then saw two small children. They passed me on the stairs from the basement to the kitchen'".

She calmed down. Yes, she had said that, she remembered now. There was no conspiracy happening, but she'd be sure to check later when she reviewed the visit in her head, to replay exactly what this Geoffrey Watson had said, in case he did know something that she'd not told him. It would mean that there was a conspiracy for sure.

"Different, the kitchen was different. Old, rough, none of it was mine, it was old fashioned, the sort of thing you get when you buy an old person's house after they've died, and they'd not done a reno for thirty years", said Juliette quietly.

"Right, yes, I understand, and the children, were they in there?" he said, writing down more notes.

Why had she said after they'd died? Not all old people died in the house, some died in hospital or a nursing home perhaps. Some didn't die at all but moved in with relatives and lived out their golden years with their loving family. Watson didn't seem too bothered, was it a Freudian slip?

"The clothes, in the wash basket, they were normal, completely normal, nothing was wrong with them", she said, trying to sound composed and not paranoid.

"The children, were they there, in the kitchen?" asked Watson again.

"No, not in view at first, then yes, they were there".

"Did they speak to you, what did they say?"

"They said 'am I their mommy'. They had an accent I think, foreign, I thought maybe German. I hear German in town, we have a German bakery. I know the sound but I'm not one-hundred percent sure, just maybe German, I may have misheard. The floor was very dusty, as if it hadn't been cleaned in years. I could see no tracks leading to them, no footprints. I looked but there were no tracks, the dust on the floor was undisturbed". Juliette felt agitated again and her heart had picked up in pace. She could feel a flush climbing up from her neck, the red rising like a slow tide, changing how she looked, making her appear angry, angrier.

"Did they speak again, what did they say?" said Geoff calmly. Just a regular conversation between two adults, nothing odd going on here.

"They asked if I was their new mommy, sorry, I already said that. When I asked where I was, the taller girl said that I was home".

Geoffrey Watson waited patiently for Juliette to calm down. When she'd finished talking, her fingers had gone straight into her ears and he made a point of not noticing, just scribbling his shopping list on his pad, trying to remember what his wife had said about peanut butter. Juliette snatched her hands from her ears suddenly and resumed. "Then I heard Phil, and I was back in the kitchen, my kitchen, I was in my home". She was now speaking ever so quietly, almost as if she didn't want to disturb anyone.

"Did Phil notice that you were flustered, you were flustered, yes?"

"Yes, completely, although I'd say freaked out covers it better. Flustered is so polite, more a minor disruption of routine. I was completely freaked out. I'd ripped the curtain off the pole and the pole from the wall, our curtain, not the other one, and my knee was hurting, a lot".

"Did you tell Phil what had happened?"

"No, I said I'd stumbled through accidentally, which I had, sort of. He accepted my explanation without question, he never questions anything I tell him, not ever, is that weird?"

"You didn't tell him about your experience then?"

"No".

"And was that it, the end?"

"No, I saw the kids again, later the same day. We went to a movie, Phil and I, and they ran in front of the car. I saw them. Phil thought that it had been foxes, but I saw them, I know what I saw. Am I going mad?"

Watson cracked a slight smile. "No, I don't think so, but you had an experience that we can't explain yet, a very real one and something way out of your personal comfort zone. It scared you, have you ever been that scared before?"

Juliette noticed that Watson had glanced slyly at the clock behind her, was he counting the minutes until the next client, the next fee? It wasn't very professional in her opinion. She was about to say something when suddenly Watson got up and grabbed an empty water glass.

"Come on little fella, outside with you, we don't allow spiders in here".

Juliette spun around. Watson had the glass over a spider up by the clock in an instant. The spider was quite a large one, dark, leggy, probably a female. Juliette wondered how many mates she'd eaten, devoured, consumed, it's what females do, death was a part of life as a male spider looking to pass on his genes. Watson carefully slipped a piece of paper under the glass, took it to the window, opened it and shook the spider out.

"Sorry, I don't know how they get in. A previous scary experience then. What did I just do?"

"Sorry, what, just now? You caught a spider in the glass and let it go".

"Good, right, just keeping you grounded. I could see that you were anxious, now you're not, distraction technique with a stunt spider, I'm sure you've read up on it. You strike me as someone who does their research".

"Yes, I do", said Juliette, surprised. "I think if you have to make a judgement on anything you should first get the relevant information, then review it, consider it and decide".

"Good plan. Most people are reactive, but thinking about what you are doing has benefits. When you were with the children, did you think, or did you react?"

Juliette thought back to the moment, but the memory seemed clouded now, as if she'd kept her glasses in the fridge and was now wearing them in a warm room.

"To answer your question about a scary, previous experience, if I may. When I was a child, my sister, Melissa, played a prank on me, we'd be about eight. We had a hatch in the landing roof, it went to the attic, just a hatch, no fancy pull-down ladder or anything. I went to the bathroom, the hatch was right outside the door and while I was in there, she climbed up and wedged my mother's fur gloves in the hatch. It looked like a hairy monster was trying to get in. I screamed; I was terrified".

"Did Melissa get into trouble?"

"No, my mom always favoured Melissa over me, always. She laughed and told me to get a grip, that was always her way, whatever happened it was always 'get a grip' Juliette".

Watson scribbled some more notes but wasn't sure how to spell tagliatelle. He usually just scribbled it to make it look ok, he always had more T's and not enough L's. "Did you have nightmares afterwards?"

"For a while. I slept with the light on anyway, a nightlight until it broke, and my mom said that it was time I grew up?"

"How old were you, when the light broke?"

"Fifteen, nearly sixteen".

Watson did yet more scribbling, he'd written down the name of a cereal that they'd seen on tv every night for a month, he wanted to try it. "Ok, I think that will do for now. I'll review my notes then we'll talk again, I'll send an appointment by email".

"Can I see your notes?"

"Not at the moment, I need to knock them into shape, make them legible", and he turned the page to Juliette so she could see the scrawly mess.

"Man, you really are a doctor", she said lightly. She felt better, less anxious, less that she was carrying something unwanted around. This Watson guy had done that, he was good. She almost asked for another appointment for the following day there and then, almost.

"It will be about a week before I can fit you in again. I can see that we made progress here today, I'm pleased, well done, Juliette. We'll sort this thing out for you, I'm confident about that".

Watson's tone was clear, it was time for her to go, no chit-chat, no flirting even, nothing overtly sexual. She didn't do that now anyway. Watson's conversation was just light man-woman, woman-man conversation, the sort she never got from Phil. She liked Watson though, he made her feel safe, he listened to her.

When Juliette got back to her car, she sat for ten minutes running the whole thing back. She was trying to make sense of some of the questions. What did the stupid gloves thing have to do with what she'd seen on the stairs, when she knew for certain what she'd seen?

Her phone went. "Hi, Honey, how did it go? What did you make of Geoff, did you like him? He's one of the good guys". Phil sounded very perky.

"Yes, good, he was good, he helped. Look, I'm not sure I really need this, it was nothing, just me being silly".

"Honey you were really spooked, and I was worried about you. Let Geoff do his job, let Geoff get to the bottom of it so we can move on, love you".

Juliette mumbled her 'love you too' reply. Sometimes it was just a reflex, but it made her feel loved when Phil did it and she liked that feeling.

"I've just been told, two nights away again. I told them, I'm getting too old for this shit, and I want to be home with you. I'm going to speak to them, put my foot down, sorry. I'll be gone when you get back, I'll call".

Juliette sat rigid in the car. She was going to be on her own in that house again and Phil, just when she needed him, wasn't going to be there, he was going to desert her, abandon her. She wasn't having that.

In the pit of her stomach, Juliette felt the guilt burning. Abigail had been fine about it and never questioned the request to look after the kids. Juliette had been vague about what she was doing, she'd covered it with 'a work thing' and left it at that. Now she was sat at what she thought of as her regular table, waiting for a menu, waiting to be noticed.

"Good to see you again, Juliette, my people must be doing something right. Is this three or four times back dining with me now, yes?"

Juliette blushed, hoping to not give the game away. "Five actually, I think you weren't here one time, but your staff did you credit. The Ferry has become my favourite place to eat and get away from everything".

"I can see that in your eyes, I won't pry but if you ever need to talk, I'm here, I listen good. My life has been spent listening".

"Thank you, it's just a life bump, you know how it is. Sometimes you just want to step off the ride, feel the breeze of change on your face a while, take a risk maybe". In her head, Juliette was seeing the words appear as if in a text to a secret lover. It was just a tease, a little bit of temptation, something not meant to be deliberate, preordained, but now the hook was set and waiting for a bite.

Angelo's expression didn't change, he was an attractive man and knew the course, although each time around the track was different. "Tell me, Juliette, have you ever been to Point Prim, not far away, beautiful views over the Bay of Fundy on a nice day, you might like it. I find it very relaxing, so I go there every Tuesday morning, rain or shine. It regenerates me, rejuvenates my soul. I recommend it to all my friends, I'm sure you'd like it".

The accent was slightly clipped. Angelo was obviously not a native of Digby County, his looks and accent suggested something Mediterranean, but his name could have been from one of several countries.

"I may just bump into you there one day then. I love peaceful places, spots where not too many people are likely to spoil the moment". Juliette knew that she was as good as advertising what she wanted to happen, but there was no guilt, no Phil, no other life. Just her and what she wanted in her life, something different, something exciting, something she could walk away from whenever she wanted. Angelo smiled but was then called away by one of the servers. Juliette noticed that all the staff were female, young and very attractive. They reflected Angelo to some extent, had he slept with all of them, she wondered?

When Juliette got home, she was earlier than expected, so she slipped in, quietly, she didn't know why. From the living room she could hear Abigail on her cell phone. She was giggling regularly and said 'no way' a couple of times. The living room door was slightly ajar, and Juliette could see into part of the room. The kids were looking in her direction, which unnerved her a bit. She was just about to walk in when she heard Abigail laugh that she'd send something to keep him going until next time.

Barely breathing, Juliette watched as Abigail raised her dress, slipped down her panties and photographed her privates. She giggled again, then hung up before standing up. In a panic Juliette rushed for the front door, opened it quietly then slammed it shut. "Hi Abigail, only me", she called, theatrically.

"Hi Mrs. Barker, I hope you had a good time. They've been very good, we sang a few songs and played charades. Other than that, nothing much happened".

Juliette was confused. "Sang, they sang?"

"Yes, we often sing. Sorry, I can't stay, I just texted that you're back, so I'll be going".

"Right", said Juliette, well aware that Abigail's phone was still on the sofa and hadn't been used since she photographed herself. This time Abigail got double the agreed rate and took it. In seconds she was gone and got into a car that Juliette hadn't heard arrive. For a few moments Juliette was rooted to the floor, then she rushed to the window in time to see a car disappearing from view, it was blue, like Phil's.

The kids never showed any sign of excitement and Juliette had long since given up talking to them properly unless Phil was around. Now they got a perfunctory 'we're going out', and they simply stood, walked out to the car, climbed in and strapped themselves up. She always reckoned that she'd have got more response from one of those ever-nodding dogs that were popular on the parcel shelf of cars way back when. The highway was quiet, it usually was. It got busier in Digby but the shakes she'd buy the kids would be worth the wait. They could slurp them quietly while she was out of the car, it would be more than enough to keep them fully occupied. The tiny parking lot at Point Prim was deserted and her heart sank. Tuesday he'd said, every Tuesday. She checked her watch and tried to relax, it was only nine forty-five, for some reason she had in mind that he would show up before ten, eager.

Angelo had been right; the view was great. It was a fine day and Juliette couldn't believe that more people didn't take advantage of such a lovely spot. A smell told her that at least one did, one who didn't pick up after their dog, sharing their smelly gift with the other visitors for some time after the event. She eased her shoe off and wiped it clean on a mossy tree, but the smell was in her nose now, and it followed her about. The Point

Prim trail meandered a bit and there were several spots where you could go and not be easily seen. One had a bench, that would probably do.

Now that she was there, now that this was happening, Juliette began to feel uncomfortable, panicking almost. She heard a footfall ahead and saw the shape of someone with curly black hair, quite stocky. Her breathing got erratic, and her mind went cloudy. Was she really going to do this again? Suddenly she didn't know what to do and the only question on her mind was, 'what would Melissa do?'

The drive back was uneventful and even the queue for another shake was short, thankfully. Somehow the kids were able to suck the life out of the shake silently, not gurgling as they chased the dregs around the bottom of the cup. It was unnerving, but she was getting used to being unnerved, it was almost her normal now. In the dark of the night, with just the creaks and groans of a cooling old house for company, Juliette knew she'd made the right decision. She'd not be going back to The Ferry again, and she'd deleted Angelo from her phone. It was a stupid idea in the first place, and it must never happen again.

"It's me". was all Phil said when she answered the phone. She knew that, he was on her caller ID as Phil, he must have known that, why was he stating the obvious?

"I was expecting you. I was expecting you home actually, delay?"

The silence told her that there was more to this conversation than she'd bargained for, much more, but not now, she wasn't doing this along the phone line. "If you have something to tell me, bad news about us, I want it in person", and she hung up. So that was it, everything fitted together, everything made sense now. Outside the car was still muddy from before, she'd wash it later. It didn't take long to tidy it up. The seats could do with a wipe though, the little darlings might be able to drink a shake quietly, but gravity still carried drops onto the seat, they were human after all.

The kids looked up when she walked back into the living room, their fuzzy-felt was out again and they seemed to have been making random shapes on the board, they seemed to like it. It was unusual for them to notice that she'd entered, Juliette had been told to make sure she was in their line of sight to let them know that she was there, to not startle them. She had at first, but she'd soon given that up too, along with the kindly voice. A fright might do them good now and then. She glanced at the board with the felt crudely scattered around it. In the middle and framed by red triangles it spelt out 'dumped again'.

It was two in the morning when Phil showed up. Juliette was still up and part-way down a bottle of red, a good one. "I came straight back, they're not very happy with me over this but I felt we were too important to let it stew, what bad news were you expecting?" he said.

Juliette felt a little light-headed, and stupid too. She'd jumped to a conclusion, a wrong conclusion, otherwise Phil wouldn't be there now. "I'm sorry, I just felt very insecure and you're away all the time leaving me here, in this house". Phil shook his head; it looked like it was going to be a long night.

For a few days, a dark atmosphere descended on the house. Juliette knew that she was to blame, she'd been paranoid and didn't need Phil to remind her of the fact, not that he ever did. Paranoia had always been a bit of the thing for Juliette, that and a feeling that she wasn't in the right body sometimes, the right sex even. The thing with paranoia is that sometimes it's justified.

"How does this work exactly?" she asked the plain looking, wispy-bearded young man in the computer store, nerd seemed to fit nicely. It was one of the side-street stores, independent and tucked away in Dartmouth. You had to know where it was if you wanted to find it, or at least be very serious about seeking out what it supplied.

"This goes into a lamp USB and looks like a phone charger, it then links with your phone, and you can view it in real time, or set it to record and review what it sees whenever you want. It can send images directly to your laptop or tablet, looking at you I'd guess tablet. The files aren't huge, low res but good enough. If you have a sneak thief, or something else that's keeping you up at night, this will help confirm it".

Juliette turned the tiny device over in her hands, not sure whether to get it now after all. It was quite expensive, but she had her own financial independence and nobody but her had her complicated bank log in for on-line banking. In her hand was peace of mind, some at least, or confirmation of her fears. Did she really want to know?

"Are these popular sellers, who'd buy this sort of thing?"

The nerd was getting a bit fed up with her by now. She could see him thinking 'just buy the fucking thing, lady'. Juliette had already decided he was probably one of those incel types with sticky mags and tissues bought in bulk. "People who have problems that they want to sort out, problems that require hard, unequivocal proof. Now do you want it or what?"

Juliette picked up on the tone. "Ok, I'll take it, I'd like a USB thumb stick too, a large one, debit ok?" It was.

Trips to the city had been few and far between since Juliette and Phil had moved to Annapolis Royal. Most of what they needed was in the local stores, or there was the option of the soulless, if socially entertaining, Wal-Mart in Digby. For anything major they could even take a ride to Kentville. She didn't miss the city though, the bustle, the panhandlers at traffic lights, people of all races chattering away in their mother tongues. It wasn't that they were foreign that bothered her, she liked the diversity, it was that she didn't know what they were saying about her that made her uncomfortable. Paranoid again? Yes, Phil had often said as much.

The ride home had been bumpy on the awful roads around Windsor, boring the rest of the way. It was always a dilemma whether to wait for the Keji turn to Annapolis Royal or to go back the long way, from Bridgetown, the rear entrance as she thought of it. Either way in, it always seemed like a trek and, to Juliette, her mom's place, which she'd pass on the way, always had a negative aura. Not that she believed in that hippy crap. By the time she'd made her mind up, the Bridgetown exit had gone and so she sailed on, stopping to pick up some of the coffee moonshine on the way in. It was nice to have in to offer to guests and she was supporting a worthy local industry, it was a win, win.

"Good trip, get what you wanted?" She knew that Phil was only being Phil, always asking after her day, but to Juliette it sounded a bit like 'where have you been, what have you been doing, who have you been seeing' all the time, intrusive, unnecessary. She never asked those questions of Phil, she'd always trusted him implicitly, until now.

"Fine, yes, fine. Seems further away than ever though and the road gets worse. They must be making new potholes as a cottage industry somewhere, dropping them in the road when we're all asleep in our beds". They laughed about it together, they always laughed together about the potholes.

"Are you still good for the meal out? We're meeting the Brysons. I did mention".

"Oh, god, is that tonight? I'd forgotten, yes, fine. I think I'll do a bit of work in my office now then, just bits and pieces to get on top of it, it won't take long. Are you ok with the kids?"

Phil was fine with that, all of it, and he had a book on the go too. He always had a book on the go. The best Juliette ever managed was the Internet or a magazine. Sometimes she envied his ability to be able to concentrate long enough to read a whole book, and when you had, be able to delete it all from your head later, she couldn't. In her office with the view of the yard at the back, was a small grass area surrounded by tall trees. It was dotted with little flags showing the invisible dog fence and, in the flower bed down the left side, some border plants that she'd not identified yet. For a while, Juliette stared out of the window, her mind a blank, her face reflecting back in the pane as the afternoon light filled the room.

She looked at her reflection and wondered where the pretty girl had gone. There was a fraction of movement. Nothing big, no clear image, just movement behind her. She turned to look but there was nothing there. She hadn't really expected anything, it was the sort of movement that dancing light might produce, light that she had no control over unless she pulled the blind down and eliminated it, and the view, altogether.

Opening up the computer, she fiddled with a couple of spreadsheets, tax stuff, things that she could pop up if she needed them to cover a different screen. She plugged the camera into her own charger port on the desktop lamp. Unless you knew, it was just a charger.

The set up process was fairly simple, although in places it assumed that the new owner was competent with computers and not someone who was seeing such things for the first time. It was one of her pet hates, one of many. Every time she got used to something on the computer, knew where the things to press were and had even mastered a shortcut or two, the damn thing updated, changed everything and then hours would be needed to get back to your comfortable space. Ok, not hours, maybe, but it was an inconvenience, unnecessary, an imposition foisted on the user by a spotty kid struggling with puberty who did the updates. Nerds, like the guy in the computer shop, in fact exactly like the guy from the computer shop. Juliette looked at the image on her laptop. Spotty kid was wrong about her being a tablet-only sort of person. 'One nil to me' she reckoned, it felt like a victory, a small one, true, but a victory, nevertheless.

The kid in the store had underplayed the quality of the images from the spy camera. Juliette couldn't shake the name, despite trying to push the spying aspect out of her mind. It was stuff to spy with, so just call it like it is. This purchase was justified though, it being insurance. This was peace of mind and after, when she'd satisfied herself that she'd been right, or completely wrong, which was also a possibility, she'd never use it again. She'd throw it into the French Basin pond the next time she walked the trail. Juliette shivered, involuntarily. Was that a reaction to her lack of trust in Phil, was she even betraying him herself by sneaking off to Dartmouth and buying the spy camera? 'Come on Juliette, it's hard thinking time now. If you do this there's no going back, he can never know what you used unless it's true, unless he really is up to something. If he is then we deal with it, the same way as we've dealt with things in the past'. She shivered again, but it wasn't cold in her room, not at all.

The image on her laptop blinked, vanished and came back all in one instant. What was that, a malfunction, a virus, was this expensive thing even reliable? Juliette was annoyed, she'd declined a receipt, she didn't want a paper trail, not now, but if the thing was faulty, would the Incel remember her, give her an exchange? Juliette thought about the nerd and how she'd cheered him up and why there was no receipt. It was just her being playful, he'd remember.

With clarity of thinking, she opened up the recorded image, just to check that it was a real-time issue and not just something with the PC. Two small faces were looking back at her, slightly blurred as if in very low light. It was all she could do to suppress a scream. She slammed the laptop shut violently and gasped for breath. She was shaking, cold and hyperventilating. She listened for a footfall on the stairs, nothing. She looked slowly around the room, nothing, just her office, not yet totally personalized. It was just her place to work. In the back yard a large, black cat stalked slowly around the edge of the lawn. A flock of ducks went over, she didn't know what sort, definitely ducks though, probably from French Basin. They had lots of ducks there sometimes.

The cat annoyed her. She'd seen it before, stalking whatever in her yard. She'd also seen it shitting in the flower beds, and she'd read that cat shit carried parasites. They infected people, sent them blind. She didn't want someone else's cat shit to send her blind, she didn't want to go blind at all but, at that precise moment, it was an option. Why was the cat even coming in the yard, couldn't it smell Sonny, god knows he produced enough of his own shit to keep her busy. Never Phil though, he never picked up after him. The thought of that annoyed her.

A rhythmic thumping dragged her back to the presence, it was the water pump. Phil must be running water somewhere, maybe he'd been to the bathroom, that big old cistern used a ton of water. It would all have to go. Juliette sat on her hands, she'd always found trapping her hands under her legs comforting, it made her feel safe. Sometimes it was as if her hands lived independent lives, made their own decisions, did whatever they wanted to without asking, but when were trapped under her legs they were more under her control, less likely to misbehave.

She knew that she was going to have to open the laptop and look again, if only to close everything down, lock it and make it secure. She shook some more; she needed a moment. Opening the laptop, she kept telling herself that she was an adult, to stop behaving like a child. It was just her imagination, those faces, the two children, it was probably just a mark on the screen, an artifact of the light. She hit enter and the screen showed the room, the spy camera hadn't stopped spying just because she'd shut the laptop lid.

She stopped recording and went to the files, the one holding the recent content. The video file was dated and timed, it took everything it needed from the system, it was today's date and a little under six minutes long. Juliette was confused. Surely it had been longer? she'd had the thing shut for twenty minutes, half an hour at least. The system said not though, it said a little under six minutes had been recorded. That included the time spent setting it up.

'Right, get a grip girl'.

Clicking on the file it opened and the image showed the room, as viewed from the low angle of the lamp port. It showed Juliette in one third, not moving much, it was probably when she was looking out of the window. Then there was some sort of static, fuzziness, then it went dark, nothing.

She slid the play bar forwards, stopping every minute, nothing, she let the last thirty seconds play out. The image went from dark to light, showed Juliette looking at the screen, reaching over, taping the keys that closed down the camera, then nothing.

Juliette jumped a proverbial mile as her phone rang, shit! It was her sister, Melissa.

"So, they say I'll be able to go home tomorrow and I should be fine. They say that I'll make a full recovery and that I can have the kids back when I feel able, is that alright?"

Melissa was such a mouse, of course it was alright. Looking after two brain-dead kids was hardly a test, apart from the general thing of feeding them and their vacuous expressions, otherwise they were as good as gold.

"Good news, Lissy, of course it's alright. Nothing to report I'm afraid, they've been pretty quiet considering, although I don't know what I expected".

"You have been stimulating them haven't you, you know, interacting? I know it can seem all one-way sometimes, but they do respond. I can't abandon them, I just can't". Tears didn't sound too far away.

"No, I know. We stimulate, we chatter away all day, play music, read stories. Abigail, you remember her, she babysits and is very enthusiastic about them, they respond, a bit, she says. She'll be devastated when they go home. No more babysitter". Melissa picked up on the comment, like seeing the back of Abigail was a blessing. She was used to her sister; their conversations were about filling in the blanks more than the content.

"Everything alright, Juliette?"

"Yes, fine, the usual, you know me, mountains out of molehills. I can hear Phil coming up, I'm in the office, do you want a word? He keeps asking to meet you, and mom".

"No, you know I don't want to speak to him, we talked all this through already", said Melissa sharply. "You and I can catch up when you come over, later then Juliette, take care". And she hung up without waiting for an answer.

"Take care?"

The lid of the laptop closed as the door opened.

"How's it going, I heard you talking, who are you chatting to?"

"Nobody, just talking aloud, you know how you do, keeps me sane". It wasn't a great choice of words, and she knew it, but Phil wouldn't say anything, he wouldn't rock that particular boat, not at the moment.

"I'm just going to jump in the shower and get ready, you can go first if you like, oh, is that a new USB charger port? I could do with one myself, a life the road treats these little things very badly".

Juliette yanked it out of the lamp socket and tossed it over, "keep it, it's just a cheap gas station one, I can get another. I was just testing it; you know I don't trust things unless I see them working properly first".

Phil tossed the spy camera back., "It's ok, I'm heading to town myself, seeing yours just reminded of what I needed. I'll pick one up myself, right, you, shower, yes, no?" Juliette waved him away, so he went off to his room to get stripped for the shower. She decided to wait until she could hear the water running before going downstairs. In her hand, the spy camera seemed to be getting hotter, like a fresh roast chestnut had been dropped into her palm unexpectedly. After a few minutes the bathroom door closed and the old radio fired up, the local radio running ads for cheap chicken legs every half an hour. She slipped quietly downstairs and into the living room. The kids were there, sitting, watching, saying nothing, not that they ever did. Despite being quite sure that they wouldn't know what she was up to, Juliette kept her body between the kids and the lamp with the USB, deftly plugging in the spy camera, then pushing her phone and lead in as if charging it, the subterfuge complete.

The doorbell rang and Abigail walked in. Juliette was fine with that, the bell was a warning, in case she and Phil were 'busy', not that that happened much, spontaneously at least. Right from the off they'd both said for Abigail to treat the house like home, and she did. "Hi Mrs. Barker, you look nice".

"Juliette, please Abigail, no formalities here".

Juliette had said for Abigail to drop the Mrs. Barker routine a dozen times, but she hadn't, and it was starting to grate. If she really was banging Phil, she wouldn't be sorry to see her go, besides, if what Lissy had said, they wouldn't need her for much longer anyway. Then it would be back to just her and Phil. The thought didn't exactly fill her with glee, in fact it worried her. The kids didn't react when Abigail arrived, but Juliette could tell that they'd become happier, despite it being her that had been making a fuss of them, both scrupulously receiving exactly the same amount of attention. Phil came down the stairs, he looked quite smart, almost the man she fell for. "Ready?"

Juliette went through the 'call me' routine for Abigail, but Phil was getting testy. "Come on, I'll have to put my foot down to get there in reasonable time". It occurred to Juliette that she didn't actually know where the 'where' was in this case, just Digby somewhere. They were just buckling up when Phil announced that he'd left his wallet in the house and dashed back. Juliette stared straight ahead, she suddenly felt exposed, alone, abandoned. Maybe Phil had really lost interest in her? She checked her look in the rearview mirror, she looked ok. What could she do to keep his interest? She had to unbuckle her seatbelt again, but with a bit of wriggling she managed to get her panties off and into her handbag. It had worked before.

It was probably less than a minute when Phil got back, patting his pocket with the now recovered wallet and holding Juliette's phone, complete with wire and USB charger-come-spy cam. "I thought you might want this. I know you feel naked without your phone", and he smiled, passed the phone over and started the car. Juliette smiled and thanked him, but she now felt very exposed. The drive was done mostly in silence, with Juliette suspecting that Phil knew what the USB was for, and that was why he'd pulled it. "You ok? You've been very quiet since we got going, anything I've done wrong?" asked Phil.

"No, nothing, I've just been a bit edgy, the kids make me edgy. I wish they could speak, it's a basic level of human interaction". She didn't know where that had come from and she felt guilty at having said it, but it was how she felt.

"Maybe they will speak, with the right situation. The doctor thought so, they don't really know the problem as such, they function, just not as kids should do for that age".

"I suppose so. Was Abigail ok, when you went back in?"

"Yes, why shouldn't she be?" It was an odd thing for Juliette to say, even for Juliette. More silence descended, a really frosty one. They took the off ramp to Digby, then made their way slowly down into town. It was quite busy everywhere, people were out cruising, shopping, heading for food, the usual things that make up a bustling town. Juliette didn't register any of it, she rarely did unless she was driving. She would often look up in total surprise when they got to their destination.

"I see their car, I hope we didn't keep them too long", said Phil, finding a parking spot.

Juliette snapped back to the present, then panicked when she saw their dining destination, The Ferry.

"Here, really, I've heard bad things about this place, can't we go somewhere else?"

"What, no, you have to book to get in at the weekend, besides, I've heard very good things, come on, don't go all flaky on me again". It was quite blunt, an instruction and Juliette almost demanded that she be taken home straight away. It was only the prospect of walking in and catching Abigail on the floor with a man that stopped her. She shook her head, as if trying to clear it. Phil was already out and heading for the door, he didn't even open the car door for her. Juliette caught up as Phil deliberately paused to one side on the step to let a large group of young people out, they smiled and thanked him, nice kids, all Abigail clones. "Sorry", was all Juliette said when she caught up, but Phil ignored her.

They stood just inside the restaurant waiting. It was noisy as people chatted, pop music played quietly in the background and plates clanked as they arrived or departed. Atmosphere they called it. The hostess arrived, she looked cheerful but busy. On seeing Juliette, she recognized the look she'd given her and just led them to the table where their friends, Phil's friends, were waiting. Juliette switched to charm mode. The Brysons seemed pleased to see them and dismissed the wait as trivia, Phil citing the kids as a delay while the babysitter arrived. "Kids, eh?"

After a few minutes Juliette felt herself relax and she started to enjoy the evening. She chided herself for the whole spy camera thing and getting testy. At one point she got nervous when Angelo came to the table, introduced himself and wished them a good meal. He didn't acknowledge Juliette other than as a part of the group, she was fine with that, she admired his discretion.

After the meal and as they drove home, narrowly missing a stupid deer that made a suicidal dash over the highway, they chatted about the evening, about the Brysons, just chatted like they used to. Juliette's head was clear, sharp, without suspicion, she liked the feeling. Once they got home, Phil waited in the car for Abigail, she had no ride home again and it was only fifteen minutes away. Juliette went inside. The kids were still up, they seemed to notice her, that was something. Abigail was paid, gathered up her stuff and left, having said how quiet a night it had been.

Juliette chatted to the kids and poured herself a generous shot of coffee moonshine, sitting on the sofa and sipping the drink while doing a large-piece jigsaw with them. She knew that she was mentally counting, but Phil appeared at almost the time she'd estimated, and all was well.

Phil didn't linger and Juliette didn't encourage him to, the kids went to bed, and she turned in, eager to visit social media land, a place where things happened but you weren't involved. As she undressed, she realised she was lacking her panties, how had she forgotten them, she forgot nothing. After a moment of panic, she found them in her bag, and it all came back to her. She didn't feel proud of herself. Sleep came surprisingly easily, but then she woke up with a thought. Her spy camera, she didn't remember picking it up from where she'd left it in the car. She padded downstairs, trying not to make a noise and wake people. On the sideboard the charger lead and spy cam lay where presumably either she or Phil had left it. She took it and crept upstairs, slipping into her office and leaving the spy cam next to her computer. 'Tomorrow', she thought, 'that stupid thing is going in French Basin.'

Juliette felt a fraud, sitting in the waiting room, mentally preparing to tell Geoffrey Watson that she really didn't need his help anymore. Sure, the first visit had gone well, very well, but since then she'd had time to rationalize what she saw, or thought she'd seen, and it didn't add up. It was just her imagination, her mom said she had a very fertile one, yes, fertile, that was what she always called it before sending her to her room to 'cool off'.

Clearly, this Geoffrey Watson didn't have much of a turnover. The waiting room was as shabby as his office, two tatty chairs, a stained table with a selection of magazines, some of which seemed just wrong for a shrink's place. She browsed 'Guns and Ammo'; it was as bad as she'd expected. 'Body Builder Monthly' was just stupid and the true crime thing was unbelievable, then she found that she'd become engrossed in one particular story. It was about a serial killer who'd picked off his relatives one at a time, not close relatives, but distant ones. All members of his family who were in wills and supposedly blocking him from getting what was rightfully his. She slipped the dog-eared mag into her bag for later, just as Geoffrey opened the door to call her in.

She sat in the chair and waited while Geoffrey reviewed something on his computer. After a couple of minutes, the silence was killing her, and she was about to speak when he snapped shut the lid on his laptop and looked at her as if surprised to see her there.

"Sorry to keep you, I just had a little loose end to tie up. How are you, Juliette?"

"I'm good, great, spectacular in fact. After last time, I went away and thought about things and I don't think I need to be here, not at all. I now know I was just imagining everything. I have a very fertile imagination, everyone says so".

Geoffrey Watson looked at her with smiling eyes, he must have heard this a thousand times, she thought. "I tell you what, Juliette, let's talk some more today and see where we are then. Nothing would please me more than to have you walking out of here with a spring in your step and a clear head, we both want that, Phil wants that too, you know he's worried about you. What do you say?"

Juliette had expected this and had already decided that she would agree, if only to convince Geoff, Geoffrey that she'd got it all sorted. She was about to say yes when an almighty rumble emanated from Watson, and he apologized. "Slightly upset stomach, sorry. Look, I need the bathroom, do you mind? I won't be five minutes".

Juliette felt as if she was on the back foot. How could she say no, so she just said 'of course', and added 'is this included in the bill' as a joke. Geoffrey Watson smiled and promised her an extra few minutes tacked on at the end to catch up. She heard Watson walking away, it sounded like a short corridor, then there was the thump, thump of someone climbing stairs. She hadn't realized that there was an upstairs to the office, she'd assumed it was something else up there and not connected, curious, maybe he had a small apartment up there, somewhere to take his lover. Juliette found that she had been counting ever since the last footfall had stopped. She eased around the desk and opened the laptop. If there was a password, well ok, if not then just a peek at her file would be illuminating.

Despite his protestations about being disorganized, Watson's filing system on the laptop was excellent, although his security was awful. Within a few seconds she was browsing her file, it appeared to be the only one active. The rest came up as archived, and that part of the computer was password protected. It didn't matter, only one file was of interest to her. Her file had a number of folders, each dated. Three were for before her actual first visit, that was interesting in itself. The one for today had two parts, one with a few target notes, indicating the direction he'd intended to take the conversation, the other one had a video clip. Juliette wracked her brains thinking what the video might be. At any second, Geoff's loud feet would announce the return of the inquisitor and with that her chance. She clicked the video file, which took a moment to buffer. She hovered the cursor over the little exit X, ready to shut it all down in a moment, the video launched. She watched it in silence and forgot all about counting.

The camera must have been on the shelf opposite or similar, the clip showed Juliette flicking through the magazines in the waiting room. She hadn't realized at the time, but her skirt had ridden up a little and the angle just showed her panties. Was he a pervert this guy? She was about to click off, but then the image of herself had picked up the true crime mag, flicked through briefly and had then slipped it into her bag, oh no.

A muffled thud shook her into the present and by the time Geoffrey was back in his seat, she was too, legs pinched tightly together.

"Sorry about that, last-night's curry I think, it always disagrees with me. Right, we'll press on then, did you find anything of interest on my laptop?"

What manner of professional psychiatrist was this. Was he just fishing, or did he really know, did he have cameras everywhere? Juliette didn't panic, her head was sharp, she decided to brass-it out. "I had a quick look, natural curiosity I'm afraid. I see you caught me stealing your magazine and I also note that I flashed my panties at your secret camera, inadvertently I might add, sorry about that".

"Really, I haven't reviewed it yet, I didn't have the opportunity. I'll look out for the booty moment especially, unless you want me to delete it now without seeing it, I'm happy to".

Juliette felt the blankness coming on her. It was like a view where a thin, different coloured film coats the image, moving slowly across the screen until the image that was once in full colour is now sepia. She had no idea why it happened.

"Juliette", the voice was sharp, loud and jolted her back to colour. "Sit down". She had no choice but to comply, Geoffrey Watson had full control of her. She was his to do whatever he wished to her. She wondered whether to undress while she awaited instructions. In a quieter voice Watson asked her to sit again, and started talking to her as if everything was normal, for him it was. "Why did you keep the real crime mag and none of the others?"

"The others weren't real". The answer had flown from her mouth without getting any authority from her brain to do so.

"You haven't asked why you were filmed".

"I assume to see whether I was in love with guns, muscle or murder?"

"Quaintly put, but yes, you're quite right. Look, I'm sorry about the embarrassment, it isn't meant to be voyeuristic. I will delete the clip once we've thought more about your reading choices. Real you say, who for?"

"The victims, the perpetrator, the people who deal with the fall-out, the police and the shrinks that have to fix people".

Watson was scribbling in his cheap jotter again. "How did I do?" she asked.

"The children you saw, what do you think happened to them?"

She'd forgotten entirely why she was there. The children, was she their mommy? Yes, that was it, were they real then? "I think they died, I don't know how or why, but I think they're trapped in the house looking for comfort, for a mother".

More scribbling. "Can you be their mother?"

"What? No, of course not. They're not real, not in a life sense. How can I be a mother to ghosts?"

A barely audible noise came from the cell phone on the desk. Watson picked it up, stopped the sound and looked up. "We're good for a few minutes, yet. The kids on the stairs, they are ghosts then, do you believe in ghosts?"

"I don't know. Something must happen though, when you die. Too many people report seeing them, they can't all be as nuts as me", and she laughed to make sure that this Geoffrey Watson understood that it was a joke, about her being nuts.

"Are you still set on this being the last session? I think we've made some progress today, we're getting close to understanding what happened and, more importantly, why".

Juliette realized that the hour had flown by. Where had it gone, it was only moments earlier when she'd been invited in. "One more, perhaps. I'll think about it".

"Good, I'll leave that with you then. You make the appointment when you're ready, you have to really want to come to me though, and this time we'll see if we can keep you awake".

Juliette was confused and Watson could see that she had no idea what he was talking about.

"You slept, for about forty minutes. You spoke, quite a bit actually, but you were asleep. I know deep sleep when I see it".

No, this wasn't right, Juliette never just slept, napped, dropped off, never. What was this fucker up to?

"Honestly, I can show you the session video, you do remember me asking your permission the first time, to record the session so that I can review it later? Nothing sinister and you didn't accidentally reveal any more underwear".

Juliette became very composed. "Of course, yes, that's fine. No need for me to see me sleeping, gee, what do you think of me? I'm sorry, I've had trouble getting a full night since the event".

Once she got back in the car, Juliette reached for a handful of gummies, to calm her down, they always worked. Then a thought struck her, she'd slept what, forty minutes in front of Watson in that comfy chair, had he really not tried to look up her skirt while she was unconscious? No, he wouldn't, surely not, he was a professional, he'd even offered to delete her earlier flashing in the video, he was very clear about it. No, he wouldn't peek, he didn't, he wouldn't. But what if he did? She called Melissa.

The children continued to unnerve Phil and he felt guilty about it. He also feared for Juliette following her experiences, episodes which he couldn't explain and wanted, with the best will in the world, to believe when she'd finally told him the story. Then there was Melissa. Juliette said she'd gone to stop at her mother's, had been released from hospital into her mother's care. This bugged him a lot. If she was that sick, how could Juliette's equally dotty mother possibly look after her? It also bothered him more that he'd never been allowed to meet or speak to either Juliette's mother or sister. He was having genuine doubts that they were even real, and he wondered whether he should call Geoff Watson and say so.

When Juliette appeared, fresh from her second session with Watson, she looked perfectly normal. She didn't seem to want to engage about it, so Phil said he had to go out for milk and a newspaper. Juliette shrugged and said she'd got work to do. She had planned to talk things through later, but clearly Phil wasn't all that interested. Once parked far enough from the house that he wasn't going to be seen, Phil called Watson and explained the complicated domestic arrangements involving Juliette's mom and sister and asked what to do.

"Just play along with it, she'll be more open after a few more sessions, if she comes", and Watson told Phil how he'd left it to her to decide. He didn't want any pressure applying. "Remember, we agreed?" To keep up the ruse, Phil had to go to a gas station for the milk, the best newspaper he could get was always full of one-sided BS and he generally tried to avoid it.

The lightest tap at her office door told her that Phil was back and now loitering. If she didn't call him in, he'd open the door a little and call in to her anyway. "Nearly done, come in if you want, I have no secrets, not from you". She was trying to be jolly, jaunty, trying to claw back some personal credibility. She'd seen Phil's looks, she knew how his mind worked, where it was poking. The door opened and Phil walked in cautiously, as if Juliette might have an inappropriate web site open or something. "I thought we might take the kids around the gardens, it's a nice day and they seem to enjoy the stimulation, or perhaps that's just me", he said.

"Sure, it will be nice, I could do with a break and some fresh air, the work is getting stodgy. I might look around for something else, I've been thinking of it for a while, maybe not home-based, what do you think?"

Phil didn't think anything, Juliette had never really explained what she actually did, only outlined her role and in the broadest terms. He knew that it was some sort of political communication thing, working with consultancies. That was what took her out on field trips, sometimes even nights away but not recently, not for a long while.

"I envy you the choice, I'd love a change. I don't enjoy working away and I hate leaving you and Sonny".

"And the kids, I hope you're at least getting a bit fond of them?"

"Yes, and the kids, but that is temporary. I don't want to invest too much emotion in the situation, I'd only end up getting attached and they'll be going home to mom very soon, won't they?"

It was a loaded question and one that Phil hadn't meant to ask, because Juliette always got defensive and rambled on about her duty to her family, her sister, the children. He waited for the fall-out, but it never came, instead she just smiled and followed him downstairs. They were both surprised to see the kids on the sofa in their coats, ready. It wasn't the first time something like this had happened and it spooked Phil to his bones but, oddly, Juliette just took it in her stride.

The gardens were nice, they always were unless it was raining heavily. The hundred or so bucks for family membership had been totally worth it, they seemed to change every week as new blooms emerged. Phil found it relaxing as a place to walk, especially early before too many tourists arrived. Juliette seemed to like it too, although she'd always choose the French Basin walk if she was alone, it seemed to have a hold over her, nearly as much as Keji. But a trip there was more a hike for them, and it was always buggy.

"How is Melissa doing?"

Juliette was immediately on the defensive. "Why?"

"Just asking, she's family, well sort of, and I'm concerned, it's normal".

"She's ok, doing well. Mom says she'll be doing some therapy soon, stuff to help her cope, to be able to get out more, live".

Phil was surprised, that was more than Juliette had said about her sister's situation for some time, if ever.

"Glad to hear it, do you think these two miss her?" It was an innocent enough question, but barely had the last word slipped out of Phil's mouth that he realized how it sounded.

"Fuck off, Phil. You just want to dump the kids and run, I know it, don't think I don't know it". In her temple a vein started to throb. The kids, who had been walking a short way in front stopped, turned and stared at her. "See, they know it too, you've upset them now with your negativity. Come on kids, let's go home. Phil doesn't mean it, not really, do you Phil? Backed into a corner of his own creation, Phil admitted his error, confident that no matter what he said, Juliette was too hysterical to listen and the kids too stupid to understand. Satisfied that a wrong had been partially righted, Juliette walked the kids back to the car, Phil bringing up the rear and having to walk briskly to keep up. That was another thing, why did Juliette always insist on driving here, it was only a five-minute walk from home?

"Sorry, I didn't mean anything, you know that; I was just asking. I mean, it's not like we've met but I still feel your concern". Juliette ignored the prompt, Phil knew the situation, there was zero chance of him meeting either her mom or Melissa, neither deserved his ignorance. As they got the kids packed in, it always took longer than the walk would, Phil casually mentioned that he was working in Cape Breton soon and that he'd offered Abigail a lift to college in Antigonish, was that ok?

"Sure, of course, why wouldn't it be? Yes, makes sense, she'll save on fares and time, no, good idea, yes".

The response wasn't quite what Phil had expected, better in many ways, but he was still treading cautiously. "She's meeting her mysterious boyfriend there", he said, conversationally. "She mentioned it last week when I ran her home, quite a chatterbox that night, I couldn't shut her up".

"Probably just very excited about a new life without any restrictions. I know I was when I went to college". A cloud entered the conversation. Juliette's college experiences had always been a touchy subject and Phil had accurately read the warnings to back off. What had she done, taken on the whole football team or something?

"Next Monday, she goes next Monday. It ties in nicely with work, I couldn't not offer".

"No, right, good, no problem. She helps us, we help her, symbiotic, good citizens. Will you stop over in Antigonish or drive on to Cape Breton after?" For Juliette it was a perfectly reasonable question. Despite what she'd said, she wasn't very pleased that Phil had offered to drive Abigail to college. She saw the logic as he was, as he said, working 'out that way', whatever that meant. Cape Breton was miles past Antigonish.

"Not sure, traffic, you know. There's a B&B I can use on the way, if I have to, all approved by the company, but I'd rather be back here with you. I'll be away a couple of days anyway. To be honest, I wish I'd never agreed, I think she might try to convert me from the dark side on the way, I don't think she approves of us living in sin".

Juliette relaxed, Phil joking about the holier-than-thou Abigail was what he used to do all the time. She was probably just making whole mountain ranges out of tiny molehills again. She decided to put aside any fears she had, silly fears, and to work hard to get things on an even keel again, including booking her next session with the deductive Doctor Watson. The mental joke made her chuckle.

Monday soon came around and Juliette had been good the whole time. When Phil was busy with the car and his work stuff, she decided to be a good girl and lend a hand, getting all his toiletries together, she knew he needed them. Phil was quite fussy about smelling right and having clean clothes available. Sometimes he came home sporting new underwear, the old ones discarded as being too shabby. He also had a pack of medication for a skin rash that he never spoke about. When packing, he usually did everything himself, preferring to leave Juliette to get on with her work, she thought he was probably not willing to ask for help in case she snapped at him. His wash bag was in the wardrobe in his bedroom, on the top shelf and she struggled to reach it. Instead of nipping downstairs for the small, foldaway step, she used an old wooden coat hanger to reach it, easing the bag in her direction. Before she could grab it, it fell and it span, depositing the existing contents on the floor. Mouthwash, shampoo, hand cream, all in travel sized containers, and a new packet of condoms, unopened, pristine.

For a moment, she didn't know what to do, then, thinking on her feet, she dashed to the office, grabbed a chair and used it to put the washbag back where Phil had kept it. She'd only just got back into her office with the chair when she heard footfalls on the stairs.

"Nearly done, I'm just going to have a quick shower, got to stay nice and clean. You ok, you look a bit off".

Juliette tried to recompose herself. "Tummy bug I think, it's nothing". Satisfied that she was alright, Phil went off to the bathroom leaving her alone with her thoughts. She needed to talk to someone.

Her mother wasn't answering, as usual, so she tried Melissa on her cell.

"I need your advice, are you up to talking to me?"

"Go ahead", said Melissa, sounding well.

Juliette explained about everything, including her now confirmed suspicion about Phil and innocent little Abigail. "What do I do?"

After a short silence, Melissa spoke. "It's happened before, sis, you know he's got to go. Just dump him, face him down when he gets back, deal with him".

Juliette was shocked. "You think I should just let him go off and bang that tramp then?"

"Too late now from what you tell me, it'll give him more to feel guilty for, and he is guilty. You know that now, you've seen the proof. Let me know if you need me to help out".

Juliette agreed, but detected that Melissa was fading a bit, so she hung up and went back to her computer.

'Damn', she thought, 'I should have used my phone for a photo of the packet, evidence of what I saw, something to show him when I confront him'.

Through the wall the sound of running water told her that Phil was busy, so she dialed the number and waited.

"Abigail, Juliette, no, no problems, Phil's just getting himself ready. Look, I was thinking, with you off to college and you've been really great for us, so I wanted to give you a gift, if you don't mind".

Abigail was surprised. She'd got the impression that Juliette wasn't keen on her, not everybody was. "Ok, thanks, can Phil bring it when he comes over, or do you want me to call in as we go"?

"Call in if you don't mind, that would be nice, more personal. I expect you're very busy getting ready, big step, lots to think about in a new life".

Abigail assured Juliette that it was no trouble coming over and that it would be nice to say goodbye in person, she sounded very genuine, very warm. She said she'd be there in twenty minutes, she'd get a ride over, her mom had to go out anyway, so it was no trouble. The sound of running water had stopped, Phil would be out soon and into the bedroom to get ready. Juliette decided to use a psychological approach, confront Phil before he dressed, he'd feel vulnerable. The tell-tale creak on the floor outside her office told her of his progress to the bedroom.

She rushed across the landing and into the steamy bathroom, he never, ever put the fan on, no matter how many times she told him, but no matter now. For a moment she forgot why she was there, then she remembered. In the bedroom, Phil was humming something or other as he dried himself. She knew that he'd just drop the wet towel on the bed again, she'd told him times without number about that too, but still he did it. Opening the door quietly, she stood behind Phil who was so wrapped up in the job in hand he never noticed her. "I know", she said.

Phil turned sharply around, he had a look on his face as if he didn't recognize her, what was this?

"I…".

"Sorry, it took longer than expected". It was Abigail, all fresh faced and pert.

"No worries, Phil's just tied up at the moment, it won't be long now".

Abigail smiled, she always did that when she didn't quite get what had been said, as if the nuances were not strong enough.

"Come in, sit please, coffee?"

"No thank you, Juliette. We have a long way to go, and I hate using public washrooms, you can catch all sorts of germs".

"Me too, you're right, you never know what you might catch. Crabs jump", and Juliette laughed. "Big day, exciting times, have you said your goodbyes?"

"Oh, yes. Mom is weepy, but I said to get used to it and sent her on her way. I'm a big girl now and I won't come running back every five minutes or be on the phone every day. I'm going to stand on my own two feet and live a little".

Juliette felt lost for a moment, this Abigail might have been her right before she went to college, before she said she was going her own way to her mom, before…

This time, Juliette took her own reading material with her for what would be her third and definitely last appointment with Geoffrey Watson. It was a version of Alice in Wonderland, a sort of fan-fiction thing she'd seen at a Comic-Con in Dartmouth once and bought. She'd deliberately chosen it to see what Watson might make of it, if he noticed. The door to the treatment room, as she kept thinking of it, opened and a young man came out. He had multiple piercings and heavy tattoos running all the way up his neck, it was hard not to look. The door closed again.

Juliette glanced at her watch, which was a waste of time because it hadn't worked for years. It had been very expensive though, so she tended to wear it more as jewelry, almost making a statement. She knew that she was early, but surely it was her time to be seen now. She wanted it to be because she felt so liberated, but still she waited, this was so unprofessional. Another five minutes and I'm walking, she thought. Then the door opened. "Juliette, I thought it was you, come in, you're a little early but that's ok. How's everything?"

"Fine", she said, as she slipped her book into her leather bag, making sure that the cover and title was clearly visible. She processed what he'd said. Early, she wasn't early at all, the car clock said so. Behind Watson's chair was a mantlepiece with an old clock on it, the sort of clock you see in a shop that claims to sell antiques, but that actually contains things nobody in their right mind would buy, she had a similar one at home.

"I called Phil yesterday, no answer and it didn't let me leave a message, is he ok?" Watson wasn't looking at her as he spoke, as if not wanting to make any eye-contact. It was disconcerting.

"He's away again, his phone broke. He said he'd pick one up on the road, a place in Kentville I think he said. He never mentioned it when we spoke last night on his hotel phone, so I assume he did. Try a text, up in Cape Breton he sometimes loses signal, a text will get there, eventually".

Watson didn't reply immediately, which Juliette felt was a little odd. If he was that concerned, he'd at least thank her for her explanation. "I think we're doing well, Juliette. Today I want to examine any reasons you might have for your anxiety. Phil mentioned a sister, Melissa, you did too, are you close?"

Juliette tried hard not to panic. Melissa was fragile and not to be upset, and she didn't like the idea of Phil talking about Melissa out of turn. "Melissa had a bit of a bad spell in her life, she let things get on top of her but she's ok now, we speak regularly, we always have. Yes, I'd say we were close, very close".

"Tell me about her".

"She's everything I'm not. Very confident, not in the least bashful. She has a beautiful body, you can see I'm a bit gangly, not Melissa. When we were kids, we used to entertain each other, Melissa would tell me stories, things she'd read. Her memory was so good that she could recite to me the whole book, remembering every detail. I was always a bit slower than her, she was the sharpest kid around, so sharp".

"She sounds great. I have a brother, but we're not close, he never calls me and I'm sure he screens his calls because he'll rarely pick up if I phone. I always wanted us to be closer, wanted to be just like him but he's tall and handsome and I'm, well, I am what you see".

This was different, Watson was giving details away, personal things, was that what he expected her to do, follow suit, tell her secrets to him, all of them?

"Give me a specific childhood memory involving you and Melissa".

It was an expected question, but Juliette felt her head fogging again, 'not now', she willed. "We used to do little plays, just short performances. I always played me, but Melissa was lots of different people. We had a large wicker basket full of charity shop clothes and we'd dress up, not me but Melissa, I was always me. It was great fun, we laughed a lot until mom took the basket away one time, I don't know why".

"You never asked why?"

"Yes, of course, she said it had got stained. It made no sense, but my mom wasn't someone to discuss things with".

"Do you like your mom?"

Juliette felt giddy again. No, she fucking didn't, but if she said that now, Watson would twist it like a knife, it would be a blade in the guts worked for maximum pain. "How is my mom relevant? She wasn't even my real mom".

"Just building a picture, Juliette, you see I think your experience on the stairs comes from back in your childhood. There'd be an event which sometimes sends signals to your brain, confusing you. Have you ever experienced a fuzziness, like a hangover but without the other things, just a head fog?"

The guy was good. Had he got the head fog idea from Phil, it was what he called them. Had he blabbed during one of their little beer sessions when they both laughed at her for being nuts? "No", she lied.

"Has there been any repetition of the kids on the stairs or anything you can't explain?"

"No", Juliette repeated, this time with more force.

"I sense you're being defensive with me, and that after we've made great steps to sorting this thing out. I spoke to a colleague, she was very interested in your case, your symptoms. She has ideas, would you be open to her attending a session?"

"No".

"No". Juliette looked around; she was in her own kitchen. She stood for a few seconds then her legs went, leaving her spreadeagled on the floor. A robin sang outside, she liked the sound of robins.

June 2019

Now that it was done there was a lot to sort out. Juliette wrote a list. Lists helped her to focus, lists could be checked off when each component had been completed then, when everything was finished, the list could be signed off and destroyed. The list she had so far wasn't complicated for now, but it would be, later.

Two trips in two days would normally have been considered a treat for the kids, even if it was to the same general area and even if they had to stay in the car. As far as lists went, that bit was the easiest.

Selecting which items would go was easy, because Phil had already done most of it. Juliette realized that, over a period of time, his personal things were no longer around. At first, she didn't read anything into it, they very much lived portions of their lives separately, it had been a condition. It was only after taking the opportunity to ferret around when Phil was working away that Juliette realized that he was moving out, one suitcase at a time. That was the red flag really.

The note was a bonus.

To pre-empt the inevitable questions, as soon as she found the note she took the kids around to Abigail's house and showed it to her parents. They were stiff as a board. They confessed to turning a blind eye to their daughter's shortcomings, her drug use, which Juliette tried not to show surprise about, and to her wicked life. They apologized to Juliette for the situation, Abigail was, they said, dead to them.

Next Juliette played the distraught partner to Phil's dad. He swallowed the lot, offered to 'be there' if she needed him and condemned his son as always being what he called a skirt-chaser. It was as easy as that. The only sticking point had been Phil's employer, who was more concerned about his client suffering than the loss of Phil as an employee. Juliette scanned the note and sent a copy over, as proof that Phil had fled.

As notes went it was simple, which meant it could be taken several ways. The slant Juliette used was that Phil had found someone younger, better than her, an upgrade, and it worked well.

"You seem a bit down Juliette, everything alright?"

Juliette had been getting her regular cut done and Carole, her hairdresser, was always chatty. Some would say nosey, but it went with the job and Juliette used Carole as a confidante. For Carole, Juliette was just another customer to gossip about.

Juliette reached into her bag and handed Carole the note. There was a brief period of silence then Carole confirmed that she'd always thought Phil was no good and that Abigail was too good to be true. The note had confirmed both. Carole then repeated an Abigail story that made Juliette blush.

The next day Juliette was out with the kids shopping and the jungle drums had been beating all night. She got sympathetic looks in the store aisle. On the street, an older lady she'd never met touched her arm and told her things would get better. "You'll see". Inside a week everybody knew who had dumped who and why and the suggestion was that Annapolis Royal was a better place without that pair.

And it was.

In her jewelry box, the one Phil had made for her with twenty compartments for what little jewelry she had, she carefully placed his silver Saint Christopher in the secret compartment Phil was so proud of. She put a fine gold crucifix next to it. It vaguely crossed her mind to wonder what the monetary value of her possessions might be now, if she ever needed to fall back on them in harder times. There must be people in the city who would buy that sort of stuff. Happy that the items in the box were in the right order, she put it back on the middle shelf of the kitchen dresser. It was a risk, if they had burglars, it would be easy to find, but it was wrong to hide it as if some sort of stigma was attached to it. The only important thing was to keep it out of reach of the kids until she could hide them properly in her special place.

Juliette didn't have any awareness of how long she'd been stood in the kitchen looking at her jewelry box, and it was only a noise by the front door that made her look up. Waiting at the door, the kids were dressed to go out. Behind the glass she could see a short, dumpy figure and then heard the knock. Despite the image being distorted, what she recognised was the professional old lady, Mrs. Rose. Her distinctive red beret gave the game away.

Juliette grabbed her leather bag and opened the door.

"Hello Mrs. Rose, sorry, I was just checking out back. We were just off out".

"I heard, Juliette, I heard about your partner, Phil, running off with that girl and I'm shocked. If there's anything you need, you know where I am, anything".

"Life goes on Mrs. Rose, we'll be ok, but if you know a good child minder, I'd be grateful. Just for the odd few hours".

For all Mrs. Rose's best wishes, they didn't extend to spending any time looking after the two kids who she'd been told were 'troubled', but who she'd never actually seen.

"I'll put the word out, I'm sure someone will want the pocket money".

"Thanks, in the meantime we press on. I have to arrange the locksmith and all that sort of thing. I don't want that man sneaking back anytime, you understand?" and she started down the path alone, closing the door behind her. Mrs. Rose had been trying to peer around Juliette, but her house was her sanctuary, and no old busy body was going to go telling tales about bad décor or a random dust bunny that she might have missed.

"Well, come and see me if you need to talk, or I'd be happy to pop around".

"Will do, but I'm doing some renovation at the moment. I'd like to host a little party at some point, just a few friends for tea and cake, and I include you in that select group".

Mrs. Rose smiled and walked off back up the road, her red hat bobbing up and down as she went. Juliette watched for a few moments to see whether she looked back, she didn't. Crisis averted. Bundling the kids into the car, she set off without any firm destination in mind. It was some way into the journey before she realized where she was.

Ten-mile Lake Provincial Park was empty, as usual, and Juliette eased into the parking spot still shaking. The kids hadn't moved, but were watching her as they always did, it was very unnerving. She pulled her phone out but, as usual, the reception was poor, one bar. Getting out for a few hours had been the thing, mostly to put Mrs. Rose off, but now that they were out, she wanted ideas of where to go, she couldn't stay there, Melissa would be angry. She started the car and headed off to Liverpool.

As towns go, Liverpool pleased Juliette. It was nice, comfortable and she'd seriously considered moving there to get away from everything. Parking up, she walked the town and looked in the windows of a couple of realtors checking prices. Then they found a chicken place, got a take-away and went to eat overlooking the river. A gaggle of rough-looking Canada Geese went by, they seemed to fascinate the kids who watched, rapt, until they'd gone. It was the first time that Juliette had ever seen anything get their attention that way.

The ride home was via an alternative route, just for a change. It was quite long and boring in places. On one road, the poor condition had her weaving all over avoiding ruts and deep potholes, it was a road she'd never travelled before. She saw one car as she went between Shelburne and some sort of mine, then it got better, quicker, and soon she was in Weymouth and back on the highway home.

As she passed her mailbox, she realized that she'd not checked for mail recently and went back. The brown envelope inside was curious, it was addressed to her, she never normally got any mail, just flyers.

Once back in the house the tv went on, she made up drinks and left the kids to it. Pouring a large glass of wine, she sat at the kitchen table as the house creaked all around her. The brown envelope had been sitting in the middle of the table since she got back, like a letter bomb waiting to go off.

She opened it.

She laid the money out in piles, stacks of five hundred. When she'd finished, she had twenty-four stacks. The note inside said that it was Abigail's college fund, that it was the best they could do to right the wrong and hoped it would ease her pain.

Juliette cried for a while but, after a few glugs of the wine, collapsed into hysterical laughter.

The music could be heard from way down the road, even with the windows up, Juliette gunned the throttle, ever aware that the local police were anal where the speed limit was concerned, but certain that the sounds of John Cougar Mellencamp were emanating from her house, she was right.

Barely checking the road, she ran inside the house, sprinted upstairs to her study and yanked the plug bodily from the wall. The music weirdly ran on for a few seconds before a wall of silence engulfed her. Juliette was startled but realized it was just in her head, her brain filling in the lines of the recently stopped song before reality caught up. Taking a deep breath, she plugged the music system back in and waited for the sound, nothing happened, the light came on, the display lit up, but nothing played. She wasn't sure what had made her spin around suddenly but there, in the door frame, stood the kids. They'd followed her indoors and had just silently insinuated themselves in the scene, it was what they did.

"Right, ok", she said, skipping back downstairs but missing the last three and ending up in a heap at the bottom. Juliette cursed her stupidity, why was she worried? Nobody was going to steal the car, or from it, this was Annapolis Royal, not Philadelphia. Limping outside, she attended to the still running car, retrieved her bags and checked around for anything that had wandered. Her ankle hurt and she could feel the throbbing of a swelling happening, she'd need to hot and cold it for a while, but at least it wasn't broken. As she blipped the car lock and turned with the bags in each hand, she almost fell again, this time over the kids who had appeared silently behind her and were not moving. "Shit, you two, come on", she said, brushing a gap between them and hobbling on inside.

She dumped the bags in the living room, the kids following in, sitting where they always sat. "Ok, drinks, back in a minute". The kitchen felt cool, cold even, which was ridiculous as it was warm out, very warm. Then it struck her that Sonny wasn't around, getting under her feet, over-happy to see her. It was something of a relief, she didn't think her ankle could take an excitable dog. Assuming that he was asleep somewhere, she poured juice into the kids' cups, flipped on the lids and poured herself a generous glass of white. The sun was just about over the yardarm and besides, it was no one's business but her own now.

Juliette's ankle was starting to feel a bit better. It was just a slight sprain, probably, and she could walk on it reasonably well. There was no need to fill a bowl of hot water or break out the bag of frozen peas after all. Limping into the living room, there was no sign of the kids, now what?

Seeing the basement door ajar, a lot of thoughts went through Juliette's head, but she managed to keep them in check and went down the stairs. As she reached the bottom, the kitchen door slowly closed just as she reached the light switch. A quick flick and her strip light was brightly illuminating the laundry, she really should get an electrician in to fix the switch at the top of the stairs, she thought.

Nothing appeared to be amiss, the other doors were shut, their chute bolts firmly in place and out of reach for smaller people. Turning, she was half-way up the stairs before she realized that the light was flickering. The hairs on her neck began to rise, like a cat's fur when it's faced with a sudden threat. She quickened the pace and reached the kitchen door. It stuck, initially but she barged through, panic starting to get a hold. There, in the middle of the kitchen floor, lay the inert form of Sonny. The kids were stood over him, looking at the recumbent pet, but showing no signs of emotion.

Juliette rubbed her forehead, none of this made sense. The dog wasn't there when she did the drinks and the basement door had been bolted too, it always was. Nor was it there when she'd descended into the basement, she was quite sure. So how was it that her dog, whom she wasn't really that fond of if she was entirely honest, was now laying on the kitchen floor motionless?

Tentatively she moved forward and nudged the dog with her toe, pain shot up her leg as her ankle complained about the unnecessary activity. Sonny was no longer an issue, he was dead.

September 2019

Juliette was focusing on a spot on the wall. She reckoned she'd have to do something about that spot, it was unsightly, and it wasn't who she was.

When Phil came back, she'd discuss it with him, maybe they could redecorate again, he'd want to keep her happy, so he'd likely agree.

The spot had a shape, it reminded her of a parrot sitting on a perch. Juliette liked parrots, their colour and energy, the way they could talk, it intrigued her. She'd even thought about buying one, an African Grey, they were the best talkers they said, when she'd researched it on the web. Then she thought about grey for a while, the colour, and decided that her parrot, who she would call 'John', would have to have colour. She'd trade off less ability to speak for bright colours, just to brighten up her life.

For an hour, the spot on the wall had been bothering her, it had changed shape and didn't look like a parrot now, more like a monkey, but not a cute one. This monkey had fangs and, if it could, it would bite you, snarling, breaking the skin, you'd bleed. Juliette didn't like that type of monkey and her mother had been wrong in making her hold the thing just for a stupid photo in the first place. She thought it would be less fragile, but it broke very easily, and her mother never shut up about the compensation she'd had to pay the owner. That was why Juliette never had pocket money, it was her own fault.

The parrot was back now, it was probably just the light.

"Right", she said, announcing to nobody. "Time to get on".

Today she was going to dress in white. She liked white, it was clean, fresh, pure. It signified a new start. Rummaging through the drawers and wardrobe, she selected the perfect outfit. It was one she'd not worn for a while, one that Melissa had given her, because she'd decided white was not for her. Juliette understood why now.

The store was busy with lots of single people by the look of their carts, all meals for one, limited amounts, not much dietary balance. Juliette believed that what you ate shaped you, defined you, she always wanted to buy antibiotic free, organic, locally produced. That meant nothing from the

USA, if she could help it, all dreadful people in her opinion and she wasn't supporting them. She realised that she'd made an unfair generalization about people from the US and would have to think about her position there again, when she had a free moment.

"Juliette, I've not seen you around for a few days". It was Mrs. Rose, looking as neat as usual, almost like a character from a novel. She'd be a librarian maybe, someone who dressed to look the part. Yes, the persona of a librarian, an older one, fitted Mrs. Rose very well.

Juliette was confused. She'd passed Mrs. Rose out on the street only the day before, when she was doing her power walking, keeping fit and available. She hadn't stopped, but she'd said hello as she whisked past. Juliette liked to keep up a brisk pace, it was the only way to make the power walking work, to keep her trim, healthy. She decided to ignore the obvious error. Mrs. Rose was older, probably getting forgetful, senile even. It happened; people got befuddled. That was a good word, she was glad she thought of it, befuddled, it perfectly described Mrs. Rose.

"Juliette?"

"Sorry, Mrs. Rose, miles away. How are you?"

Mrs. Rose didn't show it, but Juliette knew what she was thinking, was Juliette mad?

"Very well, very well, my cousin has been visiting. She's been living in Delaware recently, she quite likes it, but I think she'd love to come home at some point, if she can persuade her partner to give up her fancy lifestyle.

'What did Delaware, what did Delaware' Juliette had the old Perry Como song in her head, and it wouldn't go away. Now she'd spend all day trying to remember the rest of it, she wasn't even sure that she'd remembered the first bit right, she rarely did.

"Juliette?"

"Another two days and Phil will be back, he's away on business, I barely see him these days".

Mrs. Rose had a look on her face, as if Juliette had answered a question that she'd not been asked, but she was sure she'd been asked how Phil was. That was how conversations went with a friend, well not a friend perhaps, an acquaintance, someone you know casually.

"If you ever need to talk Juliette, you're always welcome to drop by. I'm there for you and if you ever need to go clothes shopping, I'd be happy to go along, I think you should treat yourself, that brown dress you always wear must be getting tired, or do you have more than one?"

Juliette knew then that Mrs. Rose was losing it. It was very sad the way older people slipped away mentally; it wasn't going to happen to her. She had a pact with Phil. She smiled at Mrs. Rose, a sympathetic smile, understanding even. It wasn't her fault, the poor old dear.

"That would be lovely, yes, we must, you're probably right. Sorry, I must get on, we've got guests coming tomorrow, old friends from university. Not seen them for years, so I'm sprucing up the old place, windows open letting fresh air and pure light in. I'm looking for a picture to cover a stain on the wall. I fancy a Lewis copy, or a relaxing wharf scene with boats laying idle in the setting sun".

Mrs. Rose smiled her confused smile again, poor old dear.

At the till, the checkout girl glanced at Juliette as if she'd never seen her before, but she'd been shopping here like, forever; surely, she must remember her? Seventeen beeps, that was right, she had seventeen items. She'd been very careful about that, seventeen was her lucky number, seventeen was when she left home, and her life got better for a while.

"What?" said Juliette to the girl on the till.

"Forty-two dollars and ten cents, please", she repeated, her voice giving away her impatience. It was very rude, and Juliette had a good mind to ask for the manager, but she let it go and paid, even then it took three goes for the girl to get it right, they have no education these days, they can't even do simple math without using electronics. Juliette decided to let that go too, perhaps she was stressed and not ready for having a jar of nickels and dimes to pick through, but why waste good notes when the change built up? It was legal tender, suck it up, dumbass.

Of course, she didn't say 'dumbass', she just waited while the till girl counted out the coins. She was slow but that was to be expected, in Juliette's experience so many people were.

"Two dollars short".

It was very blunt, even for a shop girl, and Juliette was about to insist on a recount. She knew exactly how much there was in that jar, and it came exactly to her bill. She'd been very careful with her choice of purchases to make sure, had she missed the tax on something?

"I've got this", said Mrs. Rose who'd appeared behind Juliette.

The shop girl seemed relieved, happy to get Juliette out of there. When she got outside, she turned around to thank Mrs. Rose but she was alone, never mind. She'd be sure to thank her later, perhaps even bake one of her cakes. She was a wonderful baker, everybody said so, Phil loved her cakes.

The parrot stain was a monkey again. It was staring at her, it had been for a while and there was a smell seeping through the house, her house. One of those supposedly fresh items must be off, she thought, she'd check the dates on everything until she found it, then she'd take it back and complain.

On the kitchen table, the shopping bag sagged. At the bottom of the bag a small piece of pork was obviously the culprit, it was going green. How could they sell meat that was so far gone? She fished it out and decided to chuck it out back for the raccoon, he wouldn't mind a bit of smelly meat. She put the rest of the shopping away, but it was only when she opened the fridge that she realized how dark it had become, it was night, what had happened to the day?

The waft from the fridge told her that something else had peaked and gone over, so she cleared the fridge of everything and cleaned it thoroughly, she always had cleaning fluid available, it had a soothing smell and reminded her of happier days, of calm and peace. Everything was bagged up and replaced with her new supplies, she felt hungry, so she ate a block of cheese. She loaded the trash bags into her car and took them to the dump, it was quiet there, it always was. That was the last of the bags, the smell should go now.

The parrot was back, she really was going to have to look seriously into where she could get a parrot, she needed some brightness in her life. When Phil got back, she'd ask him, he'd know.

Early October 2019

Juliette didn't hear the door open, nor the change in the room as multiple police officers entered, all yelling at once. She didn't know what they were saying, it didn't sound like English, but she knew that the Hispanic fruit pickers went home after the picking season and didn't spend the rest of the year in law enforcement, so it must have been.

Strong hands forced Juliette forwards, her chin hitting the dusty floor as her hands were roughly shoved up her back, the police weren't taking any chances.

"Look at this place, how can anybody live like this?" said a male voice, one of the cops. Because she was pinned down, her breathing was on the edge of coughing, and she thought she might have picked up a bug. She didn't know who'd made the comment, but assumed they were discussing another case, her house was always spotless.

As they lifted her, painfully, and led her from the house into the bright lights outside, a number of white things passed her, people in all white suits, head-to-toe in white, strange. It was almost fancy dress; Melissa would have loved it.

The car was ok, a nice model, she liked how spacious it looked. They pushed her inside, making sure she didn't bang her head, but she had anyway. Inside it smelt of pee, vomit and cleaning fluid, not dissimilar to the brand she often used. It wasn't built for comfort in the back of the cruiser, but she didn't expect to be there very long, just until they realized they'd made a mistake, apologized, and let her get home to Phil and the kids. They'd all be hungry later and expecting a meal.

As they pulled into the station, she saw someone she knew, a reporter that she'd spoken to at the French Basin Trail once. She waved at him, but he looked back sternly while a man next to him tried to take photographs, she wasn't sure of what, but it couldn't be her, besides, they covered her head before she got out the car which was thoughtful as it was drizzling slightly.

There was a lot of messing about inside the police station, and she patiently waited for them to finish, so she could listen to their explanation for the error, they'd all laugh about it then, but it was getting so silly now that she was considering talking to a professional. When they mentioned having a lawyer, she said no, because the whole joke had been going on too long now and they were sure to see that, without her having an expensive legal team to point it out. Then they locked her up, in a small but well-lit room, again not very comfortable, no magazines to read, nothing.

She was only there for less than two minutes when two women came in and stripped her naked, bagged her clothes and made her put on one of those new paper things, disposable. It made sense because nobody would want to wear someone else's paper suit after it had been used. It was good to see that the police, or whoever managed them, was thinking about these things and taking people's feelings into consideration for a change.

Sitting in a well-lit room, it occurred to Juliette that this might not be a mistake, that perhaps she had done something bad at some point, but how could they know about that? She'd been so careful, and it was self-defence, in a way. She never should have kept him, she should have put him in an institution, he was dangerous, he'd raped both her and Melissa, or had that been their real mum he raped? Stories about her mother went through her head, cruel stories, she always put her fingers in her ears when her adoptive mother started telling Juliette her stories.

A cold shiver went through her as something brushed her leg.

"We need our mommy", said the shorter of the two kids looking up at her.

Juliette couldn't figure out how they'd managed to get in. She didn't remember the door opening, but the police must have realized that, with Phil away for most of the day, she was the only person around to take care of them. Juliette wasn't scared of them these days, not like that first time on the stairs. Perhaps that was when it had all become difficult, but it could all be explained if she got to talk to a reasonable person, there must be one wherever she was.

This seat in the little room wasn't built for comfort either, it was just a seat. Mass-produced, meant for transient bottoms, not prolonged sittings. Juliette shuffled a bit, she was getting pins and needles, her bum was going to sleep, perhaps she should mention it.

"Juliette, are you listening? We need to know, Juliette".

She snapped back into the now, it happened from time to time and, even if now wasn't a good time to do it, she had no control over it. It just happened without warning.

"Can somebody tell me why I'm here? I've been very patient with everyone, many people wouldn't be, but this has gone too far now".

The two police officers looked at each other instead of answering her, then she realized she must look quite a mess. Her good clothes had gone, and her hair must look like a rat's nest, what would they think of her?

"Juliette, stay with me here. We need some answers, Juliette, we need to know where".

"Where what, what are you talking about? Can we get on, I've got to go home and do supper, Phil and the kids will be expecting it".

There was that look again.

Juliette noticed that there was a woman next to her, she didn't know who, but they must have been introduced because she was talking to her. Her tone was like she knew things, information that Juliette had never told anyone before, not even her fake mom, oh my god!

The now slapped Juliette hard across her face. The now was going to stick around for a while, the now was going to tell the police officers what they needed to know.

To Juliette's eyes, the two police officers that were talking to her, asking her lots of questions, were very different. The young one seemed to be a bystander, watching, learning perhaps. The older one, but not that much older, led. He had a face that had seen life, seen death, she wondered what his story was. He seemed a bit tired, worn around the edges, perhaps that was what police work did to people. She didn't know, she'd had no real dealings with the police before and she wasn't going to let this mistake thing put her off them, in her view they did a great job.

"Juliette, try to keep focused here, we're going to help you get this cleared up. Can we start at the beginning, Juliette, right at the beginning, can we start with the first?" It was the older officer.

"What's your name?" she asked, interested, maybe a little flirty even, although she hadn't really meant to be. It was an instinctive reaction to talking to a man she found attractive, and the officer was attractive in ruffled sort of way. It had worked with Phil; it had worked every time before. This was a man she could talk to, trust.

"I'm Sergeant Cross, I've been seconded from Halifax to help out here, to talk to you. We need you to work with us on this, help us to understand. We need all the details, can you do that for me, Juliette?"

So that was it, they needed her help as part of a team, why hadn't they made that clear from the start? "Of course, I'm always happy to help the police, what upstanding citizen wouldn't help if they could?" She paused a moment, Sergeant Cross, he looked very dependable, he'd be a George or perhaps a Howard, good, solid and reliable names?

Juliette started to breathe heavily, her shape and face changing slightly then she started at the beginning, the very beginning and the officers just let her run with it. No questions were asked, no clarifications sought, for now, they just let her spit it all out and, when she'd finished, she realized that she felt a little better for doing it, different.

As event after event entered her head, Juliette was able to provide names and dates, all the while that nice Sergeant Cross was making his own notes, although it seemed to be largely made up of ticking a list. She noticed him looking as she spoke, sly glances, so when she'd finished, she gave him her best smile. She'd already noticed that he wasn't wearing a ring, and she was intrigued, maybe she had a shot now that Phil had dumped her?

"And that's everything, Juliette, nothing else you recall, anyone you might have visited professionally or similar?"

Juliette thought for a moment, then continued as the Sergeant carried on making ticks on a sheet.

It was hard to listen to the recordings without both horror and sympathy and not a little amazement, that a seriously disturbed woman had done what she'd done, and nobody had thought to ask the right questions of her before. None of this had come to light until Mrs. Rose had spoken up. Juliette Barker said she'd killed her real mother, adoptive mother, her sister's children, a Mrs. Lester, Mrs. Lester's son, a restaurant owner, a psychiatrist, her partner Phil, and their babysitter Abigail. The latter's disappearance was the catalyst for Mrs. Rose uncovering the truth, or at least a part of it. She even claimed to have killed her sister, Melissa, too after she'd let her down, but that was unconfirmed. They couldn't find any record of her anywhere, but there was a Melissa West that had been a roommate at college for some years. They were looking for her now too, along with anyone else who might have been involved with Juliette Barker.

"How much of that can we believe?" said Cross to a senior officer who'd been watching the process and had entered the room after Juliette had been taken back to her cell.

"As far as we know her mother is dead, she died when Juliette was very young that was why she went into care. The psychiatrist, Geoffrey Watson and very much alive, he did treat Juliette for a while, but she stopped attending. The restaurant owner is fine too, he knew who Juliette was but had only spoken to her once. He said she'd eaten alone in the restaurant a few times but had stopped coming. Apparently, she was a big tipper, which was why they remembered her".

"And the rest, do we have evidence of any sort?"

The other cop seemed keen to make assumptions and that wasn't Cross's way, he suspected that was why Gordy had sent him over to 'help'.

"We don't, not yet, but now we know where to start we will have. She's obviously a nut job, she's going nowhere soon".

"I'll need to do the whole interview again with her legal people present, we need to double-check everything. It looks bad but until we can confirm anything, Juliette Barker isn't guilty of any crime".

"You've got to be joking me, look at her, she's completely gone. Besides, she said she doesn't want any legal representation at the moment, we have to respect that".

Cross wasn't happy, this felt like someone being railroaded and he said so. If Juliette Barker was disturbed, it was their duty to bring in the right people. He was also trying to rationalise what he'd heard; he was in that numb period you get when the true horror of something can't be suppressed anymore, but he'd deal with it one way or another, he always had.

Juliette sat in her cell swaying gently, in her head a robin sang like they did in the morning in spring. The now, she realized, had stayed with her long enough for her to tell the police, in very precise detail, most of what had happened. From the death of her sister to the death of Abigail for her affair with Phil. They told her they'd need a field visit, to identify where the remains were buried. She'd said she was good with that, as if accepting a deformed muffin for a few cents less. The nice one had also said she should get legal advice, so she would, he seemed to care about her welfare more than the others. She took that as a good sign for when this was all done. All men were so transparent.

In his notebook, Howey Cross wrote 'Juliette Barker is clearly not responsible for her actions and any court would be duty bound to rule that way, but she should still get locked up, taken care of, until she passes, until her own life goes the same way as those she said she'd taken so easily.

November 2019

Cross apologised to Crystal for having to take the call then listened in disbelief. On the say so of her psychiatrist, Juliette Barker had been remanded to a low-security facility and later had just wandered out. The plan had been that he would continue to interview her after a thorough psychiatric assessment. Excrement was currently hitting multiple fans out Annapolis way, thankfully he was back in Halifax and well away from the fall out, but that didn't alter the fact that Juliette Barker was at large and, potentially, a danger to the public.

November 2019

Mrs. Rose had seen the activity at the old Lester house, as she'd always think of it, and had wondered whether she should say anything about the house to the new people or not. It had been some time since Juliette had gone, vanished, poor Juliette, troubled Juliette, she never heard anything else. Then she thought about it a while and decided that the new people must be told if only to make them aware should anyone ask questions. She'd just drop by, say hello, and offer a warm welcome to Annapolis Royal.

She tapped lightly on the door. Now that she was there on the step, her nerve was failing her, and she nearly turned around and fled. A young woman came to the door and, oh my goodness, she looked so like Juliette, only the hair was dark, the build perhaps a little slighter still and she didn't have quite the look that Juliette aways had. If anything, this woman looked controlled.

"Hi, I'm Melissa, you must meet the kids. Say hello to Mrs. Rose, kids", she shouted to an unseen presence in the house.

Mrs. Rose caught immediately that she'd not mentioned her name, then she felt a tightness in her chest, her head was swimming and she started to slump. Melissa stepped forward and deftly caught her, carrying her into the house and pushing her into an old armchair, thick with dust. Mrs. Rose was barely conscious throughout, but she knew enough now to be terrified.

"Right", said Melissa, as she went to work…

CHAPTER SEVEN

July 2022-Back to the Present Day

At her computer, Mori Guier filled in what she called her victim spreadsheet, it made depressing reading. Her little cabal of collectors had been busy at first-light right to the end of May, sending her weekly counts and a few photos, images of crumpled bodies as birds lost their lives needlessly. Thankfully, the Nova Scotia counts were nothing like as bad as some big cities, but they were still bad enough. What bothered her most was that nobody would listen, nobody. It was just as if it was being allowed to happen because nobody could be bothered to try to stop it, but she would, one way or another.

Mori still hadn't heard back from Environment Minister Josh Hennigar's office about what they were going to do about it, in fact another glass edifice was in the latter stages of construction now and by fall it would be lit and killing southwards migrants before many even got to adulthood. She decided to write again, snail mail because emails never got answered with anything other than a standard 'thank you for your contact' reply. What she needed was to get the wildlife community more engaged, educated and as irate as she was that this was being allowed to happen.

At the back door, Chico, her rescue cat, stood expectantly. He knew she'd cave and let him out, she always did and then when he'd had a look around it was food time. Life was good from a rescue cat's perspective. "Ok, don't go far and don't bother the birds or no more". The door was barely open before Chico was out and gone from sight, scattering grackles at the feeder as he went. From the only tree in the neighbourhood, a noisy Blue Jay told the rest of the bird world that there was a predator at large. The jay didn't know that the predator was called Chico, nor did it care.

The birding tour was spread out all over the place, so Roy Simmons had to raise his voice to get some attention. Everything had been pretty par for the season so far, and his Graytop Birders tour had gone pretty well, with decent weather. That the key birds had shown up, and that the tour's nine participants were getting along together, was a bonus, sometimes they didn't. It was a pretty mixed group, all retirees spending their kids' inheritance, all enjoying late summer guided birding and a bit of whale watching thrown in.

The whole 'Graytop Birders' thing had been a bit of a joke at first, and it was one of the older birders from Ontario who'd suggested that there was a burgeoning market for simple, familiar tours with the chance of something interesting. And now here he was, trying to get his people together as they spread out all over the West Light area of Brier Island. Just then he saw a distant blob heading in their direction. Simmons called it a harrier, and the heads duly swiveled as his guests' newish top-of-the-range binocs got a good airing. The harrier breezed past them, at one point not more than fifty metres away, the silent flight accompanied by the motor drive of Gerard Robichaud's camera, as it machine-gun captured the moment. Simmons' brain was automatically trying to age the bird, it seemed to be somewhere between adult and immature, although lacking the rustiness of an immature Northern Harrier. It looked odd and were he alone, he'd spend more time figuring it out, but…

In the distance, a rain band was heading their way, and it was getting late anyway, so Simmons called everyone back to the transport and they headed to the hotel to freshen up and get ready for supper. After being beset by strong northerlies off the strangest weather front the Maritimes had ever seen, or so said the weather guy, it was good to have been out all day and not trying to find shelter all the time.

Westport Haven Hotel was good for their purpose, and a couple of the folks had a wander along a back trail before the metaphorical dinner bell went. After, it would be drinks and then the log. They all seemed enthusiastic about everything. A dotty old woman in the group had been very bossy initially, very demanding, but now she was calming down a bit and seemed to be enjoying herself. Simmons was convinced that there was some birding tour rule that each trip had to have at least one dotty old woman and one domineering old man.

Supper was good, they were all ready for it, and soon the beer and the wine was being ordered while Simmons kept a weather eye on the time. This lot would need to be up and at them for their early breakfast before their trip with Maritime Bird and Whale tours. He zipped through the log, pausing only for various people to note that a species was new for them, there seemed to be quite a lot but then they were doing coastal birding and most of the clients were from inland Canada. As they trickled off to bed, one of the guests, Gerard Robichaud, was obviously waiting for a word. "Something I can do for you, Gerard?"

"The harrier, Roy, what age do you think? I'm confused, I know harriers because I do a hawk watch and have done so for many years. I don't think I've ever seen one quite like our bird."

Robichaud appeared to know his birds well and Simmons was surprised that he'd even taken an organized tour such as the current 'Maritimes Avian Wonders' tour. He assumed that he was either lonely, or just taking advantage of being ferried around without the hassle of doing it for himself.

"Yes, I wasn't sure either. Not a juvenile, just not rich-rusty enough, but not quite adult either, maybe last year's bird, maybe it had delayed its moult?

This seemed to be an answer of sorts and Robichaud thanked Simmons and went off to bed. Simmons decided to update his trip diary and fetched his laptop, it was more comfortable in the lounge than in his little and cheapest room. "Can I get you anything?" He looked from being engrossed. That was the other great thing about Westport Haven, the staff were very attentive.

"Thanks, no, just taking a quiet moment to catch up. I don't remember you from last year, er…?

"Melissa. No, I'm only seasonal. I love it here, nice and quiet, very out of the way".

"Not so quiet when you've got a bunch of excited birders all talking into your ear", said Simmons, half in jest.

"I suppose not. One of your ladies is very excited about seeing whales tomorrow. You will for sure. I go out when I can, I love whales".

"Yes, me too although I'm usually busy spotting for the birders. Do you mind, I just want to update this then I'm off to bed, early start tomorrow and lots to do".

"Sorry to disturb you, I hope you enjoy your trip. I might be there myself if my sister shows up, man trouble but you don't want to know about that. If I don't see you tomorrow, I'll try and catch you next year, if you come back".

"I will, it's already booked. Nice to meet you, Melissa, I hope your sister gets herself sorted".

"She will, I'll help her bury her past".

Simmons watched Melissa walk away. She was attractive, slightly mysterious even and if he hadn't got a bunch of people to look after, he'd certainly have liked to have stayed another day and chat to her some more. He half-wondered whether her sister was also, what? enigmatic, he supposed. Maybe he might find out tomorrow.

The next day could not have provided better weather for the whale trip. Thankfully the whales were well offshore and the birds cooperating nicely. Naturally the phalaropes were very popular, the skipper of 'Ocean Greyhound' easing his boat into a large, mixed flock for photos. Northern Fulmars were called a few times and two different South Polar Skuas came in and harassed the many Great Shearwaters following the boat. Charity Haines, the owner of Maritime, had been happy to let them drop a bucket of dry chum off the back, creating a food slick that many Wilson's Storm-Petrels happily bounced over. The whales had been great too, and Simmons suspected that they would be a tour highlight for some, despite the great, mixed birding they'd enjoyed. From the back of the boat Simmons kept people busy as he called the birds, both for his eager group and the summer tourists.

For the southern part of the tour, visits to different sites on Cape Island had got them the hoped-for American Oystercatchers along with thousands of shorebirds. In Yarmouth County, a night at the Red Cap and subsequent mid-tide visit to the wharves gave them three species of tern, while a Sedge Wren not far from town and found earlier in the summer by one of the local, top birders, had remained and they all got good looks and shots.

As the boat eased into the wharf, Simmons skipped off first, ready to offer a hand to those who might need it. The tip box was getting plenty of attention and the chatter flowing. Now it was time to herd the cats back into the transport and hit the road, or more accurately, the ferry. A comfortable night in St John, New Brunswick would set them up for the next leg of the tour and Simmons hoped that the Grand Manan section would be just as good, and that his clients would still desire to see more migrant birds. It was and they did.

As was normal on trips, during meals and at the bar, people discussed their best birds. Being inlanders, most liked the alcids, especially seeing Atlantic Puffins at just a few feet and seemingly a lifer for most. Some were happy to get to grips with confusing warblers, others locked onto the many shorebirds, one lady picking out a Baird's Sandpiper on the beach at Pond Cove, Brier Island. The only topic of conversation on Gerard Robichaud's mind, however, was the harrier. He seemed obsessed.

The long drive back to Toronto, with bird and comfort breaks enroute, was another way of keeping prices down. They didn't add much more to the trip list but stops in Ontario for a Cerulean Warbler and a stake-out Ruff wound up the tour nicely and they all departed happy customers. All had promised positive reviews on Trip Advisor although, in his experience, only a few ever actually bothered. Simmons' next trip was a bit more ambitious, ten days in BC and Vancouver Island but at least he had a week to prepare and so he was quite relaxed about it, right up until he opened his laptop up at home and checked his emails.

Gerard Robichaud had posted his harrier shots to a Quebec birding site and Hen Harrier, from Europe, had been mentioned. Hen Harrier, wasn't that the same as Northern Harrier? A quick search told him that it was, or was not, depending on where you stood. The American authorities had been slow to embrace a split regarding the two harriers, something that had happened in Europe in 2016. This was not unusual; the Americans were always more reserved in this department. He pulled up a recent paper about the ID, but it was inconclusive, it did point out that their Northern Harrier is genetically closer to the Cinerous Harrier of South America, than it is to the Hen Harrier of Europe. A further web search failed to establish whether Hen Harrier had been recorded on ABA soil before, if not, if it was one, he'd found a first. It was on something called the Earlham Institute web site that he finally found out how to tell the two 'species' apart. It said 'females differ from each other by having slightly different markings on the underparts'. No shit, Sherlock!

Further down his lengthy new email list, he found another one from Robichaud, informing him that he'd researched and identified the bird with input from various bird forums and that he had written it up and illustrated it with his photos. Another email from his friend in Nova Scotia, Greg Barnes, who'd seen the eBird checklist for review, called him a 'clown' for not identifying the find of a lifetime and a double 'clown' for not alerting the Nova Scotia birders about it, but also congratulations. He finished by asking where these Eurasian migrants had come from. First the pratincole, now the harrier, what else had they missed?

Simmons pulled out his trip notebook, and as he opened it, a slip of paper fell out. 'Call me if you're this way again, M' and a cell number. He thought for a moment before the penny dropped, how had that got there? Oh, right.

Returning to the matter-in-hand he reviewed his notes. His scribble was bad any day of the week, it looked like it had been written by dipping a spider in ink and letting it dance all over the page. Also, it said 'Northern Harrier-1, but check it later to rule out other.' Opening up eBird, he found the Brier Island checklist via the hotspot and there was Robichaud's checklist with the Hen Harrier and a series of photos and notes, he wasn't even mentioned. Clicking on Robichaud's profile he saw that, not only had he eBirded the trip, he'd also shared some of the checklists with others in the group, but not with him.

He answered Greg Barnes first, apologizing for being a bit slow with the harrier but explaining that keeping an eye on excitable birders and finding firsts were not compatible. He would, on this one occasion, put the record into eBird himself too, although he stressed that tour leaders don't tend to use eBird on tours because that might allow would-be clients to find their own birds. It was a tongue-in-cheek comment but broadly true. Next, he contacted Robichaud and said he was happy to co-author a note on the harrier for North American Birds, as it was he who called the bird before any of the tour had seen it, again thanking him for taking good photos. It was a backhand way of saying, ok my friend, your photos were very important in making the identification, but I found it, or at least saw it first and I'm the tour leader and you should have included me in your checklist. Simmons felt a bit mean putting things that way, but something about the tone of Robichaud's email had rubbed him up the wrong way.

He got no reply.

The house was clearly empty. After carelessly losing Juliette Barker, even though it was nobody's fault, the tiny police detachment in Annapolis Royal had been given the rough edge of many tongues, not least Carmel Morrell's. Now they were supposed to be looking for Barker again. Activity had been reported at her old property, but it seemed to be secure and had been derelict for years.

"What now?" asked the constable. He was relatively blame-free, thanks to his rank.

"We investigate this broken door", said the sergeant, before breaking the door. He'd been there before and knew what to expect, or so he thought. In the family room, the near mummified remains of what appeared to be an elderly lady tied to a chair threw him, and his stomach, with spectacular results. The constable was more composed and called it in. Soon the property was again swarming with people, all with a job to do, all feeling the atmosphere of the house pressing down on them.

Carmel Morrell put the phone down. The sergeant in Annapolis Royal was fairly new, promising and probably not to be blamed, but she was still angry that a missing person had been found bound to a chair and had been for some time. The forensic people had sent a message ruling out suicide, The message seemed sincere and lacked the appropriate irony the situation called for. She had a call to make.

"Howey, what is possibly the body of Mrs. Rose has been found in Barker's house in Annapolis Royal. The identification will need to be confirmed by DNA, yes, she was that bad. Annapolis Royal are confident that it will be Mrs. Rose, she had a distinctive red beret which was present at the scene. It seems that the previous investigator didn't check the property in 2019, when she vanished, although it was six weeks before she was reported missing. With this being the Barker property, it's worth someone taking a look and rattling a few cages. I'll leave it with you, but I'll talk to the sergeant who was brave enough to let me know".

Cross held his phone a little way away from his ear and waited until she'd finished. "Very well, thank you, Ma'am".

"Sorry, yes, how are you and all that sort of thing. I'm worried, Howey, worried that Barker is involved in this, somehow. It's a screw up and unpleasant things might have to happen to those responsible. Take Crystal, go and make a nuisance of yourself and, if anyone questions it, give them my direct number". Morrell knew that when the press found out, and they would, senior police officers, her, would get doorstepped on it and need to be able to say it was being looked at by experienced officers, and it was.

The click told Cross that she was gone. He was minded to go in mob-handed but Darren was out. "Crystal, with me please".

It was unusual for someone from outside a regional force to get involved, but at least the officer sent had history with the case, having met Juliette Barker in person. That there would be objections was a given, but when senior people order it, you comply as reluctantly as you can, depending on the officers involved. When they got to the precinct, Cross and Roberts were shown to an office where a slightly matronly woman occupied the chair, boxes were piled everywhere, she appeared to be moving in. Cross did a double-take when he saw her. "Howey, Crystal, please take a seat. You're staring, Howey, I'm Tiff's mom, Constance, we've never met".

"No, not her mom, surely you're Tiff's big sister", said Cross and Constance O'Toole played up to it, making a flirty joke of her own.

"Would you two like ten minutes alone?" asked Crystal, feeling a bit left out.

"Make it a couple of hours and we're talking", winked Constance. Crystal rolled her eyes theatrically, herself now playing along. "Right then", said Constance. "Mrs. Rose. I have some details here for you, Carmel said you'd ask. Forensics reckon the body has been there around three years which is amazing really, but it's not the first time the house has stood empty that long, according to people in the area. Following Juliette Barker's arrest and disappearance, a young family moved in, but we have no idea who they were or whether they left before Mrs. Rose met her end".

"Or if they were involved. A family?"

"People said that there was a woman and two kids although they only saw the woman, dark haired, not Barker, we did ask that question". O'Toole knew that there would be more to come for the force not finding Mrs. Rose in good time and even though she'd been told that she was not to blame in any way, Constance O'Toole knew how things worked where the public were concerned.

"Mary Rose, has the next of kin been told?"

"Yes, I put together a sheet for you with the address of the Rose property, the key holder, a neighbour, and a few details about the lady herself. She seems to be the generic old lady type, her husband, Henry, died three years after their marriage, she never re-married. The only next of kin we can find is Alanis Higby, her niece. The two were estranged and she's in shock at being the sole beneficiary. She lives in Moncton, address on the sheet".

Cross took the sheet and skimmed through it. "When I spoke to Barker, there was no mention of a car. Did Mary Rose have a car?"

"Yes, but we've not found it yet, I'm talking to people now. Her property has remained empty since she went missing, I think the municipality wanted to have her declared dead so they could sell it off on the tax sales. I had a look myself, a neat if now dusty old lady's house. To answer your next question, Juliette Barker did know Mary Rose, although everyone around said she'd not been in the Barker house since a Melissa Rylance inherited it, I checked and I'm still looking for her full details. I do know that it was also once owned by someone called Muriel Lester, again we're checking on what happened to her, but a sick relative was mentioned, and she supposedly went off to tend them. That might just be local gossip though. I can also tell you that Mrs. Rose was babysitting when Melissa Rylance vanished, I know that for sure because I was the one who told her, I knew Mary back then, but not very well. I added the date Rylance vanished".

"Babysitting?" asked Crystal.

"Yes, two girls as I remember, went up for adoption soon after. I only called by with the bad news because I knew her, and a local lad didn't fancy it. I have nothing on the kids, you know how they are about that".

"Two girls, did you have a name for them? Geoffrey Watson, any chatter about him?"

"No name for the kids, I don't know if anyone local knew them. As for our Geoffrey, there was lots of chatter at the time, but I'm told that he kept his head down and got on with being the person who was responsible for her escape. Whispers about what she was supposed to have done leaked out at the time. It's holes in a dam that I don't have enough fingers for".

"Thanks Constance, very efficient. You look like you're moving in, I presume Madam pushed for the changes she felt necessary?"

"Yup, so here I am with a target on my back and a pension not too far down the road. I know that Madam has already spoken to you about the case, and that it's active, which is why she told you to come over for a look. I'll forward our case file directly to you and I'd appreciate being kept in any loops as Madam sees fit, although I suspect I'll spend my remaining days in the police dealing with minor vandalism. Can you believe that someone stole a memorial bench plaque from the Botanical Gardens? Heaven help us".

"I'll do my best".

Locks had already been changed at the Barker house and so they had to collect a key from the duty sergeant before gaining access to the crime scene. The place definitely looked unloved. Cross had seen photos of the inside before, the mess that Juliette Barker had lived in, somehow, but the outside he'd expected to be normal, it wasn't, it brooded. Both shivered as they entered the place, the memories hanging in the air seemed to cry out to them. "I might have to bring Moira over for a look, she has qualities in situations like this".

"Careful, Howey. You only just got the big chair; we don't want spiteful locals telling tales".

"All the same, I don't think we're going to take anything from here that we don't already have in print, but we'll have a little poke around just to get a feel. What we do need to do is talk to Geoffrey Watson, Barker's shrink. He's one of the reasons she's on the lam, although he was very dismissive of those detaining her, rightly too as I remember. We'll leave Mary Rose's place, it sounds like it's been checked properly, we need to know about her car though".

When they arrived at Watson's business address, the term 'unprepossessing' came to mind. It didn't look like the sort of place an expensive shrink might work from, but you never could tell. After taking a place in the waiting room, Watson was in with somebody but had found time to see them after, the detectives leafed through the elderly magazines. Cross had already scanned the room and noticed the camera, so he made a deliberate ploy of placing a random magazine in his inside pocket. Crystal saw him do it and guessed what he was up to. They waited in silence. Presently a young woman came out of the office, gave them a brief smile and slipped out of the door. Watson, bulkier than Cross remembered, bid them enter and take a seat, as if they were a couple in a relationship seeking answers, which in some ways they were.

"You might not remember me, but I came in from Halifax when Juliette Barker was in custody. You recommended low-security detention, which didn't work. Barker vanished and hasn't been found, and we're reopening the investigation into where she went and whether she committed any crimes. I'd appreciate your insight".

"My planner tells me that you had an August appointment already booked. Would you like me to cancel that now?"

"No, not for now. We might need a more formal meeting with you later, it pays to have options".

'As you wish. I do remember you actually; you seemed a bit preoccupied by something else at the time. We psychiatrists spot these things, sorry. How did whatever it was that was on your mind work out for you?"

Cross ignored the prompt, "During your sessions with Barker, did she seem unstable at any time? I assume you have notes from your consultations with her".

"I assume I don't have to remind you about patient confidentiality, Staff Sergeant Cross. Unless you've acquired a court order, my files on Juliette Barker remain confidential".

"I expected you to say that, and no we don't have a court order, yet Geoff. You seem to be resistant to our investigation".

"Can you blame me? I've had a lot of mud slung my way after Juliette absconded, much of it from our police service. My marriage suffered, my practice suffered, and I had to endure personal abuse. You'll appreciate that when I recommended a low-level security establishment for detention, a place that might help, not scare, Juliette, I didn't expect the place to be so lax that they gave her the keys to a car and a sat-nav".

"A bit of an exaggeration, but I do understand", replied Cross, reining in any sharp replies. There was no point in getting Watson's back up further.

Watson turned abruptly to Crystal. "You, Sergeant Roberts, what are your thoughts on the case, from a woman's perspective?"

"Do you think Juliette is still alive?" asked Crystal. Her insights were not open for discussion with Watson.

"I don't know. After she absconded, my official involvement in the case was terminated. Apart from the vitriol, nobody has said anything more about her to me, until now". Watson certainly seemed to be carrying quite a chip on his shoulder, Cross couldn't really blame him for that.

"Following your sessions with Barker, did you ever consult?" Cross had resumed the questions, making sure that Watson couldn't wrest the initiative, which shrinks are wont to do.

"As it happens I did, with a colleague in Halifax".

"Do you have a name?"

"She is bound by the same patient confidentiality as me and, no, I don't intend to offer a name".

Crystal stood and walked over to the wall behind the desk, admiring the certificates. "Impressive, you seem to be over-qualified for an out-of-the-way place like Annapolis Royal, Dr. Watson".

"Please, don't use doctor, it makes me sound like Holmes' sidekick. To be honest I get very tired of telling people that, they think it's so hilarious. To answer your question, I'm here because my wife preferred it here and where she was happy, so was I. After the incident we became estranged, and she moved away. I'm hoping to build bridges, but it takes time. I decided to stay here and try to recover my reputation, in the hope that she might return, do you see?

"Understandable and I'm sorry things panned out that way. I don't think the local police did anyone any favours, least of all you. Putting aside the patient confidentiality aspect of the Juliette Barker case, if I, as a layman, wanted to read open-source information about the types of afflictions that might make people think they've committed crimes, where might I look?"

Watson was a bit surprised by the question, it wasn't the sort of policework he'd come to expect. "An interesting question. Purely hypothetically, a layman might do well to research schizophrenia but also Histrionic Personality Disorder. The former is well-known, but the latter not so much. It's very much a specialised area, something we're learning more about all the time".

Cross gave an almost imperceptible start when HPD was mentioned, but quickly rallied and continued. "During your sessions with Juliette Barker, did she give you anything that isn't covered by confidentiality, anything that might help us find her? So far, she's been very skilled at not being found".

"I can't think of anything. In both sessions we covered the reason for something that bothered her. I had hoped for a third session, which she had booked, but it didn't happen. I thought that her childhood might hold the key, it often does. She really looked up to her sister". Watson was still cool to the police in general, but he found that liked Cross, his approach seemed less judgemental.

"Sister? Her sister, I thought she'd lost contact?", said Crystal, surprised to hear talk of a sister.

"No, no, she's alive and well, Juliette told me they talked often".

"She's mentioned in the witness statement transcript, Juliette said she'd had no contact with Melissa for some time and we've not found her. Did Juliette just tell you what she thought was real?"

Watson was shaken, surely not? He needed to review his tapes and he would, as soon as the police had left. "Er, I didn't hear the police transcripts, I was supposed to, but I didn't, then I was dropped, as I said".

"We need to know what she said about Melissa, Geoff, we need an idea of what she might be thinking and how her missing sister might be a part of the problem. This sounds like paranoid schizophrenia to me". Cross was getting a little impatient, but he could see that Watson was softening. Important information was in Watson's notes, and he wanted access to it. Carmel said she'd back him, maybe it was time to test her backing.

When he next spoke, Watson's attitude changed completely. He was struggling with the thought that he'd not seen that Melissa was possibly a construct. "Sorry, I'm sure you can see you've caught me on the hop here. Can you give me a little time. I'm a bit confused and I want to go through my notes and transcripts in detail. If I send you just the references to Melissa with anything sensitive regarding Juliette redacted, will that help?"

Cross agreed that it would. "Juliette Barker nearly finished my career, officers, even though it wasn't me who was supposed to be watching her. I'm very wary of mis-stepping again, I hope you can appreciate that. Give me a little time and I promise I'll get anything that I don't think is covered by the patient-doctor confidentiality to you".

"Soonest then, please, we don't want another Mrs. Rose somewhere if that is avoidable".

"Mrs. Rose?" said Watson, confused. Cross explained and Geoffrey Watson looked panic-stricken. He clearly didn't like what he heard and now had panic in his voice. "I'll email something before you get home, trust me".

"We appreciate it. Geoff. I think you still have a part to play here. If we were to find Juliette, would you be willing to get involved? She probably trusts you as much as anyone".

"Involved, really? In the questioning and helping you find the key to get her to open up. I thought I was persona non grata with the police these days".

Cross shrugged. "As lead investigator, you're not persona non grata with me".

"So, I'd be onboard, informed and expected to play a role in getting to the bottom of everything?"

"Yes, that about covers it". Howey Cross had been waiting to dangle the carrot, he'd almost done it before playing the dead Mary Rose card. Watson was obviously shaken, but he was still surprised at how quickly Geoffrey Watson had lunged for it. "Oh, one more thing, why did Juliette Barker come to you?"

Watson looked surprised to be asked. "Juliette made the first appointment, she called me, sorry, I assumed she'd said that".

"Not a referral then?"

"No, the request for a consultation came directly from Juliette Barker, nobody else was involved that I'm aware of". There was a short pause as the information sank in before Watson showed them to the door, having recovered a bit of composure. Just as they were about to go, he smiled and politely asked for his magazine back. Cross played stupid, patting his pockets. He handed it back and even managed a light blush.

"The magazine, why?" asked Crystal as they made their way home.

"To see whether he was watching. He was and likely always has, so Juliette Barker is on a tape somewhere. Whether he realises that that was what I was up to doesn't matter now, he can't deny it. Any thoughts?"

"One minute, and Crystal set her phone to record and talked dates and places into it. "I figured that the person he consulted with might have been a former fellow pupil, a long shot but worth it. We know she's a 'she and in Halifax', we now know when he studied, thanks to his diploma. All we have to do is find out who was at his college at the same time, find out where they are now and extrapolate and we'll have a pool of people to approach".

"Nice", said Cross handing her his phone. "Just scroll through to the folder marked 'Barker' and take a look at the certificate in the photo".

Crystal gave Cross a sideways glance but scrolled through the folder anyway. One set of certificates told her that she'd found what she was looking for. "Do you know her?"

"Tina, yes, she's a friend. We'll still have the confidentiality thing to deal with, but we're a bit further along the route now, and we can try".

"And you took these photos, why?"

"I wanted to know what the qualifications looked like, real ones. Tina knows, it was some time ago and knowing what real certificates looked like was a gap in my knowledge. Don't worry, I asked her first, I just didn't mention that she was to be my baseline and I didn't know then if I'd ever need to use them for reference, but at the back of my mind was Moira. I figured that if she ever needed any help of any sort, post-natal and after the bleed-out trauma, I'd know a real from a fake when seeking help".

"A bit sneaky but very caring and thoughtful. I assume that Moira was fine, because you never mentioned otherwise, and now they've come in useful. Best case scenario, what are we looking for from this case?"

"The killer of Mrs. Rose and perhaps the redemption of Juliette Barker, if she didn't kill her or anyone else".

"Clever thinking there, Howey boy?"

"Not at all, just taking an objective view of things, hot babe".

"Hot babe, where did that come from?"

"The same place as 'boy', so either stop using that term or get used to being called 'hot babe'".

"I quite like being called hot babe, especially by you. Did Moira really offer to fetch me for a threesome that first night I stopped over?"

"She was joking, winding me up. She didn't mean it, but she knew I'd react. I wish I'd never mentioned it now".

"But you did, Howey. Pity she didn't ask, if that was the only way to get you on my body count, I might have considered it".

"Crystal!"

"Really, Howey boy, you're so easy to wind up. Moira was right".

"What, what do you mean, Crystal, what did Moira say?"

Crystal didn't answer, instead stretching her long legs out and pretending to nap. The chances of napping on the lousy parts of the highway between Annapolis Royal and Kentville were miniscule, but she tried anyway, it didn't work. A little further along the highway, Howey reached over with his free hand. Crystal sat upright with a start. "Howey, you know I won't resist you, but what about Moira?"

"What she doesn't know won't hurt her".

"But I'd know, I could never look her in the face if she asked me directly".

"Crystal, let me do this".

Crystal reached into the bag on her lap and handed Howey a Boston Creme. After a post-vacation enforced abstinence, it tasted fantastic.

"You'll never get away with it, copper, when the boss girl finds out it'll be curtains for you, boy", said Crystal in a mock Chicago accent.

It was a funny moment, spontaneous, something that never seemed to happen with Darren much these days and Cross wondered what was troubling him, because whatever it was, only Darren could tell him.

Despite the fact that it would make a long day even longer, Howey called Tina from the car, asking if it would be convenient to drop by, she said it was but what was it about? He gave her the briefest of replies, not wanting to risk her saying no and hoping that once they were there, she'd be a bit more helpful than Watson.

Tina had no sooner put the phone down than it rang again, "Hello, long time, Geoff, how's things?"

"Hey, Tina, sorry. Life, kids, work, you know how it is. Look, to the point here, Howey Cross, a policeman, came to see me. He's smart, can add two plus two and I think he might want to talk to you, just a heads-up".

"About?"

"That case I discussed with you, about three years ago now, Juliette Barker. I know I don't have to ask; I can rely on you being professional if he calls by".

"Yes, you can, but I should tell you that I know Howey socially, I know his wife Moira better. What did you tell him?"

"Nothing, I cited patient confidentiality naturally, but I did suggest areas he might look to help understand the issues. That he's digging into the case again is fine, I welcome it and I'll help as much as I'm obliged to, I just didn't want him to catch you unawares".

"If he calls by and asks questions, is there leeway? I remember the case, a serious case, or are you asking me to say nothing?"

"I'm just pointing out that he might ask questions, I totally trust your professionalism in this, I always have, that's why I always ask you when I want to consult".

"Thanks then, Geoff. If he comes over, I'll see what he's after. The patient, is she still at large? I heard nothing after she vanished".

"I don't know, I had no more contact, it's just that there's been an incident, here in Annapolis Royal".

"Incident? Expand".

"I heard that an old lady was found dead in suspicious circumstances in Barker's house, recently. That's why the police are door-knocking again".

"In your opinion, the patient, is she dangerous?"

"Yes, I think she might be, but she doesn't know anything about you".

"My name never appeared in any notes you made then?"

"Er, yes, but there's no way she could know that, she never had any sort of access to anything I didn't want her to see. I keep security very tight here".

"Ok, well thanks again. Got to go, a patient has arrived and is waiting, I'll have to knock a few dollars off if I don't get to him soon".

"Thanks, Tina, sorry to have bothered you", and Watson hung up.

Tina Peck walked to the door, musing on the conversation with Watson. She wasn't at all surprised to see Howey on the doorstep accompanied by an attractive female officer. She ushered them in.

"Tina, this is Crystal Roberts, a sergeant in the Kentville detachment. We're working on a case where serious incidents took place. We spoke to a colleague of yours today, Dr. Geoffrey Watson, although he told us not to call him Dr. Watson for obvious reasons".

Tina was impressed. Howey had laid plain why they were there and what they had. The only variable was the pretty officer with him who she knew had a connection to Terence Ferry. She was surprised that Moira hadn't dropped Crystal's name into a conversation at one of their sessions, she could see that there was a chemistry between Howey and her. She decided to sit back and let things take their course.

"Crystal, hello. Geoff just called; he said you would be coming to see me. I take it his was the set of credentials you wanted to check against mine?"

"Sort of, yes, obviously he checks out. How much do you know about a woman called Juliette Barker?"

"Geoff would have cited patient confidentiality, I'm sure. I can tell you that Geoff sent me notes and asked me to confirm his diagnosis".

"Histrionic Personality Disorder?"

"Yes, but I can't give you any details. Her notes showed the markers we use to diagnose HPD, I never actually met her".

"How common is HPD?"

"In mild forms, not that uncommon. Where it can dominate your life, less common".

"Did Barker's HPD dominate her life?"

"I don't know, I never met her".

"You know that Moira had the same diagnosis some years ago?"

Tina didn't much like that Howey was apparently trying to get her to break Moira's confidential conversations with her, not that her diagnosis had been discussed. Howey could see it in her face and continued. "I'm pretty sure she doesn't have HPD, but I'm not qualified to say so, you are. If she's not already spoken to you about it, she will".

Tina relaxed a little. "I don't want to discuss another patient, potential or otherwise, even if she is your partner, Howey, but Juliette Barker is very different from the Moira I know, very different. I think that this is where this is going, as much as any questions being a part of your investigation, am I right?"

When Howey said 'yes', there was a little gasp from Crystal who felt that she'd become caught up in something uncomfortable. They both looked at her. "Sorry, not the way I expected the conversation to go", said Crystal. "Look, should I really be here for this? I can wait in the car, there's still a doughnut left".

"No, it's ok, we're done here. Thanks, Tina. Can I ask, would it compromise your integrity if we consulted with you, professionally? We'd need to clear it with upstairs but, hopefully, that will just be a formality."

"You mean hire me? To do what?"

"To help us understand, objectively, what intense HPD might do to an individual, how they might think and how someone like that might be able to vanish, almost at will. I won't ask after specific patients, but I will ask how HPD might manifest itself, so I know better what we're dealing with and what to expect when we catch Juliette Barker. I intend to tell Moira about this conversation later, if you have any concerns".

Tina was a little annoyed with herself for thinking that Howey was trying to manipulate her. He was being totally professional, and he was as transparent as he always was, but he was understandably worried. She almost wanted to tell him not to worry, but she didn't, instead she gave him a card and said to make an appointment.

"I wasn't ready for that at all, you might have warned me", said Crystal, once they'd got back on the road.

"I didn't know where it might go myself. I assume you think it a good idea to hire Tina, if Madam agrees?"

"What? Yes, she seems very composed and confident, cute too".

Yes, she's all those things and the current beau of Josh Hennigar, so no ideas, and if you do get ideas, don't tell me about them".

"You know I'm straight, right? But if you do have a little fantasy about me and now cute Tina that does it for you, I don't mind. Josh Hennigar, really? Well, I never".

"Crystal?"

"About three years ago and not long after you spurned me, Josh and I were quite close".

"He was married then?"

"Yes, yes, he was, just about. Listen, I'd prefer your friend Tina not to find out about that, if that's ok with you?"

It was, but it might end up being a complication further down the line if Hennigar was ever investigated by them for anything. Both phones pinged at the same time, it was Darren. 'Juliette Barker reported as having been seen in Liverpool recently, local police recognised her after the fact, no longer in the area though, they said they looked'.

"I think it's time to shelve everything and give the Barker case our full attention, I'll talk to Madam", said Howey, "Agreed?"

Crystal nodded. 'Josh Hennigar', she thought. 'Well, I never'.

Howey Cross was deep in thought when he pulled into the yard, he had to pull up sharply as he passed through the open, inner gate as, parked where he normally parked, was a small SUV that he didn't recognise. As he approached his front door, he could hear laughter and the dulcet tones of his dear sister. He braced himself for ridicule. "Shhh, he's here", said Angela as he walked in the door. She often did that to suggest that the conversation and laughter were all about him, which they generally were.

"Angela, a new car, does that mean New Zealand isn't happening?"

"Short-term lease, Howey. I sold the camper, and the other car has been borrowed, possibly permanently. I hope the person who borrowed it has the sense to get it into the shop, the brakes are shot". It was typical of Angela to not tell him that someone had stolen her old Subaru.

"I'll assume you didn't report it and that you might know who it was who borrowed it, which is why I didn't get asked to tap into the system, interesting". Cross could see that he was right by Angela's face. It was likely a temporary resident of The Orchard who'd taken the car with whatever intent.

"I just came over to drop off some papers for Moira, I could have emailed them, but I was nearby, and I don't like to send sensitive documents over the Internet. Moira was telling me about Brazil and the Trans guy who tried to pick you up and you never noticed that there was an Adam's apple involved. It's good to know that our keenest minds are out there keeping us safe", and she laughed. Howey knew she didn't mean anything by it, but she had a very blunt way of dealing with him that he'd just had to learn to live with.

"Actually, Angela, I'm glad you're here. I'd like a serious conversation, here or in the office if you have time".

"Would it help if I confess now, or do you want to go through the whole waterboarding thing just to follow procedure?" Angela put on her 'serious' face as she turned to Howey.

"Angela, you know we only interrogate suspects that way on Thursdays. No, it's sensitive". Moira saw Howey's face and realised that it wasn't anything for the kids to hear and, perhaps, her. She gave Howey a sign that it was fine and started to get the kids ready for bathtime. Howey ushered Angela through to his study and shut the door.

"If you don't want Moira to hear this then it must be serious. Go on, although I guarantee nothing".

Cross explained in sparing detail about the Barker case, without naming her. When Carmel had said to go through the women's refuge system to look for Barker it had hoped that he might get valuable insights, a way in of sorts, from his sister. Angela listened passively. Howey might be her brother, but her involvement in spiriting away women in need wasn't something for the police.

"What are you asking me, Howey? You know I won't divulge anything, the whole system is based on trust, that's why it works. I don't trust the police, you included, in this, sorry".

"I don't want case details; I'm looking to understand how extensive the invisible network is. How I tap into that network is my business. When I brought Yvonne Wilding to you, she vanished very efficiently. Over the years I'm sure that very many more abused women have done so, thanks to you and the organisations you have access to. The person we're looking for, she can only have become invisible with help. My guess is that she moves around a lot and has done so since she vanished. We think that she still uses the network when she needs to because it offers anonymity. I suppose my question is, how big is the network?

Angela had been taking in what Howey was telling her and was torn. She knew that he wouldn't ask for anything unless the case was serious. The thought that someone unbalanced was hiding in the system didn't surprise her, she'd dealt with a few like that but, generally, they were just troubled, not psychotic. "I know of perhaps seventeen people out there who do what I did in Yvonne's case. They get no official funding but the known refuges, like The Orchard and the rest do help. There might be others, unofficial ones that I don't know, does that help? I have nothing else, but I will ask a few questions for you, but only if I think it's safe to do so, and only because it's you that's asking and I know you. Individually, I won't compromise anyone".

Cross was relieved. Angela could be very stubborn sometimes, but she'd seen the gravity of the Barker situation and shared his concern. If she found anything, he'd have to find a way of making sure it looked like solid policework had got results and not the result of information leaked from the system.

"I'll miss you, you know", said Angela, giving her little brother a hug.

"I'll miss you, too. It's a long trip, I'll worry that you're safe and when you've made the move, we will visit, promise. Tell Moira yourself, I can feign surprise when she tells me".

Angela said nothing as she walked out of the office. "All sorted?" asked Moira, keen to know what it was all about.

"I've got to press on, sorry, too many crazy deer out there. Moira, I'll see you at The Orchard for the interviews then. Got to dash", and Angela was gone.

"Did you get what you wanted?" Moira was still digging.

"Sort of, for the case. I wanted to know how many women's refuges there are, unofficial ones. We have some doors to knock on and I wanted to make sure that the right people do it".

CHAPTER EIGHT

End of July 2022

There was a light on inside the house, which was a relief. Howey knew that Sheila Moffat, the midwife who delivered Moira went to bed early, but he reckoned that at five in the afternoon he should be ok. He'd had the photo that Sheila had lent them in his pocket for a while without once finding himself in the area. Now he was looking for a quick drop-off, but Sheila was lonely, and he knew he'd be lucky to get away with only half-an-hour. He knocked and waited, then heard the footsteps behind the door. It opened a fraction, still on the safety chain, before Sheila saw who it was and let him in.

"As promised, your precious photo coming back, Sheila, and Moira thanks you again for the loan. She got a professional copy made, she's very happy to have it".

"Come in, Howey, you can stop a few minutes, yes? I know you're busy and you have a bit of a drive in front of you. You wouldn't catch me taking on rush-hour traffic, it's bad enough as it is".

"I can stop a short while, Sheila, but, as you say, a bit of heavy driving to get home".

Tea was offered and declined, potential bladder issues if stuck in traffic cited. Sheila still had her photo album on the coffee table, a mark showing the page where the missing photo resided. Even before Howey had sat down, she had the photo album open, and the photo was on its way home. Something caught Howey's eye, there was a space where a photo had been, but now wasn't.

"Do you prune your albums, Sheila?"

"If you mean, did I used to take out the photos of those little ones that didn't make it? Yes, I did. It doesn't feel right to me to have a photo of someone who has passed. I know it will sound silly, but I didn't want the healthy babies infected. I used to give the photos to the parents if they wanted them, they usually did".

"I noticed a space by Moira's place".

"Yes, that was her twin sister, Julieanne. Her aunt told me that she'd passed later, which was how Moira ended up being raised alone. I wasn't surprised when her mother went off the scene, but I was surprised at the child's passing, she'd seemed the livelier of the two at the time".

"You're saying that Moira had a twin sister? She never said".

"She must have been told when she was very young and forgot. Children blank things out in my experience, she probably has that feeling, deep down, that she is disconnected somehow. Twins are usually close, like yours, they sometimes seem to work as one while being in two different bodies. I've always wondered why there isn't more research into it".

Cross deliberately didn't tell Sheila that Moira forgot nothing, more or less ever. He knew that her gift had been a long time in the taming, if indeed her mind had been truly tamed by their relationship and the responsibility of motherhood.

"Did you send that one back?"

Sheila fidgeted a bit, and Howey could see that there was something going on unsaid.

"No, but before you ask, I don't have it now either. It went missing one way or another, I don't really know when or how. I can tell you that the sister was a blonde child while your Moira was dark and that is very rare. If Moira didn't tell you about her, if she remembers her at all, then she'll have her reasons".

"No, of course, if she wants to tell me she can, not that it is very relevant, it just seems odd that she never even hinted. Do you remember anything more about her mother?"

"I do, we all thought that she was a little fragile at the time and probably wasn't up to raising her alone, no father was mentioned but that wasn't so unusual, and I was never judgemental, some were. Mothers in those circumstances, and without the emotional support of a partner, go one of two ways, they struggle along doing the best they can, or they go for adoptions, whether to a willing family member if suitable or through the wider system. I suppose it wasn't so bad for the aunt that had only one child dropped on her in the end although she must have said yes. I heard that they became very close".

"They were. So, her birth mother is dead?"

"Perhaps, I don't know for sure, my memory is slipping these days, that's why the photo albums are such a comfort. Howey, do you mind? I was about to cook supper. I'd invite you to stop and eat, but I know you can't".

"Sorry, yes, I'll get along, beat some of the traffic perhaps. Thanks again for the loan of the photo, we'll pop by next time we're over with the terrors. You take care".

Sheila was up in an instant and almost marching Howey out, something he hadn't expected. From the kitchen he could hear the dishwasher running, the way it does after you've cooked and eaten. As he departed, he turned to say goodbye again but found that the door was almost shut. Sheila had clearly been rattled.

The traffic was what it always was, chaos. As he cleared the city and hit the highway home, he relaxed a little bit and started to mull over the situation. He was very sure that Moira would have mentioned a sister to him, and equally sure that she would have remembered having one if she'd been told, so what to do? By the time he hit his drive, he'd decided to pick a moment and ask.

The terrors were waiting for him and still full of beans. Moira was busy with something on her laptop, which she closed as he walked in. "How is Sheila?"

"Seems very well. No more rare birds, or at least she didn't mention any. I didn't stop long, she was wanting to eat and ushered me out quickly".

Moira gave him a long look, the sort that peeled back a few layers of the conversation and saw something lying underneath. He knew that once the kids were asleep there'd be questions. After an hour of over-excitement, eyes drooped and beds were filled. Once Howey had put them down, he joined Moira on the sofa. It was as if she'd just been waiting for him like a Venus Flytrap, he found it slightly disconcerting. Her expression said, 'talk to me'.

"I never knew you had a sister", he said, jumping right in and giving Moira the chance to explain. The sheer shock on her face told him another story. "Sheila said you were one of twins, a sister called Julieanne, she died at some point, she didn't know any details".

The change from shock to tears took seconds, and Howey struggled to console her as she shook through crying. Eventually she calmed a little, but she looked awful, pallid, red-eyed, a mess of snot and tears. He fetched a clean towel, one of the ones they used for Trixie when she stayed over and got muddy. For a good five-minutes Moira buried her head deep in the towel, occasionally shaking it in disbelief.

"I wasn't sure whether to say anything. I felt sure you knew and had decided I didn't need to know, which I don't".

"I didn't know, I didn't know! How could I not know something so important, something so fundamental?"

"Now that you do, well, what about it? I know you'll try to dig and find out, and with the Internet it should be possible to find out something. Will you be ok?" Howey tried to frame the question as concern for her wellbeing, not 'will you go mad on me?'

"I will, it's just a massive shock but it explains a few things, bits of me I've never been able to figure out. I'll need to think about this, possibly on my own, but not tonight. I'm going to mix up something to put me out cold. We can talk more tomorrow night, when my head stops whistling".

Howey had learned not to ask about Moira's potions, as he called them, although she assured him that they were all legal, somewhere. Later, as Moira slept silently, Howey laid in bed wondering. Images of Juliette Barker kept sitting in front of him and the fact that she'd claimed to have a dark-haired sister, Melissa. It was the wee hours before sleep welcomed him, and when it did, he dreamt.

He was back in Annapolis Royal, standing behind a glass window looking at a bedraggled creature sitting in a soul-less plastic chair. She clearly had little idea of what was happening, but she'd occasionally talk to someone, a shorter person or someone who was laying on the floor that only she could see. He flexed his shoulders and entered the room. Juliette Barker looked at him and her shape changed subtly, despite the circumstances she went into boy alert mode.

"Juliette, try to keep focused here, we're going to help you get this cleared up. Can we start at the beginning, Juliette, right at the beginning, can we start with the first?" It was the new officer speaking.

"What's your name?", she asked.

"I'm Sergeant Cross, I've been seconded from Halifax to help out here, to talk to you. We need you to work with us on this, help us to understand. We need all the details, can you do that for me, Juliette?"

"Of course, sergeant, always happy to help the police. What upstanding citizen wouldn't help the police if they could?"

Juliette started to breathe heavily, her shape and facial expression changing slightly, then she started at the beginning, the very beginning.

"And that's everything, Juliette, nothing else you recall, anyone you might have visited professionally or similar?"

Juliette thought for a moment, then continued as Sergeant Cross carried on making ticks on a sheet. All the time she spoke, she was looking down, looking at something that wasn't there.

"Juliette, one last question. Who are you, really?"

Slowly, Juliette Barker raised her head. Her hair darkened, her shape barely changed, and the face of Moira was looking back at him, smiling.

Howey could feel his heart pounding in his chest, and he was gasping for air as he woke with a start. Next to him the sleeping body stirred slightly, but then settled back into sleep again. He got up and went to the bathroom, his T-shirt was saturated with sweat and his hands shaking. Catching his face in the nightlight-lit mirror he looked haggard, old, as if some of the horrors he'd seen during his career had carved memory lines into his very skin.

Behind him the door opened quietly, and Moira walked in. She didn't acknowledge him but flipped the lid and sat to pee. He didn't dare move or say anything. When she'd done, she stood and went back to bed. Howey gave it a couple of minutes before flushing, then, not wanting to make a noise opening drawers in the bedroom, grabbed a T-shirt out the laundry basket and slipped back into bed.

As he tried to sleep, the image kept coming back to him, and details bounced around in his head, making connections, forming patterns, he didn't like it.

"I'm not mad you know", said Moira, unexpectedly.

"I know, I thought you were asleep", he whispered.

"I am", and then all was quiet except for the subdued sound of her breathing.

CHAPTER NINE

Early August 2022

"I'm sorry to have to ask, Pauline, but one of our seasonal staff seems to have upped and left right after I paid her, she was only casual but very good. Last I heard she'd got a ride off the island and away. I wouldn't ask otherwise, you know that". Kirsten Stockley had been reluctant to call her friend at Tiverton, but she really needed help. The hotel was nearly full and even with herself working tables too, they'd never be able to manage the evening meal rush without help.

"No problem, I'll come straight over. Who went? Only you really should get your staff officially; someone will find out you have been paying cash in hand and at below minimum and you'll be in trouble". Pauline Stockley had come with Kirsten to view the Westport Haven Hotel when she was interviewed for the manager job. She'd loved the place, the affordability of life there, and had moved to the neighbouring Long Island.

"Melissa, the one who needed her roots doing, as you so graciously pointed out. I did hire her officially, actually, she had a SIN card and everything, but I haven't processed her yet. I'll not be bothering now. Next season I'll be more established and hotel income might be less scary. Absentee owners don't help, they don't see what we do to keep viable. I've a good mind to walk myself".

"Now then, Kirsten, let's have none of that, you love it here as much as I do. All we need to do is find you a burly fisherman hung like a horse, and you'll soon forget your woes".

"Thank you, Pauline, you have such a lovely way of putting things, but I think I'll pass", and she laughed. They'd been close for years, so less than subtle jokes were often the norm between them.

That evening it was crazy busy after two minibuses full of Indians, two families, decided to eat there before carrying on their tour of Nova Scotia. The women looked lovely in their saris, so colourful, and they were all very polite, and generous when it came to tipping. When the last of the people went and the cleaning up was finished, Kirsten and Pauline grabbed chairs and a well-deserved bottle. "Here you go", said Kirsten, as she handed Pauline a hundred-and-fifty dollars. "Tips, and what I would have paid Melissa".

"Excellent, I had a quiet evening planned but now I'm up one-fifty, you can call me again. This Melissa, did you fancy her?"

"No, not my type, but she was interesting. If I was to use a word to describe her it would be enigmatic, she gave off an air of absolute control. We never spoke much so I don't know her full backstory, I do know that before coming here she had a relationship that ended suddenly when she caught him on the job as it were. Heaven help him and his bit of fluff is all I can say. She said it was what sent her here, I felt sorry for her which is why I took her on".

"Come over on your day off, you can tell me more about her and I'll use her in my next bodice-ripper, I'm casting around for ideas", said Pauline, although she'd already started to plot a new character in her head, based on what Kirsten had told her.

"I wish I had your turn of phrase, then I wouldn't end up running around places like this, still each to their own. More wine? You can stop over if you want".

Mori Guier was updating her bird deaths spreadsheet for FLAP Canada again as the news played on in the background. When Josh Hennigar appeared, her ears pricked up. Hennigar's office still had yet to reply to her request for a meeting to discuss the ongoing bird deaths in downtown Halifax, it was so ignorant of them. The news item was talking about some bird reserve that Hennigar had opened recently and how it was progressing. It showed a clip of the opening and the worthies present. More interesting was the side news that his new partner, Tina Peck, was the President of the Nova Scotia Bird Group. Mori was suddenly much more interested. Clearly Ms. Peck didn't seem too keen on the publicity, but having Hennigar's ear was no bad thing. In her younger years Mori might have been of interest to him herself.

As a relatively recent arrival in the Maritimes, originally hailing from Winnipeg, Mori felt that she was coming home. Her folks were Maritimers born and bred, only moving west when work called. Bringing with her what she called her 'FLAP' mentality, it had taken her a while to discern whether there was a similar building-collision bird-deaths issue in Halifax. She'd missed much of the spring, and because her handful of local recruits to the cause were more of the robin fondler type rather than concerned birders, she didn't have any solid data on the potential problem, but that was changing as more and more reports came in.

Mori found the bird group website and joined on-line. It was always better to be looking from within with these things. Not surprisingly, her digital welcome pack contained zero references to building and light bird deaths, but an index to all the historical newsletters had her slowly reading an account from the 1970s. It was, pun intended, quite illuminating.

Hope Atwood had been the wife of a Lighthouse Keeper, both had retired when the light became automated. Hope had kept a light diary, writing up items of interest, including pieces about whales, both offshore and dead on the beaches. She was a beachcomber and had found numerous curiosities of various sorts, including a profusion of sea glass. She'd also had a passing interest in the birds, not to a very specific level, more taking in lost strays. One feature of her diary was mention of the 'buckets of birds' that they got during migration. Her account mentioned the need to go out at dawn with buckets and pick up light-attracted birds, many of which would become gull or Mink food if not rescued, many were already dead.

Mori was frustrated that there weren't any more details, tangible facts that she could incorporate into a topical article for the FLAP Canada newsletter. It was a couple of hours later when she realised that she'd spent the whole morning browsing the historical newsletters. Opening her email inbox, she was delighted to see that it had been a light night, not a great one for movement as borne out by the BirdCast prediction. She added the seven known deaths to her database then went looking for the NSBG President's email address, it was time to see whether there was any help there or not.

If Hennigar's office kept stalling, well there was more than one was to skin that particular cat. As if reading her mind, Chico jumped up and sat on her lap. He really was a very good boy.

The idea of having two small stands of wheat, one for food and one for wildlife had seemed a good idea at the time, but the logistics of using a scythe to take in the food crop, cutting, stooking to dry then separating the wheat from the chaff were now a reality and Howey Cross was fit to drop. He was grateful for the shade offered by the cheap Canadian Tire gazebo, provided, according to Moira, for the workers' comfort. So far, thanks to a hand injury incurred by Darren, and Moira being busy with the vegetable plots, he'd been the only labour available for the reaping and, while losing yourself in manual work was sometimes nice, he was beginning to think it would also be nice not to.

"Nice job, boy", said Moira laughing and bringing home-made lemonade.

"It's amazing, it looks like a small area but once you start swinging that scythe it just seems to grow. I'm beginning to think we should devote more of the crop to wildlife, like as much as there is left to cut".

"No, we need this crop, we said, we'd take a little and give a little, otherwise we're just messing about. It's good for you, sat down at work all day doesn't keep the Cross body honed, your lovers will start to complain".

"Lovers? After this I'll need a quiet lie down somewhere".

Moira laughed and lay back on the hay-bale seat she'd made, the thick cotton tarpaulin moulding to her body shape. Howey joined her, putting off getting back to it for a while. "Nova Scotia, I know you said you washed up here and liked it, but I've often wondered why, what drew you?" It was something Howey had meant to ask Moira several times, but it had usually slipped away when she'd distracted him.

"My mother was here, before I was born. She had me and my sister in British Columbia, you know that, but I think I, we, were conceived and carried in Nova Scotia somewhere. I've never been able to find out where though. I was told that we came back to Nova Scotia, but I remember nothing about it, I was very young when I went back to BC to live with my aunt".

"Do you know even roughly where your mom was in Nova Scotia?"

"No, my aunt told me that they'd lost touch for a while, then she'd showed up pregnant, she was looked after and left. I have no details about her, none, and the only person who could have supplied any never would, and she's gone now".

"Is it important to you?"

"Not in the scheme of things, no, but I've naturally wondered who my mom was and what happened that she didn't want me, us. I wonder how like me she might have been, maybe lots, maybe not at all. Perhaps I'm like my father, there had to be one".

"I did say before that can do a little digging if you give me any details you have".

"Like I said, I have nothing, besides, I thought that was illegal?"

"Technically, it is".

"At one time I'd have been on my knees thanking you for the offer, but I think the past should sleep undisturbed. I don't have the same demons anymore, you sent them packing when you took me on. Stirring a potential Hornet's nest might not be prudent".

Howey was surprised to hear the reluctance in Moira's voice. She normally wanted full details, gained either by deduction or explanation, not wanting to know didn't fit the Moira persona, the real Moira that he knew and loved.

"Ok, was she called Magowan, your mother?"

"Not sure, Magowan was my aunt's name so maybe, if that was the name she used. I know it sounds odd for me to not want to know now, especially after I spent a lot of time looking myself, but I worry that there might be something disturbing, disrupting. I want my life to be this, be us and the kids. I don't want a spectre from the past peeping around the door, whispering".

"Finding out you were a twin, I saw how that affected you, is that part of the reason why you don't want to chase down who you are?"

"Yes, but my twin died, and that's the end of it as far as I'm concerned. In a way I'm glad they never told me, I might have fixated and become unstable. As a child I could be difficult, sometimes, self-absorbed as if in a bubble. Nobody knew about disorders back then; they said I was just either energetic or subdued. In a way I had to be my own self-help support group, so I started being other people, someone I could ask questions of, even though I knew it was me answering. I sound terrible, don't I? a real nut-job. Luckily my aunt was a progressive thinker, and she gave me enough rope to run, but stay safe. I wish I'd understood that better. I miss her and wish she could see us, see what a great job she did in raising me".

Howey was beyond happy with the conversation, the fact that Moira was lucid, sane. His biggest worry was that she might be unstable and slip one day, become lost in her own head and exclude him and the kids, mentally. Conversations like this were his way of doing a health-check, he was sure Moira knew that too.

"Right, boy, get back to work. I want that crop in and stooked before the rains come. Got to go, I left the kids with the chainsaw trimming the low branches in the woodlot, they'll be getting low on fuel now".

Cross looked over to where the kids were playing and laughed at the image of Phoebe telling Vinnie where to cut and where to stack the brush. He was quite sure Moira hadn't bought them a 'my little chainsaw' set to play with, yet.

"Don't forget the Newells are coming over, they said around four", said Howey.

"I hadn't forgotten, I wonder if Darren would react to me wandering around in the buff the same way you did when you thought Hinzi was naked in our yard, that was so funny, we both still laugh about it".

"Yes, well, just throw something on to cover up the best bits before they get here, I need to talk to Darren, and I want him focused".

"What about you, are you going to put a shirt on so that your rippling muscle doesn't turn Hinzi's head?"

"I don't see that happening; besides, I think you mean muscles".

"I know what I mean", said Moira heading back to the vegetable patch laughing.

Attacking the crop with renewed vigour, Howey ran things through his head. Moira might not be keen to know anything else about who she was, but it wouldn't hurt for him to have a little look. Just to get an idea, if he had the opportunity.

CHAPTER TEN

Early August 2022

The sudden quiet in the station told Howey Cross that Carmel had arrived. Two visits within a month, he was surely blessed! The door opened and the woman herself breezed in. "No need to get up", she announced. Cross said nothing, he hadn't intended to after Moira had told him that standing up in the presence of anyone or holding the door for them was enforcing the patriarchy, he wasn't sure whether she was joking or not though.

"We spoke about your team checking the refuge system, how is that going?"

"I covered it in my most recent update, we're working through them while pursuing other cases in the interest of financial expedience, Ma'am". Carmel gave him a look that, if delivered by Moira, might mean trouble.

"I have information that Barker spent time at The Orchard at one point, using an assumed name, Rosemary, although I understand that they all pick their own names there. Has Moira had any more recent dealings with The Orchard, a place managed by your sister?" There's a bit of an edge there, Cross thought.

"Yes, they're in the process of replacing Angela through her choice, she's going over to interview the candidates at some point, I assume you know all their names?" This time the look was worse; he was playing with fire and he knew it.

"Howey, we're not making progress here. Juliette Barker is a danger to herself and others, we need her secure". Carmel sounded desperate.

"I agree entirely, but she's very adept at slipping through the cracks, so we're operating a policy of mortaring over cracks as we go. Eventually we will be in the right place at the right time, and we'll have her. I might need to get a court order to free up Barker's patient notes from her shrink, Geoffrey Watson, will you authorise the request? I hinted that you would to Watson".

"Why, do you think there might be clues as to where she is in his case notes?"

"I was thinking more about who she is". Morrell wasn't sure what he meant. She'd read the police interview notes thoroughly and everything pointed towards Juliette Barker being a psychotic killer. 'Why' wasn't their problem, the lack of supporting evidence would be though.

"If you really need it, yes, you can have it. Watson, what's he like?"

"Family man with issues there, sensible, professional. He probably has her on CCTV too, I know he films patients while they wait for him".

"Voyeur?"

"No, I don't think so, more to see what they are like in unguarded moments".

"Barker is adopted, I'm pushing buttons trying to get you the real mother's details, but the adoption service simply does not want to play ball with us, I've had problems with them before. They did say that her real mother and adoptive mother were dead, but I take that with a pinch of salt. They said her sister died when they were babies, and we know from Watson and Barker's original statement that that is possibly not the case. I'm after the documents for the dead child anyway, if I get them, I'll let you know. We have a missing flat mate in Dartmouth to think about too, Isabelle Fisher, I have sparing details, and of Phil Kendrick, a former partner".

Cross had felt a chill creeping over him as Carmel told him Barker's history and he could see the striking similarities between the early lives lived by Juliette Barker and Moira. Morrell didn't appear to have noticed, so he asked the obvious question. "Let me guess, we can't find him either?"

"No, but we do have a charge sheet. He was arrested for assault on Barker and charged. He got a slap, and they got back together and lived in the apartment that Fisher actually owned. Whether together with her or after Fisher vanished is unclear. Barker also reported a rape, when she was fifteen, a non-blood relative who, well you can guess. Add Robert Tambling to your list. I'm waiting for more details there.

"Are we suspecting Juliette Barker of killing upwards of three people, likely more?"

"We are and that's why we've got to find her. The other thing I need to mention, Dan Bush. I'm getting interference from our political masters".

"We expected that, American, rich. He'll have someone on the payroll, even if only at a low-level, someone keeping their eyes and ears open and Bush on speed-dial. Darren has been working on this with input from Crystal and Regis. I know she's the lead on the case now, but our priorities have shifted somewhat. To be honest I'd rather focus the whole team on Barker".

"No, keep both enquiries going and ask Darren to update me directly so I get anything before your routine updates get sent. The cold cases are so close to being wound-up, even if we can't nail Bush directly for his involvement in the deaths of Robbie Parkes and Steven Clement, we can make sure mud gets thrown in his direction, one way or another. You saw the lab report on the arrow?"

"I did, prints from Cox and Dylan Morgan were on it, you'd think it would have been wiped first. We both know what probably happened, I think we always did. Regis suggested that the arrow was kept as a keepsake, something defining closure after it killed the man who was responsible for Beth's death. We think Cox wanted us to find it, maybe out of guilt, or possibly so that we could just accept the facts and move on. Do we do anything with Cox now? We already have Morgan as the executioner".

"Leave that with me for now but I think so, the arrow is damning evidence to have in his possession, but you can't very well dig him up and charge him. Ultimately, it will be his reputation that gets a life sentence. I'll spin something".

"Madam Morrell, you sound more like Josh Hennigar every day".

"I'm glad you mentioned him, what do you know about something called 'Flap Canada'?"

"I know that F.L.A.P. stands for Flight Awareness Program, but I've not come across it or anyone in it in Nova Scotia, as far as I know. I can ask around. Why?"

"Just something we're watching. We wouldn't normally bother with legitimate groups, but there's been some chatter about Hennigar, and as our Environment Minister we have to make sure he stays in one piece".

"Really? I can't think of any birders or bird-related people who would get violent like that".

"Nobody would punch out a guy who shot rare birds then?"

"Clive is different, Cape Island is different, you know that but even Clive wouldn't attack a minister unless he suppressed a rarity on Cape Island".

Carmel rolled her eyes. "I don't think I'll ever get this bird thing at all. I like birds, but chasing after them just to see them, sorry, no".

"What does capture the imagination of Madam Carmel Morrell then?"

"Life, Howey".

"Most people fill their lives with something, birds are just one of those things. While you're here, I've been asked about the mount, the bird with the arrow, can it go to the museum? I know a curator of skins who would be beside himself to get it".

"I suppose, although what he'd do with it is beyond me. I saw the photos it's very tatty. Well, got to fly, lunch with the government and talking about funding- yippee. Get me Barker, Howey and do it quick".

"Ma'am".

Just as she got to the door Carmel turned to face Cross. "You do know that Regis worked out of Annapolis at one time, use him, local knowledge, he'll appreciate it if you do and Dr. Peck, that's a no, stick with Watson, hire him if you have to hire anyone".

Cross nodded. "I did know that fact about Regis and we are consulting freely. I trust Tina Peck more than I do Watson, but I respect your decision. Do enjoy your lunch, Ma'am".

Cross started to count to ten. At nine, a tap and a swinging door announced the presence of Leah Brown. "Madam looks well. How old would you say?" It wasn't a question that Howey had ever considered. Carmel had the same sort of fine complexion that both Crystal and Moira enjoyed. He didn't much fancy guessing at the age of any of the women in his life, they could be a bit funny about that sort of thing, especially if you got it badly wrong.

"How is brother Kent doing?" said Cross, moving the conversation in a different direction, "I miss him".

"You asked before, still fine, really enjoying being in Yarmouth County and learning lots. He said to remember him to you, if you asked".

"He's only seconded for six months, not banished. Tell him I want him back here after his stint in the south and not to go getting his head turned by the fleshpots of Yarmouth".

"I will, but go on Howey, how old do you think Madam is?"

Cross knew that Leah wouldn't leave it unless he had a guess. "I don't know, it takes a few years to get the top job and we don't think that she slept her way up the ladder, I'd say a conservative fifty?"

"Slept her way up the ladder? Really, this isn't a movie star we're talking about. She's fifty-four, Howey. She'll retire in eight to ten years; I heard her say it once. I'd say the job is between you and Crystal if you're both very good and keep your noses clean. Something to think about and if you do get it, you know I'm willing to come along for the ride, and a better salary".

Cross was surprised, more that someone else thought that a certain amount of career grooming was happening rather than at Madam's actual age. He thought for a moment and realised that he'd only ever seen Carmel as his boss at one time, the big boss of police and not a woman. A part of him also thought it wrong to think of a gay woman in the way a straight man might think about an attractive woman. It was wooly thinking, at best.

"You seem very well-informed about Carmel, do you have inside information, have you yourself dallied there? Now I'm getting an image".

"Never trod that line, Howey, but imagine away, it's good for a girl to know that a man she admires is thinking about her. As for Madam, I work with press releases, so I know lots of things about lots of people. It's the media and admin mafia, Howey, we know all your little secrets and what works for you. We probably know a lot more than you do about the very people you work with every day. Don't worry, we don't share unless asked something specific that won't upset anyone. Do you like Carmel?"

"Yes, I do, she's refreshing". He knew that it was an odd thing to say.

"Interesting, refreshing? It sounds to me like you are a bit wary of her. You know you've looked very tense recently, Howey. I'd be happy to rub your shoulders for you, you know that, and if you wanted a happy ending, you'd only have to say".

At one time, Cross might have stammered a weak retort, but he'd got the measure of Leah and her suggestive humour, so he just smiled and ordered Leah back to work and to keep her hands where everyone could see them. She liked the joke.

"How's it looking over there? They were pretty quick". Moira was asking the obvious question of Crystal; she could easily see that the house had arrived, the workmen were all over it like wasps on candy.

"It's going. They reckon it'll be a few weeks yet. It helps to have contacts in the trade, also known as Daddy, and I was lucky in getting that cancelled place, it was just what I was looking for".

"I hope you don't think I'm being rude, but I was going to plant a shelter belt between us to give both of us some privacy. I don't know if Howey mentioned it, but I like to wander the farm in the buff on fine days, I find it liberating".

Crystal laughed. Howey hadn't mentioned it, but she could well believe that Moira would think nothing of dropping her kit and getting stuck into feeding the pigs. "What does he say, when he comes home and there you are in all your glory?"

"Nothing much now, but when it first happened, I thought I might need to put something in his tea".

"Poor Howey, I don't think he anticipated his life being so full of surprises. I know he loves it; he says so at work. Never a dull moment, which is nice because work often isn't very pleasant".

"He's been a bit preoccupied recently, is it just being Staff Sergeant or is something about that case bothering him?"

"Sorry, Moira, not talking shop, I prefer the horrors of work to stay there".

"So, there are horrors at the moment, interesting. What time are your builders packing up?"

"Early, they have to go to another property until the electricians have been in, why?"

"Want to help me feed the pigs?"

Crystal wasn't sure that Moira was being serious, but she had that look that said 'well'?

"You mean strip off and wander around with you, in the nip?"

"Yes, I'm going to. It's a warm day, the bugs aren't a problem and, like I said, I find it very liberating".

While Crystal didn't consider herself shy, it's no good being a shy looker in the police, she wasn't feeling too confident either. Moira shrugged and started to divest herself of her garments as Crystal watched. When she was bare, she asked, "how do I look?" and then just headed outside into the pleasant breeze. For a moment Crystal hesitated, then followed suit.

It was an odd feeling, but Moira had been right. It did feel liberating and being naked, with Moira, was only like being in the girl's changing rooms, right? After about half an hour, and with the pigs fed, Moira fetched drinks and they sat chatting on the bench by the front door.

"Ok?" asked Moira laying back and enjoying the sun.

"Yes, actually. I'm not sure how I'd be if Howey showed up though".

"He'd be cool with it, see it as a joke. I'm sure he'd enjoy the view too; I know I have".

"You know I'm not bi or anything, don't you Moira?"

"I know, but that doesn't mean I can't admire your body, feel free to admire mine, we're the pinnacle of female perfection", and she laughed. Crystal joined in but was getting fidgety.

"So, are we going to surprise Howey when he gets here? I dare you", said Moira, looking at Crystal with a sly grin.

"Ok, yes, we're friends as well as colleagues and it'll be a joke and he won't talk about at work, will he? he'll just laugh".

"Laugh and look, expect him to have a good look. I find it especially interesting to see you like this because it was nearly you, rather than me, remember".

"I was never in it once he'd met you, I told you. I was too late, and Howey didn't see me as attainable. That was my fault, I'd got a reputation for being a bit blunt with men who tried it on. Howey never did, never even flirted. Perhaps if he'd seen me like this, he might have got the hint, but it would have caused a riot in the cafeteria".

Moira laughed. Crystal the ice queen was thawing nicely.

"I like you Crystal, I like that Howey likes you and that you're fitting in so well with us, like Hinzi and Darren and hopefully Terence, if he's the one".

"Has Howey seen Hinzi naked, does she do the same when she's here?"

"No, but we did do a little trick on him once", and Moira told Crystal all about the nude apron and the pink clothes and how Howey had become flustered. She didn't tell Crystal that Hinzi didn't wander around in the buff in front of anyone but Darren.

"Right, I see. Er, Howey, when's he back?"

"In about four minutes".

Crystal shrieked and streaked for the outbuilding, grabbing a pair of old dungarees off a nail and doing her best to cover up, despite several missing buttons and a back pocket. Moira followed her as Howey arrived.

The drive home wasn't normally very stressful, but Howey Cross found himself getting irrationally angry at a truck that slowed for every single bump in the road. 'What's the point of owning one of them if you can't drive the damn thing?' he yelled to nobody.

Stopping at the first gate, he pressed his transponder, he could see the tip of Crystal's house easily. After all had been agreed, he had a slightly nagging feeling that perhaps some distance would have been better. It was as if he had a nice blanket that he sat on with Moira and the kids but now they'd all have to move over and let someone else sit on the corner. He knew that it was all a part of his anxiety and the stress of the Barker case. It was stopping him sleeping some nights.

The track felt smoother than normal, which was odd as he'd not graded it for a while, and they'd had some rainy spells. He got out of the car just as Moira wandered past the pig shed, naked and with a bucket. He laughed. It was a nice day, why not? Skipping inside, he divested himself of his clothes and went to join her. As he walked towards the outbuilding by the pig shed, Moira came out laughing and dressed in dungarees, followed by Crystal, similarly attired. They both started giggling.

Howey felt the anger rise in his chest but reined it in and just walked past the girls and into the pig shed, saying 'ladies' and nodding as he went. Moira immediately saw that the joke had backfired. She had intended that they all stand there naked and slightly embarrassed, but Crystal had lost her nerve at the last minute, hence the dungarees. Crystal fled to the house to get back into her day wear, Moira followed Howey into the pig shed.

"Sorry, it was just a joke. Me being me, I'm afraid". Howey had found another pair of overalls and was covered up.

"No, no problem, a joke, I get it. It's just that I'm Crystal's boss now, and, well, I have nothing to hide. It undermines me, sometimes you need to think of the bigger picture a bit. It's not just us anymore".

So that was it, Crystal had invaded their space despite being invited to do so. Moira apologised again and they went back to the house in time to see Crystal walking back down the lane to her car and future home.

"If it's any consolation, like I said, we were all supposed to be naked, but Crystal's nerve went. Bad joke, bad me, I'm really sorry".

"Forget it, I have work to do, shout me when supper is ready", and Howey went into the office, closing the door. A noise from the terrors' room announced the end of nap time, so Moira set about feeding the family. Supper was a solemn affair. The terrors saw that something wasn't quite right and behaved, even Vinnie understood that daddy wasn't very happy. Once the eating had finished, Moira bathed the kids and put them to bed. Downstairs, Howey industrially cleaned the kitchen.

"This is something more than just a prank, come on Howey, we talk, remember?"

"I can't talk about this; it's work and don't want you involved". It was blunter than he'd intended, but the message was the same.

"I understand, I just want to help, if I can, but I'm guided by you. Crystal won't tell anyone or even mention it, I'm sure. I think she understood your anger, I know I do".

"Do you though, Moira? Sometimes I worry, but I carry it because that's what men do. I can't always lark about; I can't look at the funny side. I have to get on with it and I have to make sure the likes of Crystal and Darren can go home at the end of their shift and put things out of their mind, but I can't. It's always there, always. Then I come home, and I'm ridiculed. Any credibility I might have had has gone because you thought it would be funny. And what if Crystal had been naked too, what then? Do we form a menage a trois just to play out your fantasies? I've got more work to do", and he got up and went back to the office.

Moira was dumbstruck. They'd had minor tiffs before, but this was serious, this was her life and happiness being damaged and for what, a prank and not even an original one. The temptation to seek solace with something that would take off the edge was overwhelming. She grabbed the bottle of white from the fridge, the one she'd been planning to serve with supper, then reached for the glasses, taking two instinctively. The sound of the bottle and the glasses hitting the stone kitchen floor had Howey out in a second. He bodily lifted Moira and took her into the other room, before going back and cleaning up.

When he was happy that no glass remained, glass that could slash a toddler's foot or dog's pad, he went back to deal with Moira. She hadn't moved.

"Butterfingers", he said.

"No, not paying attention. I was going to pour two glasses then it struck me that you didn't want to be with me anymore and I can't even think about that".

"Good, because that is not the case. I told you; I'm carrying something at work and I'm finding it claustrophobic. It's not you, nor your prank. It's me, I feel like I might snap some days".

"Talk to me then, share the load, you know I can handle it".

"No, Moira, you can't, not this. Can we just make up and get back to where we were before?"

"Okay", said Moira in a small and insecure voice. They went to bed and tried to shut the door on the black cloud that was following Howey Cross around, but Moira could feel it seeping around the edges, finding a way in.

The next morning Howey was out early, before dawn. He did that sometimes, when he wanted to get on top of things before the troops showed up. Moira worked hard on convincing herself that things would be ok, that they'd talk it through later. A knock on the door came from Crystal, she looked worried.

"Come in, he's gone in already, do you have time to chat? I could really do with someone to talk to right now". Over coffee, Moira told Crystal about Howey and his heavy load speech. Crystal listened, all the while weighing up how much to say. Howey hadn't told them to not discuss the Barker case specifically with Moira, but she also knew the history of his fears, over whether Moira might be troubled, might become like Juliette Barker. That was why Howey had asked her to run the rule over Moira during the Martin Perry case and then as now she'd seen nothing but eccentricity. In the end she decided to tell Moira a few unsavoury case details, it was the only way to head trouble off before it had the chance to take root. Moira was crying by the time Crystal had covered everything. Through her snivels, she thanked Crystal for being so honest with her, and told her that she'd not pass on anything to Howey. Then she hugged her with such intensity that it was palpable. Crystal responded, hugging back and telling Moira it would be fine, she hoped she was right.

When Howey got home, Moira was on the front deck with the kids, they were making a wicker basket out of grass. Phoebe checked with her mom, before leaving the work detail and greeting Daddy. Any atmosphere hoping to get a foothold had been dissipated by the attentions of a small child. He joined them on the deck, Phoebe showing him how to weave while Vinny just got on with the job in hand.

"Good day?" asked Moira.

"Yes, a good day. You?"

"We've all been very busy. Supper is cooking, I thought something Thai as I'm still planning our next family extravaganza but with options, vacations, time and workload permitting. Is that ok?"

"Sounds intriguing, you can tell me more when the child labourers have hit their respective pillows. I want to have a talk later anyway, it's time we did". On seeing the look of barely disguised panic on Moira's face, he continued. "I want to share some of my heavy load, I've been thinking about it all day. You're right, we share, we talk". Raw relief flowed through Moira, and she involuntarily started to sing. It was a French language nursery rhyme and Howey watched amazed as the bilingual trio set about harmonies.

Supper was a lot jollier, before eyelids drooped, and their pits called in the terrors.

A glass each was waiting when Howey got back so he settled in to taste it and wonder where, exactly, he should start. "Your Histrionic Personality Disorder, you once showed me a bottle of pills and said you'd taken steps. I've never asked since your diagnosis, but do you still take the same dose, has the doctor increased or decreased it?"

Moira thought for a second, then went into their bathroom. Moments later she was back with a small pill bottle labelled 'Buspirone', which she handed Howey. "Count them", she said.

He examined the bottle, contents thirty pills, one to be taken as and when required. He counted out twenty-nine. He examined the bottle more closely. The expiry date was November 2020. "This is the same bottle?"

"Yes, I tried one, but it wasn't for me. I was going to tell you earlier, but you never asked. I've never felt the need for a pill, not since we got together. The closest was probably last night, and even then, I resisted. I refuse to be a slave to medication".

"What did the one pill do?"

"Made me drowsy, not with it and I need to be with it. My mind didn't shut off either, which is what I expected. I didn't want you dating a cabbage, I had to be the real me if we were going to work".

"How did you deal with anxiety? Did you see things, or think you did, was there any lost time?"

"I didn't take them long enough to find out, but I looked them up like you have already. I decided to self-medicate by diversion therapy. You and birds are my diversion, and now the terrors too. It worked and the only time I've been really anxious was when I thought you'd had enough of me. It's always been my greatest fear".

Cross took a slow sip of wine and told Moira all about Juliette Barker and his fears. He didn't say he'd asked Crystal's advice, but he knew that Moira would easily join up the dots. At times during the story, Moira gasped as she saw herself in Juliette's shoes. She knew how fine the line was between eccentricity and lunacy.

"What made you want to tell me now?" asked Moira, her breathing shallow, expecting a twist.

"I needed to share the load or explode. I needed to know that you were ok. The prank just got to me. Crystal apologised again and we joked about how cold the wind was, that sort of thing. I've been feeling a bit resentful about her being next door too, irrational though it may seem. I think we need to maybe plant some trees to give us back our privacy. I already said for her to call first and not just wander over, then I thought more about it and told her to ignore me. I still want for us to be able to wander around naked if we want to though, I want to keep the spontaneity. Am I being selfish?"

Moira reached for her laptop and showed Howey the order for forty, three metre tall Black Spruces. "And with the small cones they might attract White-winged Crossbills when they wander our way. This size are a bit expensive to buy and plant but worth it, yes?"

Howey looked at the order, arriving in six weeks and including installation. He felt tears start to well up. His nutjob partner was no Juliette Barker after all.

"I think you should look for another diagnosis, or at least have the original HPD confirmed. I don't think you're HPD, you clearly don't. I hinted to Tina that you might talk to her, will you?"

"You spoke to Tina about Barker's HPD and thought of me? Now I can see why you were so wound up. How do you know that I haven't already talked to her?"

It was an unexpected answer, Cross was happy with it and left the conversation open-ended. "What now?" he asked.

"You trust me".

CHAPTER ELEVEN

August 2022

When Moira had arranged for Hinzi to babysit while she went to do interviews for the management of The Orchard, she hadn't bargained for Phoebe insisting that she wanted to go with her and then Vinnie insisting that he didn't. She was almost there when she realised that this was the first time that the twins had ever been apart, actually apart, it made her nervous for them. "Are you ok, Phoebe?"

"Fine. Why are you sad?"

Sad? Moira hadn't realised that she was radiating sadness, but her little girl had seen it. "This place, The Orchard, it has a place in my life, a place I'll tell you about sometime. My friend started it but she's dead now, you remember I told you people die?"

"Yes. We're organic, it happens".

Organic? Where had she got that from?

"Why is Aunt Hinzi different?"

At first Moira wasn't sure how to answer, then she realised that Phoebe was picking up on her mixed-race parentage. "Her mom and dad are from different parts of the world; she is made up of those different parts. Long ago we all came from one place, deep within Africa. Remember, I showed you Africa on the globe?"

"Yes, why aren't we all black people then?"

"We evolved to fit our climate over millions of years, we don't need our skin to be black in the northern hemisphere. I could tell you all about the genetics of the thing, but you're not supposed to be ready for that yet".

"Ok, tell me another time. When Aunt Angela leaves us, she won't come back will she?"

"I don't think so, will you miss her?"

"Yes, but we can Facetime".

Moira shook her head. When she got pregnant, she hoped all would go well, and it did. Then, after the birth and the buckets of blood episode, she hoped that the kids would be normal, and they were. She also hoped that her kids would take the good bits of both parents and be better than the sum of their parts, and they seemed to be. She was sure that there had to be a lump in the road somewhere, and that that lump might be having a daughter just like her. She pulled into The Orchard and looked at it for a moment. "Don't worry, I'm here", said Phoebe. Moira felt emotional. Memories of Justice and some of the other people who passed through The Orchard flashed through her mind. Back then she was a human pinball, pinging from place to place. Had anyone told her where she'd be in a few years' time, would she have believed them? Probably not.

Angela was ready, as she always was, and the list of candidates had been boiled down by her to three, with Moira sitting in on the final round of interviews. She'd have been happy to leave it all to Angela, but she'd said she wanted Moira there and that was that. Eastbeach was pretty much as she remembered it, although there appeared to be half a dozen new builds where a nice, wild tangle had once lived. The Orchard looked clean, kept, and efficient, as she knew it would be. Angela was very organised and Moira thought her slightly schoolmarmish, although definitely not like Miss Noble, her old teacher and, later, friend. Not at all.

"Moira, you're here. I see Phoebe is joining the family firm, is everyone else well?" Angela was always to the point.

"Yes, very well, Howey sends his love and told me to tell you to be careful on your travels".

"Does he think we might get savaged by sheep or something, it's New Zealand we're visiting, not the back streets of Sao Paolo. Right, you've only read the CVs, but I felt you ought to be here, especially as whoever takes over will need to deal with the transfer and with you directly. Ready?"

"I'm ready, but you never gave me the names as I asked for when you brought their anonymous CVs over, what are you up to, Angela?"

"Names are unimportant, and I might have missed the odd CV too, we had a few more possibles that didn't feel right enough to bother you with. Whoever we choose, has to be the right fit and homing in on people's pasts isn't always a good indicator of who they are. Come on, they'll be here in half an hour, and I want more news about your Brazil trip and whether my little brother behaved himself".

"He did, he loved it. Now, give me a quick tour so I can see all the changes you've made but not told me about and we'll chat as we go". It was a jokey aside, but Moira knew there would be some changes because when Angela took on a project, it got Angela'd.

"And you, Phoebe, I want your opinion too", said Angela making sure she didn't sound like she was addressing a child.

"I like it", said Phoebe, still taking in the surroundings. Moira had been telling Phoebe all about The Orchard on the way over, leaving out the bits that she thought perhaps a bit adult for her, but Phoebe had understood the place right from the start and, even for Moira, sometimes her daughter's perception was a bit unnerving.

The interviews were to take place in one of the rooms they used for group therapy sessions, Moira looked around as she entered, the sights and smells coming back to her. The wall had new art, no doubt the work of guests who were encouraged to express themselves. One painting had a lot of anger about it, anger against men, maybe just one or maybe all of them, it wasn't clear. Naturally it was the one Phoebe gravitated to and looked at for some time.

"Are you ok, Phoebe?" asked Moira, she could see her daughter was thinking.

"Yes, this one speaks to us though, I do hope Dilys is alright". Moira looked closely, in one corner was the name Dilys in tiny strokes, in taking in the whole of the painting, the anger of it, she'd missed the most important part.

Chairs had been arranged so that Moira and Angela could sit together, close enough to read any notes, while the candidates used a sofa, a spot chosen to make them not feel isolated sitting on a lone chair. Moira never questioned the presence of a small chair for Phoebe, she hadn't asked for one though, she hadn't known until she was about to set out that Phoebe would be with her.

"Are we going to discuss the applicants first?" asked Moira, feeling a little in the dark.

"No, best not to have any preconceived ideas. Here's a pad for notes, I listed each candidate and left room for you to write".

The sheets were neatly laid out and the candidates were named; they were Tinkerbell, Daphne and Buffy. Moira understood, anonymity was a cornerstone of The Orchard and very few of the girls that passed through chose to use their given name. She herself had been Jezebel, someone from another time, another persona, almost.

Moira fidgeted a bit. "Sorry, before we start, I need to pee, oh and there was a bag that I gave you to carry The Orchard documents in, the one I had back when you visited us one time. Old, leather. It once belonged to Justice, but she gave it to me. I always intended to take it back with me the next time I came over, can you dig it out for me, please?

"No, sorry, it got purloined a while back, I meant to say. We had a girl here who got very attached to it, so I let her use it, day to day, on the understanding that it was a loan. Then, when she left, so did the bag. I'm so sorry Moira. I did put the word out that I wanted it back but, so far, no sign".

"Oh, ok. Not to worry. I think the bag has lived a long and interesting life. It used to belong to Constance Smith, the former owner of this place, before it became The Orchard. Perhaps it had its time with me and now it's gone back out into the world for new adventures".

"Moira, it was only a bag, they don't have adventures, they have uses, I really don't think they have personalities. If they did, the rehab clinics would be full of them". Moira laughed, it was very down-to-earth of Angela to view bags that way but, to her mind, each and every bag out there had a story to tell, no matter how small. "Hang on, I think I have a photo", and Angela dashed off to her office, which was really just a sitting room with a desk and a locked filing cabinet. Moments later she was back. "That's your old bag I believe".

It was, but Moira was more interested in the person holding it. There was something about her eyes that made her skin creep. "Yes, that's it, who is that holding it?'.

Angela neatly sidestepped the question. "I'll keep trying and perhaps she'll come back when passing this way again, unlikely, but some do like to keep in touch. If she does, I can ask her for the bag back, good enough?" It was, she supposed, but Moira took another look at the troubled face of the girl, before handing the photo back.

So far, none of the current residents had appeared around the place, but that wasn't really a surprise, The Orchard was all about people not being bothered by things from the outside and having space to do what they needed to. Moira went to the bathroom, then nipped to the kitchen to fetch Phoebe a drink. At the table, a wiry, dark-haired girl sat reading. It was an old book with tattered bindings and Moira recognised it instantly, it had once been hers and was one of the things she'd left behind the day she saw Justice Mellor for the last time. Wherever she'd been and in whatever persona, Moira had always left something behind so people knew she'd been there, a sort of Magowan Inuksuk. The girl looked up and smiled.

For some reason Moira felt a shudder again, but she reined it in. "Hello, I'm Moira, real name".

"Hello", said the dark-haired girl quietly. "I'm Melissa", and she cocked her head as if to say, 'you decide'.

"I see you're reading 'The Other Me'. I know that book well, it was a part of my life at one time".

"Yes, it's fascinating. I admire the author's journey, someone who had to look very hard to find out who they really were, it keeps you wanting to know more. I've already read it twice; I get almost to the end then put it down. I think she deserved to be happier, so I re-write them in my head. I like my endings better".

"Me too, that's what I used to do. I always thought that the heroine didn't look for long enough, she just gave up in the end and settled for something almost, but not quite right. Sorry, I didn't mean to spoil it for you".

"You didn't, like I said, I already know how it all ends, my version at least".

The way Melissa had said 'how it all ends' had Moira feeling even more disconcerted, almost threatened. There was something about this Melissa that heightened her awareness. "Sorry to have disturbed you, I have to get back to my meeting", she blurted.

"You're Moira Magowan, right? Angela said you'd be coming over; sorry I should have realised. This place is great, I can almost be me here and not worry about the outside world banging on my door again. I hope you found what you were looking for, have a good meeting", and with that the strange dark-haired girl went back to reading her book, Moira's book, as if Moira herself hadn't been there at all.

When Moira got back to the meeting room, the first candidate had just arrived. "Imelda?"

Imelda Smith looked a bit different since last Moira had seen her. It was almost as if her annoying little 'all about me' edges had been neatly sandpapered off. "Moira, I hoped you'd be here for this, how are you?" and Imelda hugged Moira and held her close, very close. When they separated, Moira almost expected to be kissed, but Imelda then turned her attention to Phoebe and made a fuss of her, using that baby voice that some people think is appropriate. Phoebe let Imelda get on with it, but the look she gave her mom almost made Moira laugh out loud.

"Right, enough catching up for now. Imelda, please sit. Moira, shall we?" said Angela, keen to get down to business.

Each candidate was to be given a flexible thirty minutes to make their case and field questions. At the end they were to leave before the next candidate arrived. Imelda started her pitch and Moira listened to the details. It only took her ten minutes to say what she wanted to say and ask what she wanted to ask. Her application seemed to be predicated on two things. One was availability, she lived locally, and the other was a claimed repentance at her behaviour during the whole 'sea glass' affair as it became known, where local councilors had been bought by developers wanting to destroy Eastbeach and its Piping Plovers, and she'd been one of them.

When she'd gone, Moira asked Angela, "Buffy?"

"Yes, how did you guess?"

"She was always of the opinion that she was the pretty one who fought the bad guys. I have to say, Imelda is a no. I don't trust her at all".

"I agree, she does have some positives, but not enough to trust her not to steal the fixtures and fittings. Her CV was good though. Next?"

"Yes. How many girls are here at the moment?"

"Just one, but we have three coming tomorrow. Last week we had four, but three decided to move on".

"Did that coincide with the current girl arriving at all?"

"No, Melissa has been here a while, on and off. She's quite complicated, we've had people in to help her, at her request".

"Is it working?"

"Even though it's you, Moira, client confidentiality applies, I'm sure you understand?"

"Sorry, yes, I do. Who's next?"

Daphne didn't use a pseudonym. She was bright, business-like but there was something hiding behind her slightly tired eyes that said she got it, all of it. She asked the right questions and gave the right answers, but it was very rehearsed, not spontaneous and Moira didn't get the right vibe, listing her only as a maybe. Angela said nothing. Because the next applicant had arrived a little early, they ushered Daphne out the back door to avoid them meeting, Moira showing her the way.

Moira walked back through the kitchen to the meeting room, on the table was her old book and a note saying she should take it back, it belonged to her. Pausing for only a millisecond, she folded the note and put it inside the book before carrying it back to the meeting room and the last interviewee. She wasn't concentrating on anything but the book when she walked in. "Moira?" Stopping dead, Moira realised who the voice had come from. The last applicant, Tinkerbell, was Genevieve Mason.

Moira smiled and gave Genevieve a guarded hug. Why had Angela even considered Mason? She knew that Moira had evicted her from the stables and that Mason leant so far right that she could touch the floor with her ear. There must be something she didn't know. Genevieve Mason was clearly as surprised as she was. Moira looked at her with her questing eye, Genevieve was different somehow.

"Before we start, Genevieve, I might recuse myself from the process. My evicting you from the stables could prejudice both of us from making a rational decision", said Moira, pleased at how she'd recovered her composure.

"You will not, do you think Tinkerbell is here for fun?" Angela exclaimed. "She's a genuine candidate, I know, I went through them all. Now Moira, Genevieve, there's history between you, either make up now or we can't do this, and I really think we should. I need a pee myself now, so you've got as long as that takes to clear the air", and Angela left them, and Phoebe, to it.

Moira decided to grab the high ground. "Whatever else happens here, Genevieve, I was right to move you on. We couldn't coexist and I don't want to come over all bossy, but I gave you the chances and you didn't take any of them". It was a good statement of intent and Mason could make of it what she wanted.

"Oh, Moira, I know. It was such a personal disaster for me when it happened, but it brought things into sharp focus for me too, things I'd papered over because that is the sort of thing that we Christies do. Christie is my family name; I use it now. I'm no longer a Mason, or at least I won't be once the legal process is finished. Come closer, I want to show you something".

Moira walked over to Genevieve and stood, very close. She realised that she was trying to intimidate her, but Genevieve didn't seem to notice, she just undid her jacket, pulled up her blouse and exposed her bra-less breasts. She had a long scar just below the neckline, a slash. Instinctively Moira reached over and traced it with her finger. "It's real and not the only one. After the stables went, Stephen got worse and I left him, something I should have done long ago. I came here for a while, and it helped me get myself together. I went back to my family, who I'd alienated through my stupidity and my brother stepped in to help with everything. I live in Eastbeach now, I've met someone kind and caring. You sending us packing was the catalyst for that change. Cards on the table, I can be a snooty cow at the best of times but as for the rest of it, I'm not dancing to anyone else's tune now, Genevieve has left the cult".

Moira didn't know what to say, she was shocked. How had she not seen what was just below the surface? Her gift had always been totally reliable, she saw things other people didn't, so how had she missed this?

"She showed you then, nasty business, nasty man. Tinkerbell, put those titties away now please and can we get on?" Angela had swept into the room and, in her usual way, had taken control of the situation. Genevieve lowered her top and Moira hugged her properly. "Do you need a room, you two?" asked Angela, half-joking.

They simultaneously broke the hug. "No, let's get on", said Moira, her head yelling at her, just like it used to.

An hour later Tinkerbell had gone, and the three of them were sitting in the kitchen sipping coffee or juice, according to age and suitability. "That was why I left the names off. I see you're still shaken. I'm sorry about that but I didn't want preconceived ideas, deliberate or not. I think Genevieve is what we're looking for. I agree that Imelda is a chancer, out for herself. Daphne is a survivor, and also very good, but not the one. Think about it, tell me what you've decided tomorrow". At that point Melissa walked in.

Before Angela could do an introduction, Melissa had gone over to Phoebe and was talking to her, not as a child but as an adult. Moira's instinct was to attack, but she didn't know why, instead she picked Phoebe up and gathered up her possessions, including her old book. "Sorry, I have places to be. Nice to meet you, Melissa. Angela, I'll call tomorrow, now if you'll excuse me", and she hurried quickly out the Orchard, into the Grand Caravan and away.

After a bit of distance, the monotony of the highway allowed her time to think, Moira ran things back, focusing on the bits that had troubled her. It wasn't just that she'd missed Genevieve being under the heel of her man that bothered her, she felt unsettled. "Mom, it's ok", said a concerned voice from the child seat.

"Yes, it is, Phoebe, but I have things to consider What did you think of The Orchard?"

"I liked it, I don't think I understand it though, not yet. Tell me when I'm older".

"I will, you know that, and you're right, it is complicated. Who do you think should take care of it?"

"The most deserving of a second chance".

The following day, once Howey had gone to work and the terrors had been sorted, Moira called Angela. "It's me, Tinkerbell deserves the opportunity, you were right".

"I know, but I can be a bit bossy sometimes and I see you all over The Orchard, it needed you to decide too. Good news, your bag appeared".

Moira was about to tut at the suggestion that Angela could be bossy, but the news about her bag completely threw her. "How?" was all she managed to get out.

"I put a note on the general board and Melissa knew the girl who'd borrowed it. She said she made a call, and it was left on the doorstep this morning. I'll get it back to you before we go".

"Er, great, but please don't send Melissa with it". Moira was as surprised as Angela was that that had been said out loud.

"No, I hadn't intended to, besides, she went this morning and said she doesn't expect to be back. She did pass on her best wishes to you and Howey though".

"Howey? Did you tell her about him?"

Angela must have sensed something in Moira's voice because she'd adopted a concerned tone. "Actually, no I don't think I did".

"I see, perhaps she saw it on-line or something, maybe through the birding world, nothing to worry about I'm sure". Moira was forcing calmness out and only missing by quite a bit.

"Moira, I wouldn't normally do this but I'm going to email over a photo of Melissa which I'd like you to pass on to Howey. I know it's not what we do, but since we make up the rules, this time we will".

"So, you felt it too, that sense of foreboding she gave off?"

"No, nothing quite so specific, I just want to make sure that her problems do not include you. I said she had specialist treatment, it was for HPD, I think you need to know that, Moira?"

"Yes, sorry, I'm aware of HPD. Look, I'm sure nothing is amiss, she was just one of those disconcerting people you meet from time to time. She could have found out about Howey any number of ways, I think I over-reacted but do send the photo over, please".

"I will, I said so, now I have to get on, Tinkerbell is due in five, talk later, there's things I need to tell you", and the phone went dead.

Tinkerbell due in five, so Angela had already offered Genevieve the post. Then there was the mystery of things to be told, Angela rarely waited like that. There was a tap on the door that made Moira jump. "Only me!" It was Crystal.

"Come in, no need to knock", said Moira, trying to pull herself together, and failing.

"Are you ok, you look like you've seen a ghost?"

"I'm fine, I just didn't join up a few dots on something. Not working today?"

"In later, it might be a long day for Howey, we've got people to see".

"He said".

"Are you sure you're ok?"

"Yes, I just want to check my email, I might have something of interest for you, but I don't know how", and she explained her discomfort with the girl at The Orchard. When it came it through, it wasn't a great photo and Moira struggled to match up the image to the woman called Melissa. She did a print off and wrote 'Melissa, real name' on the back. Crystal promised to make Howey aware of things and said he'd call if he had any questions.

In the late afternoon Angela was as good as her word and called back. She told Moira what was planned, and she told Moira to pick her time to tell him all about it and all would be well. "Trust me".

CHAPTER TWELVE

It was late May 2022 when George Berry caught a glimpse of a bird out back of his house, just a glimpse and he wasn't sure what it was. Hermit Thrush was the default yard migrant, but they all seemed to have moved through already this spring. He'd never had one of the 'good' thrushes in his yard, he'd not even seen a Grey-cheeked Thrush since he'd moved to Queens County two years previously.

"You look busy", said Mildred, his wife.

"A bird in the yard, didn't see much of it".

"Brown, smaller than a robin? I saw it yesterday; it's coming for the newly emerged bugs I think". Mildred, while not a birder of any sort, had sharp eyes and ears and often saw things well before George got onto them.

"Right, that's me for the next hour then. If anyone wants me, I'm going to sit in the shed with the door open". George Berry didn't really regard himself as a birder either, just someone who was interested in birds, particularly as subjects for his paintbrush.

The shed was full of yard furniture, a barbeque, a couple of bikes and various other assorted items you'd expect to find in any Canadian's shed. Behind it sat a Motus tower that students had installed before they'd even bought the property. As things went, it was one of the quieter towers and they didn't come to do the download that often. It had picked up a few shorebirds, but George was only an infrequent visitor to the website that showed the towers, and what they'd recorded. Queens county was a birding backwater as far as he could tell, and he often wished they'd bought the place in Yarmouth instead. What Queens did have was a decent artist community, and that was his real passion, art.

By fifty minutes, George was subconsciously counting the hour down. True, he was keen on his yard list, but he'd already had several Hermit Thrushes so far and he was starting to convince himself that what he saw was just a dull looking one. Then a movement amongst the shrubs caught his eye and the interesting thrush was back and feeding. George set about making sketches that he'd work up into a few rough pieces before doing a single illustration. The fresh green of the shrubs it fed under made a nice contrast on what was a subtly coloured thrush. It struck him that the absence of true rufous anywhere meant that his bird was likely not a Hermit Thrush at all, so it was probably one of the more glamorous ones.

Presently, the thrush slipped away and, despite some effort to see it on subsequent days, it didn't reappear and had likely gone. On his drawing board, the thrush took on a new life as George worked hard at his artwork getting the plumage details and shades just right. It took nearly a week until he was happy with it, but he was still yet to identify it. On seeing the bird, the artist in him had taken over and he'd been preoccupied by it. It never occurred to him to use the bridge camera on it, the one kept by the window that Mildred used to snap feeder birds to post on Facebook.

"Finished?" asked Mildred, bringing George a coffee.

"I think so, it's as close to the real thing as I can get it".

"Mildred went and fetched her tablet and opened her bird files. She then opened an image and placed it alongside George's artwork. "Pretty good I'd say", she said.

"You had a photo all this time?"

"Yes, I told you I saw it. I didn't want to show you the photo until you'd finished, you always work best from your field sketches, a photo might have muddied the artistic waters".

George shrugged, Mildred was a devil for doing that sort of thing, it was one of the things that made life with her so much fun.

"Are you going to post that on Facebook?" she asked.

"What? No, but I might put it on my artist site. It will get a few likes before being buried by some terrible crayon sketch of a cat or something".

"You should say when they're rubbish, people should have a more critical eye instead of hitting like for something drawn by someone with the artistic skills of a lemon". Mildred often scoffed at some of the dire on-line attempts at art by people with zero skill or talent.

"No", said George, "we don't do that, we encourage and then, later, the warders come and escort the poster back to their padded cell. You should post your photo though; I'd be interested in what the bird experts think".

"I'm not posting it without an identification, I don't want us to be seen as needy and lazy, people who couldn't even look in a book when I did look in Sibley. The nearest I could get was Bicknell's Thrush, but if I post that they'll laugh at us, they're rare here, only found in the north".

"Don't they have wings though, or do they walk north in spring and south in the fall?"

"All the same, George, this is Queens and I checked eBird, we've never had one here. Besides, this is old news now, it was in May, and you know how people are, they'll ask why we left it so late".

"Never too late is my motto. I'll post it on our account, and I'll say we think it's a Bicknell's, shall I? That way the experts can chip in if they feel confident enough. Lots of people who have no idea will like it anyway and who knows, we even might get another tick for our precious yard list, it can't do any harm this long after the fact". Mildred agreed, as George knew she would. He also knew that she'd been deliberately provoking him to grab the Bicknell's nettle. "I'll even add my artwork, but only in the comments, it is a bird site and not a 'look at me, aren't I talented' site, after all".

It didn't take long after posting to get three different comments effectively rubbishing the Bicknell's identification. George and Mildred weren't too disappointed, although a couple of comments might have drawn a sharp retort from some, would the page admins allow it. A few days later a truck arrived, and young people started to do things in their yard. "The Motus people are here doing their download, George, do you want to say hello?" Mildred was looking around the curtain, trying to see but not wanting to appear to be nosey.

"No, let them get on with it, it shouldn't take long. I wouldn't be surprised if they move the tower, the last time I looked they only had half a dozen pings from it". The lightest of taps on their front door got their attention, Mildred went over to see who it was.

"Hi Mildred, do you think I could use your facilities? One too many Tim's coffees I'm afraid". It was Lisa Goddard, one of the Motus people.

"Of course, come in, anytime", and she waited while Lisa kicked off her shoes before walking through to their powder room. George had been hovering, quite keen to ask whether there had been much activity, now that his asking wouldn't disturb them.

Lisa emerged looking less flustered and made for her shoes. "Sorry again to disturb you. Hi George, how are you?"

"Fine, thanks Lisa. Much to download?"

"Yes, quite a bit this time. Ooh, that's nice, I do love your artwork, George, is this the one you put up on Facebook?" asked Lisa on seeing the framed painting hanging on the living room wall.

"Yes, the famous thrush".

"It's much better in real life, and it looked exactly like this? Sorry, silly question, of course it did".

George was quite pleased at the compliment and fetched his sketch book, showing Lisa his field work.

"Very nice, George, you're wasted with website design. You really should be illustrating the next field guide, at least do a plate of common fruit flies for us, I've seen your photos on iNaturalist and the artwork on your website, stunning. Do you still think it was a Bicknell's?"

"I don't know, I've never seen one and I've not seen many Grey-cheeked either. People on Facebook certainly seem reluctant to agree with us, or even offer an alternative".

"Yep, that's social media for you, a legion of keyboard warriors hiding in a basement somewhere. Notice none of the big names chipped in, not wanting any egg on their faces if they got it wrong. Did you eBird it?"

"Not yet, we were just talking about it. I suppose I should have done so at the time".

"You should, the reviewers don't bite, and they would have a careful look at it, anyway. Sorry, got to go, three more towers to visit before dark. Thanks for the use of the facilities, take care you two", and Lisa hurried off to join her colleague who was putting the last of their gear back in the truck.

Before the truck had left the drive, Mildred was on her pad and opening the relevant checklist containing thrush sp., changing it to Bicknell's. "There, done". Then they both forgot all about it, more or less.

About ten days later, George had done a cursory check of their tower on the web site. "Mildred, come and look at this", George was quite excited and Mildred could tell. She rushed over from her baking to see what the fuss was all about. On the Motus log for their yard and in the right time period was a tag readout. It covered three days, and it recorded the presence of Bicknell's Thrush, one.

In Halifax a back-seat lurker had been watching the Bicknell's exchange with interest. Her recent postings about window kills had been largely ignored but this little thrush had been very popular and garnered lots of reaction. An idea hatched. What we need, thought Mori, is a celebrity death.

The idea of doing a newsletter for her own people had been in mind for a while. Now, with her idea fresh in her head, would be a good time to talk to the masses and see what the response was. For the rest of the afternoon she hunched over her laptop, typing away. Three spell and grammar checks later, and with the judicious addition of some very sad images, Mori hit send and her mailing list were told all about the celebrity death idea. She got no immediate response, but she was used to that.

CHAPTER THIRTEEN

August 2022

"You seemed a bit tense when we spoke, Moira. Are you wanting my professional services?" Tina Peck hadn't been surprised when Moira had called her and chatted, although it wasn't something she did with Moira very often. Following her earlier conversation with Howey, her qualified mind had started looking for cracks in her friend. Now Moira was standing outside her door.

"I'm not sure how to approach something and the Internet isn't that helpful".

"Dr. Internet rarely is, too unspecific. If it's anything professional I can refer you, as we know each other I'd ask whether seeing me with my metaphorical white coat on is appropriate".

"It's down to trust, Tina. I trust you and I'm unsure, at this point, which way I should go. Can I come in?"

"Sorry, yes, please", and Tina showed Moira into her kitchen where the smell of coffee was appealing. "Can I get you a cup, just brewed, I'm on half a day".

Coffee was poured and Moira sat at the kitchen island waiting, patiently. She looked around the apartment and could see where Josh had started to insert himself, then she laughed out loud at the bawdy joke that had appeared in her head. Tina gave her a look.

"Sorry, I had a thought. How's it going with Josh? I see his influence here".

"Yes, it's going fine. He's living here now, mostly, when he's not away with work. It'll take a while to get used to having a live-in man again, but it has its upsides and downsides". Moira laughed again, then explained the first joke, which Tina got.

"I'll give you a fifteen-minute consult for free, but if you have to come to me, professionally, I'll tack it onto the bill. Sorry, Moira but business is business and being clinical helps me deal with patients clinically".

"You mean no emotional attachment like friendship to get in the way? I see that, I like it, I do something similar myself at times". She took a deep breath and organized her thoughts. "You remember me telling you I was diagnosed with HPD some years ago? I stopped taking my medication when Howey and I got together, I haven't felt the need for it, I never really did. I'm wondering whether the original diagnosis was good. I brought the paperwork with me. Eleven minutes left, yes?"

Tina smiled. Moira was a fascination for her, but she'd never said so. Now she had the chance to look under the hood properly, to see how she worked. Moira Magowan piqued her, intellectually. "You want me to see whether you have HPD? Ok, that will require an appointment and I'm happy to add you to my client list. This then is just a chat between friends, forget the fifteen minutes. Tell me why you think the diagnosis was wrong".

For the next forty minutes Moira went through her list, written down on paper but also kept in her head. Tina listened but didn't make any notes and only asked a couple of seemingly innocuous questions. When Moira had finished Tina called up her appointment app and booked Moira in for three sessions. "I'm not cheap, sorry".

Moira waved the cost thing away. She was relieved that Tina, her friend, would be able to help her. "If it isn't HPD, and I appreciate you want to run through the whole thing to check first, what might it be?"

"At the risk of throwing away a juicy fee, I think you're probably autistic".

Moira felt relief flood through her body. Autistic she could handle. "I'd still like to go through the process, the full works, ok?"

"Me too, so my app will message you with times and dates. Is there any reason why you want to go through this again, no external pressures?"

"I need to be sure".

The checking of refuges was a slow process, made slower by the fact that resources were very limited, and Howey seemed to want to be personally involved in every visit, which wasn't practical. Even Carmel had called and told him to trust his staff, but he felt that he had a personal stake in the case, and it was dominating his thinking. "Leah, where are my sergeants?"

Leah Brown knew it wasn't the right time to joke. "Roberts and Newell are on the road heading to Bridgewater. Darren has a plan to do seven more visits, Crystal is again the Trojan Horse. Problem? You do have a meeting at ten".

Cross had forgotten, a budget meeting he could do without. "Right", he said, sweeping into his office.

"Honey, what's that brown bird at the feeder again, is it a Cardinal? I know you've been looking out for one".

Amy Pyne's relatively new boyfriend was being over keen again, but she thought to humour him anyway and keep an eye out. A friend had told her when she'd moved there that Eagle Cove sometimes got unusual birds, but so far everything had seemed very run-of-the-mill. She dropped into the armchair, a seat placed especially for looking at the feeders and waited. She'd missed it three times so far but, despite feeling dead on her feet, she was determined to get a look this time.

"Honey, you missed it, it just came in and took some seeds, it's gone now, you must have dropped off again".

Amy rubbed her eyes, it was true, she was tired a lot these days, but only because she was running two jobs to save for a trip, to see her twin sister out west. Coffee arrived, she knew that it would, and one of the old kitchen chairs was dragged alongside her as the vigil resumed. Half-joking, she tossed her old copy of Peterson, a legacy from her sister, over to Ciaran and told him to have another look through and find the bird. He'd already done this twice, but she wasn't happy with his answer. He always stopped at something unlikely, it was like he was only doing it to try to please her.

Ciaran sat back and thumbed the well-worn pages, skipping them two or three at a time until he got to the small birds. "Nope, nope, not that, definitely not that".

"Try thinking quietly, eh?" said Amy a little testily. She was annoyed with herself, Ciaran was a good man, much better than her former beaus who were self-obsessed narcissists to a man. The vocal accompaniment to the field guide scanning was reduced to a whisper in an instant, it was all that she could do not to laugh out loud. Ciaran stopped speaking and she knew where he was in the book, but he was wrong. He paused a while longer, then kept thumbing. Out of the corner of her eye she could see that he'd had kept his little finger on one page. This made her even more determined to see the bird than she felt was good for her, she had to prove him wrong.

"I think it's best to wait for it together, I can't seem to find it in the book and I'm not like you with your sharp eyes and memory. I did sketch it though; I can sketch good. I'm not going to show you my sketch until you see it, you only get mad at me".

Poor Ciaran, if only he knew her past, he might have some sympathy with her at her lack of trust, or more likely she'd hear the door hitting the frame as he walked out forever. She didn't want that, not with Ciaran.

Her coffee was now froth in the bottom of the cup, but it wasn't doing what it was supposed to, and she felt her eyes start to droop. Just five minutes was all she needed, five minutes and she'd be as good as she was before.

"It's here, now, on the small table", yelled Ciaran excitedly.

Grabbing her binocs, Amy focused on the bird, the table partially obscuring it so she could only see its back and, occasionally, its head. It wasn't a Cardinal, of that much she was sure. Resting the binocs on the window ledge, she re-focused until the table was sharp, then tried to take a few phone photos using the binocs as a lens, she'd seen them do it on YouTube. As she watched, a blur told her that the Mourning Doves had panicked again, and everything cleared the yard. It was either the hawk that came in daily, or that damn cat from next door.

Sitting back and feeling much more awake than she had done recently, she opened the phone images and expanded the sharpest. It wasn't too bad, and she'd caught part of the face. She grabbed the field guide off Ciaran who'd not said a word, such was her intensity, and she went straight to the page. "It can't be", she said as much to herself as anything.

When he dared, Ciaran opened his sketch pad, leafing through his many sketches of her, until he got to the bird. Amy started to tear up, she should have listened to him, trusted him, she had to start trusting. "That's great,

Ciaran, you got it perfectly. The book says we don't get them anywhere near, I'm going to have to call someone with a good camera, get some shots to back us up or people will think we're nuts, if we tell them".

The people she was referring to were the Nova Scotia Bird Group Facebook people. She'd seen it before where people had posted something unusual, and a few people had done what they called a 'pile on'. It was one of the reasons she'd kept a low-profile, but not the main one. Now there was no doubting their bird, but she wasn't going public until her friend Nathalie had been and got a photo of it, a good photo. She dug out her list of phone numbers, kept in an old-style address book, not trusted to the memory of a phone. Ciaran watched as she scrolled through, not wanting to ask about those numbers that had been redacted using a thick, black marker pen.

Amy dialed, but nearly didn't press the last number. Nathalie knew her, had looked after her one time when she was at a low point in her life, she knew things that she definitely didn't want Ciaran to know about. She pressed it anyway and waited. After a few rings, the answerphone clicked in and Nathalie's voice told the caller that this phone wasn't in general use at present and that she was currently working away.

Amy logged on to the NSBG Facebook page and scrolled a few posts. One guy was a regular poster and he lived in Guysborough, so not that far away. He took good photos and, although she didn't know him personally, it was worth a punt, and she could keep some semblance of anonymity too. She went to his home page and messaged him.

"It's back", said Ciaran quietly.

This time the bird sat on the side of the table for a while, then hopped onto a piece of fallen fence and started to preen. It was a Sage Thrasher for sure. Suddenly, all hell broke loose as doves went everywhere, one slamming into the window in front of them and falling on the lawn, dead. The cat from next door streaked through, grabbed a bird from near the table and shot off through the broken fence in a moment. "Bastard, bastard,

bastard", said Amy, then she apologised for swearing, but Ciaran understood, or at least said he did.

It was getting late, and no birds came back that evening. The next day, Amy was in at seven and wouldn't be home until after six that evening. Ciaran had to work too, so nobody was going to be there to keep an eye out. Had the cat got the thrasher, what should she tell the guy, Kyle, in Guysborough if he answered her message?

The next day seemed to be much longer than normal. Arriving home, Amy wearily pushed open the door, expecting to have to start supper. As she went through to the kitchen, Ciaran had set the table and something great smelling was cooking on the stove. In the middle of the table was a package, long, interesting. "I got you a little something, went to New Glasgow to get it".

Amy didn't know what to say, but whatever it was she knew she'd have to make a show of liking it. She tore off the wrapping and started to howl with laughter. Ciaran had bought her one of those water rifles that squirts a plume a good distance, certainly enough to drench a surprised moggie. "I thought you might like to sit by the window ready while I finish supper, and if that bastard cat comes back, give it a blast. Oh, and the thrasher is still here".

Amy noticed that the water rifle was already full and the liquid inside was red. "Food dye, I thought we'd make a point, we have a choice of colours". Smiling in a slightly scary way, Amy hefted the gun and went to the window. Inside ten minutes the bastard cat was back and got a thorough soaking.

Half-way through supper, a loud knock on the door made them start, Ciaran answered it. "What have you done to our cat?" said the angry voice of their neighbour outside.

"We don't want to hurt your cat, so we squirted it with water. The food dye will wash off, eventually. If it comes back, it'll get another dose until it gets the idea that being in our yard is a bad idea".

"You can't do that, around here we sort our problems out with our fists, I've been in prison, you don't mess with me like this".

"How do you know I haven't been incarcerated too?"

At that, the irate neighbour seemed to be less irate. Ciaran wasn't small, he just seemed to be a very gentle sort. "You keep your cat away from our birds and it won't keep changing colour, you have a choice, make sure you make the right one".

Mr. Angry didn't have a comeback; this wasn't how it was supposed to go. Instead, he stomped off, making a show of banging the yard gate as he went.

Amy hadn't moved throughout the exchange. Ciaran sat and started eating as if nothing had happened. "Is it true, have you been to prison?"

"Yes, I have, we all have our little secrets, don't we. Mine is a spell in prison, it doesn't matter why".

"When were you going to tell me?"

"When I knew you well enough that you would listen instead of throwing me out, I think we're there now".

"I think we need a bottle and somewhere comfortable. I want the details and then I'll see how brave I am with my secrets".

In one of the local yards, a cockerel was saying 'good day' in his own inimitable style. The bottle had long been emptied and Amy and Ciaran were curled up on the sofa. It had been a long night.

"I'll make breakfast, what time are you in?" asked Ciaran.

"Eleven till late, sorry. Will you still be here when I get home?" Amy looked worried.

"Why wouldn't I be?"

"After I told you everything, you still want to be here?"

"Can we change any of it?"

"No, but I'd understand if it put you off".

"It's history and not my business. This woman you got involved with, will she show up here?"

"No, I hope not. She doesn't know I left The Orchard, she said she had things to do in Annapolis, so I ran for it".

"And Angela, the manager, will she keep quiet?"

"I think so, nobody wants to tangle with her, but I heard that she's in New Zealand anyway so I doubt she could contact her".

"The things you told me about her, how much do you think might be true?"

"Most of it, maybe all. I don't know, in that place people feel safe enough to open up, that's the whole point of it. It was great for me, it got me back on an even keel, but she was a problem, so I left it behind, I stopped being her sounding board. Honestly, if you think about what we talked over, I won't blame you for going".

"I know I seem a bit needy, but I've fallen for you so I'm walking carefully around you. I'm not really a mouse, but I'm not nasty either. Prison was an aberration, and it was only for four months. I'll keep coming home until either you tell me I'm not welcome here, or the FBI catches up with me".

"What, FBI, what aren't you telling me?"

Ciaran started laughing. "Sorry, just joking but seriously, I'm here until you say go, ok?"

Amy's phone pinged, Kyle from Guysborough had seen the message and wanted to visit, she showed Ciaran.

"Say ok, I'll stay here and work on-line, I'll help him get his shots but what then?"

"I suppose we say people can come; I'll just keep out of the way for a while".

"Fair enough, leave it all to me. Did you refill the water rifle?"

"Yup, yellow this time. Call me if Kyle gets to see it, keep me in the loop".

"Will do and thanks for being honest".

Amy smiled as she grabbed her bits and pieces and went to work. She was happy that most things had been aired. Those things that couldn't be talked about would stay locked up in her brain for good, nobody needed to know any of that part of her past, not now, not ever.

Tina Peck read the report from the flight awareness people at FLAP, it was one of a pile of documents she'd had to wade through when she took up her role as President of the Nova Scotia Bird Group. Following another message from Mori, she'd dug it out to make herself familiar with the group and it's aims. Mostly what she got was little notes asking for advice or support for various low-level and bird-related causes, some were more ambitious though and generally outside the group's remit. The one from FLAP Canada bothered her more than the others because Mori Guier, the FLAP coordinator, had apparently written to her before, which was puzzling as she couldn't find any previous correspondence with Mori. She checked her ongoing folder, the brief notes from the previous presidential incumbents offered no insights either, nobody mentioned Mori or whether the group had ever got involved. She pinged an email back straight away.

Hi Mori – sorry, I don't seem to have had a contact from you previously and my information on FLAP is limited to a few notes from my predecessor and an outline from FLAP Canada that seems generic. What is it that you need from us, please be aware that we have limited resources, best wishes, Tina.

She didn't add that she was the current president, she wanted to keep it casual as being too formal can make people defensive. The reply came back much quicker than she'd expected.

Tina – thousands of migrating birds are dying in HRM due to building strikes, we need to do what we can to stop this. I know you have the ear of the minister; he can raise it with his boss- even go federal, hopefully we can get something done by the time fall migration starts. Mori.

So that was it, this Mori wanted her to use her personal relationship with Josh Hennigar to address the issue of window strikes. Not going to happen, thought Tina. Then a second email came with the figures for the previous fall, 643 corpses collected from the three tallest glass edifices in Halifax. The list was broken down by species, aside from mostly common warblers and small thrushes, it included two Connecticut Warblers. It changed her mind.

Josh put his wine glass down and leaned back from the table, smiling at Tina. Then his expression turned more serious, and he leaned towards her. "I'm away for a week, they just dropped it on me. I'm going to Japan, sorry for the lack of notice".

Tina was getting used to living with the whirlwind politician that was Josh Hennigar. Sometimes she had to take a step back and try to look at things from a detached perspective. It was working for her but, sometimes, she felt that she was being dragged along by momentum and not by making her own decisions. "Not a problem, I have a full diary. Question, what do you know about the light awareness people?"

"Dead birds and buildings, I've read the brief from Beatrice. If you're going to ask me what my department is going to do about it, sorry, nothing. I have no sway with the commercial aspect of politics in Nova Scotia, the developments currently under construction conform to federal and provincial regulations as they stand".

"I see, thank you for the politician-speak. Are you aware of the sheer numbers of birds involved and how widespread the problem is? This is Canada-wide, and you are in a position to make a difference to thousands of fragile lives".

"Beatrice and my people looked at it, but, like I say, it's not in my area".

"Josh, if you're going to get to the top like you say, everything has to be in your area. If I put something together for Beatrice to look at, will you?"

"No, it's not an area of politics that I can see being beneficial".

"To you, maybe not, but to the birds and those who love them it is. Get Beatrice to check out how many people buy feed, join groups or profess to be interested in the birds. A lot of voters there, Josh, a lot that might be swayed by the caring face of a politician".

"Thank you Madam President and I look forward to future cordial relations between our two offices, in fact if you have ten minutes spare, we could do a quick interface to keep me going while I'm away, the budget doesn't run to geishas". Tina was getting irritated. She didn't ask much of her partner's position and usually he was only too eager to do something that got his face in the press or on the TV news.

"I'll take that as a no then. Ok, Tina, do me a single sheet, send it to Beatrice but no promises. I told you, not an area I can have any influence in, besides,

I don't want to appear to be in the pocket of the wildlife people, it's not good for future investment. I've already had guarded warnings from colleagues".

Tina found herself dispassionately observing her partner as he made his politician's excuses. He'd said similar things before when they'd first got together and before they started to live together. For some reason it all seemed so much colder now. She decided to let it lie and talk to Moira about it at their next session, all of it. Moira was the sharpest cookie she knew, even if the recipe could sometimes best be described as interesting. In the meantime, there was nothing to stop her consulting the troops.

CHAPTER FOURTEEN

Screens started to fill up as the committee and invitees got settled for an irregular meeting. They were welcoming a couple of new committee members, both without portfolio but experienced in the birding world, only Darren Newell was absent, a prior engagement he said. The smiling face of Penny Chalmers appeared, and Tina looked very closely at the shelf behind her, just in case. "Penny, I see you have a new, er, friend. What happened to Clint?"[1]

"I retired him, he's done admirable service, but I fancied a change. Why do you ask?"

"The thing behind you, it rather dominates the backdrop".

Penny Chalmers looked around, reached over and put the item out of range of the PC's camera. "Sorry about that, I forget sometimes. I call him 'Shaft', if you want to know, I got a discount. When the man in the shop said there was fifteen percent off, I asked if I could just buy a full-sized one instead. I think I misunderstood; they were laughing for ages". At least three faces on the screen were now crying with laughter, including Moira and Barbara

---

[1] Clint was Penny's 'me time' facilitator which she once inadvertently left on a shelf where it was seen by all participants on another Zoom meeting.

Stock. Penny and her little 'friends' invariably made the girls laugh and the boys try to avoid the subject. Meanwhile Penny didn't see what all the fuss was about.

It took a while, but the meeting was called to order and when Tina announced the sole topic, bird strikes, the group involvement was news to many although everyone knew of the 'lights attracting birds' issues. Tina made her statement, most of which was simply repeating the words and numbers sent to her by Mori. Then she opened the floor for debate to see what the committee felt they should do.

"Not much I can say about this, eBird doesn't want corpses reporting", said Greg Barnes, thinking solely while wearing his eBird hat. "You can report them on iNaturalist though, which would at least get them recorded. Someone could create a corpse project just for HRM perhaps, not me though, I don't know iNaturalist very well and I've enough to keep me busy with eBird. Zelda would kill me if I took anything else on". It was fair enough, eBird was voluntary and time consuming. Tina noted the iNaturalist comment down, it would be worth thinking about, although the actual use of iNaturalist was pretty low in Nova Scotia, at least amongst birders, many not wanting to do what they saw as duplication with eBird.

"Do we have an iNaturalist guru in our midst?" asked Tina.

"George Berry uses it extensively for insects, he's a birder too so he might be willing. I know him and Mildred quite well, I can ask if you like". Penny Chalmers was only too pleased to get at least a bit involved. Since giving up the Piping Plover job she'd missed the thrill of participation, which is why she accepted the committee member without portfolio role in the first place.

"Bicknell George, he posted to the Facebook group recently?"

"Yes, that's him".

"Do we really need someone who can't identify a Grey-cheeked Thrush?" Frank Conte's ears pricked up when he heard Berry mentioned. He was one of the Facebook respondents that had poured scorn on Berry's claim of a migrant Bicknell's Thrush in Queens County.

"I couldn't see what the problem was, it looked like I'd expect one to look", said Barbara Stock, who sat quietly while the more illustrious committee members spoke.

"Really? How many have you actually seen, Barbara?" Conte was getting adversarial, which was probably a big mistake where Barbara was concerned.

"I can chip in there", said Greg before Barbara let Frank have both barrels. I've been researching Bicknell's for a bulletin note and Barbara here had seen multiple Bicknell's annually for twelve consecutive years until she moved in with Neil. Isn't that right, Barbara?".

"I wasn't going to be so explicit in public but thank you, Greg, yes, I was a fieldworker on the Bicknell's project. How about you, Frank, what's your Bicknell's tally?"

"Can I again intervene and just stay that the Queens Bicknell's was validated following George and Mildred submitting a checklist. The record was also backed up by a Motus ping, it was tagged, one of yours actually, Barbara". Greg left a suitable gap in the conversation for Barbara to respond, but she didn't.

"Ok", said Tina slowly, "can we just get back on track. Penny, please talk to George about setting up a dead bird project in iNaturalist for us and ask him if he'd be willing to do a Zoom short course for the uninitiated, like Greg, if you will. I'd like to point this Mori Guier in your direction too if I may, with your experience perhaps you could be the group's liaison?"

"Happy to, thanks", and Penny's screen went blank.

"Right, ok, I'll call her after the meeting, she seems to be having technical problems there".

"What if Shaft answers?" Barbara had decided to play the joker, mostly because it seemed to rile Conte up a bit. She knew him well enough to know that something had already got his goat, she'd find out the next time she bumped into him, she knew that she intimidated him a bit.

Tina never flinched. "I'm quite sure I can handle Shaft".

The meeting ended with lots of giggles but nothing concrete was decided. Soon the only face on the screen was Howey Cross, who quickly vacated the seat he'd shared with Moira, leaving her in view. "I bet this isn't going to be smooth sailing", she commented. "Good move to hand it off, people will keep expecting Josh to get involved and he can't, not all the time. I don't think we can do much more than support FLAP Canada and put something on the website and Facebook".

Tina listened, all the time looking to see whether she could see any cracks, she knew that Moira had been feeling what she called 'fragile' recently after discovering that she was one of a pair. Tina had worked with twins before, including the sort who seem to occupy the same space. Moira didn't seem like that, she didn't seem to be able to switch between the personalities, possibly because her twin had died. She realised that Moira was still talking. "Tina, can you hear me?"

"Sorry Moira, I was thinking, I did hand it off without realising it, didn't I. I've been wondering recently whether being Bird Group President and having Josh as a partner isn't a conflict of interests, I'd appreciate your perspective".

"If Josh can't help, is there anything you can do for him to make him change his mind?"

Tina knew what Moira was getting at. "No, nothing", she said, with a wry smile.

"Then no, there's no conflict of interest, although you might put pressure on yourself because of the role. If you stepped down, who might take over?"

"I haven't given it any thought; I suppose Darren might give it a go?"

"Good choice if he can fit it in, but not at the moment. If push comes to shove you let me know first and I'll see to it that Darren is prepared. I take it Josh is away again, are you ok?"

"Yes, fine, I was going to ask Penny whether Shaft had a brother though".

Howey could hear the laughing coming from the office, he liked it, Moira was being Moira, whatever the joke was.

"Another day, another set of refuges, I promised not to be too late back today, the Newells are coming over". Howey Cross had nearly automatically climbed into the driving seat but had then remembered being told not to hog the wheel. It might have been partly in jest, but he got the message.

"Oh, really", was all Crystal could manage.

"Sorry, you'd be welcome too, it's just that it's going to be a birdy evening, images from Brazil. I can get Moira to do a less birdy one for another time, if you're interested?"

"Ok, that would be nice. Sorry, I didn't mean to sound disappointed at not being invited, besides, I'm out tonight".

Cross took the comment at face value and promised to set something up, then settled in for the ride.

The highway was smoother than most, it wasn't that long since they'd resurfaced it, and it wouldn't be long before they'd need to do it again. It was currently in that sweet spot when a roll along it could be almost soporific. Crystal had her iPods in and was still listening to the audio transcripts of the Barker case again. Road trips were the ideal time to do it, especially as Howey Cross was fast asleep in the seat next to her. The car sat-nav said Eagle Cove was still nearly a hundred clicks away, she decided to let Cross sleep a while longer.

It was all a bit foreboding as Howey Cross drove the track home. Both gates had been left open, so he'd dutifully climbed out of the car after each, closing it, checking that the mechanism was ok, it was. As he approached home, the backdrop was more like some AI generated, dramatic scene, rather than the familiar view he always enjoyed. He parked and checked he'd got everything. Sometimes he left his phone plugged into the car system, the phone battery seemed less and less able to power the thing for much more than a few hours, so it needed almost constant charging.

When he got to the door, he could see it wasn't latched shut. In summer it often wasn't, being remote they enjoyed the liberation of being worry free that passing miscreants might try to gain entry. He pushed it open and everywhere was red. What had Moira done this time?

The door opened wide, and he could see Moira's favourite West African dress, it appeared to be standing unaided, then he realised that she was there too, his eyes just hadn't seen her. "Moira, did the kids go mad with the face-paint again?"

The dress turned and Cross was surprised to see that it wasn't Moira that was wearing the dress, but Crystal. It took a moment to take in, then he remembered that the dress was sleeveless, but the one Crystal wore had red sleeves. "Howey, all sorted, we can be together now", she said. Crystal smiled and slipped the dress off, letting it fall around her ankles. She had the same body as Moira, the same tattoos, the same everything.

"Moira, what happened?"

"I know you like Crystal, so I did some needlework, you know how handy I am with a needle. Now you can have both of us in one body, Crystal's hair and face and my body, will that do?"

"What happened here?"

"Oh, this, I can tidy up later. I've ordered a dumpster from a place in Keji. Very environmentally friendly, they recycle all organic waste, they have a place in the park where they can bury it".

"I don't understand", said Cross tasting blood in the air for the first time.

"Sorry, Howey, I thought you'd like the changes", and Moira reached up and drew Crystal's face off her own, like removing a mask. Moira's real face was red, bloodied, her eyes were wrong. "Am I losing my skills, Howey? Normally I only have to show you a flash of leg to get you ready, come on, we can be us again without any distractions, just us, won't that be wonderful. What if I do this? There we are, all ready and waiting now".

"Howey!"

The few moments after you open your eyes, and the dream recedes are the hardest time to focus. Cross looked around the car, then over at Crystal who was glancing his way as she tried to concentrate on the road. "Sorry, are we nearly there?" Things were now normal, real, there was no blood.

"Yes, you might want to get yourself, er, organised".

Cross wasn't sure what Crystal meant. He had his notes, and they would be asking the same basic questions once they got to Safe Shores, the scene of the latest possible Barker sighting, if it was her. Then he realised and felt uncomfortable. "Sorry, I dreamt".

"I saw. Don't worry about it, think of something calming".

"I dreamt that Moira has killed you and cut your face off to make me like her more".

"And that was the effect it had on you? Should I be calling Watson, see if he has a slot for you?"

"I'm sorry, I've never had a dream like it".

"Don't worry about it, I had to wake you when you started moaning. At least I had the road to concentrate on. Why would Moira, even in your subconscious, think you'd prefer my face to hers?"

"Crystal, it was a dream, irrational. I have no idea where it came from but it's not the first", and he told her of the dream where Juliette Barker morphed into Moira.

"Maybe you should see Watson, or someone like him? This is you projecting Barker onto Moira for some reason. Moira isn't nuts, how many times do I have to tell you?"

"No, I know. Sorry again for the embarrassment".

"The embarrassment is all yours, Howey but, like I said, forget it. Promise me something though".

"What".

"You won't tell Moira about your dreams; she doesn't need to know. This is between us, talk to me anytime you need to and if you need a reassuring hug, just say so. If we keep a gap between us big enough for the holy spirit, it won't be seen as sexual".

Cross laughed. "I've never heard that expression before, were you raised a Catholic or something".

"No, but Terence was. It was something he said to me one day, it made me laugh too. Leaving a gap for the holy spirit is about as effective as using the rhythm method for not getting pregnant, another one of their little inventions. Are you all back to normal now?"

"Yes, and sorry again. It won't happen again".

"Never say never, Howey, you're not past your prime yet, boy".

The house was a little rundown, but they could see that whoever had it now had made a start on improvements. Two windows were obviously recent, and the only accessible door was an expensive one with a double lock and solid panels. It seemed to be overkill, given that Eagle Cove looked to be the sort of place where nobody ever locked their doors. Cross knocked, the door opened just an inch and a body blocked the view into the house. "Yes?" said a man's voice.

"Police, Staff Sergeant Cross and Sergeant Roberts, is Amy in please?"

"What do you want with her?" The voice sounded very defensive.

"We're looking for someone and Gaby Monroe at Safe Shores told us Amy might have information we might find useful, is she here?"

Standing just behind her boyfriend Ciaran, Amy Pyne calmly whispered that it was ok and to let them in, then she went to her living room to wait. The door opened a further crack and identification was shown. When it opened fully, a large man was waiting. He did a double take on Cross then held out a hand. "Howey, Ciaran Lowe, remember me?" Cross did.

Amy Pyne was best described as slightly built. Howey and Roberts could see that she'd lived a life already, their experienced eyes able to fill in the blanks just from her face. "Is this about that woman, Melissa?"

"No, not Melissa. We're looking for Juliette Barker", and Crystal produced the slightly worn photo they'd been carting around every refuge they'd visited so far.

Amy looked briefly, then fetched a pair of reading glasses from a sideboard. "I only need them for close things", she said. "Dollar Shop pair". Taking time to have a good look, she handed the photo back. "It looks like Rosemary, I don't think that's her real name though, we didn't have real names in The Orchard".

"The Orchard? Tell me about being there and tell me about her, please", said Cross, he'd assumed that Amy had been in 'Safe Shores'. He could see that Amy was nervous with them being there, but he wasn't going to ask awkward questions, he only wanted to know about Rosemary. Ciaran was hovering close by. "Would you prefer to talk to Crystal in private?"

"No, Ciaran knows all about me, I'd prefer him and you to stay. I told Gaby about it, so I guess that was why she told you. Rosemary, she was disconcerting, changeable, yes, changeable is the right description. One moment she'd be a bit haughty, but ok. She'd go on about looking after her sister's kids, then later it was as if she had never heard of them. She attached herself to me for some reason. At first, she was ok, but after a while and when I was ready to come back here, I slipped out and didn't tell anyone. It happened there, people often came and went".

"Yes, I know The Orchard, my sister Angela runs it".

Amy was genuinely surprised, then she popped the glasses back on and had a really close look at Cross's face. With her being so near, he could smell tobacco and weed although the house didn't advertise it when he first walked in, many do if a regular user lived there. "I can see her in you. Angela's alright, nobody messes with her. She's in New Zealand, is that right? Sorry, I'm drifting, I do that a bit. Rosemary told me she'd been abandoned by Phil, her boyfriend, and that she'd left the area where too many bad memories stacked up. I thought it was just a story, but she had details, I can't remember specifics, sorry, but they were like bits of information to fill holes in a story. I remember she said she liked to walk in Keji, a park I've never been to, she liked a trail too, one with benches, ducks and something she called grass birds, noisy but only in summer. She said she had a favourite bench, one with a dedication".

"Did she mention anyone else?"

"A sister, fragile she said, and her mother, adoptive, but none of it made much sense. It bothered her lots that her birth mother hadn't wanted her. She said she'd looked for her and that she was somewhere in Nova Scotia, maybe she found her".

"You said you left The Orchard, Amy. Was Rosemary still there when you left?"

"No, she'd gone off again. I took my chance and left too. Ciaran and I have been together a while, he takes care of me, and I look after him".

Crystal asked the same basic questions again, Amy answered confirming what she'd told them. Apart from the odd extra detail, there was a dog called Sonny mentioned, she told the same tale. Cross was on his phone, looking something up. "Sage Thrasher, yes?"

Amy brightened. "Yes, it was here but we think that fucking cat next door got it, despite us shooting it with coloured water. Little bastard". For the next five minutes Cross talked birds with Amy and Ciaran, finding out that they'd also had a Yellow-breasted Chat in the spring, a nice yard bird. When she was talking birds, yard birds, Amy was different again and Crystal could see a bit of who she'd been before life had skittled her. Time was moving on and they declined the offer of coffee. Ciaran showed them to the door.

"It's good to see you're doing OK, Ciaran. Some people slip after what happened".

"I know, but it wasn't like me and it won't happen again. Amy can be a bit delicate, but I'll look after her. If you need to speak to her again, can you call ahead?" and he gave Cross a slip of paper with a cell number on it.

"I think we have what we need. If she remembers anything else though, my card is on your table, call me and take care", and Cross shook his hand.

With Cross taking a turn at the wheel, they got back onto the highway. "Most of what Amy said is on the original Barker interview tapes, at least we know for sure she's still in Nova Scotia and Madam was right about the refuges being just that. What did you think of her?" he asked.

"Ex user, clean but still blowing legal dope. She's got a lot of miles on her face and, to be uncharitable, probably elsewhere. She obviously comes from a good family, her diction and word use isn't street, private education I'd say, well to do but went off the rails. I don't see her remembering much more, but you never know, she certainly brightened up when you started talking birds. This thrasher thing, is it really called that?"

"Yes, look it up on eBird like I showed you. You've not asked about Ciaran yet".

"That was my next question", she said as she put the thrasher into eBird. "Brown, boring. Ciaran then?"

"He got involved with some people, a bit of driving, a bit of minding their stuff. I arrested him. He was easy to talk to and admitted his sins but wouldn't name names. He had a spell somewhere for his trouble, I spoke up at his trial and told them how I thought he needed a fresh start. They gave him the minimum. I reckoned he'd be ok if he got away from the area, which he told me he would. I've never heard his name since, so my hunch was good. I heard he worked out west a while, then I lost touch when Moira came into my life. Sorry again about earlier".

"Forget it, it was funny really, not the dream, obviously. Poor men, it's one emotion they can't easily hide, especially if they were born lucky, unlike us girls where everything is invisible unless we choose otherwise".

"Changing the subject", said Cross. "I feel guilty that Darren usually goes out on his own, but we go together, more often than not. We need to change that. I need you to step up there, ok?"

"Sure, but we don't click the same. I know he doesn't find me attractive, I guess I'm not his type".

"It happens and he's devoted to Hinzi, get over yourself woman".

"Careful, Howey, I can get most men pointing north with just the rustle of my stockings" and she flexed her legs.

"Crystal, behave!"

It had been a long but fruitful day, even his little incident had been put behind him, but Howey Cross still had a delicate subject to broach with Moira. Crystal had been right when she'd told him to just ask her. With the right information, it would be easy enough to cross-reference everything, a few minutes of effort for peace of mind. Howey knew that she was right.

Howey waited until the Newells retired to the cottage. It had been a fun night and they seemed to enjoy finally seeing the images from Brazil. It was the old holiday snaps cliché, but as many were of various birds and wildlife, Darren was happy. Hinzi always took a very cosmopolitan view and seemed to enjoy the architecture and beach scenes where locals of all shapes and sizes enjoyed the sun and surf.

"Tell me about your aunt".

Moira was surprised, why now? "When you say tell me about her, would you want a short resumé of her life and career, or would you prefer interpretive mime?"

"Anything. Her name, where you lived in BC, interests, history, partners, anything. I did say I'd help find connections for you if I could, but I need basic information to go on and you never offered it".

"I know, I thought about it, a lot, and decided that I didn't want to get you into trouble. Now it feels like you're pushing for information, something more is happening."

Cross knew that there was no point pretending otherwise. "Yes, in part. I'm digging in the same area as your roots, and I might turn something up. I just thought that if I did find anything, peripheral to the case, that you'd want to know".

"You want to rule me out of your inquiries?"

"What? No. It just occurred to me that if I was looking in a certain place for something, I'd find other things not relevant to the case. I'm trying to help, nothing sinister is going on, you seem very defensive about this". It wasn't like Moira to shy away from the possibility of important information, if there was any to be had.

"No, I see that, but what if there's something I don't want to know about in my family's past? I'm as settled and happy now as I've ever been, rocking my mental boat might toss us all into the sea. In many ways, I prefer my history to start from the day you saw the real me. Everything after that point in my life is real, quantifiable. Before that, and after I left BC, I have some gaps, even with my mental capacity. Do you see?"

Cross did, but he'd still like to know a bit more himself. "I'm not pushing and of course I'll respect your wishes. If you decide to give me anything at all, nobody else will see it. I'll just skim any information I get for my case for anything I think you might be able to use when, and if, you try to find your real mom. I know you want to".

"I do, I did, and I'd like to know why my aunt was always reluctant to talk of her but, like I said, what if there's a can of worms waiting to creep into our lives and devour any loose flesh?"

"That's a bit dramatic, I was just thinking more that I'd find a name for your mother and possibly where she is, if still living and the rest is up to you". Cross could see that Moira was torn. On the one hand she wanted to know more about her past, on the other she was genuinely scared that what she might discover would define her.

"This Barker case, the one you aren't telling me about anymore. Is it that one that's going to have you and your team digging around in BC?"

"Yes, we need some details to better understand things and it seems that Juliette Barker, while conceived in Nova Scotia, was born in BC. The problem we're having is verifying everything. Much of what we have comes from people who knew her. We've accumulated a lot of information about her life and family connections, things so complicated that there must be some truth to it. Nobody could keep the deception up and not get caught out".

"I could".

"Yes, you could, but you're not Juliet Barker and she's not you. When we get Barker, I want to be ready. To find her, the better we're prepared, the more we know, then we can try to think like her".

"Profiling your suspect, I see. Will you also profile me?"

"If there's a link, yes, but I don't see how there can be. There are, I'll admit, some similarities in some areas of the case, but we're talking a different period, maybe even a very different area. BC is big. I'm probably seeing coincidence where none exists, and I truly want to be able to give you a name and then let you decide what to do with it. If you want to follow it up, I'll be here with you all the way, if you don't, nothing changes".

"Let me think about it for a few days. Does anyone else know you're asking for this? Darren, Crystal?"

"This is family business and it'll stay that way, nobody but me will see anything you give me".

"No matter what?"

"I can't answer that one, honestly".

The next morning Moira was already up and feeding mouths when Cross emerged ready for work. She smiled and handed him an envelope, sealed. "This is all I have at the moment. I tried looking once before but got nowhere, although the Internet wasn't such a thing then. I'm going to try again with your agreement, ok?"

Cross said it was, thanked her and took over the feeding duties. Moira had a worried look, so he flicked a spoon of breakfast cereal in her direction, Vinnie saw and followed suit. Before long a messy food fight was underway. There was a knock at the door. Crystal pushed it open, saw what had happened, backed out and slowly closed it.

Sometime later, Cross rang Crystal. "Sorry, I had to help with the clean-up, you were very sensible in not coming in". Cross had showered and changed again, after helping clear up the mess. "We don't do that normally, but Moira was a bit pensive, and it just happened".

"Actually, it looked fun, everyone was laughing. I haven't laughed much recently".

Cross was concerned, normally Crystal was pretty even in temperament.

"Don't worry about me, a heavy night and I'm just pondering on how I might make a few life changes. A new haircut, buy some clothes, take a vacation somewhere warm, that sort of thing. Did you get the details from Moira?"

"Yes".

CHAPTER FIFTEEN

Moira had been intending to go into town with the kids, but when she heard the car pull up outside it had an air of irritation about it. She waited for a good two minutes before Hinzi walked in, she looked a bit tearful. What was it they said about house buying? It was in the top three most stressful things to do, along with dealing with a death and becoming bankrupt, or was that delivering bread? "Tell me the worst".

Hinzi was rarely bothered by things, but her getting a contact to do a pre-survey report on the house had delivered some bad news. Moira read the two-page document. It was easy to see why Hinzi was upset. Any bank would be reluctant to lend on the basis of these findings if they were in an official report. Cox's house needed a roof, a re-wire and some structural work doing and that was only from what was a superficial look-over. Lots needed doing and it wasn't going to be cheap. "He says it's not falling down or anything, it just needs work, but we'd need time to get it done, gradually, and as we could afford it. I can't see us getting the mortgage we need, not once an official report gets done, if we bother now".

"Hinzi, it's just a little roadblock, navigable. Do you have quotes, how much will the work cost?"

"Ballpark, thirty thousand, on top of the offer price it makes it untenable. I'm know I'm being silly, but I had my heart set on the property. We'll withdraw the offer and look at the other options, I'll talk to Cara".

"Offer her less, send the report and see if she'll absorb some of the costs for a quick sale. I know they don't want it dangling around and becoming a tax liability at some point".

"I thought of that, but the bank won't lend against the house until the repairs are done. It was pie in the sky anyway, it was just that it would be something we did, you know what I mean. We'd already had misgivings about the stable property, being in each other's pockets. I know we're close, but couples need distance too, we're not commune types and neither are you and Howey, not really".

Moira wasn't so sure about the commune idea, she'd often thought before that buying a mansion and sharing it with like-minded people would suit her, some days. This problem did have a solution though. "Look, I know you don't want to, but I'm happy to invest in you, give you a deferred loan for the repairs at the bank lending rate if you get that mortgage". Moira was always very clear that any financial help she might offer to anyone wasn't charity, business rates applied.

"I knew you'd say that and thanks, but like I said, this was something that we were supposed to do on our own, our thing, all our own work. I'm sure you understand. It's always been our thing that we do things our own way, to suit us, suit how we live our lives. You know what I mean, we've talked, besides there's ways and ways".

"How is a loan from Magowan-Cross International at the current bank rate, any different from the one you are half-considering getting from a much dodgier source?"

"How did you know?"

"Because I'm me and because I understand the nesting instinct. I know you and I know that your heart is in that house now. What does Darren say?"

"He doesn't, I've not told him but, to be honest, I think he was already worried about over-committing anyway. I tried to tell him the math. Commuting from Halifax won't work, we'll spend so much on gas and keeping the cars healthy that we might as well have taken the place anyway. We probably should have stuck with the original plan and bought next door from you".

"Too late now, I'm afraid. Crystal didn't hang about and got something on there very quickly, her dad is something in the industry apparently. To be honest I'm not sure whether she'll stay there. She's not getting on with Terence, I'm pretty sure they're done, and I think she might find Kings County life a bit dull for her. If you won't take our offer, you might talk to her about things?"

Hinzi could see the sense, but Moira could see that the proximity thing was still in her mind.

"I can see what you're thinking, but I'm only speculating here, besides I'm not sure it's just about taking a loan offered in good faith. Be honest with me, Hinzi, is part of wanting Cox's house to ensure more of an element of personal space?"

"In part, you know how things are. I wouldn't want any problems to arise through misunderstandings and close proximity might do that. I'll talk to Darren and try to persuade him to accept your offer, he'll see sense, you're great friends to us".

"You are family to us, and families help each other out. I'll see what I need to do and set it up in case you accept our offer, you talk to Darren, and we'll then set up a business meeting, somewhere neutral where we can all take a look at the project, obviously I need to meet with my people first, get their buy-in. You get that official survey done so we both know where are and If I think it's a bad investment, sentiment won't sway me otherwise. Listen to me, Moira the business professional, who knew? It helps to be able to be different people sometimes".

"I see that, you do become different, still Moira but different. I wish I could do that sometimes, but I am what I am and have my funny little ideas, and Darren is fine with that. How do you do it, Moira, how do you think that way?"

"I never knew the how or why myself until very recently. I think it helps to know that I'm one of two, that I always was".

"Before we eat and because we're quorate, I call a Magowan-Cross business meeting to order. Present Howey, Vinnie and Phoebe Cross and Moira Magowan. Order of business. One, the offer of a loan to aide in the purchase a property for the Newells, business rates apply, a deferred loan with pay-off options. Thoughts?"

"Ok", said Phoebe, "yes", said Vinnie, all three looked at Howey Cross. "I take it you're a yes too, Moira?"

"I am".

"What percentage of the board need to agree?"

"Oh, 100% of course", said Moira, smiling at Howey.

"And these business terms?"

"Will be decided in consultation with the Newells, they might need some flexibility, financially".

"Agreed then. Point of order, are you happy at having Crystal on our doorstep? I know it was all very quick, she seems to operate that way".

"Good point, a show of hands please". Moira looked around the table. Unanimous then. Additional agenda item, do we want to go and visit Aunt Angela at her new place in New Zealand? It will be when it gets a bit nicer there, so next February. I have a provisional offer of local paid help for the farm".

"Point of order. She's not moved yet, she's just visiting". Howey was happy to play along with the game, he knew that Moira was setting them up for a trip, but New Zealand was very unlikely.

"Noted, I was going to mention earlier. I spoke to Angela, the house is sold, their goods and chattels are in a container, and they will be flying next week. They will be in our cottage for a few days before they go and I'm taking them to the airport, you're too busy on a weekday". Moira watched Howey to see that he was ok with the news being dropped on him like that, but that was what Angela had said to do.

He never even flinched. "I'll figure something around work for the airport run, I assume you'll send me the times when you know them". His phone pinged; Moira smiled. "Have you ever thought of auditioning as a Bond villain?"

"So, Mr. Cross, we meet at last". Howey laughed, he didn't want to tell Moira that he already knew that Angela was leaving, that she'd told him a while ago. There was no need to break the moment.

CHAPTER SIXTEEN

Mid August 2022

So far, 2022 had been devoid of hurricanes, but there had been a succession of southerly storms, each bringing a smattering of scarce birds to Nova Scotia, enough to keep the year listers happy enough, especially Greg Barnes. Then a depression out by the Azores gathered pace before swinging north very quickly, so quick that most of the models called it wrong. Despite the absence of a week of dire warnings about property damage and coastal chaos, hurricanes that didn't impact on the US were hardly newsworthy, Hurricane Philomena whipped through Nova Scotia anyway. True, she ruffled a lot of trees and carried with her a lot of water, but she didn't seem to bring too many obvious birds. It was also odd for a hurricane, being very compact and fast-moving. It had been interesting for the Nova Scotia birding community to watch it progress though. Heated water all the way up to just off George's Bank had given Philomena the energy it needed to carry it through the wind shear to the south, a feature that normally did for early hurricanes. Then it thumped in, quickly breaking up over land and becoming a wet storm. The weather people had been eager to start wringing their hands at the potential destruction trail Philomena had promised, it would give the rest of North America news footage to drool over, in the end it collapsed so quickly that it barely made a footnote outside of Canada.

The more focused Nova Scotia birders had watched Philomena with interest too, hoping that her eye had a rare avian gift or three for them. Predictions were rife on the Nova Scotia Bird Group Facebook page, with frigatebirds, tropicbirds and even the rarer pelagic terns all being predicted. The hurricane's final track took it mostly over part of the Greater Antilles and then through miles of open ocean, resulting in more than one outlandish prediction.

Baccaro had seen the eye of Philomena pass right over, but to those in their wobbling cars who'd braved the storm, it appeared to be virtually devoid of birds bar a handful of hungry Laughing Gulls and a second-hand report of a frigatebird species. Naturally, the birders searched diligently in Philomena's aftermath, but most soon lost interest and went home. If the bushes weren't dripping with ticks, then the storm was a big let-down. Only Clive Mood was putting in the time and kilometres, mostly around Cape Island and the outlying sites. He was moderately happy with a Least Tern on The Hawk and his efforts had also found an out-of-context White-eyed Vireo, but that had been it until he heard an unfamiliar call, then got a glimpse of a flycatcher at Baccaro, a flycatcher that refused to show. He didn't know what it was, and he was very unhappy about that fact.

Mood was slowly warming to the Discord RBA system. It had taken a while to gain traction but had now shunted the Google group into touch, so he was trying to embrace it. The thing was, if you put something somewhere wrong, one of the snappier members, often someone out of province or their heads, would leave an occasionally disparaging comment. It was understandable that people got exasperated by repeat offenders in the rarity claim market, wrongly calling birds that turned out to be common species, but sometimes people were quick to jump in with a put-down. Mood opted for the chat channel to post his calling bird.

'It might be something or nothing, but I had a weird bird, a flycatcher type in the Alder scrub at Baccaro, the site of the old Air Force place. I'll go back tomorrow and try again, but it hasn't given a good view yet. It might just be a Great Crested Flycatcher, but it seems wrong, and they usually show better'. The hurricane had brought a few land birds, including catbirds, or perhaps people had just noticed a few more with less vegetation to hide them, it was hard to say. Nobody responded to the message and Mood resolved to just get on with it. He'd told them he'd seen something he didn't know; it was something he didn't admit to lightly and it was up to 'them' whether they bothered with it.

"We should go for a drive, Neil. Clive might be on to something at Baccaro, there's squat all flying past here at the moment and I could do with a change of scenery". Neil Porter's girlfriend, Barbara Stock, had an earthy way of putting things, at least she'd said 'squat' this time and not one of the many worse expletives she was fluent in.

"Ok, but put your face on first, I'm not taking you anywhere looking like that". The whack resounded around the sea watching blind and, although Porter had expected it, he'd not been quick enough to duck this time.

"Whoops", said Barbara, leading him back to the house for repairs to a bloody nose. "You're normally much better at the old bob-and-weave. Am I getting quicker or you slower? Don't worry, I'll drive. I should put clean undies on in case you have to go to hospital for that, you can take a pair of my dirty undies along too if you like, just in case you have to sleep alone and you want to be reminded of me".

"You mean the smell of fish, Barbara? If I'm in Yarmouth I can get that from the fishing wharves", said Porter, ready to duck this time, but she was now in what she called 'sweet little me' mood. Sadly, it was wasted on him because his nose still dripped blood. Porter didn't argue about making the short trip. Living with Barbara, while it had many compensations, could be a bit unpredictable. He rather liked it, despite the odd scuff mark and he knew she'd make it up to him.

Mood's truck was already at the site when they pulled up at the compound. The gate, which may once have fitted the gap it pretended to cover, was badly distorted, with a ragged piece of nylon rope used to close it. What they were hoping to keep in, or out, was anyone's guess. They could see the top of Mood's head bobbing up and down further out in the Alder scrub, so they insinuated themselves in alongside him.

"Here", he whispered, and pointed to a particularly dense spot with Alders embedded in a tangle of thorn. A movement had them raising their binocs, but it was a Grey Catbird, Mood shook his head, that wasn't the bird. Nothing stirred for a while, so they kept slowly moving around until they each had a view into the scrub that satisfied them. A quiet whistle from Barbara had them edging slowly her way. A pale olive-grey bird was just visible, moving slowly, flitting down low in the dense vegetation and only giving bits and pieces of a view. After a couple of minutes, the view ended when the bird called once and moved to an even denser clump. They retreated to a non-disturbing distance.

"What the fuck was that?" asked Barbara, she could see why Mood hadn't called it.

"A washed out Great Crested?" asked Porter, he was better with distant seabirds than anything that hid in bushes.

"It looked a bit small and slight. No clear yellow on the belly but maybe that wouldn't be there on a bird with bleached plumage, not that a bird now should be that bleached. The truth is I don't know. I'm glad someone else has seen it, I thought I was losing it", said Mood, relieved.

"We need a photo, and a recording, that call wasn't right either. You two ease it my way and I'll give it a bash. I've got my new camera with eye-detection, I'll try to get a shot", said Barbara, hoping her new technology might just give them an edge. For the next two hours, they sneaked around the bushes trying to find the mystery bird. It was close to calling time of death when it flicked between two patches to an isolated clump. "Right, you little fucker", said Barbara, nominally under her breath, but loud enough to be heard at Baccaro Light.

Even though they knew the bird was in there, it still took a while to get eyes on it. Barbara used the camera, but it wasn't always easy to find the bird in the viewfinder and when she did, the tangle had the focus hunting all over the place, but she got shots of a sort. Without warning, the flycatcher got up and bounded over the scrub, and the road, and into even trickier cover outside the compound. On the back of the camera, most of the images looked like gnats had died on the lens, but one had found the eye and had got most of the head. "Obviously a *myiarchus*", suggested Porter, which nearly got him a slap from Barbara for not talking properly. Mood said 'obviously', as if dealing with a twelve-year old.

"Ash-throated?" suggested Barbara, but Mood insisted that the bill was wrong. Then he told them the story of how he'd seen one once on Cape Island years ago, a bird that nobody believed him about and one that led to some falling out with some name birders. "They soon shut up when I posted the photos", he said, obviously still annoyed.

"We need to post this lousy back-of-the-camera image to Discord, someone might know", said Barbara, not happy at giving up after all the effort. "Best not to say anything about my photography limitations though, eh Neil?"

"I'm not aware of any", he said, diplomatically.

The back of the camera image was posted, and they were chatting about it when the bird flew back over the road and into the favoured scrub. "At least there's a chance of someone else seeing it now", said Mood. "Only you two bothered to come though, I'm not sure anyone else deserves it, whatever it is". Nobody on Discord responded quickly, as the deeper thinkers took their time looking at the photos. Unusually, the regular 'jump in with both feet' crowd seemed to find them to be on the cold side this time. "Are you two looking again?" asked Mood, he wasn't, he'd got things to do.

"No, we're not really twitchers, we just wanted a ride out. We'll go and look at the sea a bit from the light, then we're going to Cape Island where we'll look for oystercatchers and later, I'll get treated to a fancy coffee and piece of cake at the café in town. Isn't that right Neil?" It was.

As they were munching a splendid muffin in Salty Shores, a Discord message popped up from a name neither knew, them not being twitchers as such. It was from Hugo Ridley, and he'd speculated that, in view of the hurricane, the flycatcher might possibly be a La Sagra's Flycatcher from the Antilles. At least he was having a punt, whoever he was. He then let himself down a bit by adding 'if it's genuine'. Barbara could just picture Mood reading that jibe and oiling his gun on the front porch while his girlfriend suckled a pig. They looked up La Sagra's Flycatcher and there was a very similar bird looking back at them, then they played the call and bingo. "Well, fuck me", said Barbara. Porter restrained himself from answering, he'd got into trouble in the past for trying to take Barbara at her latest profanity in the literal sense.

'Clive, did you see, La Sagra's Flycatcher. Who is Hugo Ridley?' she texted Mood.

'Lobster food if he keeps that 'if it is one' shit up,' texted Mood back, but he'd included a smiley face icon, so it was probably only partially meant. Half-way through the second piece of cake, the phone was pinging like a pinball machine, so Barbara muted it. People were desperate for more updates. 'Get off your asses and go look', was posted by Mood. Barbara snorted coffee out of her nose when she saw the message and even Porter laughed. The comment didn't stay up long though.

The next day about fifteen cars were parked up along the road, as birders scattered all over the compound looking for the bird, including Hugo Ridley. Some present were treating him with awe, he was the top Canadian lister after all. Others kept their distance, well aware that in some cases, cash was often a primary factor in having a big list, not necessarily talent.

Despite a lot of searching, the flycatcher wasn't found, although a couple of people claimed glimpses. The same pair were getting a reputation for glimpsing things that had apparently gone. Everyone eventually gave up, for most, Baccaro was a three-hour drive from home.

Mood scrolled through the eBird reports the next day. His, Barbara's and Neil's checklists hadn't been validated, yet. The two birders who'd claimed it had put 'continuing' as a description. That wasn't going to fly in this case and the 'continuing' comment sparked some entertaining chat on Discord.

A couple of days later Mood went back for another look, not really expecting much. He had the place to himself and put his Bluetooth speaker into the middle of an Alder. Stepping well back, he played La Sagra's calls, a download from Xeno-Canto and not the one on the Merlin app that many had tried and failed with. A little 'weeeik' call some way off told him he'd had a nibble. Out of the corner of his eye, he saw a bird come over the road and into the scrub nearby, so he readied his camera. It took a while, but when a bit more calling happened from a spot not far from him, he pointed, checked and then focused, just as the La Sagra's popped up right on top of the bush. It was only there for a moment, but he'd got it. Back in the truck he looked at the image. He took a phone shot and posted it to Discord. 'Continuing' he wrote, wondering whether Ridley had got home and unpacked yet. Sadly, after that last appearance, it wasn't.

Hurricane Philomena, so disappointing initially, had turned out to be a bit of a giver after all, if not to all and sundry. On Sable Island, the residents there were treated to point-blank views of a Nova Scotia first, a Brown Noddy. It stayed three days but nobody else managed to get to see it, Sable isn't somewhere you can just twitch, and their transport was reported to be having issues.

Perhaps just as intriguing as the La Sagra's and Noddy was a handful of iffy photos from couple of non-birders who'd just moved to Carleton, near Yarmouth. They were both doctors and had been recruited from Europe to help fill the rural void in medical care as General Practitioners. Their large property had lots of flowers; they'd bought hummer feeders as soon as they realised they had them visiting. In the Facebook group 'New to Yarmouth', they'd posted a few hummer shots and asked what species they were. Inside a week they'd bought their first field guide and were shopping for winter feeders.

Three days after Philomena had gone through, Zofia, one of the doctors, posted a blurry image of a yellow hummingbird at the feeder but that wasn't in their book, at least not on the hummer page. A lot of people on the site said it was a 'goldenfinch', or a 'yellowedthroated', another said, more lucidly, perhaps it was a Yellow Warbler. The post was two-days old before a guy called Jose, a group member from Costa Rica of all places, said it was a Bananaquit. When you looked at the image properly, there was more than enough to identify it. Discord near melted.

The homeowners were contacted and were happy for people to look for their bird, even going as far as moving a hummer feeder to the front yard and removing the rest. Locals and a few visitors from afar looked often, but the Bananaquit was never seen again. Hurricane Philomena might not have supplied the species dump many had been predicting, but she had given Nova Scotia three new provincial list additions, even if nobody in the eBird top twenty got a sniff of any of them.

Moira loaded everyone into the Grand Caravan. She texted Howey and told him of the dip and how she was heading over to the Birchinalls' place with Hinzi and the kids. She always liked to catch up with people when she was down that way and, with Lenny and Marge Barnes up in Halifax for a few days, the Birchinalls were the only people around on a weekday.

"Can we drop into the Farmer's Market on the way back?" asked Hinzi, Moira was happy to; she'd probably pick up bits herself. The Birchinalls were happy to receive guests and made a fuss of the kids, but soon enough they said their goodbyes and made for Dayton. The market wasn't too busy, and a slow pick got them what they wanted. Moira was just about to head back onto the road, and then to the highway, when she saw someone getting into an old Honda Civic and driving off. The licence plate had one of those faded plastic covers on it making it illegible.

"Moira?" Hinzi had seen the reaction.

"Sorry, I just need to call Howey and we'll get on". She got no answer, so she sent a text. They were an hour up the road when Moira's phone beeped. Hinzi read it "Text not sent, tap to switch to SMS". Hinzi tapped. The reply came straight back, 'keep checking your mirror, if you see anything you don't like, let me know'.

"You're sure it was her, the same woman?" Howey Cross didn't like to question Moira's memory recall, but it was a process and he had to follow it, no matter who it involved.

"Yes, she made an impression on me at The Orchard, made me jittery. She knew your name and she knew we were together. Should I be worried, I have a shotgun licence, somewhere".

"Moira, no joking".

"Am I laughing? I got one years ago to do competition skeets with another girl, we got pretty good. I kept the licence up; I've just never mentioned it. I won't allow anything to happen, you know I won't. Don't poke the she-bear, not if you want to keep both arms".

Cross had never seen Moira quite like this. "We don't even know whether this Melissa has done anything wrong. I agree that we'd like a sit down with her based on what Angela sent, just to check her out, but unless she is seen anywhere near here, I can't see what we can do". He was worried that Moira was getting too involved. If the woman was Juliette Barker in disguise, she'd kept well away so far, so she'd be unlikely to break cover now. It wasn't even established that Barker had committed a crime either, all her supposed information from her police interviews had been a dud. That they'd not found any solid evidence suggested that she'd made everything up, that she was delusional.

Crystal walked in; she could sense the tension. "I did a full drive around, nothing of note. From what you say, Moira, this Melissa didn't see you in Yarmouth. I called Angela and she can't say for sure that she never mentioned Howey's name in casual conversation, he is her brother. You have your stamp on The Orchard, so of course she'd heard of you".

Moira realised that Crystal was right, she was applying the sort of cold logic that she herself was very good at, not so long ago. "I'm sorry, you're right. I overreacted and let my imagination run away with me a bit. I'm sorry, Howey, I didn't mean to cause a panic". Howey hugged her and told her that it was fine, that they were fine. Crystal watched, then made excuses and left. Seeing their raw love for each other was a bit much for her at the moment.

Late August 2022

"I had a thought". It was Darren who had been trying to look for angles with the dead hunter cases. "When Beth Cox died, does anyone know why Coates was in Ontario?"

"I think that is a gap in our knowledge, why, do you think he might have been up to something there too?" It had actually occurred to Crystal that Coates might not restrict his nefarious activities to Nova Scotia, but she'd neglected to write a note to self at the time, which was very unlike her. If asked, she'd quote mitigating circumstances.

"It's worth checking for unsolved incidents around the area and date. I'll do a system search, mention it to the boss while you're out with him, will you. I could do with the Brownie Points", said Darren, half-joking.

"Oh, come on. Just because Howey has gone up a notch doesn't mean anything changed. I admit, my being here might be a bit of a distraction, I am the looker here, but all the same, Howey is still Howey. You tell him once you've done some digging. I'm sure you'll get a pat on the back if you find something".

"Maybe, but I never seem to catch his ear like you do these days. Maybe it's the aftershave, I should switch to your perfume, it might make him more aware that I'm here", and with that Darren went back to his desk. Crystal wondered whether Darren had a point, but the evidence hinted more to Howey settling into a new role, establishing boundaries and probably being seen to do so more rigidly with those who were regarded as 'his' people. Her phone beeped; it was Terence messaging that his trip had been extended a couple of days until he'd reached his objective. It occurred to Crystal that she didn't actually know the details of what her boyfriend did, and so had no idea what objectives he had to achieve.

Darren decided that Crystal was right, away from work Howey was still Howey, any perceived favouritism was in his head, but if it continued, he'd have a quiet word. He started an unsolved crime search covering eastern Canada for the past five years, he reckoned that he might as well take the broader view and, if he came up with some interesting, potentially Coates-related activity, it might provide the evidence they needed to think about Coates' paymaster qualifying for extradition. 'Dream on', he thought.

Darren realised that it was a big ask, but apart from a couple of unsolved murders involving priests who were not seemingly related to fishing, nothing else stuck out. He opened the case files anyway. As far as he knew, Coates had never had a grudge against the clergy.

"Crystal, with me". Howey Cross was breezing out of the office, expecting Crystal to get a wiggle on to keep up. If anyone else had talked to her in that tone, it wouldn't have ended well for them.

When she got there, Cross was already in the driver's seat and setting his phone up with the directions. For some reason CBC news always fired up when he connected his phone to the Android Car-play thing. "Where to, boss?"

"We're going to see Watson again. I called ahead; we have an hour of his precious time so think whether there's anything we should be asking him".

"You mean we're going without a good reason and without a thought-out strategy, that's not like you, Howey".

"I have a couple of questions, ones he will be able to answer. I want you to observe before stepping in at any opportune moment. I just thought that you might have been mulling things over too and have come up with a strategy of your own".

"Right, ok, will do. Oh, and Darren has an idea about Coates, what he might have been up to in Ontario when Beth Cox died might be relevant, he's checking into it. A good idea I'd have thought". Crystal had fed Cross Darren's idea to see his reaction.

"Or a waste of time, but I suppose we need something, we're stagnating with that one a bit. I messaged Peter Burns, he's still reluctant to get involved any further until he feels well enough, understandable. It was only a courtesy contact anyway, none of us can see where his difficulties with Bush can help us. Darren might be onto something when looking at the broader picture. I asked Kent to gauge the state of lobster fishing for us, he's in the right place to talk to the right people, his ear is to the ground in case the names of Bush or Coates come up. He says hi by the way".

"Good, because we need something more there, I'm lead on the case, and it makes me look ineffective if nothing happens. The Coates case is stagnating because we're putting so much into the Barker case".

"Are you questioning my leadership, Crystal?"

"What? No, just stating facts. Don't be so freaking paranoid".

"No, you're right. Sorry, my bad. Moira's reaction at being a twin has got to me. She's ok now but it shook her and, when I thought more about it, me. You know there's a lot of similarities to Barker's life with how Moira was raised, it's been on my mind a lot recently".

"Similarities perhaps, but very dissimilar people from what I understand of Barker. If you're in a dilemma, perhaps you should step back and let me and Darren deal with the case?"

"No, I don't think so and I know my fears don't really have any substance, it's just that I've always kept a weather eye on her, my natural, protective nature. Let's change the subject, How's things with you? Not seen you socially recently, is Terence keeping you busy? Not that I meant anything by that, I just meant occupied. Sorry. How are you two getting on, I wasn't prying, is he moving in?"

Crystal laughed. That was more the old Howey Cross, blustering when he got something wrong. "We're ok I suppose but I'm still spending a lot of time alone while he does his stupid projects. Just as well I have the house to keep me busy, you should all come over and visit, I can give you directions, just bring a paintbrush with you. Going back to Terence, I still don't really know what he does, do you?"

"Environmental consultant he told me. Advises industry on best practices to keep them legal. It sounds interesting although I didn't know he had to travel that much. I'd have thought most things could be remote these days".

"No, he said he has to be there, wherever there is this week".

"There is a way to find out where he's been recently", said Cross, furtively.

"I don't want to pry, it's still early days for us, things are much slower than I expected", said Crystal. Then after a moment's thought she added, "How?"

"He's a birder and I guarantee that he'll put checklists in eBird for wherever he is, it's what birders do. All you need to do is to look at his profile in eBird to see his latest checklists, I'll show you". Cross pulled into a gas station; the car had been running on fumes for the past ten kilometres. He pulled out his phone, navigated the app to the Nova Scotia top 100 and scrolled down. He knew that Ferry had been birding the province hard since returning, so he should be in the top fifty at least. His scheme was thwarted when he saw no hyperlink giving Ferry's profile, so he showed her his, and how it worked. "Odd that, not many give up the chance to say who they are and let people see their birding heat map".

"Why would he not have a public profile?" said Crystal, a little concerned.

"Lots of reasons, maybe he never got around to it, didn't think about it, or someone gave him stick for a rarity sighting that nobody else caught up with. People go quiet on eBird for all sorts of reasons, some prefer to become anonymous. Text and ask him, he'll tell you, I'm sure". The answer was light, but Howey being Howey did wonder himself why the apparently outgoing Terence Ferry was an eBird man of mystery.

"Ok, sent. Let's see what he comes up with". Howey clambered out to fill the tank. As he got back in, Crystal looked at him, interrogatively. "Darren, are you treating him as least favourite for a good reason?" Crystal hadn't meant to broach the subject, but now seemed as good a time as any to give it an airing.

"Am I, I did wonder but I expected him to mention it directly. I'm trying to be scrupulously impartial. Regis advised it, he recommended being aloof".

"You're taking staff sergeant advice from someone who drove you up the wall to the point of walking? Maybe you should ask Trump how he got such a natural tan?"

Cross laughed. The orange one was deliberately not mentioned around the precinct. One of the other officers had a prized MAGA hat in his locker and trotted out the 'drain the swamp' rhetoric at regular intervals. "Point taken, I'll see Darren out of work, shoot the breeze, drink a beer and have that chat".

"Sounds great, can I come? I promise I won't let you down. I can drink beer and pee standing up and everything".

"Maybe", was all Cross would say. The exit to Annapolis Royal was getting closer and he wanted to get his head ready for the inevitable game of mental chess that Geoffrey Watson was bound to insist on. As they drove on, Crystal was fiddling with her phone having just had a text. "Anything interesting?" asked Cross.

"eBird, just digging like you showed me. Sudbury, I know that Terence is somewhere near Sudbury, he said he'd been there for three days".

"Right, not that far from Manitoulin Island then. Nice, a Sharp-tailed Grouse site although I've never been".

Crystal gave him a look. "There are birds with tails that are sharp, isn't that dangerous?"

"No, not unless one backs into you. Right, now search species maps for the grouse, change the details to narrow down the time period then look for pins on Manitoulin, it sits in Lake Huron. Each pin will be a bird checklist, open the pin, find the absentee boyfriend, easy".

Crystal navigated the app easily and was pleased to find Terence's checklist and he had seen a dangerous grouse. "He got one, and some Sandhill Cranes. Only one checklist thought, he must be busy".

"Now you know the area, you can search around for more recent checklists, I'll show you later, we're here".

After being kept waiting a little longer than they were happy about, Watson ushered them into his consulting room apologising for the delay and citing a run of consultations that lasted longer than expected. "Have you found her?" he asked.

"No, not yet, but I wanted to keep you updated. My boss has asked us to keep you in the loop. The advice I've been given is to tap into your extensive experiences of similar cases, although none will come close to Juliette Barker, and I wanted to go through our transcripts of our interviews with Barker and get your take on them. Can I take it by doing that, we wouldn't be breaching your patient confidentiality obligation?"

Watson seemed to swell a bit, or at least he sat up straighter. "No, the interviews are your intellectual property, I think. Can I see them?"

"Ah, there we're told that while we can read out selected parts of the interviews, we're not to allow you free access. We have the same basic data protection issues, sorry".

"Oh, I see, actually that's quite correct. Ok, read on and I'll answer as best I can".

Cross handed Crystal a couple of sheets, he had sheets too, both had the office schedule printed on it, waiting for their comments. Crystal produced a pen and waited for Howey's lead.

It took about forty-five minutes, including a bit of backtracking before they thanked Watson and left.

"You crafty so-and-so", said Crystal as they got underway. "No plan, right? Did you come up with that on the fly?"

"What, we asked some questions and Geoff answered them. That he thought his answers were comments on Barker's statements is basically true. We found out that he doesn't have much more than we do, so we don't need to waste more time with him at the moment. It also told us that, while he thought her sister was a fantasy, Phil and Abigail were real. That Phil seems to have been in another place at another time doesn't matter. Abigail Smith is missing and has been since late 2019, now for the difficult bit".

"Her folks?"

"Her folks".

"Juliette's sister, we're not treating her as missing at the moment, perhaps we should be, given the circumstances?" Crystal had been bothered by the conflicting evidence over Barker's sister, she was very much a grey area where the investigation was concerned.

"We know that she was real, but she's not showed up in the system. Alive, she could be anywhere in Canada, it's a big ask". Cross had had the same difficulties regarding Barker's sister.

"What if she was a victim and Barker is covering her tracks by telling people she talks to her?" Crystal turned off the sat-nav, they'd arrived.

"From what I've read, twins can work as a pair. I read a case history where twins had been separated at birth but lived almost parallel lives, despite being raised thousands of miles apart. When they were finally united, their similarities, both physical and in their life choices were uncanny. That we don't even have Melissa's adoptive family name is a drawback. We can only deal with what we see, for now. Right, solemn face, let's see what Abigail Smith's folks have to say".

Cross and Crystal climbed back into the car. Crystal looked back at the neat cottage home, its windows shaded with snowy white net curtains, its door firmly closed. There was no sign of any occupants waving them off, although she was sure their departure was being monitored.

"That was difficult", said Crystal, trying hard to reconcile what had just happened. "How can parents disown their children, just because of a bit of promiscuity and drugs. What happened to Christian values?"

"If they're not interested, you can't force them. I'll admit that them not having kept any photos of Abigail is taking the cult to extremes, but that's what it is, a cult. We might find her on Facebook, we should get something from there. Fancy some lunch?"

The cafe was busy but the staff smiling and attentive. The menu looked pretty good, but Cross was wary of ordering anything too calorific, Moira had already pointed out the spread. "Are you ready to order?"

Crystal went for a bagel and coffee, Cross for a salad. "Won't be long, we're busy today, seems like most of the town is eating out", and the waitress bustled off.

Crystal looked at Cross. "Tell me they spoke to people in here", she said.

Cross shrugged. "I don't think they did. I don't recall any statements taken from here. Let's finish lunch, then we can have a chat".

Their meals arrived and they tucked in. Around them the other tables slowly emptied. "Anything else I can get you?" asked the server, they appeared to be the only ones left. The last of the other customers had just gone and, while trying to sound attentive, the woman in front of them told a different story with her body language.

Cross and Roberts showed their IDs. "Can we have a word? It's about Juliette Barker. Did you know her?" She did.

Laura Towle was very talkative, and very informative. She seemed to revel in being involved, as if Annapolis Royal was so quiet that being embroiled in a messy murder inquiry was just what she wanted as a leisure activity. Cross asked the questions; Crystal wrote it all down. Her last comment had them thinking. "She loved Keji, she once told me that Little Kempton Lake there was where she left all her troubles".

They mentioned Abigail Smith and Laura continued to talk. Crystal wrote it all down again.

"Have you been here long Laura?" Crystal was wanting to add a few details to her notes.

"Too long really, I own the place. Did anyone tell you about the woman who lived there before, the one who they think died near Digby?" They said no and Laura started to talk again, it was a long story and took a while, but Laura's gossip potentially added flesh to the bones of the story. Melissa Rylance and Muriel Lester became people to find out a lot more about.

Back outside, Cross and Crystal looked at each other over the car roof, before getting in. Both thought that they'd found something interesting. It was a lead, of sorts, the first lead they'd had in many days. Cross took a deep breath. "Text Darren with a summary of what we have, I'll catch Madam later and discuss. I think, if my memory serves, that Little Kempton Lake is in Queens County, the park's split between Annapolis Royal and Queens. I'll talk to Constance O'Toole about a search and liaising with Queens and we'll need to go in with dogs". The car had an air of excitement, things were moving in the right direction. Crystal got busy texting, as Cross pulled the car out onto the road.

Darren replied, 'great news, brief tomorrow then, I'll set it up. No connections found for Coates in Ontario, a surprising number of dead priests though, I came up with seven, all retired. Somebody is going to have their hands full'.

Crystal looked up from the text she'd been reading out. "If we search Keji and find bodies and if one of them is Abigail Smith, then our search changes from looking for someone who might have killed someone but is delusional, to someone who did kill, but how many?" Cross had been thinking exactly the same thing. "After tomorrow's brief, I'll set the wheels in motion. Any bodies there aren't suddenly going to run away. It won't be cheap, a search time, dogs and handlers, the works, it's time for Madam to put her hand in her pocket.

"We need to update our profiles for Muriel Lester and Melissa Rylance too, the adoption agency is another place where Madam can wield a little influence". Crystal sounded optimistic.

"If she has a mind to", said Cross, effectively shooting her optimism down with his tone.

CHAPTER SEVENTEEN

Late August 2022

When Howey Cross got in to work next morning, it took a moment to remember that he'd already planned to send Crystal and Darren out together more. It had been deliberate, agreed with Crystal and at Leah's suggestion to, she said, 'dispel any rumours'. He knew what she meant. He'd been out on the Barker case with Crystal several times, with Darren left on his own and feeling a bit left out. It wasn't deliberate and he'd said so when he scheduled their trip to check refuges in Halifax and Dartmouth following a brief to discuss the previous day's news. He didn't expect much from their trip, the places closer to the city weren't easy places to hide in, but they had to keep at it, they had to find Juliette Barker.

"Just following up on yesterday, Ma'am". Cross had found Carmel a bit intransigent when he'd spoken to her after having got back from Annapolis Royal. He could see that they were much closer to understanding both Barker and what she might have done, but while his request for a search and cadaver dogs had been met with coolness, asking for a push on the adoption agency was met with pure ice.

"Sorry, Howey, but what I said yesterday pretty much stands. Your waitress might have given us some ideas, but without solid evidence Keji is a huge place to look. Even just the Little Kempton Lake area, it would take a lot of officers a long time to search it and we don't have access to dogs at the moment. We need Barker to lead us there and so you need to find her. I'm just being realistic; you know that, and I want this thing wrapped up the same as you do. Getting anything from the adoption agency needs help from the judiciary, which I can't see happening. How's Moira?"

Any persuasive arguments that Cross was about to employ had been scuppered by a simple question. "Er, fine, no, spectacular. She has a project of some sort on the go, I don't know what, I never do until she's done but she's very enthused".

"Good, she has an excellent mind, she needs to keep it busy, I know, I'm the same sometimes. Find me Barker, Howey, then we'll find money to dig, we just won't need as much. Nice work with Watson by the way, thank Crystal too". The phone went dead.

Darren had left a pile of papers, each containing short notes on the dead hunters' case. Cross was feeling less than enthused about it, mostly because he knew what had happened, or thought that he did. On one slip a name came up. Michael Garrity, Smiling Mickey to his friends, was someone who had physically fought with Kenneth Coates once, it was suggested that he might be worth talking to. There was an address included, somewhere in Lunenburg County and worth a shot, anything to get out of the precinct. Something Greg Barnes had said recently in the bird group came to mind too, but he couldn't remember what. He grabbed his coat and told Leah he'd be out for a few hours.

Five Years Ago

Smiling Mickey took another slug of whatever it was Tom-thumb had brought along, it was awful but had the desired anesthetic effect. The shack was supposed to be for dominos but, while it looked like a hotbed of keenly fought domino challenges, in the cupboard at the back was a shelf with various bottles of maturing home brew, all labeled in order of conception. Some were now more than a month old.

"What did they give you?" asked Tom, not that he didn't know. The news of Smiling Mickey and his run-in with the game wardens was all over the county.

"Two-year ban, eight hundred dollars, keep the guns".

"Could have been worse".

Smiling Mickey did what he'd got his nickname for. Tom was right, if they really knew what he'd got up to in the past he'd have been looking out of a locked cell door, again. "I'll bide my time, keep my nose clean and get my own back when the time is right, I'm a patient man", he said, and he smiled the famous, insincere smile.

'Someone is going to pay for this', thought Tom, glad that it wasn't him this time. Smiling Mickey had held grudges from sixth grade and, as he knew to his own cost, he always got his own back.

Late August 2022

September was supposed to be when the winners of the Sable Island trip raffle were heading out for the day hoping to find rare birds. Scheduling the day had been bad enough, the only serviceable flight having to fit them in between taking and bringing back scientists. Avian flu was being studied, Sable Island was isolated and so a good place to study it but that meant windows for the trip were at a premium. In the end the winners agreed to defer the trip until the spring, when, hopefully, things would be less frantic. Greg came up with a plan 'B'.

"Never heard of it", said Darren Newell when Greg Barnes asked about a place called Coot Drop Island. Greg's interest had been piqued when he came across a local newsletter piece doing one of those rehashed history things. A Halifax man had visited Coot Drop Island and had reported seeing lots of birds. He'd even shot some, it was the 1950s when they did that, and the luckless birds had ended up in Halifax Museum. Manly Stanley had later shown Greg the skins to confirm the ID, the single trip haul had included a Prothonotary Warbler and a Western Kingbird, along with a few less common migrants. The problem in finding the place had been that Coot Drop Island wasn't the real name of the place, it was actually called Pine Island on the maps, and it was out offshore from LeHave somewhere.

Greg had been intrigued enough to want to set up a little trip, just for a look-see, a birding adventure. He was an avid island birder and Coot Drop Island would be a new eBird location for him and everyone else, by the sound of it. He put out a few feelers and waited. A friend of a friend of a friend then put Greg in touch with a local boatman, known to locals as 'Smiling Mickey', who was willing to take a group over to Coot Drop Island. He was told it would be a minimum one-fifty for the boat, on landing, and that they'd get five hours ashore, the tide dictating that they'd leave port at 04:30. He put the trip up on the Discord chat channel and had six takers. Greg was pleased, it was enough for the trip to go but his dad, Lenny, had declined due to not being overly fascinated with scrabbling across slippery rocks to spend five hours on a small island, hoping for birds.

The day came around and the small crew duly assembled. The skipper was a bit rough, spat a lot and refused to engage in conversation but that wasn't that unusual. It was a steady run out in a boat that didn't strike everyone as being particularly well kept. The seats were wet, an axe wandered around the floor at will and a hole in the side, thankfully above the waterline, was bunged up with an oily rag. A handful of spent shotgun shells that surprisingly hadn't gone over the side when used, rolled around the floor and contributed to the overall redneck ambience.

Greg was only on nodding terms with two of the intrepid explorers, Antigonish birders Bill White and Chesney Robinson who, it transpired, had been recruited by Frank, just to make sure the trip ran. Frank Conte, Jerry Buckley and David Cantwell he knew well. On the way out, the group had chattered away, getting to know each other better, chewing over the birding possibilities of a new place. Soon they left the shelter of the bay and were out into the exposed and open ocean. The island was a dot in the distance, more because it was relatively small than because it was miles away. Greg had established that it would take about twenty minutes or so to get there and that it would be a rough landing, there was no beach on the images he had, just what looked like wet and slippery rocks.

Naturally everyone birded very keenly on the way out, the sum reward, apart from gulls, being a single Common Loon and a Black Guillemot. As the island neared it looked quite attractive, one end had a series of healthy-looking bushes and a couple of trees. The image on Google Earth had showed what looked like a pond at the other end, a migrant magnet if ever there was one. Twenty feet from the island it was clear that the landing was going to be a bit of a lottery. The swell, not obvious as they chugged out, was magnified by the proximity of the rocky shore. The rise and fall was perhaps only a metre or so, but the footing was iffy, and the rocks were slippery. Lenny had been right to give this one a miss, despite Greg's badgering.

The skipper drove his boat straight into the rocks where it stopped with a thud, then he leapt out with a rope and ran sure-footed and goat-like over the rocks and onto the coarse grass above it. "Come on then", he said, with no charm. One by one, the birders cautiously got out, then slipped and slid a bit as they headed for firmer footing, but all made it unscathed onto the turf. Greg had already collected the money and the skipper was obviously waiting for it.

"Pick-up around one-ish then?" said Greg, starting to doubt the wisdom of paying the ferryman for only half the trip.

The skipper didn't answer, instead he pocketed the money and started back to his boat, Greg had a bad feeling about this. When the skipper had nearly reached the boat, he turned around laughing, then shouted, "you bastards stopped me hunting five years ago and I said I'd get the birders back sometime, so there you are, revenge is sweet. Good luck finding a ride off, enjoy your birdies everyone", and with that he turned to leap into his boat, slipped, smashed his head spectacularly on a rock before plunging into the water and slipping under the boat.

Jerry Buckley dashed forward and grabbed the rope before it followed the skipper into the water, then they all just stood there.

"Shouldn't we try to save him?" said David Cantwell.

Still nobody moved. There was an air of uncertainty to say the least.

Frank Conte walked forward and took the rope that Buckley was still holding. He deftly tied it to an elderly lobster trap and turned back to the group. "Look, he's gone, dead, there's nothing we could have done, it was an accident, we all saw it. I suggest we call the police; they'll probably call the coastguard, and someone will take us back, or one of us can skipper the skiff".

"What about birding the island?" said Buckley, ever the practical one.

"Good point, it'll take the police a while to get organized, let's have a look around while we wait for help".

"Anyone got a signal?" asked Greg. Nobody had.

"I suggest we have a kick around anyway, in case he's either washed up somewhere or even crawled out", said Bill White. "We're here now, we should do a search. If he's dead, he's dead but if he's injured somewhere we have a responsibility". It was a good point and so they conducted a search of the island that included checking all the vegetation on the off chance that Smiling Mickey had managed to crawl ashore and hidden in a bush, he hadn't. Then they wandered around the island all waving their cell phones at the sky trying to get a signal. They didn't.

In birding terms, the Coot Drop Island jaunt had been pretty good, dead angry man aside, and although nothing spectacular was found, it held a good mix of spring migrants, a few year ticks and was a nice change of scenery. Cantwell offered to take them back, he'd worked a small skiff in his youth and assumed it was like riding a bike, but with an outboard. Getting into the skiff was done very carefully, two at a time for support and avoiding the still pink rocks as best they could, they being a stark reminder of what careless footing might bring.

"I took some phone shots of the scene including the rocks", said Buckley conversationally. "Quite a bitter sort of guy, that one. We should be in signal range soon, who's going to call the police?"

"I will, after I've had a word with dad", said Greg, not sure whether to feel awful about the guy dying or happy he'd been hoist by his own petard. They were over half-way back when he made the call, explaining everything. Lenny said he'd get right back to him, but it was Howey Cross who called, telling Greg that local law enforcement would need a statement from everyone.

"What about the guy?"

"Someone will go out and look for him, but I suspect he's communing with lobsters somewhere. Unless one of you held his head under or pushed him in, I wouldn't worry, this will just go down as an accident".

As they headed to shore, they saw a cruiser arrive with the blue lights flashing. The mood of the boat turned sombre, as what had happened to the boatman finally sank in, then Buckley called an adult Little Gull passing close by, with a couple of Bonaparte's, and the mood lifted. On shore the bored officers listened to the story and just took names and addresses. Cross lingered on the periphery, clearly his chance for a chat with Smiling

Mickey had gone. Greg told him of Mickey's attempt to maroon them on the island, and why. It figured, given what Cross knew of Mickey's proclivities. It didn't look like he'd be a big loss to society.

Not wanting to head home, Cross pulled up a list of women's hostels and refuges, selected one in the area and put it into the sat-nav. If nothing else, a visit to 'Last Chance' in Chester would be one less place to look at, if they cooperated.

Last Chance was quite a surprise. Clean, modern, and clearly well looked after. Inside he found someone in a suit who seemed to be in charge, She called herself Tracey Johnson. He showed his ID and started asking questions. The woman was polite, but Cross could feel that he wasn't welcome, that was one of the reasons why he preferred these visits to include Crystal. He looked carefully for a reaction when he showed the photo of Juliette Barker to Johnson, but she just shook her rather attractive red locks. "Any reason for the tinted glasses?" he asked.

"Conjunctivitis, pink eye. I hope I'm not still infective, I can take them off if you like", she said, reaching up.

Cross said that it wouldn't be necessary, thanked her and left her to it, she seemed keen to get back to work. As he drove home, he instinctively rubbed his eyes. At a gas station he filled up, grabbed a coffee and carefully examined his eyes for signs in the rear-view mirror. 'Maybe I'm a bit tired' he thought, before getting off back to Kentville. When he got in, Leah had left a pile of papers on his desk for him to deal with, neither Darren nor Crystal had called or texted with anything and now he was sure he had a sore eye. He pulled up their expanding list of refuges to check and marked up 'Last Chance' as done. Then he red-penned the name Michael Garrity from the Coates file and settled back to tackle the backlog.

"Does anyone know where Tracey is?" Mary Bennet, the manager, had looked all over 'Last Chance' but there was no sign of Johnson or her own spare suit. It was her own fault; she should never have left her office unlocked.

CHAPTER EIGHTEEN

Early September 2022

The knock on the door was loud, it demanded attention and made Mori nervous. Her landlord was generally quieter when he knocked and, although he'd promised to drop by and look at a tap that was dripping, he wasn't expected until later. She looked through her peep hole and saw a man. "Hello, yes?"

"Mori Guier? I'm here to talk to you about FLAP Canada".

"Who are you?" She looked again and saw an ID card with the man's photo and saying that he was some sort of policeman. She opened the door a fraction. "What is it?"

"I wanted to have a little chat about something to do with FLAP, I'm from Josh Hennigar's office".

Finally. "Just a moment". Mori nipped to her phone and texted one of her helpers that a man had arrived from Hennigar's office and that she was letting him in. The door opened and she welcomed the man in. "Do you have a name?"

"Can we sit, have that chat?" To business then. The man sat and Mori started to talk dead birds, he let her.

"Your organisation monitors bird strikes, yes? Windows, lights, windmills and that sort of thing?"

"Yes, I was just going to give you the figures for Nova Scotia, they don't include lighthouse strikes and the windmill people don't talk to us. You see it wouldn't take much to make an impact, to do some good and there's thousands of us all over North America all waiting for action". Mori was quite pleased to get some of her arguments over so early in the negotiations, as she thought of them.

"Are all of the people involved concerned citizens like yourself?"

"Yes, I suppose so, just ordinary folk doing what they can".

"I read about you wanting a celebrity death, I didn't quite get the context".

"Oh, you get my newsletter. Sorry, I was being rather cynical, I don't wish death on anything. Don't worry about Chico, he's harmless, he'll just sit on you for a while then lose interest and wander off".

The man was trying to ease the large tomcat off his knees, which was having the reverse effect he desired and Chico, who knew how not to be moved, flexed his claws ever so slightly. The man jumped.

"Chico, bad boy, no treats and no out", yelled Mori in what she thought of as her firm voice.

"To go back to the celebrity death?" said the guy as he brushed cat hairs off his pants.

"Yes, if we had a rare bird like say a Bicknell's Thrush get picked up it would become the banner species for our campaign. I don't wish ill on any bird, but it would help. Mr. Hennigar hasn't responded to our messages until now".

"I see, well thank you Mori and good luck. One question, your cat, you let it out?"

"Yes, he's a rescue cat and he can get very antsy if he can't go out, I know what you're thinking but he's a good boy, I feed him well, he's never caught a bird, he wouldn't".

"No, of course not. Thanks again for the clarification, I'll be off then".

"Give Mr. Hennigar my best wishes, we need more like him".

When the nice man had gone, Mori sent an email to Tina Peck, thanking her. Tina read the text and wondered what had happened.

Storm Ulrika, when it hit, had Crystal's largely empty new house rattling like a crate of empty beer bottles on the way to re-cyc. Her generator had kicked in just as they said it would, so she had power for now at least. She didn't need heat, in fact were she able to, she'd have had the air conditioning up high such was the humidity. Her home Wi-Fi wasn't working but her phone still had a connection, so she decided to try to learn some more eBird. It was an area of her life where friends and her partner had a mutual interest and she felt she ought to know at least how it worked, so she didn't feel totally at sea the next time it was discussed.

After refreshing her glass of gin, a recently discovered comfort for the increasingly frequent times spent alone, she opened up the app and sat back to see what all the fuss was about. With Howey's help she'd mentally filed clues as to where to go within the app, places where she could see what birdies they were seeing in Nova Scotia. On the 'Top 100' page for the province she scrolled down the list of anorak-wearing sad people, smiling when she came to people she knew.

It was interesting to click on and then see each individual profile. Some of the birders had pretty dull resumes, others injected a little humour with a different sort of image or tongue-in-cheek self-deprecation in their little biog. Moira kept making references to stunned owls, just to wind up Greg Barnes, apparently. Howey kept making references to his inexperience with birding despite being active for a few years now and far from slow. Even the terrors had their own accounts, although it was clearly Moira who updated them for them, but Terence, he didn't want to be known.

Since she'd first found out about his lack of openness where eBird was concerned, she'd put it down to an element of shyness and the fact that he was new to Nova Scotia birding, in a way at least. She'd meant to ask him about his list personally, but he'd barely figured in her life recently and she wondered whether she was wasting her time with him. As far as his lists were concerned, she could see a number, for Nova Scotia at least. She changed the parameter to Canada and was surprised to see that her Terence was in the top twenty-five life listers in Canada, which meant he must have done an awful lot of chasing or been lucky enough to use his time working to bird as well. Another question to ask the indefinable Terence Ferry when he got back.

Suddenly the room lit up and various things announced that Nova Scotia Power had done their thing, despite the weather, and they were now being fed the electricity they needed. Eventually the house modem caught up after spending an eternity wearing flashing green lights. Once the blue ones were on, Crystal switched to her laptop, and continued her education in eBird. A thought occurred to her. If Terence was so high in the country top 100, then he must have lots of checklists in there somewhere. She texted Howey asking for an example of any rare bird in Canada, telling him she was trying to learn eBird. He texted back with something called a Red-flanked Bluetail from British Columbia. Her mind's-eye gave her the image of a bird, small with red sides and a bluetail, it really was that easy.

It took her a while to figure out how to see individual bird records again, and not the species accounts although the images that came up for the bluetail confirmed her initial impression of what it might look like. After a bit of trial and error, she finally found the right species map and scrolled the list of observers until she found Terence. Even though it had been pretty simple, once you'd grasped the logic, Crystal was inordinately proud that she'd found out that Terence had been in Vancouver in January 2013. An amusing thought popped into her head, and she imagined all those 5G-chem trail nutjobs out there desperately conflicted as to whether to report that they'd seen a rarity, knowing that the information about where they were and when on any given day was freely available to anyone.

It was with some disappointment that Crystal closed down the laptop when the power was lost again. She'd spent some time picking through Sibley, then looking to see both whether a rare species had occurred in Canada, and whether her boyfriend had seen it. In most cases, where the bird had been seen in the last ten years or so, he had. Terence Ferry sure got around a lot. She reached for the gin again and was surprised to find it empty. One more for the bottle bank. The lights stayed off, so she went to bed and slept the sleep of the slightly inebriated.

The next morning and sporting more than a little hangover, Crystal sat eating breakfast with Howey and Moira. Her fuel supply was getting low, and the farm had a fancy back-up generator and capacious fuel tank, so she'd accepted the breakfast invitation despite the possibility the terrors might go full toddler on her and chuck food around, but they didn't. "Any idea how long before we get power?" she asked as a general question.

"It won't be long, they're usually pretty good around here, probably later today. You're looking a bit red-eyed, didn't you sleep?" Howey was only vaguely interested. He had farm things to do and so was rushing his breakfast to leave enough time.

"The wind noise kept me awake, so I was reading late".

"Proust, Wells, Adams?"

"No, a new Nova Scotia author, a crime writer actually. Quite good. I also had a wander around eBird for a while. I can see why it's so popular now, it's like a little league for birders".

"Some treat it that way, yes, but the main and very serious purpose is data gathering. We now know more about our birds, their populations and distribution than ever before", said Howey, seriously. He stood up, cleared his plates, and headed outside for his bout of manual labour. The women watched him go.

"Welcome to the sect, Crystal. Now all we have to do is sacrifice a goat and cover you in its blood and you're ours". Moira liked to add a bit of silliness to the conversation. Howey was way too serious when it came to the citizen science thing.

"Before you fetch the knives, I don't see me taking up looking at birdies, but I can see the overall picture, and I can see that eBird is a tool we can use, professionally".

Moira laughed. "True, people that decline being tracked by web sites have sold their souls for a place at the birding top 100 table. Did you find that bit? Most illuminating although not every birder participates in eBird".

"I saw that. Terence is in there but there's no profile. I can't understand why a profile isn't mandatory, how can you tell whether someone knows what they're talking about if you can't see what they're like or how many birds they've seen?"

"Howey asked the same questions before we got him. Some people just don't want more information out there than is necessary, not that I'm saying people are hiding anything. Not everyone has a 'look at me' attitude. Moira was sounding quite sensible; she'd obviously had the same thoughts as Crystal at some point.

"You don't seem to have many species in Nova Scotia, Moira, just a couple more than Howey. I thought you'd been birding for a few years?"

"I did a reset when Martin Perry killed his brother and I emerged into the real world. You got a glimpse of me in the transitional phase in that cafe in downtown Halifax that time. I felt that if I was going to walk in the real world I had to start afresh, for my reputation and my soul. I only kept one species from that time, something that represents the new me". Moira looked slightly wistful, surely she didn't miss her previous persona?

"I know I won't know what it is, but what species?"

"A Carolina Chickadee, a provincial first. I was lucky in finding it, but it also confirmed that I was good enough to walk with giants, or at least three steps behind. Then Howey happened".

"Howey happened, yes, I remember it well".

Suddenly there was a competitive element to the atmosphere, something both women knew would surface from time to time and there'd be, as there was back then, only one winner.

Moira had already decided to head off things at the pass. "Why did you decided to wander eBird, really?" she asked.

"I just wanted to connect with Terence, to vicariously experience his presence just like those birds he'd chased had. I was feeling low, maybe a bit neglected".

"He's not the one, is he?" said Moira, shrewdly.

"No, I don't think so", answered Crystal, a little sadly.

"Melissa, the boss wants a word when we're clear". The busy steward had passed on the information, as requested, but now he was busy either feeding hungry faces or trying to explain why something wasn't available on the Pictou to Wood Island, PEI, run.

"Did you tell her?" The boss was annoyed, when people were told to see him, he expected it to happen.

"Yes, she said she'd be there, and I left it at that, I was serving so I couldn't follow her around or anything, if I see her can I tell her the problem?"

"Yes, there's a mix up with her documents, Human Resources want to see her to iron it out. Probably them screwing it up rather than anything Melissa's done, she seemed very sharp if a little old for such a low-paid job, how old do you reckon?"

The Steward wasn't that interested in playing guess the lady's age but threw in a thirty-five anyway.

"Close but no cigar, she must have led a blameless life. If you do see her, tell her it's nothing to worry about, thanks".

"Will do, but don't be surprised if we don't see her again" said the steward disinterested, as he cleaned down the serving area before doling out the next, and last plate of Cumberland Sausage.

CHAPTER NINETEEN

Early September 2022

Howey Cross was surprised to get an internal message from a cop, James Godden, working out of Guysborough. His surprise was compounded by the fact that the cop cited reading the notes regarding the two outstanding cold-case hunter files Cross's team were working on, Kenneth Coates being the tenuous link to both deaths. As Staff Sergeant, Cross was now routinely seeing the bulletins each time one was issued, previously he'd only seen bits of bits as his bosses felt relevant. The bulletin was nicknamed 'Tales from the Fridge', a nod to the nature of the cases. What it did was inform the wider law enforcement management that cold cases had been reactivated or closed down, solved or otherwise. It made interesting reading.

Godden's email quoted a friend of a friend conversation whereby Kenneth Coates had been involved in the roughing up of an independent fishery owner who'd, allegedly, been less than civil to Dan Bush. It was another slender lead to Bush, who seemed to be the common denominator in his cold cases. The rest of the bulletin was only vaguely interesting, although Cross was sure that Madam's hand would be behind all or most of the rejuvenated investigations. This gave Howey the impression that he and his team were a part of an elite group, hand-picked from on high. It was surprising how much was going on, from a drugs thing in Dartmouth through to a Catholic Priest dying in suspicious circumstances, all cases now getting the fullest attention from law enforcement.

After spending ten minutes reading the bulletin, he decided to forward the whole to his sergeants to keep them in the loop. There's no such thing as too much information. Knowing he was banging his head against a wall; he called Wild Caught Fisheries again and identified himself. The voice on the desk recognised him and confirmed that Dan Bush was not in Nova Scotia and, no, they were not aware of any future dates when he would be available for interview. In the background, he heard a voice before the person on the end of the phone changed. "Mr. Bush likely won't be back any time soon so stop calling".

"And you are?" asked Cross, not willing to let it go.

"Martin Atkinson, plant manager. Mr. Bush has been advised that you want to talk to him, but his legal people are dealing with it, so there's really no need to keep calling here, we're a very busy plant".

"I see, thank you, Martin. In that case I'll be along at some point to talk to you, don't disappoint me when I drop by. We staff sergeants can get very testy when that happens. When we meet, we'll be having an informal conversation, or you can get legal representation if you think you need it and we'll bring you along to the Amherst precinct, have a nice day", and Cross cut Atkinson off before he could say anything. Pleased with his decision to kick a few local tires, he texted Crystal and Darren to let them know what he had in mind and then went back to reading the bulletin. Something there was bothering him, but he didn't know what.

When Crystal pushed open the farmhouse door it was once again a scene of chaos inside, but this time lacked the flying food element. Moira was busy feeding kids, cleaning up and trying to get Howey out of the way. He was insisting that there was no rush and wanting to lend a hand, but Moira would have none of it. It didn't help that she needed to head to Annapolis Royal for some business appointment, and she was running late. "Crystal, take my man away, will you? He's getting under my feet again".

"Come on Howey, bad people to chase, leave Moira to it, she has everything under some sort of control. Is it tonight you're stopping over with Barbara and Phil, Moira?"

"Barbara and Neil, yes, the kids need the mental stimulation and heaven knows I do too. Howey said you'll be out late again, so I thought we'd go for a wander. Barbara loves the kids, Neil might too. Cape Breton way today, is it?"

"Yes, and we'd better get a move on. Howey, get your ass into gear, lots of highway miles to do today".

Cross knew when he was being ganged up on and allowed himself to be chivvied out the door. "Lasagna in the fridge, plenty of it to share", called Moira as the door closed.

"I'd have been happy to drive in and go from work", said Crystal as they climbed into Howey's car, aware that by leaving her car at home again, she'd lost an element of independence.

"Makes no sense though, we're both coming back here after. Why, is there a problem?"

"What, no, not really. What do you expect to get from this Atkinson guy at Bush's fish plant?"

"Nothing for now, but a visit by us will fester with Bush and it might tempt him to react. Besides, I've pencilled in two different women's refuges to pull in on the way back, just to looksee and talk to whoever operates them".

"I see, that explains why it's me and you, and not me and Darren again. He seemed happier these last few times out, chattier. I was worried that we might not get on, but we do, I'm pleased. What will Darren be up to, anything useful?"

"I asked him to go to Annapolis Royal this afternoon, knock on a few doors independently, try all the local stores and get a feeling for things first-hand. After our luck with Laura Towle, there might be a few more little mines of information we've not tapped into yet. People don't always know what they've seen or whether it's relevant until someone asks them the right question and I hate to say it, but the Annapolis crew on the original investigation forced our hand on this. He knows what he's about and he can do the French Basin, too. If he has time, he's going to poke around Keji, he wants a year Red-shouldered Hawk".

"Birding again, right? I wasn't suggesting Darren wouldn't know his job, just showing interest. Should I call ahead and speak to Atkinson, make sure he's there when we get there?"

"Not yet, let's get nearer then call. It will give him less time to try to avoid us, I don't want to give him any wriggle room. He was there three days ago; I spoke to him again and told him we'd need a face-to-face although he was still playing the 'I know nothing' card".

"Maybe he doesn't, he might just be a minion".

"He's worked there since the plant opened and runs the show, I think he'll be in Bush's inner circle to some extent and, while he might not be involved in anything shady, Bush will feel the interest. If we get told we're intimidating him, we'll know we're doing something right there".

"But that's not the case you're really interested in, you're more focused on Juliette Barker, so this Atkinson visit is just a reason to poke a few ants' nests and see what crawls out?"

"Yes, it is".

Once they'd hit the highway north to Canso Causeway Howey relaxed, he hated the racetrack that leaving greater Halifax entailed, then there was the ever-present roadworks at Truro where bridge repairs were taking forever. A stop for coffee gave some respite, but soon it was back on the hard miles. Twenty minutes after crossing Canso Causeway, Crystal called Atkinson. "Shit, he didn't come in today. The girl I spoke to said he's on his way to Cuba for a week's vacation, short notice, she says he got a great deal". Cross didn't comment, he just found a place to turn, and they headed back first to Guysborough, then to New Glasgow. As they went along, Crystal used her phone to find the flight and passenger list, Atkinson was on it. "Legit then, but it smacks of him running away. We can always meet him off the plane when he comes home".

Cross was thinking something similar, although Atkinson wasn't legally required to talk to them and probably wouldn't if they doorstepped him at the airport. His mind switched to Juliette Barker, not that it had strayed much from that case recently. Every day he saw her in his head, her face, how it changed, became something else when she saw him- he worried that he might be becoming obsessed. He knew why he felt that way, but he didn't want to address that issue, not now, hopefully not ever.

Guysborough took longer to drive to than the time they had with the facility manager, who didn't want to get very involved. She'd reacted when Cross had shown his ID and become very defensive when he explained the reason for the visit. Crystal saw what was happening and took her to one side, giving her some of the less palatable case details while Howey was sent to wait in the car. Despite the gravity of the case, she still wasn't very willing, but she did say that nobody matching the photo Crystal had showed her had been there recently. Crystal knew that offering a crumb, albeit a negative one, was just a way of keeping them at bay, she also didn't think it was the sort of place a nutjob would get into easily, they seemed quite formal.

"Before you packed me off to the car, I got the feeling that that place wasn't likely, too by the book. Did she tell you anything?"

"She looked at the photo of Barker and said no, I believe her. I didn't realise it was some sort of church-run thing. She said they save sinners who want to be saved, which I thought was odd, and another thing, one of the residents, did you know that Tiff was undercover?" The question was asked more as an accusation, as if Howey hadn't told her everything.

"What? No, I didn't know but that makes sense. I tried tracking Tiff down for a chat, make sure she knew we still had her in mind, but I couldn't find her in our system. Then I got a station sergeant who said she was in Bridgewater but not available. I suspect the hand of Madam here".

Crystal apologised for her tone, but Cross understood, and said he'd have words with Madam when he next spoke to her. "The next place is more like a commune, sort of like The Orchard but more joss sticks and embroidered smocks". Howey had made a joke, the first one of the trip, which was unusual for him. Normally there'd be more light banter, some laughs and a few bad jokes.

"Is something else bothering you, boss?"

"Juliette Barker. What must her fragile life have been like to end up as she did, besides, I've been sensing something from you. Being with Moira taught me to look for the signs, you seem to be uncomfortable with me".

"Really, you can see it, crap, I thought I was doing a good Job of hiding it. I suppose we could go back and forth a bit about it, but I think I'll just get it off my lovely chest right away. I still feel bad about the whole nudity trick we played on you. I know you said it was forgotten and to move on, but it plays on my mind during my long, lonely nights".

"Terence is away again then? I meant it when I said it was ok, although I was furious at the time. Moira has few inhibitions, I like it in her, it's one of the things that make her very different. Sometimes it doesn't occur to her that other people don't have that same personal confidence, if you like. I know I reacted a bit too strongly, I should still be apologising to you, after all it was you that was exposed to me in all my glory".

"I just wish I'd not chickened out myself. If I'd gone through with it, I'm sure it would have just been a big laugh, something shared between just us three, almost a dirty secret. It's like I missed a tiny opportunity to be a part of what you and Moira have, just for a moment. I envy what you have, I'll admit it".

"I did wonder at the time why you backed out; you have nothing physically to be embarrassed about. I think maybe that was a factor in my reaction, as much one of disappointment rather than shyness on my part and you're right, we would have laughed and it would have been something personal, intimate without being sexual. I said forget it and I meant it, you're just missing Terence too, it's natural. Where is he?"

"Finishing a difficult project, he says. He texts more than he phones now. He said he has three more days to go yet, I'm not feeling a great connect there. Oh, I meant to ask earlier, I have a set of shelves to put up at home, can I borrow some tools, a drill thing and a hammer?"

"Do you know how to use a drill?"

"No, but how hard can it be? Men use them all the time".

"If we get back in time I'll come over, it won't take long. I can bring the lasagna too, if you like, Moira always makes enough to feed an army. Right, we're here. This place might be a possible bolthole, more relaxed than stalag Guysborough".

The large, rambling building that housed the refuge was exactly what Cross had expected it to be. Slightly shabby with an air of insouciance. The manager, although she laughingly called herself the head witch, was amiable but largely out of it. She was happy to lead them around and spent more time talking about their craft output than answering questions. They had a pottery sideline which helped finance the place, from the look of some of the pots, their customers were going to be quite disappointed. When they showed them Barker's photo, they both noticed a slight shift in her demeanour. Juliette Barker had clearly been there, but the head witch had no idea when exactly and they had no records of any sort. It seemed very in keeping with the whole place. For the next thirty minutes they tried to talk to various residents, but most shied away once they were shown the badges. Only a Karen had an opinion and not a very favourable one. Yes, she remembered Juliette, although that wasn't what she'd called herself, and she was a snobby cow who thought herself better than everyone else. With that the Karen wandered off, muttering. Cross thanked the head witch, left a card and was about to go when a voice said, "I know you". Cross looked around to find Dora Westbury walking towards him.

"Dora, how are you?"

"I'm good. Howey, are you here on duty and would it be inappropriate to give you a hug?" Then she grabbed him and hugged him like a long-lost lover.

Cross broke free and explained about the case, then he introduced Crystal, who'd been observing Dora and how she'd reacted to seeing Howey, it was fascinating. Dora looked at the photo. "I did see her, a few months ago. Quiet, but a bit of a 'me-me' type. She had a loan from the help fund, a couple of hundred which she swore she'd pay back at some point. Most never do, it usually ends up in their veins".

"Sorry, Dora, how would you know?"

"I do the books here. The head witch is pretty useless, so I come over when I can, make sure the spending is under control and just keep an eye on the place. Think of it as me doing my civic duty".

"Do you know where she went?"

"No, but not far on a couple of hundred dollars. I don't think she was a user though; you get to recognise the signs. She didn't look quite like this when she was here, she had red, wavy hair although, come to think of it, it might have been a sort of dark blonde when she first arrived. Is this one your women Howey?" and she indicated towards Crystal.

"I'm like you, Dora, just an adoring fan", said Crystal, flashing her eyes and fluttering her lashes.

Dora laughed. "I'm only teasing him, I'm sure he knows that. Howey, leave a card and I'll call if I see or hear of her again. The refuges work like a spider web. Someone moves the web in one spot, and we all feel it twitch, sooner or later".

Crystal gave Dora a card and a look while Cross blushed slightly, before they walked back to the car. "Well, that was interesting", said Crystal, referring to Dora and her obvious interest in Howey.

"A case before you came over, she was jilted, I was sympathetic. I'm baffled and surprised in equal measure. You, her, this female interest in me was never there before I met Moira, now I get flirted with by hot chicks, I don't get it". It certainly was a puzzle although one woman of his acquaintance was not on the list, Hinzi.

Crystal was giggling, Howey was right. Dora's looks at Howey were a bit obvious, and then there was Leah back in Kentville, although he seemed to have navigated those shark-infested waters well enough so far. "Get over it, Howey. Since you settled down and produced a litter you've become unthreatening, almost attractive, a babe magnet. You know that's all we girls really want".

The very idea was enough to make him laugh out loud, they both did, and soon any lingering awkwardness about anything was long forgotten. Crystal called Darren and, putting her phone on speaker, updated him on progress. He said he'd had a mostly boring day of talking to old ladies who knew nothing, but who all wanted to give him cake and coffee and mother him. He did have a couple of things to check out though and would brief later, no birds to speak of.

Cross asked what the things were, he felt he couldn't not know.

"I'm following up on some talk about an incident with a deranged kid, long ago, he lived in the Barker house. It might be nothing, I spoke to the detachment admin and he's going to dig out the file for us, it's all still on paper. I also spoke to Mary Rose's beneficiary. She said that the municipality had billed Mary for the removal of her car from the French Basin trail parking lot, I remember the car, a green Subaru- it was there for months. I dropped by the municipality, but they contract these things out. I contacted the tow company and they said they'd get back to me, they haven't yet but it sounds like the car was sold. The nice girl I spoke to said that was what usually happened with unclaimed vehicles. I have a VIN number so we can check that".

"You've been busy, great work Darren. Anything else?"

"Just a few two-and-twos making four and based on chatter. Something about an assault, back in the day, by some sort of weird kid. It's likely just local gossip but let me have a look first".

"Ok, sounds interesting. Can we talk later? Lots of miles to do yet".

"Sure, but I'm finishing early today, got an appointment, I did book it in advance", and the line went dead.

Crystal looked over, her expression asking what they were going to do, they had another refuge to pull in, if they could.

Cross read her thoughts. "Home, we've done enough road-time today, besides, we've both got lives outside of our careers to enjoy. You with Terence and me with Moira and the terrors, my life just happens to not be home tonight".

Crystal didn't respond, and Cross got a feeling of indifference to her current situation once again. He didn't ask, but he was pretty sure Terence wasn't going to be a feature in Crystal's life for much longer.

It was late afternoon when they pulled into the farm. "I've got a few animal-related chores to do, I'll be over in about an hour".

As he got on with the pig feeding duties, the inevitable text from Moira arrived. 'Sage Thrasher relocated in Eagle Cove, two observers. We can go at the weekend; we can rationalise your twitch circle and stretch it a bit'. Taking a quick peak at Sibley, he looked at the unremarkable-looking bird before texting back 'three hours each way again is a maybe, unless there's anything we need to do out that way, Orchard-wise'.

'Good thinking, I'll get back to you on that tomorrow, enjoy the lasagna, be nice to Crystal'. Cross smiled. Of course, she knew he'd offer to share the lasagna.

'Me again, just heard it was only seen by lad and dad, you know who'. Moira was telling him that the two birders who claimed to re-find the Sage Thrasher were a couple of newbies from Manitoba, stringers, without actually saying it. Very diplomatic, not that she needed to be.

When Crystal got home and flopped on the sofa, it took her a moment to remember that Howey was coming over to put up a shelf and bringing food, but an hour would give her time to tidy up, shower and to dig out the shelf kit, which was in the back of the garage somewhere. She'd only been in the house for five-minutes but already the garage was packed to the rafters. It was a good ninety minutes before Cross showed up bearing food, but the oven was now nice and hot, and the lasagna duly deposited to warm up. "I'll just get this done and then we can eat, yes?"

"Yes, you carry on, coffee?"

"Coffee would be good, thanks".

It ended up being only a ten-minute job, it was a simple shelf kit and went up very easily. Standing back to admire his handiwork, he heard Crystal arrive with the coffee, turned and didn't know what to say. She had a cup in each hand and was completely naked. "I know you said that it was all ok now, but I felt I owed you a look, so please look, take as long as you like. To be clear, that's all this is, just a look and, when you've finished admiring the view, I'll go and get dressed and we can eat. We're even now and we have a sort of moment to remember. One question though?"

"Er, yes Crystal? "Said Cross, retrieving his jaw from the floor, or so it felt.

"What's that in your pocket?"

"Screwdriver?" said Howey weakly, before bursting out laughing, Crystal laughed too, then went off to get dressed. Later, over lasagna, she looked for a reaction, but Howey wasn't saying anything, and she worried that she'd messed up badly again.

"Did I do wrong?"

"No, I get it and I'll certainly remember it, unexpected as it was. Can we finally draw a line under it now though? We're even".

"That was what I thought, you know that's why I did it. Will you tell Moira?"

"Absolutely, at some point".

"Good".

"Will you tell Terence?"

"Absolutely never".

"This weekend, I thought we'd go to stop with your mom and dad, it's migration time, there must be some birds for you down there". Zelda had been surprised at how little Greg had been off chasing recently. She knew that he'd had a few ticks, but he'd not said anything to her about how his big year was going despite her showing interest, occasionally.

"A few maybe but, apart from the biggies, it's been a slow year. Unless we get a real hurricane dump of birds, I reckon I'll be a dozen short of three hundred, twenty or more shy of the record. Pity about the Bananaquit and the Sage Thrasher, but I wasn't going for it without it being seen by trusted birders".

"And I guess with it being an El Niño year and wind shear high off the Carolinas there's not much chance of getting that bird-filled hurricane now? Pity Ulrika didn't bring much, too far offshore though, it needed to brush the eastern seaboard and pick up high-altitude migrants". Greg stared at his partner in amazement. "What? I might appear to have lapsed into a coma, but I do listen actually when you're rambling on about such things", she said.

"Obviously, and yes, the blocking weather will likely keep a bird-laden storm away now. After the Coot Drop Island adventure and Sable being cancelled for this year, I sort of decided that this wasn't going to be the year. I've not missed much since, but I'm sticking to the plan and there's not been a deal within range. I still need Dickcissel and there's been one at Chebogue Point for a few days, a good enough reason to visit, I suppose".

"That and it's your parents who live there and they like to see Leo regularly and even you. I want to catch up with Marge, lots of girly things to talk about. You can take your dad out; he likes it when his little boy mansplains things to him".

"Yes, that too, and I don't mansplain anything, I'm very careful not to and whenever you mention it, I take great pains to explain how careful I am about not doing it. Dad might want to go to out for more than an hour or two, there might be birds up the French Shore or we could go to Baccaro to sea watch, is that ok?"

"I think your mom would be delighted, maybe you can get Don to take you out in his new boat, he's taking paying customers on local runs now, I saw it on the bird group Facebook page. He could get you that Cory's you're missing, maybe even a Long-tailed Jaeger, it's the right time of year for them, I expect a few immature birds are out harassing Black-legged Kittiwakes. Don't give me that look again, I told you I listen. Don't give up on the year list yet, just stretch your chasing range line a bit. I want you to do this for me and Leo now, I want you to be able to tell him all about it when he's old enough. You might even write it all down so he can read about it for himself, because this sure as shit is the only chance you're going to get for a few years". Zelda often had a way of making things clear like that.

"You're saying that I have your blessing to chase for my total and you won't be pissed at me?"

"Go for it, while you can. Like I said, it will be your last chance for a while, trust me on this", and she patted her belly.

"Oh".

It had been Don Amirault's dream, since he'd first discovered a love for sea birds, to own his own boat capable of 'getting out there'. He knew it wasn't going to happen, but it did no harm to have a dream, to have something you'd really like, provided reality didn't slap you back too hard. In his mind he'd managed the next best thing, to get out on fishing boats regularly but, the problem was they were fishing and not chasing birds and he wanted to chase birds, seabirds. He'd also done seabird surveys on contract, but they were drying up as money got tighter and, again, the seabirds weren't the reason for the surveys, the fishery was.

A part of his plan for learning sea birds, something that he'd considered in his early years, was to join a boat going somewhere, whether a cruise liner, or a container boat, even a proper, long-term marine survey vessel if he could work it. So far that hadn't happened for a number of reasons, the prime one now being his relationship with Mary Kenney. So, his dream remained a dream and, he reckoned, might always be just a dream. Mary knew and felt guilty at holding him back, but also a little pleased.

The lottery ticket bought by Mary in April 2022 had been a joke, it was, she said, her little contribution to his dream of getting a boat. Then he won, or at least their ticket did. When the news of their good luck broke, and they'd tried very hard to keep it quiet, the inevitable hard-luck stories hit their mailboxes from people they'd never heard of. It was a lot of money, life changing money. Enough to pay for a dream come true. Don had naturally insisted on splitting the money equally with Mary, then he intended to use most of his half try to buy a recently de-commissioned seventy-foot cutter.

"The boat can cruise at 31 knots, has sleeping quarters for ten, a full galley and all the bells and whistles an ex-Coastguard boat comes with. I won't commit all of my share of the winnings to the project, the rest will go running the thing, but I have ideas.

"What will you call her?" asked Mary, as she had the photographic guided tour of his intended pride and joy.

"I thought 'Ledgerunner'", said Amirault, "because we'll be out there birding the ledges, doing sea bird surveys, of our own and breaking down the boundaries of sea birding in Nova Scotia and Eastern Canada".

"We, just me and you?"

"We, as in me, you and those paying a fee to the new Sou'west Nova Seabird Tours, unless you come up with something snappier?"

"Tours, taking birders out for real deep water pelagic trips, or are we talking just Puffin patting?"

"Both, I want to tap into the Canada listing market and grab the minds of those who want to see Puffins too. I want to get contracts for real survey work, species protection, including banding and fitting transmitters, maybe even DFO work if they can find the money. That's the plan, but only if you buy into it, we're a two, not a one".

"I've been on boats all my life, what makes you think I'd want to work birding tours on one? Especially as I have enough money to chase my own dream".

"I'm sorry, you're right. In all the excitement I never asked you what you wanted to do, what your dream was, sorry, I got caught up in the moment, it's all been a bit crazy".

"My dream is to be with you doing whatever makes you happy you fool, I was teasing. I think I need lessons because I thought it was obvious from the tone of my voice. I think the boat name needs work though. Have you done a business plan? We need to turn over at least fifty-thousand dollars a year as a small business and you'll need to be able to get supplies and gas at cost. Then there's sundry equipment to buy, survival suits, we'll need at least twelve at around two thousand dollars each, then there's setting up the credit card system and getting a tie in with local accommodation, what?"

Amirault was seeing things a bit more clearly now. "I thought just getting a boat was enough, it isn't though, is it? I've got my skipper's licence, but we'd need a second qualified skipper too, and we need a company manager. Which one shall I put you down for?"

"Both, but first we need to buy the thing, cover the logistics of owning it and do some sea trials. I don't think we'll be up and running this year, but we could do a few inshore trips late summer. That open deck area, if we modify it, will hold thirty-five easily, at sixty-five a head, less seventy for chum and around four-forty in gas at current prices, that will turn seventeen-sixty. Say another two hundred in insurance and we could offer snacks to cover that we could clear fifteen hundred per trip".

"Mary, will you marry me?"

"Aye-aye, skipper".

"See, I told you it was worth going to see your folks. Marge has started a new batch of knitting so she's happy, you and your dad got to ride in 'Ledgerunner' and see a few birds, so you're both happy and Leo nearly patted a skunk at Chebogue Point".

"Are you happy?" asked Greg. "We said to wait a few years after Leo arrived".

"Yes, well, I changed my mind and when little Esther pops out, we'll see about taking a pair of pinking shears to your pipes".

"We will?" Greg swallowed, apprehensively.

"Oh yes", said Zelda, firmly.

CHAPTER TWENTY

September 2022

Darren was just wheeling his chair towards Howey Cross's office when a voice said, "better make that two, Darren". It was Carmel Morrell. Behind him, Leah had already seen what was needed and had Kent Chivers' chair, the big one they had to buy especially for him, scooting towards the office.

The door closed and the brief got underway. Carmel had pulled rank and had one of the regular chairs, Darren was sat in Kent's chair, it made him look like he was sat in one of those huge chairs they stick in front of nice views at scenic spots, the ones that are a blot on the landscape but nobody at the municipality responsible for them can see it.

"Ok, I'll assume you take time to read my notes when I send them, Carmel. If we cover anything here that I've missed, please speak up". Crystal and Darren wriggled at the informality of Howey with the biggest of bosses, but he seemed unfazed, and Carmel just nodded in agreement. "I've done a list, and yes, I checked it twice, before any bright spark chips in. I think we have questions still to answer, some might not have answers".

"Before you continue Howey, can I just personally thank you all for your work on this. I did read the notes and I appreciate how much effort is being put in. Darren, thank you in particular. I know you've not only been a major contributor in the collection of information about Juliette Barker, but you've also kept the station afloat when Howey is out".

"Thank you, Ma'am, but we're a team, we share any credit and shoulder any blame together".

Both Crystal and Howey looked at Darren in astonishment. "What?" he said, scowling theatrically, for effect.

"Moving on then", said Cross, shaking his head, slightly. "I want to know whether Barker had access to a car and whether that car belonged to Mary Rose".

"She did have a car; it was repossessed around two months before her arrest. She'd not made payments. I checked, it's since had three owners. Sorry, I only got that information just before the brief", and Darren smiled apologetically.

"Ok, Mrs. Rose's car has had a not dissimilar life. It was sold after the owner failed to claim it, the tow people bought and sold it. The new owner had it six weeks before the engine blew, couldn't be fixed apparently. He had it taken to a breakers yard, they recycled it. It's likely that one or both cars were used by Barker at some point, but we can't prove it". Cross ticked his sheet.

"Howey, I'm confused about Barker's sister. Is she alive or dead? If Barker told Watson that she spoke to her regularly, can we believe that?" Despite trying to keep up with the dribble of information the team was accumulating, the status of Melissa remained unclear.

"I think, Ma'am, that we should assume that both Melissa and Barker's mother are still extant until we prove otherwise". Crystal had been trying to trace both through conventional means without success.

"I'm having trouble with the whole refuge thing. I accept that Barker used and is using it, but I can't see how a deranged woman can vanish without help, either from a friend or relative. Someone must have picked her up near the detention centre and moved her somewhere, she hasn't been hiding in refuges for three or more years", said Darren.

"Darren is right", said Cross. "I've had similar thoughts myself, the trouble is, apart from the professionals who dealt with her, there doesn't appear to be anyone else who might ride to her aid. It could be somebody inside the facility?"

"I checked them all out, Howey, nothing amiss there". Carmel knew that she should have mentioned that little detail before.

"The way I see it, if we keep at the refuges, keep narrowing the circle, we'll corner Barker, if she's still in that circle. Do I have your permission to get Annapolis involved more, Ma'am. I'd like Constance to keep an eye out there, Barker has an affinity with the place for some reason although she won't go back to the house, of that I'm sure". Cross was only interested in shutting doors to Barker, but he couldn't do it without local buy-in.

"Leave that with me, Howey. I'll do what I can". Carmel shuffled some papers. "I have some information from fisheries that might interest you. Dan Bush doesn't own any lobster licences in Nova Scotia, he recently transferred them to Dan Bush Junior. Call me cynical but that might be so that he doesn't have to fulfill the residency that the licences stipulate. I got Bush senior's immigration details; I'll send them over. Looks like the game there has changed, slightly".

"Excellent, thank your admin please, Ma'am", said Cross getting him a stern look. "I'd like the same information for Martin Atkinson, the plant manager, and, I suspect, his Nova Scotia fixer. can I leave that with you, or should I chase it down myself?"

"Leave it to me Howey, you go and talk to junior, he'll be in Cape Breton at some point". Morrel checked her watch. "Got to go, meeting with people from adoption agencies. I might have more information for you later", and Morell left them to it. The mood in the room relaxed.

"What next, boss?" asked Crystal.

"We keep going with the refuges, Darren gets the short ride to Annapolis to ask more questions and to follow up on that assault that was mentioned. Gossip or not, we need to know the long and short of it. Madam seems pleased with us so far; it feels like we're getting closer".

"Howey, I do have a couple of hours off tomorrow, Hinzi and I have a thing, it's on the schedule". Darren's voice made it clear that, whatever it was he was doing was going to be done, case or not.

"No problem, make an early start and talk to Regis about policing in Annapolis, it might be an idea to pay our respects to those officers who were around when Barker did her thing".

The meeting broke up and Crystal read the room, grabbing Kent's vast chair and hauling it grunting through the door. "Good work with the cars, Darren. Was there something else?"

"Yes, thanks. The offer, we discussed it and would like to say yes. I've been told to get over any discomfort and to view it as any other business situation".

"Moira will be delighted; can you drop over to sign the forms? She's had them ready, she knew you'd see sense".

"Tomorrow, like I said, Hinzi and I have a thing, in Halifax tonight, so we can't make it until tomorrow".

"No problem, I'll let Moira know, enjoy your thing".

"You found time to talk to Mori about window strikes, you lovely man, I'm so pleased, thank you".

Josh spent a moment trying to figure out what Tina was talking about. He remembered her talking about the window things, but he was sure he'd made it clear that he wasn't going to get involved, then it clicked. "No, it was Security who went to see her, she was flagged as a risk, but they must have been happy that she wasn't, I heard nothing more".

"Security risk, an old woman with a cat, are you serious?" Tina's warm glow was cooling rapidly.

"Yes, something about a celebrity death".

"And you thought that meant you? You prick, she meant a rare bird to raise awareness, not an environment minister that shirked his responsibility because it might not be good for his career".

"Steady on, Tina. I didn't send anyone, I don't have any input there, I just remember seeing a note somewhere after the fact. You can apologise now for calling me a prick, at least you didn't append 'little'".

"I'd have thought that was taken as read. I saw the same newsletter your security team took to be a real and present threat. You probably got a copy too; did someone bother to look? I'm annoyed and disappointed Josh, and angry, really angry".

"I'm sorry, really, it wasn't my fault, I'll fix it, how can I fix it?" Tina told him.

"Political news now, and the Environment Minister, Josh Hennigar, considered by many political commentators to be something of a highflyer in the Provincial Government, has released a statement regarding the issue of bird strikes and buildings. In it he stated the Provincial Government's commitment to conserving wild organisms and that he backed naturalists in their campaign to get developers and property owners to take voluntary action to help cut down what he called an appalling mortality rate so easily avoided".

"In other news, police in the Atlantic provinces are still searching for retired Catholic priest Father Seamus O'Connor...".

Howey Cross was still in his work suit, it was crumpled, he felt crumpled too. He'd eaten alone again; Moira was still preoccupied with whatever. It had been like this for a week, but when he'd asked, she just reckoned it was bird stuff, even though she'd handed some of it off. Hinzi walked in with the kids, with Trixie slowly following behind. "Did they behave?"

"Yes, they do like Miner's Marsh. Phoebe, do Sora", and Phoebe did a perfect whinny, smiling at how good it was, then she looked at daddy.

"Bad day?" she asked, she really was mini-Moira.

"Bad day".

Suddenly Moira was there, she gave Howey a kiss and handed him a USB. "Sorry, I had to get this done- my head was just full of it, sorry. Right, everyone, ice cream", and in an instant the house was their house again. Hinzi smiled apologetically, whatever was going on, she'd been a willing part of it in covering kid duties. Cross looked at the USB tentatively, how bad could it be? He excused himself and fired up the laptop. The USB contained a lot of files, each having a number and a title, he opened the first and was surprised to find an electronic family tree and reference to someone fishing off Vancouver who was a Magowan. The tree then fanned out with multiple branches, before retracting sharply. The only extant name on it was Moira with her date and year of birth, the was rest left blank. So, this was what she'd been up to, she'd gone through the whole Internet and found links to people with her name and from the area where she was raised and created a family tree.

Back in the kitchen, ice cream was mostly hitting mouths, but a bit was on the floor and Trixie was lapping it up. Moira was beaming but Hinzi had slipped away, if Cross had to describe her behaviour recently, he'd have said furtive. He made a note to ask Darren if everything was ok. "I found her, Howey, I found my mom I'm sure of it. She was in Annapolis Royal back in 1987 but she went to BC to have me, us, in December, the birth being 10th January 1988, my birthday. She came back with both of us to Nova Scotia but to a Dartmouth address. She took me back to BC in June 1988 then vanished. I can't find any trace of her yet, but I'm still looking".

Cross could see how much this meant, it was a little bit of the puzzle, a sliver of identity. "Father?"

"No, not stated and my aunt never gave a clue, but you'd think he might have been in Annapolis Royal somewhere, she lived there long enough for the timing to be right".

"Do you have an address in Annapolis Royal?"

"Yes, on the stick, she rented a room, the basic details are on the stick. I only got this because all rentals in the year of my birth were filed with the municipality. One of the houses is still there, I checked, that was why I really went over. Howey, it looks sad. If it didn't sound crazy, I'd say it was tired and weeping, unloved. I didn't dare knock on the door, but it looked empty anyway. The other road has been swallowed up; the old houses gone to new builds".

"I didn't get past the first file, tell me the address".

Moira knew something was about to be revealed, but not in front of the kids, not in front of Phoebe, she felt things. Moira noticed that Phoebe hadn't touched her ice cream since the conversion had begun. "Later".

As the kids went about their bedtime routine, Howey sat with the laptop and scrolled the rest of the files. It wasn't intentional, but the last file he opened had Moira's possible mom residing at either 285 Bay Avenue or 68 Belleview. The first address chilled his bones, but the timing didn't fit the worst-case scenario, not at all, it was months out, had she made a mistake? There was no mention of wine when Moira rushed in and sat next to him on the sofa. "I know you have something to tell me, I know it's bad and I know you're contemplating sugar-coating it but don't. I need to know everything; I need to make sense of things".

Howey closed the laptop, there was no way he could do this gently, it was too heavy, too laden with issues, so it had to come out. "The address, the sad house is sad for a reason. We found a dead woman there recently, murdered. It was Juliette Barker's house, still is. Darren found out from local people that a woman there had had an incident happen years ago, we don't have the date yet, but we will soon. The incident involved an assault, but nothing happened, and no charges came of it. With your files and information that we've only just got from Annapolis Royal, I should be able to lay out a timeline".

Moira was pale, drained. "My mother was assaulted? Was she raped, am I the child of a rapist?"

"I don't know, your timeline doesn't fit, but there is the possibility that the incident happened to Juliette Barker's mother and that she's the result of the assault. Tomorrow I'll bring a DNA kit, I want you to give a sample, I want it on file as much to rule things out as to make a case, are you ok with that?"

"Yes, of course. Is it possible that whoever did the assault on Juliette Barker's mother also assaulted my mom?"

"Yes, but before we know anything we've a lot more to find out. I'm sending a team over tomorrow; I'll be going with Crystal. Speaking of Crystal, I want to tell you something".

"She dropped her drawers on front of you, right?"

"Yes, how did you guess?"

"I didn't guess, I knew she would at some point. What did you do, did you have a good look?"

"Yes".

"Good, she has a great body. Did you tell her that you'd tell me?"

"Yes, I said 'absolutely', and she said 'good'".

Moira was smiling. "What?" asked Cross.

"You've seen Crystal naked and you're still here, so I'm fine with that and she's happier to have paid a debt although not so much because of Terence. I might have misread him".

"Really, why".

"I can't put my finger on it but then I've had this to do, still have because I won't stop digging. When I have my answers I'll apply my skills to it, if he's still around. I think Crystal will dump him and soon".

Howey tried to look surprised at this, initially, but he'd thought as much after recent conversations. Crystal hadn't been happy for quite a while, and something had to give. Turning back to more important matters, the primary issue on his mind, he said, "If you get your answers, mom, dad, some history, what will it give you?"

"Some more blue sky in the jigsaw of life. I might not have the full picture that matches the lid of the box yet, but I'll have fewer gaps. It's less important than it once was, the future is the thing, but I'd still like answers, good or bad".

It was a good answer, Howey thought. A better answer than he'd feared. "Can I ask something, about Hinzi, and I don't want to sound self-absorbed or anything".

Moira smiled. "Why hasn't Hinzi ever flirted with you, right?"

Cross was once again astonished. He'd not even hinted. "Yes".

"Where did this come from?"

"I bumped into Dora Westbury recently, and she flirted. Leah at work flirts, even Crystal flirts with me sometimes, when she wants her own way but never Hinzi, she never has".

"Do you find her attractive?"

"I like her, she's great, fun but attractive to me, no, I don't know why. Moira, you have that look that says you're about to tell me something that you think I won't understand".

"Does Darren flirt with anyone?"

"No, he's devoted to Hinzi, he's just Darren".

"Darren and Hinzi are devoted to each other, it's as simple as that. Can we leave it there? It's really not our business and if it makes them happy, I can cope with Darren not salivating when he sees me".

"It never occurred to me until some people went on a flirt-fest with me".

"Why would it? It's what you call a private life and their business, just like what we get up to is our business. There is something going on with them at the moment, but that's up to them to tell you, it's certainly not my place, I might put a foot wrong". Moira gave him a stern look; Howey knew he'd get nowhere trying to winkle it out.

"Let's get back to your family tree now, after what you just said it looks a lot less complicated than real life". He opened up the laptop and they went through the various branches. Nothing was obvious, nothing stuck out but then not all the branches had fruit, yet.

"Well, this feels a little odd". Regis Muir was sitting on the opposite side of a desk, a different desk from his own but in the exact same place his had previously occupied in this office.

"I suppose it must. Are you still enjoying being here? I'm sorry we can't offer more than three days a week, budgets, you know the score". It was the first time Cross had called Regis into his old office, most previous conversations had been simple 'how's things' and 'hello's'.

"To be honest, Howey, I could do with a bit more to do. I know you did this for me, Carmel said. I do appreciate it, but I think I have more to offer than just being a tidy-up guy. If there isn't anything else, then I might call it a day". Cross could see that Muir was being serious, and he understood. So far, he'd not involved him in the Barker case, but that was going to change.

"How well do you know Madam?" he asked.

Regis gave Cross a shrewd look. "She's a colleague. I knew her before she rose to the top, never socially but we spoke often. You know she was instrumental in guiding you here, I'm sure she told you so. She wouldn't risk you finding out by accident and being pissed at any perceived manipulation, although that is what it was".

"Do you know why?"

"She sees you as a talent and I think it helps that you finally settled down with somebody, the responsibility of a partner and kids. She always said you'd never think twice about taking a risk, now you do".

That was an interesting viewpoint, and there was more than a little truth in what was being said. "And what about Crystal and Darren?"

"I was told that they were good officers; I looked them up. Anything he wants is what I was told, I took that to mean you should be allowed to construct your own team if they'd come from the big city to Kentville, which you have. Tell me you haven't called me in for careers advice?"

"No, I have a job for you, something that requires experience and subtlety. I won't ask if I can trust you, because I know I can, but this is delicate, it might be uncomfortable, professionally".

"For me or both of us? My career is already done".

"For you personally then. I want you to dig into something and find me what I need. I'm the only one who will know what you're doing, everything is on my authority, and it involves using your contacts from when you served in Annapolis Royal".

Muir half-smiled. "She said if she gave you the tail of a worm you'd give it a good pull. I know where you're going with this, but I'm wondering whether it is relevant to the Barker case alone, if not then the worm might be best left to go on its way. I assume you got the locations of my previous postings from my file, Leah said you'd requested it".

"Actually, you told me once in conversation, not directly, but you knew Annapolis Royal much too well, you had to have spent time there to have such an intimate knowledge. I knew that Leah would tell you, which is why

I asked for your file. How you reacted would tell me whether I should use you or not".

"I can see why Carmel likes you. What else do you know?"

"That Carmel was in Annapolis Royal, that she moved over to Halifax in 1988 but there's bits of her timeline I can't fill in, she's missing the best part of a year. I thought that you might know why".

"Is Carmel a suspect?"

"No, not at all, she's a part of the jigsaw, to paraphrase Moira. I have the sky, now I need to finish filling in the figures in the picture". Just as he finished using the jigsaw analogy, he felt a mental click as a piece of that jigsaw found a home.

Muir looked like he'd got hold of a grenade, one that Cross had taken the pin out of and then handed it back to him. Was this what she meant when she said, 'anything he wants?' Then he saw his own bigger picture, Madam had done this, she'd been instrumental in everything. Cross moving over, his retirement and subsequent part-time involvement, everything. Reaching into his jacket pocket he pulled out an envelope marked for the attention of Staff Sergeant Howey Cross and handed it over. Cross took it, almost as if he'd expected it.

"You know I'll pull on that worm until I have it in a jar, Regis".

"There was an incident. Carmel was destined for great things, but something happened, and she took a leave of absence. She never came back to Annapolis Royal, resuming her career in Halifax which turned out to be a good move. I investigated the incident, off the record because there would be a stigma, it was something that opponents to senior, female police officers might exploit. She dealt with her situation, I dealt with the Annapolis end, and it was done. If you'd asked her directly, she might have told you".

"Maybe I just needed corroboration. The incident, she was assaulted, raped, and had a child, correct?"

"There I can't help you, Howey. Carmel and I agreed that the subject was closed, and we've never spoken about it since. My assumption has always been that she went away to have a termination, itself something of a career roadblock in Nova Scotia, given the traditionalist attitude of many. She never told me the result of the assault and I've never asked".

"Ok, I get that, but I need a name now. I need to know who assaulted her and where".

"For professional or personal reasons?"

Cross laughed, he might have known that wily Regis Muir would ask that one, difficult, question. "Personal".

"Meaning that Carmel won't be included in any reports or investigations, that the only person who will be affected is Juliette Barker, when you finally catch her? I need your assurance here; I need to trust you with this". Muir was almost pleading, although Cross could see that having the situation out in the open, if only limited to themselves, was the sharing of a weight he'd carried for years.

"Absolutely".

"Graham Lester, son of Muriel Lester of 285 Bay Avenue, Annapolis Royal. Having read the transcript of your interview with Barker last time, I'd definitely ink in those names on the list of misdemeanors but not by Barker, I'd suspect Melissa Rylance, the woman who went missing and left behind two children. Can you guess who one of those children was? I'm sure you can. I'll just shake your hand now, Howey, and be off. I'll do an office tour and say goodbye, I'm pretty sure I've done what I was placed here to do. If you ever need a chat, come over, you're always welcome, and bring the family, anytime".

Cross stood and shook Muir firmly by the hand. Now he had something, a time bomb really. How he deployed it depended on circumstance, the right circumstance. He'd know when. His door opened and closed. "Did you fire him?" It was Leah Brown, looking formidable.

"No, we talked about a case that he worked on then gave me his resignation letter, it's here if you want to read it. I think he just wanted to help with the transition, he had the detachment's best interests at heart. He said he felt I would be ok, and it was time to go".

Leah walked around the desk and gave Cross a light kiss. "Thanks, Howey, I'll make sure everyone is aware and there's no whispers".

"The perfect Communications Officer and great to look at too".

"I can shut the door if you have three minutes spare for me", said Leah as she slipped out laughing. She shut the door, anyway, correctly surmising that Howey Cross had things to think about.

"Do you have a SIN number?" The hard-faced woman at the hostel was trying to be compassionate, but a life without such a luxury meant it didn't come naturally to her and she sounded a bit fierce.

"No, well I do but it's back in the flat and Geoff, the reason I'm here, isn't going to give me anything. I really just need a few days, a week maybe. I have a cousin in BC who will let me stay there but not just yet. It's complicated, do I need a SIN to be here, If I do, I'll just move on".

"No, just things the trustees think we need, but we do need a name, I can't just call you room six now, can I?"

"No, yes, it's Abigail Smith".

"Smith, is this your real name?"

"Yes, why wouldn't it be?"

Lucie Rivers had seen a lot of girls come and go at the hostel. This one was a first timer for sure, and in need of a bath and a meal and a little bit of help. If she said she was Abigail Smith, that would do for her.

"Ok, Abigail Smith, room six. House rules, no men, no drugs, no bad language. Smoking is done outside, meals are at seven, one and six. No alcohol either. Do you need a doctor?"

"No, no, I've been sleeping rough for a while, sorry about how I look, I scrub up quite well given the chance".

"There's a cloakroom at the end of the corridor, you should find something in there that will fit. It will be clean, but I can't guarantee that it will be fashionable. Welcome to The Gateway, Abigail, welcome to Antigonish".

"Thanks, I really appreciate it and if you need any help I have a business management degree, before Geoff, I managed three chain hotels".

Rivers looked hard at Abigail Smith, she did have something, a certain confidence and she was well-spoken, a cut above the usual dregs that got washed in, but could she trust her? "I'll bear that in mind, we're always glad of extra hands, particularly when they belong to someone responsible".

"I don't expect something for nothing, if my skills are of use then use me. Apart from Geoff, nobody is going to come banging on the door looking for me".

"We'll see". said Lucie, while already wondering if she'd found someone to cover for her, allowing her to finally take a day off.

"Where's Crystal?" Moira was looking around Howey as he came in the front door.

"Home, why?"

"I expected her to eat with us, or is your long day together quite enough? If I was in close proximity to Crystal all day, I'm not sure I could keep my hands off her".

"Moira, really. I manage very well thank you, my self-control is impeccable".

"Unless it's Boston Cremes, eh?" How did she know?

"I need to talk to you about something personal, difficult. Are you ok with that?"

"Talk, eat, no drink tonight. You're getting a fine set of spare tires there, my fault I know, I don't exercise you enough". Despite Moira joking, he could see her apprehension.

"I spoke to Tina as part of the Barker investigation. I hinted to her that I thought you'd been seeing her, we did talk about it, I wondered how it was going, I don't want to pry".

"And I thought that my little clues might be too subtle".

"Did you really think putting your appointments on the wall planner might be too hard for me to figure?"

"No, not really. Long story short, she thinks I'm autistic, a savant with an eidetic memory. It explains everything, well nearly everything, falling for you is inexplicable apparently. People like me are very rare, I'm special, I always knew it".

"Not HPD then?" asked Howey, cautiously.

"No, nothing like it and she's baffled why my previous head doctor came up with that. She called it a lazy diagnosis. I didn't tell her that when I had it, I was in one of my more detached phases and living in an opium den".

"This new diagnosis, did she talk about how it might affect you?" Cross wasn't too worried, but still wanted reassurance.

"She did, she said my taste in men would be questionable and my fou-fou needs plenty of daylight. I asked whether I would be allowed to buy a bolt gun for when the sheep become chops, and she said best not".

"Seriously though, you're ok?"

"I am, I'm not a psychopath and I'm not schizophrenic and I'm not nuts, so all good and, you know, I feel a weight lifted". She wasn't the only one to feel that way.

CHAPTER TWENTY-ONE

Early October 2023

Lenny Barnes had been scrolling Facebook looking at the Armitage Meadows photos, it was really taking shape and was now accepting visitors provided they were bird group members. When news of the reserve had been made public, the group had seen a forty-two percent rise in membership. He scrolled up and down looking at the latest developments, the blinds looked good, at the back of his mind he knew that he was putting off having a difficult conversation, especially as the person he was turning to for advice was his own son. Taking a deep breath, he dialed.

"Son, I've got a bit of a dilemma", he said in all seriousness. Greg Barnes was used to his dad joking about, so this was new, unless there was a punchline coming.

"Ok, go on".

"I met a guy at Pinkney's Point, they call him Dilbert, a nickname, I don't know his real name. Anyway, he has a little skiff, and he took me a ride out into the marsh, this was back in June".

"Congratulations, Dad, no longer a landlubber. Why are you only telling me this now, are you embarrassed?"

"No, it isn't that. He showed me a nest, there's a pair of Least Bitterns breeding there, and he said not to tell anyone, and I haven't, apart from you now, obviously".

"And the site wasn't visible from any public vantage point?"

"No, I tried every angle. It's too far and it's hidden, you can only get there at high tide by skiff and it's a ways in". This was one of those little problems that people with the responsibility for recording birds got from time to time, the decent rarity that isn't available because of extenuating circumstances.

"Did you take documentary photos at the time?"

"Does the Pope shit in the woods?"

"A 'yes' would have done, Dad. Ok, so it's all documented. Will he take you out again next year, to monitor progress?"

"I didn't ask, I think so, but that's not the point, I had to sit on a rarity, and it doesn't feel comfortable".

"That would be the sharp beak".

"Very funny, what will people say if they find out I kept it quiet?"

Greg sighed, if people would only read the eBird FAQs he wouldn't get the same questions over and over again. "Dad, when you do a checklist, you can check 'not for public viewing', you can hide it. Obviously, I know you've not done the checklist yet and this was back in June?".

"No, I haven't and yes it was. I know I could have hidden it but that feels worse, secretive. People are going to call me a suppressor or worse when they find out. I'd rather have found a way to get everyone onto them, a good bird like a Least Bittern, tiny things. I guess lots still need it?"

"Not really, they breed at Amherst, hard to see but they're there".

Lenny sounded shocked. "Really, I thought they must be super-rare here. Do you need it for the year?"

"Nope, we went Amherst as a family back in late June. We did some shopping, walked a few trails, I had one sat out making noises".

"I didn't see that on the rare bird alert".

"No, because, in the same way that you don't see American Oystercatchers as a rarity, even though they're only found in one spot in Nova Scotia, so you don't see Amherst Least Bitterns flagged either. Same thing, rare but breeding and annual but only just there. Hide your checklist when you put it in and ask to keep tabs on the birds next year. If you really want to you can write a nice piece about it for the bulletin. I can help you with any big ornithological words that might confuse you".

Lenny sounded deflated, thanked Greg and hung up. "What did he say?" asked Marge.

"He was frankly sarcastic, told me to write it up later and hide my checklist. I don't know where he gets it from".

"Mirror, mirror on the wall, who is the most sarcastic of them all?"

Lenny realised what Marge was saying and laughed. "Seems he might be a chip of the old block after all", he said.

"If he really is yours", said Marge.

With the weight of suppression off his shoulders Lenny called his new friend Dilbert in Pinkney's Point. "Those Least Bitterns, if they come back next year can I go out again?"

"What do you mean, come back, they're there every year, have been for the past ten or so".

"Oh, right, can I go out again then? I want to monitor them; see how they do".

"Sure, we can fix it up. They get babies then those dirty bastard gulls eat them, or the mink find them, never seen a baby get old enough to fly".

"That's nature I suppose. At least they don't get bothered by hunters, not out of season as they are".

"Not anymore, not since Coates pissed someone off bad". Lenny's ears pricked up, he knew all about Kenneth Coates, Howey Cross had asked him to keep his ear to the ground.

"This Coates was a bad guy then? Sorry, I don't know the name".

"You would if you upset his rich friend, or you was a duck anytime".

"Rich or not, the law applies, surely? I know we're a bit redneck down here, but the law is the law".

"Yes, I suppose but them rich Americans think they can push people around and Coates was only too willing to do it for them. My friend Steven stood up to him, the American, and he paid. Everyone knows it was Coates, but the police don't seem to want to know, hunter cold case they called it, accident, someone hunting and a stray shot. Stray shot my ass and the gun that killed him stayed in the family, I heard that, we hear things. You want to see them tiny bitterns next year, you call me in June, and I'll fix it up. Don't tell no one though, people might take against them".

Lenny thanked Dilbert and looked at his notes, years of being a police officer had resulted in his jotting down the salient details of the conversation. He called Howey Cross.

"Darren, come on, let's go and talk to people". Howey Cross had been in his office for two straight days, trying to get the growing amount of paperwork into better order. Crystal was in Halifax for two days too and he wanted to talk things through, so Darren would have to do. He sat in the car and waited, then realised how his thought process had worked and felt awful. There was a division, one that had widened after Moira had talked about the Newells' domestic arrangements. It was odd how the thought that they had such an emotionally exclusive relationship had affected him. Maybe he was feeling excluded by his best friend?

"Sorry, Howey, I chanced a pee in case we're on the road for some time. What are we about?"

"I'm not sure, I thought we might drive and talk, away from the office, away from the others".

"Ok", agreed Darren, a little rattled by Howey's attitude. "I can't believe a cat got the Sage Thrasher, that would have been a great bird to see in Nova Scotia. I was ready to roll before we found out it was lad and dad who'd claimed it, no photo, never is".

Cross ignored the comment.

"Moira said there was something with you that I had to ask for myself. Is this secret a thing for me to get confused about?"

"Maybe, look, I'll come straight out with it shall I? we're competing in the Canadian National Dance Championships, freestyle event".

"What?"

"You know, dancers compete for cash prizes, we're in it and doing ok, we're into the next round of regional heats".

"What, dancing, you, dancing?" Howey had an incredulous look on his face. He'd never seen Darren do so much as tap his foot to music, let alone a soft shoe shuffle.

"I knew you'd be like this, that's why I never mentioned it before and I'm certainly not showing you the costumes".

"What, dancing really, in costumes, really?" Howey didn't seem to be able to get past this surprise.

"Come on, let's get going. Places to go, people to see", said Darren, a trifle huffily.

Cross got the car underway again, heading for Windsor and a refuge to check and tick off. Darren sat checking his phone. "Bastard, Lenny had a Least Bittern at Pinkney's Point and told nobody, a message from Greg".

"Yes, I know, he also made a contact there that knows all about Coates and Steven Clements, shall we swing around and go and find his contact for ourselves?" asked Cross.

"Ok, yes, and the Mute Swan is still there, we could pull that in, what do you reckon?"

"Isn't it an escape?" said Cross, as he looked for somewhere to haul the car round and head off south.

"Nope, wild and free and quite magnificent".

"Magnificent, a Mute Swan...?"

"They all count", said Darren.

There was a short silence as the kilometres shot past; something seemed to be preying on Cross's mind. Eventually, he spoke. "Moira also spoke about your relationship with Hinzi. About you being totally devoted, aren't we all?"

"Certainly, just as you and Moira are, it's just that Hinzi and I are different, or we like to think we are. Don't ask me to explain it, I can't, I'd rather talk about the dancing".

"Go on then explain how I, top cop Howey Cross didn't know that you danced for money".

"And trophies. We didn't, we do now, it was something we both wanted to do, and we found we were quite good at it, we might even make the finals but I'm not counting sequins before they're sewed".

"Are you teasing me?"

"Yes, because it's none of your business. We work well together, sometimes we bird together although you'll always go with Moira, which is right. People, couples, have things that belong to them, exclusively, I'm sure Terence and Crystal are the same. It's how it all works".

I wouldn't be too sure about Terence and Crystal. I can't see him lasting much longer", said Howey.

"Really?" Darren sounded bemused. "She never mentioned, we don't have chemistry but that's ok, we have respect. I think she finds Kentville a bit quiet, she misses the big city and a big police detachment, she said so when we talked ambitions".

Cross was surprised. Crystal had never mentioned either her ambitions or missing Halifax. "What about you?"

"I love it, and if you move up again and become Chief of Police, it might happen, I'd go for your job. I enjoyed doing it while you were in Brazil, it might take a few years maybe, when Aldrick retires, unless he doesn't come back. I assume you enjoy being in Kentville?"

Cross did, but only because the family was close. Some days, when the most exciting thing to happen was a come-hither look from Leah, he missed Halifax too.

When they got to Pinkney's Point after a long and boring drive, the Mute Swan was there, and it did indeed count. Dilbert, or whatever his real name was, flatly refused to repeat what he'd told Lenny though and closed his door on them.

"Pull in a refuge, while we're here?" asked Darren. They did and it was another blank.

The list of refuges to check was getting smaller and, naturally, the more distant ones were going to be the last to take a look at. Trying to figure out which way Juliette Barker had gone after New Glasgow had been akin to sticking a pin in a map, which is exactly what they did. In Cross's office, one wall had a large-scale map of Nova Scotia covered in pins, blue for nothing, red to do, there was virtually nothing for the very far north either way, yet.

"We could get the locals up there to do it for us", said Darren. "They only have to take a quick look; it'll save us miles on the road".

"I don't think so, that was how she slipped away before, locals not having all the details and missing something. I know it's a hard slog, but I feel we're getting close. Are you still ok to visit Atkinson tomorrow?

Sorry you're alone again". Cross's phone pinged. "No Crystal until later and I've got to go to a meeting, I tried to cancel but Madam said not this time".

"I'm fine, I still need Eurasian Wigeon for the year and there's one at North Sydney. Two birds, one stone".

Clayton Payette walked into the busy hall, paid his entrance fee and started to browse. Trade stalls dominated, the most popular was Browning, the name endured. At one end of the Legion hall, a gun show buy and sell was in operation, with a few hunter clones busy picking up rifles and staring down the barrels as if they knew what to look for. The guy tending the stall was tall, bearded and with a 'works outside' sort of complexion. "Busy?" asked Payette.

"So-so, a lot of people here with deep pockets so far, it's what you get at these things. Really, I'm just minding the store for my brother".

Payette browsed the neat row of guns. He was thinking to replace his old rifle, but every time he saw the modern prices he vowed to keep it for another season. When it stopped dropping deer first shot, that was the time to look for something more modern. One of the guns was very nice though. He asked to handle it and the guy handed it to him. Payette was careful how he handled it while he did the barrel-look thing. "Nice, how much for cash?"

"It's a nice gun that one, I nearly didn't put it out, I'm minded to say it's not for sale and have it myself".

Payette knew it was just a sales pitch, he'd been around long enough to know bullshit when he heard it.

"How much then, if you were to consider selling it?"

"Eighteen hundred, it says so on the tag".

"For cash?"

"Eighteen hundred and I need to see your papers. We don't sell without".

Payette had been turning the gun over and over. He noticed that where the serial number was looked a little damaged, but he got three of the numbers. He took out his wallet and took out two hundred from a bundle and his gun licence. He'd budgeted for two thousand if he saw what he was after, so it was easy math. The guy took it and counted it anyway, then scanned the licence. Payette waited until he was happy and waited for a receipt. "Got a cover for it too, here, worth a hundred and fifty but it comes with it", and a nice cover was handed over. Payette slipped the gun inside, carefully. Happy, he left the gun show and headed for his detachment office. Time to check in.

'Howey, Clayton Payette here, at Amherst. Just letting you know that I think I have the gun that Coates owned. In for ballistics now, there's some delay, might take two weeks or more. I hope it is the right gun, else I'm eighteen hundred down, although I will be one new gun up. I'll be in touch when I know more. I must have been to fifteen gun shows since we talked, but if it's the gun, it'll be worth it'.

Howey showed Darren the text before replying. 'Terrific news, thanks Clayton. Just closing in on something here, a big case. Keep me informed and thanks again'.

"Ma'am, Tiff just reporting in. I've not got long; I don't want to be seen on the phone. I had a whisper that someone matching Barker's description was in a neighbouring, off-grid refuge for two weeks, that was a week ago. Before that, a contact thought she might have been in Sheet Harbour more recently, but that she was going north of Canso Causeway next".

"We've had a couple of near misses; we had a potential sighting of a person of interest in Yarmouth but found nothing. That person had an old Honda, does that match with what you know?" Carmel was reluctant to give out too much, not that she didn't trust Tiff O'Toole, it was just that the less you know, the less likely you are to slip up.

"Yes, the Sheet Harbour woman had a Honda. I didn't get a name, my contact is a recovering user and prone to lapses, but I think the guess that she's heading into Cape Breton is probably good. I'm moving myself soon, I think a headcase type here is getting interested in me and I don't want to get into a situation".

"Move quickly then, Tiff. See whether the Cape Breton tip has any legs if you can, we need a break in this one".

"Will do. Oh damn, got to go. Sorry, got to go, Ma'am".

A ping told Cross he had a text message. 'Howey, intel suggests Barker's heading to Cape Breton, it might be wrong but if you can, check out refuges there as a priority. Carmel'.

Howey Cross showed Darren the text. "It has to be Tiff", said Darren.

"It is Tiff. If Madam thinks it's good, then it's good. You volunteered to do the Cape Breton run alone, Darren, are you still ok with that? We're going to Shelburne and the last red pins in the south".

"I know and I'll check out whatever refuges I can. What do we do when the pins are all blue?" Cross didn't answer, he didn't know himself.

CHAPTER TWENTY-TWO

Early October 2022

The sign at the gate was modest, hand-made and just told people that the place was for fallen angels. Sydney had a drug problem, everywhere had a drug problem, it also had a port, both attractions calling those susceptible to temptation like moths to a porch light. Darren Newell realised that he wasn't in the right frame of mind to do this, he'd been sent to visit Dan Bush's fish plant, to get answers, to ask faces directly where Martin Atkinson was now, and he felt pissed at his boss for being sent on his own. He was supposed to talk to Dan Bush junior, but, surprise, surprise, junior wasn't there having been called away. He texted Cross with the news but got no reply.

At the second refuge on his list the door knocker bothered him. It was obviously purpose-made, brass, obscene to some eyes, but he, sort of, understood the iconography. He took a photo of it with his phone to show Howey later, then used it to attract attention. Sounds behind the door told him that people were there, so he waited. He was about to knock again when the door opened and a smart-looking, well made-up woman roughly in her mid thirties with designer glasses waited for him to identify himself. He could see that she'd deduced his profession immediately, it was as though officers of the law weren't infrequent visitors to the establishment, or unexpected. She expertly checked the ID before asking him in. "Sorry for the delay, a guest has an unruly dog that insists on trying to shag the leg of any visitor. I'm sure you appreciate not have that work suit inconveniently stained, Darren".

"Thanks for the consideration er, miss?"

"Yes, come through to the office. Can I assume that one of our guests has been badly behaved somewhere again and that you have come here to discuss it with them?"

"Actually, no, not as far as I know, this is more just a box ticking exercise. I really would appreciate a name".

"Call me Vivienne, then. You came here from Kentville, really, I have people who hail from that neck of the woods and yes, I do ask for some personal details of our guests, I know many such places don't. We're not too formal here, not at all judgemental, but we do offer help, if we can. To do that effectively, we need basic details. I should advise you that there are areas where I will not, or cannot, answer questions about. I'm sorry to lay the rules out like this but it saves time for both of us. Now, what do you want?"

Darren could see that honesty was the best policy here, so he told Vivienne about their search for Juliette Barker, that they needed to speak to her as a matter of urgency and that they were picking their way through the refuge network because they thought she might be in it, somewhere. Vivienne listened intently, she seemed to get it straight away. "You have a photo of this Juliette Barker?" Darren offered the only image he had. Vivienne looked at it for a moment, but her face never changed. "She doesn't look like this now, she has cropped, red hair, various tattoos and calls herself Leslie. The dirty little dog is hers".

"Juliette Barker, she's here, now?"

"Yes".

"How can you be so sure?"

"Because I used to be a sergeant myself, in the Sydney detachment and not so long ago, before I became disenchanted, before you ask. I'll fetch her".

"Be careful, I only told you bits".

"I understand, just give me a moment". Vivienne lifted her leather bag and strode out of the office with purpose, Newell watched as she went through a door that led to the back of the house. He called Howey.

"Where is she now?"

"The manager has gone to fetch her".

"Describe the manager". Newell did.

"Go after her, now!"

Darren stood for a second, 'fuck!' Then he ran through the same door that Vivienne had taken and tripped over a yappy dog. A very short woman with red hair was trying to get hold of it, she was a head shorter that Juliette Barker would be, but Vivienne wasn't. "Where did she go?"

"Vivienne? she went out the back door".

Darren flew out in time to see the white rear lights on a dark saloon come on, it was reversing out of a spot on the other side of a small courtyard, maybe thirty metres away. He ran towards it, but the car sped out and hit him, knocking hm over and onto the loose gravel, then it stopped. For a moment, all he could smell was exhaust fumes and he felt sure that the car was going to reverse over him. Suddenly, the car sped off, showering him in gravel, a piece catching him just above his left eye and causing bleeding. Sprinting back through the house, he dived into his car and went after the saloon, taking a calculated guess which way she'd gone.

The phone went and Darren pressed answer using the hands-free. "Are you ok, what's happening?" It was Howey Cross, sounding frantic.

"In pursuit, call back up. Dark saloon, maybe a Kia, being driven by a smart, dark-haired woman. She's wearing a black business suit, white blouse, pale shoes, heading to the 305".

"Is it her?"

"Yes, sorry, I've got flashing lights behind me". Darren sounded flustered.

"Put yours on then".

"Right, yes, sorry, I took a bit of a whack, not thinking straight, oh shit!"

It looked worse than it was because of the blood already coming from Darren's brow. The airbag was mostly pink, and the officers attending were being sympathetic as they helped him out. Darren had swerved to miss a car pulling out and ended up destroying an innocent roadside tree, a new one, so it had slowed him down and given way before his airbags had joined in the fun. Radios were chattering away, and the car had decided hitting trees wasn't good for it, pumping out steam. Darren's cell phone had a disembodied voice coming out of it as it resided in the passenger footwell. A young officer dug it out and handed it over before moving back a safe distance. "Howey, I lost her, I hit a tree, sorry".

"You're ok though, nothing injured, you're ok?"

"Just a bit shaken up, I might need a rental", which was a bit of an understatement.

The phone went silent, and Darren could picture Howey Cross in his office in a pose he sometimes struck, one of deep thought and concern. In the background the local police radios continued to chatter. Darren's ears were ringing a bit, then he heard the word 'pursuit'. "What's happening?" he asked another officer.

"It looks like they're chasing your person of interest, out on the bypass".

"Take me there, now".

The young officer never even paused. This was way better than attending cars turned over by druggies looking for things to sell, or redneck fights where the beer desensitised what little brain they had. The police car tore through a suburb and soon found the open road. Traffic was light although they could see taillights blinking on some way upfront.

"Darren!" yelled Cross.

"In pursuit with local, Howey, talk to people if you can".

Cross understood and had the head honcho of the Cape Breton detachment on the phone in moments. Oddly enough, he seemed more annoyed that they didn't know that Kentville police had been sniffing around his patch without telling him, than the possibility that they'd get Barker. The mention of Carmel Morrell soon sharpened his senses though, Cape Breton was RCMP, they knew all about her.

Cross tried to tell Darren that he'd smoothed the way, but the phone was dead, no signal, stupid topography. After ten minutes and with the rest of Kentville now crowded around the speaker waiting, Darren's voice came on. "Got her".

CHAPTER TWENTY-THREE

Early October 2022

"Staff Sergeant Cross, we have a match and you said to call as a matter of urgency. I'm sending the information over now". Cross thanked whoever it was from forensics that he was speaking to; he'd not caught the name clearly. The results popped up in his email and he automatically hit print, despite the sign by each printer in the precinct about wasting paper.

Crystal and Darren arrived when summoned, Crystal dragging a chair behind her, it was her turn. Today was going to be a day for answers, but first they needed to know what the right questions were. Despite the economy drive, each officer had a folder with a wad of documentation. Since the re-arrest of Juliette Barker, things had moved on apace. "I suggest we get up to speed with this new information", said Cross, stating the obvious. "Starting with a DNA match, top sheet". This was new.

"Ten-Mile Lake is between Annapolis Royal and Liverpool", said Howey Cross as looks of confusion spread over the faces of his officers. "In September 2018 the remains of a body was found there, a woman. It was a mess; animals had found it sometime before, there wasn't much left, a few bones. We had no DNA match at the time and no head was found either, so no dental. It went unidentified until very recently when something else came to light. Melissa Barker went missing in 2018 and Juliette Barker had a period of treatment, grief counseling, which ended when she moved to Annapolis Royal. The reason we've not found the Barker sister is because she's already dead".

"Do we think Juliette was involved in her sister's disappearance?" asked Crystal, looking to make all the right connections.

"We don't know yet. I need to speak to Watson about that line of questioning. If Juliette flakes out on us, we're not getting anything, I've seen her flick-flack between personalities before. If we can show her that we're trying to find out what happened to her sister, that might keep her with us long enough to piece things together". Cross knew it was dangerous ground and while Juliette Barker was never going to be let out into the wider world again, giving her some eventual peace of mind over her missing sister might be worth it, especially as she believed Melissa was the one behind the crimes she was being charged with. "Darren, are you with us?"

"Sorry. Howey, I was just remembering something. A thought struck me. It says here that Melissa Barker had been driving a Toyota Echo when she went missing, and that they never found the car. I have a mental image, sorry. I'll need to think a while, carry on".

"Wildings, you're thinking the Wilding brothers, right?"

"Yes, remember their place? Wrecks all over, some burnt out. Did we get the details from all of them? I remember that some were so far gone as to be unidentifiable, but I can't remember which ones, we need to see photos".

"Can someone please get me up to speed here?" asked Crystal, who felt she was very much sitting on the outside of the conversation.

"A case in Queens, two brothers raped and killed a number of women over a period of years. The missing women were put down as runaways by local police, but one uncle knew different and killed the Wildlings. It was complicated, you need to read the report", Cross explained. "Ok, Crystal, call up the case files, I'll dig out the number, Darren take a look at the photos and see if you can find an Echo. I need to speak to a shrink about a strategy". Cross felt the case buzz that he got from a murder, it was something missing since he'd downsized to Kentville, as he thought of it.

Watson took just over an hour to get there. He'd cleared his diary after Barker's arrest and the police were being as good as their word in involving him in the interview process from the start. He nodded to people as he walked through to Cross's office, he was on first-name terms with a few now. "Geoff, come in, a development".

"As you hinted when you called. I was coming over anyway for the scheduled interview".

"We now think that Melissa Barker was murdered, sometime in 2018. We got a DNA match to a dead woman and Juliette. It happened before Juliette received treatment for depression and before she moved to Annapolis Royal in 2019, do you think it might have been the catalyst for how she behaved after?"

"Quite possibly", Watson mused. "I can see how Juliette might have compartmentalised her treatment period as being Melissa's breakdown. Does she know yet?"

"No, and this is why I need to know what to ask. I don't want her to clam up or become Melissa, I need Juliette focused".

"You have enough evidence to convict her, even if she can reasonably plead not criminally responsible due to her illness, a plea I will support. Do you need to put her through it?"

"We thought some form of closure for her over Melissa might help her going forward?"

"You mean having found the reason for her psychosis, she might then be able to live a normal, if incarcerated life? My professional instinct says don't go there. Accept the closure of the missing person case but leave Juliette to whatever memories she has".

This wasn't what Cross had expected, he thought Watson would be more detached, more professionally curious. It was true that the missing person case would be marked resolved, but was it right not to tell the only living relative the truth?

"What if she volunteers any information relating to Melissa's murder?"

"How reliable would it be? She's a fantasist, it's part of her illness. Without forensic evidence it would be hard to take anything she gives you seriously. No, I'd say as her psychiatrist and for her own good, steer clear. Get whatever you need from her to close your case then let her live what's left of her life".

"Ok, thanks for that. I'll be in there with her in an hour and I want you in my ears, so I don't misstep. If you want to walk into town and grab some food or something in the meantime, feel free, or there's Miner's Marsh right behind us, a nice head-clearing place to walk. I'll see you later".

Watson mumbled that a walk would do him good and left Cross to it, he called Darren in as the printer behind him spat out a single sheet of paper. "I need you to do something for me, You'll need to involve Constance O'Toole and take forensics. I need to talk to Madam to clear it, but you get underway, and I'll have the warrant by the time you get there. I might be wrong, so here it is in writing if you need it later", and Cross handed Darren a signed sheet with instructions. "Send Crystal in".

When Howey Cross entered the interview room, Juliette Barker stopped chatting to her legal representative who seemed a trifle uncomfortable. Barker did a double take. "Sergeant Cross, how are you? It's so nice to see you again". It could have been two old friends meeting up unexpectedly in a coffee shop.

"I'm very well, thank you Juliette, you're looking well yourself".

"Clean living, more's the pity", and she laughed at her little joke.

Cross was more than surprised at the woman before him. She was sharp, aware, attractive even given the clothing limitations applied by her detention centre. A far cry from the bedraggled creature he'd first seen in Annapolis Royal. In the viewing area, Crystal watched along with Geoffrey Watson, then Carmel arrived. Everyone in the room, including Watson, was in direct contact with Cross via a microphone and earpiece. It was snug in the watching room, Kentville precinct wasn't built to hold a lot of people. They watched in silence.

"Juliette, do you know why you're here?"

"If it's my driving, I'll admit I was going a little fast, but the stinger really wasn't necessary. I saw the flashing lights and was looking for a safe place to pull over".

Howey Cross laid a number of photos on the desk, arranged in a fan shape, they were, as best he could reckon, presented in the order of events. Juliette leant forward and browsed, as if inspecting vegetables in a market. She reached forward and picked up the picture of a young woman, Abigail Smith. "Ah, I see, I suppose you want to know where they all are?"

"That would be a start, Juliette. Now do you know now why you're here?"

"Yes, bad things happened I'm afraid".

"Yes, they did. I'm here to try to unravel them, are you happy to help me with that?"

"Like I said the last time we met, what upstanding citizen wouldn't help the police, although I was sitting down at the time", and she chuckled again. Cross wondered whether any medication was involved. It didn't look like it outwardly, he'd never thought to ask.

"Great, ok then, first of all can we talk about you. We know a bit about your family history, how you and your sister were adopted, but we have gaps, and you know how the police are, we like to fill gaps. Talk to me about college first". In Cross's ear Watson cautioned him to keep Melissa out of the conversation for now. He nodded that he understood.

"College, I loved it, had a great time. I graduated and took up conflict resolution, independently and based online. Customers would contact me, and I'd be able to advise them how to deal with conflicts, industrial at first, you know the sort of thing?"

Cross agreed that he did. "At college did you have relationships?"

"Yes, a few. I was a bit of a gal at times but then I settled down, with Phil. It went ok at first but then he left me for some slut. I was naturally upset, Melissa was too, she quite liked him and was happy for me. It made her quite ill for a while. When I found out that I had a house in Annapolis Royal, things in my life improved".

"Did the improvement last?"

"No, it went downhill a bit after I had an episode, but I got help and came through it. Often that's all we need, a little bit of help". Juliette asked for a coffee, not from Howey Cross or the other officer in the room, but by staring at the large mirror on the wall facing and the faces hidden behind it. Crystal went to arrange for it to happen.

"Do you like the area, Annapolis Royal?" Cross felt it a fairly neutral question, but he could hear Watson draw breath sharply.

"I do, it's an historic town with lots of walks. It gets busy with tourists, but they go off back to their lovely homes and leave us alone. I know I can't go back there; I can't go anywhere anymore. I'm thinking very clearly now Howey, it is Howey, isn't it?"

"Anything else you like about the area?"

"Keji, it's right next door and lovely to explore, honestly, you could get lost in there. Have you enjoyed visiting the bits I took you too?"

"You haven't showed us anything yet, are you willing to, Juliette?"

"Oh, right, yes, sorry. I do love Keji though, it's my favourite park in Nova Scotia".

"Did you ever get to any other parks?"

"Careful", said Watson, he could see that Cross was hoping Juliette would volunteer the information about her sister.

"I have, one local one but I can't go there anymore".

"Why not?"

"There are locks on my door, silly, and I don't like to. I did go back again but I didn't know it was where I was. Once I realised, I got out of there as quickly as I could".

"Staff Sergeant Cross, she's getting agitated, move away from that line of questioning or you'll lose her". Geoffrey Watson wasn't happy. Carmel said nothing, as Cross had requested.

In the interview room, the outer door opened, and Crystal carried in a coffee and a few cookies on a cardboard plate. Juliette took her drink and sipped, then took a cookie. She gave Crystal a small smile of thanks as Cross waited to resume.

"Talk to me about Mary Rose, Juliette".

"Mary, really, I never knew her first name, I always called her Mrs. Rose. She lived locally; I saw her from time to time. She knew my real mom, her name was in her planner, it said 'Mrs. Rose found my planner and returned it' so when she introduced herself to me, I already knew the name. She was sweet".

"Do you know what happened to the planner?"

"I put it in the recycling with virtually everything else, when I found out that my real mom hadn't wanted us. It was in the house in a box full of old photos and papers. Someone had put it in the basement, there's a little room down there, almost a spare room. I found all sorts of bits and pieces from down the years, even a genuine Maudie. I got a good price for that from a dealer, I needed the money". Juliette smiled, a little conspiratorially.

"The house in Annapolis Royal?"

"Yes. I had big plans for that place, but after my episode, my plans got sidetracked. Howey, you seem to be skirting the issue here. If there's something you want from me, ask, and don't worry about the people over there chattering in your ear", and Barker nodded at the mirror. Behind the mirror, Crystal's phone buzzed.

"How long did you live in Annapolis Royal, Juliette?"

"January 2019 until late last year, on and off", she answered, and she smiled again at the mirror.

"Excuse me, bathroom break", said Geoffrey Watson. Crystal stood aside as he left the room.

"Ok, Howey, Watson's gone", said Crystal into his earphone.

"Tell me about Ten-Mile Lake Park, Juliette".

"Finally. You found her, didn't you? She said you would after you and I met last time. Don't look so confused, you must have found Melissa or why else ask about that park? I went there in June 2019, and I remember everything, I assume you'll want details?"

Cross said that he did, and Juliette told them all about tracking down her long-lost sister and arranging a meeting and a picnic in August 2018. She said some men came while she was walking the trail to the meeting place. Juliette saw what one of the men did and fled, she got away because she'd parked in a different part. "I got particularly flaky after that, I felt guilty that I'd not helped but, if I'd tried, they'd have got me too. I never reported her missing, she wasn't, I knew where she was". After a few more details, Cross was ready to wrap it up for the time being but suddenly Juliette asked him to thank Geoff for her. "I'd be a real mess in more ways than one without Geoff", she said and winked.

Cross got to his feet. "We'll talk again later today if you're ok with that, Juliette. Thanks for being so helpful".

Juliette threw Cross a flirty smile, "anytime, Howey".

As Cross made his way back to his office, Carmel stopped him. "I hope you're right about this, Howey".

"Me too", was all he said as he walked past the officer posted outside and entered his office.

"What is this, they said I can't leave, am I under arrest?" Watson was blustering, a show of indignation tailored for the occasion.

"Sit, please. No, you're not under arrest, however, I'd caution you to not try my patience here. We have forensics looking at your flat in Annapolis Royal, the one above your practice. People think they can clean a place very thoroughly, they think redecorating can help too, but if someone has been there any length of time their DNA will also be there. Tell me why you helped Juliette Barker?"

Watson sagged; he didn't have it in him to tough it out. "I thought she was innocent and wanted to help her. When she got out of her confinement she came to me. I was going to call the police, but she pleaded. I was going through a bad patch at home and with my career, I couldn't not help her, she was very persuasive. After that she'd come to me from time to time, spend six weeks or more with me, then go off again for short periods. She isn't a murderer, she isn't responsible".

"Her body is though", said Cross.

"No, I got through, Melissa isn't there anymore, I got through".

"We'll continue this conversation in the interview room. Do you want legal representation?"

"Yes, I think I'd better", said, Watson.

"Hello again". Juliette Barker straightened up in her chair, she completely ignored Crystal. Behind the glass viewing screen Darren watched, making notes, next to him was Kent Chivers, who was back in Kentville temporarily, to learn.

"Hello Juliette, should I call you Juliette? I know you have a number of names", said Cross, looking at her kindly.

"I'm Juliette Barker, but sometimes I'm Melissa Barker. What day is it?"

So much for Watson's insistence that Melissa was gone, thought Cross. "It's Tuesday", he replied.

"I'm Juliette then".

Howey Cross laid the photos on the desk again.

"I'm sorry, I can't help you".

"Who can?"

"You'll need to speak to Melissa", and with that she somehow changed, became more deliberate, her face told them that she wasn't Juliette anymore. "Hello, have we met? You know I think we might have".

It took four full days of gentle questioning to get answers, because some days only Juliette Barker was there, and she was genuinely perplexed. It was only when Melissa showed up, and often not for very long, that they got some answers, not good answers, not for the victims, but answers all the same. And then they were done, or thought they were. Melissa refused to come out, but Juliette asked casually whether they'd like to know a bit more, before telling them about her real mother, and Mrs. Lester. None of it explained the things she saw, or thought she did, only Melissa could do that.

The M on the tree was faded, but they found it because Melissa showed them where it was. "I suppose I should have been a bit more random, but I probably wasn't thinking straight", she said, casually. The digging team found most of what they were looking for.

Howey Cross looked up as Leah Brown wandered in. "Madam is very pleased with you". She placed a bunch of folders on the desk and gave Howey a smile that lacked ambiguity.

"Darren made the capture, he deserves the credit for staying at it, on his own and far from home".

"Have you told him this?"

"I have, certainly. You said Madam was pleased, have you spoken to her personally then? She only seemed relieved when I called".

"She's outside now praising Darren and Crystal; your turn next I expect".

'Oh good', thought Howey, slightly desperately, as he watched Carmel approach.

The door shut and Carmel sat silently for a moment before bursting into tears. Cross instinctively went over and kneeled, holding her, feeling her convulse as she got things out of her system. He held on until she calmed down, stopped sobbing and started to apologise for making his jacket's shoulder wet. "Catching Barker is only the start of the process for me, am I right, Howey?"

"Yes, in as far as we can close a lot of missing person cases, we can also make sure that Juliette Barker is looked after- but she'll never be free from this, Melissa Barker has to be locked up too. My investigation will only deal with the Barker elements, there are no others that I'm intending to include, although I have blanks where other aspects are concerned". He leaned back and then stood up, moving to a chair next to Carmel's. He didn't think that sitting behind his desk was appropriate for this. Carmel dabbed her eyes with a tissue, sniffed and squared her shoulders.

"Ok, well then. I was a young officer in Annapolis Royal. I saw what I thought was a break-in happening and attended, it was the Lester house. It turned out that Muriel Lester had a son, he attacked me.". Carmel started to sniff again; the memory wasn't a favourite one.

"Why didn't you report it at the time?"

"Muriel came back. I knew her, not well, nobody did, but I knew her. She was distraught, she kept her son in the basement, he'd got out. She pleaded with me, and I felt sorry for her, he was all she had. Like I said, I was young. I'd also only just found out that I was pregnant, a bit on the late side to do anything about it, I was always irregular, sorry, you don't need to know that. Anyway, I was pregnant, and I foolishly thought I could be a cop and raise a family, I already knew my own sexuality by then, but I thought I wanted kids and saw it as serendipity".

"Did you speak to anyone?"

"My partner, a new relationship at the time and she didn't want to know after. I was lost, so I went to my sister in BC, had the babies and returned to Nova Scotia when I could, but not to Annapolis Royal. One of the children died of natural causes, it was hard, and I struggled. My sister took in the surviving baby and made a good case for adoption, and I agreed. She was quite firm about the terms. I found that I still had career opportunities and was now in a new relationship, which I didn't want to burden with a child".

"So, you left the child to be raised not knowing who it's mother was?"

"Yes, and I know it sounds cold, but my sister is the fluffy one, or was, and I knew it was right for my daughter. Over the years I asked about her, naturally, and she did well, they said she was brilliant. Once I got back and in uniform I was intending to talk to Graham Lester and his mother, to make sure he wasn't dangerous, to make sure nobody else got attacked. If it had been someone without some self-defence training that he'd attacked, well it had been bothering me for some time what might have happened. I followed it up, but I heard he'd died at sea, his mother was no longer there either, something about a sick relative. I never did find out everything and if I'm honest, I stopped trying, with Graham Lester gone, dead, so had my problem".

"Did you try to contact your daughter after your sister passed?"

"I did, but she was having an unstable time and I shied away, but I always knew where she was, how she was. Being a police officer has its benefits sometimes. Then her life changed, and I thought again about getting involved, but after so long it didn't seem right, and she was happy, stable, safe".

"If it's any consolation I don't think you have anything to regret about things, we're all allowed to make life mistakes, I don't think there's any ramifications for you". Cross was being deliberately conciliatory; he could see that Carmel was distraught.

"There should be though. Had I pressed charges there and then, Graham Lester wouldn't have committed an offence again and Juliette Barker might not be locked up now". Suddenly Madam was Madam again, although her usual immaculate make-up needed attention.

"Not so, according to a professional psychiatrist who has looked at the case, Juliette Barker is a schizophrenic and always has been. Graham Lester could have been charged with his first assault, but you know how it works and the chances are that he wouldn't have been, not over thirty-years ago. Had you made a complaint, it would have tainted you in the eyes of the police service, and I hate to say that, but it was true back then. Thankfully we're getting better at dealing with cases of assault against women and that is because the service has had a strong woman at the helm. Without you, we might still not be taking attacks of women seriously. Your biggest issue now isn't whether reporting Lester's attack on you would have made a difference, it wouldn't, but how to deal with your grown-up daughter, if you intend to. I have the DNA results, Carmel, I haven't told her yet".

Morrell was amazed. Cross seemed so calm, collected and as if discussing some case to which he had no connection, whereas she was on the verge of dropping to bits right in front of him.

"If I choose not to have contact?"

"I'm a staff sergeant in the police service. I do as I'm told, but I also do what is right if asked directly. If you say things stay as they are, then I take confidentiality very seriously, but she'll find you, she will, you don't know her like I do. From my point of view, I get what's left over either way. I have to carry a secret that she will one day find out and I'll have to justify not saying anything, and not saying anything could jeopardise our relationship. If you do decide to be a part of her life, I have that to live with too, both personally and professionally. I'm entirely guided by you in this matter".

"Do you have a preference, a plan?"

"I have two, one for each eventuality".

Driving home had been done on automatic, thankfully the road had been quiet. As he opened the gate, he saw that Crystal was home and that Terence's car was there too. Maybe they were going to be alright after all. The kids were playing with some fuzzy felt. On a green board 'Alcid' was spelt out, next to it was 'Pig'. Moira walked through from the kitchen and held him tightly; it was only then that he realised how much he needed that hug. In his mind, and ever since the conversation with Carmel, he'd wondered whether today would see the defining moment with his Moira happen, would what he had to tell her make her flake out? It might. "Things are afoot, I see. We'll talk later and if you're wondering, 'Alcid' was all Vinnie's work. Pat the kids, feed the pigs, supper in forty-five and then we'll settle down, ok?"

Pigs, yes, he had to feed the pigs. It was a nice evening, he stripped to the waist.

Crystal had been online making notes when she heard the car pull up outside. Quickly closing her laptop and putting the pile of scrap paper covered in names and dates into the kitchen drawer, she waited.

"Sorry it took longer than anticipated again". Terence Ferry had just walked in, he had what Crystal thought of as a certain coldness about him, he usually did after one of his longer trips. "Has work been busy?"

"Yes, very. You should have called me before coming over".

"Oh, yes, sorry. It's not working for you, is it?"

It might as well have been a slap with a hand full of rings, it was impossible for Crystal not to flinch, but she quickly recovered. "No, not at all. Sometimes we're great together, at first, but sometimes isn't enough. I'd say it's not you, but it is, sorry".

Ferry took it all in immediately and Crystal could tell from his expression that her agreeing to finish it wasn't a shock. "If it's any consolation, I made important changes to my work, I don't think I'll need to go out of Nova Scotia for now".

This was a surprise, nothing had been said about the possibility of a near-normal life before, about Terence making her more of a priority, but she'd made her decision, and that was that. The door key sounded excessively loud as Ferry placed it on the kitchen counter, before picking up the key next to it, and they were done. "Good luck, Crystal, I hope you find whatever you are looking for".

Crystal muttered a 'you too', desperately trying not to be a weak female about things, even though her moist eyes were betraying her.

Ferry smiled and left, the door closing ever so quietly. Looking from her kitchen window, Crystal watched as Ferry headed out of her drive and away. She counted to a hundred, then pulled out all her loose sheets. For the next three hours she single-mindedly compiled all the information she had, then she strode over to the farm, knocking, even though both Moira and Howey had insisted that she was family and should just walk in. Howey walked up behind her, he was covered in pig shit and shirtless. "Crystal?"

"Howey, we need to talk".

"Later, give me an hour". Crystal understood.

Howey had never seen Moira so nervous. "If you want to pop a gummy, I won't mind. I know there's a bag in the kitchen cupboard".

"They're Jelly Babies, I got them from the English shop online. The terrors needed to taste what real candy is like". It was quite a snap back.

"Oh, right, sorry. You can still change your mind you know? This has to come from you, you were the one who was abandoned".

"I know, don't think I haven't taken this to pieces and put it back together a hundred times. What will I say to her?"

Cross understood her dilemma, but this had to happen. Moira could never settle if she didn't meet her biological mom at least once. "How about,' hi mom, why did you abandon me to be raised by my loving aunt after having been raped?'"

"Stop it, you make it sound so reasonable and unbelievable all at once. Did you ask her why when you found out?"

"Carmel is my boss; she is the all-powerful one who could break my career. It's not the sort of thing even a Staff Sergeant can do".

"Why, you know she has the hots for you". It was said in a very accusatory way, something he'd never heard Moira do before. "Sorry, that wasn't fair, but you know what I mean".

"Actually, did I mention? She's gay".

Moira started to laugh. "No, you didn't. Ha, one experience with a man and she turns to the furry cup, makes sense".

"There's more to it than that, she'll tell you, I can't because I don't know everything. You only have to be Moira Magowan here, Moira the fully formed woman I pledged to love until forever".

"You're right, I know, but I've never been so nervous in my whole life. Can I ask a favour?"

"Sure".

"Can you look after my Bowie knife for me? It makes my skirt pocket bulge".

Cross laughed, there was still a bit of the real Moira in there, then.

The café was basic, it met a need for coffee and stodge for those that had a gap to fill. Howey stopped outside and waited while Moira gathered her wits. "I'll be three doors down waiting in the car. If I see you running down the street with Carmel's head tucked under your arm, I'll start the car and we'll skip town. The kids are old enough, they can fend for themselves now, agreed?"

Wordlessly Moira got out and walked into the café.

The ride home was conducted in silence, but not a brooding silence, more one of relief. Cross knew that Moira would speak when she was ready and, if not, well he was ok with that. At home, Hinzi was on the porch with the kids. They were doing some sort of complicated hand slapping thing while singing, Darren lazed in a chair nearby. Phoebe stopped when she saw her mom get out the car.

"Anyone for refreshments?", said Moira brightly, "I'll fetch lemonade and cake", and she bent down, stroking Phoebe's hair before scuttling off.

"Is she ok?" asked Hinzi, surprised that they were back so soon. Cross shrugged; he had nothing else to offer.

"She's ok", said Phoebe, "she'll be fine now".

Moira came back looking a bit happier, but her eyes still showed some of the strain. She handed round the treats before dropping into her favourite lawn chair. "I know you're all worried about me and want to know details, but there's not a lot to know. Today I met a woman who is my mother, but we have no connection, just blood. She chose a path that she could live with, I think I understand. My sister was a cot death, unexplained, it happens. Now I know a little more about her but she'd barely had a life so there isn't much. I'll mourn and celebrate her on my birthday but there'll be no sadness, it's just life".

Moira took a moment to compose herself, Howey could see that it still had a raw edge to it, despite the brave face.

"I have a life here, my mother has a life where she lives, we have Howey as the common denominator. She is career driven for reasons she explained as best she could, I have my family, all my family right here.

Sorry kids, there isn't going to be a new grandmother in your lives. I talked, she talked, and it all made perfect sense. I know who I am now, I know who my sister was but not what she might have been, and I know how we came to be. Sorry to disappoint".

Howey inwardly breathed a sigh of relief. He wasn't sure how much Carmel might tell her, it sounded like she'd told her almost everything and that was good, if not entirely palatable.

"Dancing?" said Howey in an exaggerated voice, before finding himself pelted with cake from all quarters.

It was pitch black outside, a proactive choice to help migrating birds and busy moths. If the moment been in a movie, a distant owl would be hooting, but this wasn't a movie, this was real life. If you looked hard inside the farmhouse, you could see a faint glow emanating from the kids' room where a nightlight gave off a few comforting rays. On the porch of the farm, two people sat, embracing. Nothing had been said for a while, the only sounds coming from the very occasional car that went past their distant gate and the odd Spring Peeper that had got the dates wrong.

"If I wanted to stay here and wait for the sunrise, would you wait with me?"

"Yes, if you made a good case for it".

"Good answer, Howey. I feel sorry for Juliette Barker, she had possibilities but a little flip of a switch in her head and events beyond her control condemned her to a difficult life. Did our similarities scare you?"

"Terrified me, but I work best that way, fear motivates me, it always has. You might see similarities with Barker, but I see huge differences. The only similarities for me are the geography and being one of twins. Was a father mentioned?"

"A party, some guy, a drunk mistake and she thinks a bit of bad luck in the rubber department. It would have been nice to know but it's not that relevant, not now, not after all these years. I know you've been watching me carefully over this; looking for signs, you have since we got together. I can promise you that I don't have anyone else but me in this head, despite my personas. I won't say that I'm sane, different, yes, but sanity is overrated in my opinion. Sanity gives us people who walk away because it's the best course of action for them. It hurts that I can't feel empathy with Carmel, but I do understand the sanity of her choices. I do feel some empathy for Juliette, but I'm not mad you know".

"I know, you told me not long ago".

"I did, when? I don't remember".

"Never mind, I do".

It was idyllic sitting on the porch, bathing in the moment, but then the skies opened, and lightning started hitting distant spots and it was time to go to bed. The sun would rise whether they waited for it or not but, with this being Nova Scotia, it was fifty-fifty whether they'd be able to see it for the rain clouds or the fog.

"Ma'am", said Howey Cross as Carmel Morrell knocked on his open door. She walked in, closed the door and took a seat.

"Can we put this one to bed now, Howey?" There was a tone in Carmel's voice that said that she was glad it was all over and, while finding things out hadn't been as joyous as it might be, the world hadn't ended as she once feared it might.

"My report is finished; I haven't sent it yet".

"So, the Barker story, do me a breakdown. Actually, no, go further back".

Cross had anticipated something like this, he'd written it down to get it right, it was that complicated.

"We believe that Melissa Rylance was raped by Graham Lester. We also believe that Rylance killed Graham Lester and also killed Muriel Lester, two unidentified bodies were in the same general area that Juliette Barker took us to, we presume them to be the Lesters. Melissa Rylance went missing after giving birth to twin girls. She remains missing.".

Carmel looked pale and Cross knew that she was thinking back to dark days.

"The daughters were to be fostered together, but they ended up being separated, Juliette was raised by Elaine Barker. Juliette tracked down Melissa and arranged to meet at Ten-Mile-Lake where she said she saw her sister raped and killed by two men, possibly the Wilding brothers. That sent her over the edge".

"Darren did well, picking up on the car there", said Carmel sadly. The Wilding case had taken its toll on much of the police services in Nova Scotia.

Cross continued. "Juliette Barker moved to Annapolis Royal alone after the trauma of her sister's unreported death. Phil Kendrick was never with her there. We've not got him yet though; we may never find him. The children she was supposed to be looking after in that house appear to be figments of her imagination, too. Barker, in one of her sane periods, understood that she needed help and went to Watson, who tried but failed to help her. Later she sank into a pit of destitution and despair as her demons caught up with her. Shall I continue?"

Carmel nodded. It was all beginning to make some sort of twisted sense.

"The shallow grave at Keji also held the body of Abigail Smith, a local girl who Barker killed, believing that she was having an affair with Phil Kendrick, her parents believed it too when told so by Barker. It seems that Abigail Smith was a bit of a rebel due to her parents' fundamentalism and tight control of her. They even gave Abigail's college fund to Barker, out of guilt at her perceived behaviour. We also found several cats and a dog in the burial area; they were close to the graves we believe are the Lester's. She's admitted to killing a restaurant owner, Angelo Jones, at Point Prim. He's alive but we do have a missing person, a dog walker and, from his description, he's not that dissimilar to Jones. He was reported missing when his dog went home alone. At the time it was presumed he'd slipped and ended up in the ocean, we can't prove anything either way".

"And earlier?"

"We also think she may have killed Robert Tambling, a Dartmouth man who was questioned about an assault on Juliette but released without charge. Old flat mates, Isobelle Fisher and Melissa West are also missing, possibly dead at Barker's hand. Her new psychiatrist, Tina Peck, knows what we need and will keep asking. We can't find her adoptive mother anywhere, but she wasn't included in Barker's statement, she would only refer us to Melissa. Tina has reluctantly recommended hypnosis as a way of bringing Melissa back to the table, and of getting more from Juliette".

"Do you think it's a good idea?"

"I think that Melissa is the devious one and I wouldn't believe anything she said as that persona. Juliette is also talking about a missing woman that she found documents for inside the house, possibly a relative of Muriel Lester. It might be a fantasy, some of her claims clearly are, but I've sent a team in to look. Constance is running the search".

Carmel nodded again, it was a lot to take in; Cross had a good point regarding the Melissa Barker persona, who would be best kept out of things, given her history. "Anything else?" she asked.

"Darren found the bench that was Barker's safe place at French Basin, it had a stolen plaque from the Annapolis Botanical Gardens on it. A search behind it found a bag with a crucifix belonging to Abigail Smith and a St Christopher, which we have yet to identify the owner of. We might get something on that when we show it to Juliette".

"I suppose I should feel lucky that mine turned out ok", said Carmel, sadly.

"Yes, and with that in mind you're invited to supper, if you have a window".

"I'll say no, but please thank Moira. It gets too complicated, I might have to get someone to discipline you, one day", and Carmel made a small laugh. Cross wasn't surprised that she'd rejected the olive branch, in offering it, Moira had predicted the same.

"No problem, if you ever change your mind, the invitation remains open. That about wraps up what we have. We know that Barker was in and out of Annapolis Royal after escaping custody, Watson took her in. She also moved around the refuge system, sometimes taking short-term employment in various seasonal posts. A list is appended, we have gaps, but I don't think that matters now".

Carmel read the cheat sheet Cross had prepared again. "Good work by everyone, it was a difficult case for many reasons. I've decided to retire when I'm sixty, so you and the rest of the contenders have a few years yet to keep shining. Tiff is back shortly; she's leaving her current refuge today. Sorry for stealing her like that but it did give us a few snippets".

Cross wasn't going to complain. "Geoffrey Watson, what is going to happen there?"

"He'll be charged with perverting the course of justice and anything else we can think of. He won't serve a custodial sentence, but he's ruined, professionally".

"Should we regard him as a victim too?" Cross tried to sound detached, but he felt played by Watson.

"A generous thought but no, he knew what he was doing. You know that she's pregnant, yes?"

"Yes, I know. And the child, when Juliette gives birth, are we presuming it's his?"

"One bridge at a time, Howey", said Carmel trying to read his mind, she knew that there would be more twists and turns in the case yet.

"On another matter, do you mind if I call Darren and Crystal in, Ma'am?"

Carmel clearly hadn't been expecting this, but she agreed.

Howey opened the door and nodded to his sergeants, who both headed in, closing the door after them.

"Ma'am".

"Ma'am".

"Something to tell me?" asked Carmel, with a quizzical look.

Crystal opened a folder and pulled out a number of printed eBird checklists, then she unfolded a map onto Cross's desk. It wasn't a map of Nova Scotia; it had half a dozen scattered red dots on it.

"What's this?"

"Ma'am, I think you might want to talk to your colleagues in Ontario". Just then a tap at the door had Leah sticking her head in. "Howey, Ma'am, Tiff just came in, she's got someone with her, someone who came with her voluntarily and who you'll want to talk to".

"Who?" asked Cross, a bit annoyed at the disturbance, given the gravity of the subject they'd been discussing.

"Melissa Rylance, Juliette's Barker's sister, she's in the interview room now. With her sister safely in custody, she wants to tell you all about it".

Carmel, Darren and Crystal looked at each other, in surprise.

"Right", said Howey, and he went to work.

Across the table in their little interview room sat a dark-haired version of Juliette Barker, at least as far as Melissa Rylance's unsettling disposition was concerned. On the desk in front of her sat two planners, of the sort people used before smart phones came along. They had a different story to tell.

Crystal and Darren carried out the interview, a process watched by Cross and Tiff, but not Carmel who had places to be. When presented with the poor photo of the woman from The Orchard, the one Moira had had a bad feeling about, Rylance confirmed that it was her before apologising for not coming forward sooner. "I was pretty scared".

Methodically, they went through times and dates, places and people. The planners told the story of their mother, also called Melissa and of how she was raped by Graham Lester and how Mrs. Lester had taken him away to a relative described in the planner only as 'Vivienne". It said, in their mother's hand, how Mrs. Lester had said the house was hers and that she was never coming back. The bodies in Keji suggested otherwise.

It took well over two hours but, if everything checked out, they'd finally have all the sky and all of the faces of the people in what was a very complicated jigsaw. All the information had been freely volunteered by Melissa Rylance, including how her crazy sister had contacted her and her birth mother, how she'd backed out of the picnic after speaking to Juliette on the phone, but she assumed that their mother had gone ahead with it.

"Just one last question, Melissa", said Crystal. "The planners, your mother's planners, how did you get hold of them?"

"Ah yes, well, you know that the house in Annapolis was supposed to be for both of us? It was in Mom's will".

"Yes", said Darren. "It was being rented out for most of the time".

"Well, I did visit, just once, when it was empty before Juliette moved in. There were boxes of papers in the basement, in a sort of spare room. I was looking for information about Mom, anything really. I found the planners there and decided to keep hold of them. They were in Mom's handwriting, something she'd used personally, it was a connection".

Darren nodded. "It's just that we understand that Juliette also saw the planners when she lived in the house, but she can't have if you had them".

"Oh, I see. Well, I only took a couple, I left the rest. I was already thinking I'd have to move, fast and light. Juliette was getting scary, even then". Melissa sat back from the table; her hands folded neatly in front of her. It all made sense.

When the interview finished, Howey Cross entered the room. People now had things to do, a story to research, he sat. "Forgive me, Melissa, but your face is familiar, have we met?"

Rylance laughed. "Yes, Howey. It was when you worked out of Halifax, we met in a bar one evening and got chatting. I gave you my number, but you never called".

"Oh, I'm sorry, I don't remember".

"I do, sadly I'm blessed with the sort of memory that never forgets a thing. Say hello to Moira for me and tell her that the book ending is exactly what

I hoped it would be, she'll know what I mean". Cross said that he would, but he didn't really know what book she was referring to.

"Will you visit your sister? she's not coming out you know".

Melissa Rylance did the smile again. "No, I don't think so, besides, I have a partner out west, Gerry, I'd like to spend some time with him".

"Please don't go missing again until we've finished everything".

"Tiff knows how to find me, but I've told you everything I know, it's time this thing finished".

In Howey's office, four officers debated what to do next. "Do we have anything we can charge her with?" asked Tiff.

Cross had to admit that Melissa Rylance was only guilty of keeping out of the way, not a crime, and there was no hint of anything else, she'd checked out clean. Juliette had now also admitted to killing Mrs. Rose, there was nothing more there to pursue.

"So, what about the body in the park? It's obviously not Juliette's sister", said Darren.

"I'll talk to the lab, but I presume that there's enough similarity between mother and daughter DNA that it's probably the mother. I'm doubting that the Wildings were even involved", Cross answered.

"Wow" said Tiff, "what a first case. Is it always like this around here?"

"No", said Cross.

"No", said Crystal.

"It has its moments", said Darren.

Crystal walked around the back of the farm, following the noise. On the patio, the Cross clan were having a water fight using old washing up liquid bottles, Howey appeared to be losing, judging by how wet through he was. "Grab a bottle, I filled one for you", spluttered Moira as a squirt from Vinnie hit her square in her face.

"Not stopping, got a hot date", yelled Crystal above the noise. "I'm just dropping this off".

Moira stopped what she was doing, and the rest followed suit. Crystal extended her arm and offered an old leather bag to Moira. "Forensics dropped this off at the precinct earlier, they said it was for you".

Moira took the bag and Crystal beat a hasty retreat; she didn't trust Phoebe not to give her a covert squirt. Moira looked the bag over, then inside, it was empty.

"You ok?" asked Howey, looking a bit concerned.

"Yes, fine. This isn't my bag, I got mine back from The Orchard. This is nice though, I'm in two minds about whether to keep it".

Three jets of water hit her right where cold water might best make you jump.

CHAPTER TWENTY-FOUR

24th October 2022

Howey Cross drove the track home; it had been a long and difficult day. Both gates had been left open again, so he'd dutifully climbed out of the car, checked that they were working properly and shut them behind him. As he approached the house, heavy clouds promised rain later. The farm seemed quiet, subdued, even the animals knew that rain was on the way.

When he got to the door, he could see it wasn't latched shut. It often wasn't, so he pushed it open and everywhere was red. What had Moira done this time? The door opened wide, and he could see someone who looked like Moira from behind, a little bit skinnier perhaps. The person turned and Cross was surprised to see that it was Melissa Rylance, it took a moment to take in. "Howey, all sorted, we can be together now. I knew when we met in the bar all those years ago that we'd hit it off, some day", she said. Melissa then smiled and slipped her dress off, letting it fall around her ankles.

"What happened?"

"I know you've always liked me, so I did some handiwork around the place. You know how handy I can be, or perhaps you don't. Now you can enjoy me and my body without worrying whether you're betraying someone. Do you like my body, will it do?"

"What happened here?"

"Oh, this, I suppose we can tidy up later, after, although it might be wise not to stick around long. People will talk, they always do".

"I don't understand", said Cross tasting blood in the air for the first time, he knew that he was in shock.

"Sorry, Howey, I thought you'd like the changes. It's too late to change back I'm afraid, it's all been a bit final for those involved. I hope you're not going to disappoint me; I hate being disappointed, it can bring out my dark side".

"Howey, I heard a noise". Moira was wide awake and shaking him. Cross was out of bed in seconds and running down the stairs two at a time. A shadow dashed across from the kitchen heading for the front door, he grabbed it, threw it to the ground and started to pummel the body with both fists, ignoring the screams. "Howey, stop! Enough".

On the floor the body was still. Moira feared the worst, then it groaned and coughed. The lights went on, the burglar was probably mid-twenties, it was hard to tell. Cross went to put him in the recovery position, the burglar whimpered like a dog, expecting more punishment from an angry master.

"Howey, we need to call an ambulance". From the kids' room came the sound of crying, the kids never cried.

Cross looked down at his hands, they were bloody, three knuckles were split and bleeding profusely. The kid wasn't moving much, he'd been beaten senseless, beaten not far short of being dead. Moira came back, the kids were still grizzling, they'd heard the screaming from daddy and didn't like it at all. "I called Crystal, she's coming over".

From behind the window, Carmel looked on, but her face gave nothing away. In the interview room, an officer seconded from Halifax was setting things up, not making direct eye contact with Howey Cross, a second officer waited patiently. "Interview taking place in Kentville Precinct Kings County on 25th October 2022, nine twenty-two, am. Sergeant Ramsey Willox and Constable Cameron Lewis attending. For the tape can you please confirm your name".

"Howard Edward Cross, but I prefer Howey".

"And do you know why you're here Howey...?"

MEET THE AUTHOR

English by birth, Canadian by choice, Mark Dennis has done many things during his life. Working in a warehouse, motor mechanic, trailer builder, sample management guru in a pharmaceutical research facility and, his dream job, Warden of a Country Park. Through it all he has always been an avid birder, never happier than when outdoors and scanning the bushes or staring at the sea. Spending many hours behind a keyboard writing complex novels may be considered counter-intuitive, but he does sit right by a picture window and always has his binoculars handy for regular scans of the yard.

As well as the Nova Scotia Birder Mystery novels, he also writes a murder-mystery series set in his old hometown of Nottingham, a fantasy science fiction series, a number of birding memoirs, travelogues (with Sandra) of their birding adventures and some useful site guides for birding in South-west Nova Scotia. A recent novel, and a subject quite close to his heart, is a dystopian near-future story of what might happen when the climate change waters rise, titled 'Survivor'. Busy Guy!

Mark lives on Cape Sable Island, Nova Scotia-the very same 'Cape Island' mentioned in the Nova Scotia Birder Mystery novels- with his wife, Sandra. He still gets a shiver of anticipation every time he crosses the causeway from the mainland to their island home because you never know what might be there!

For more information about birding on the island, see Mark's blog at https://capesablebirding.wordpress.com.

For more on his books and other writing, see https://markdennisbooks.wordpress.com.

A Note on Images

Cover photo: Baccaro Light, Shelburne County, Nova Scotia, by Sandra Dennis. Sky and dead bird images are royalty-free photos from Pixabay, with thanks to the photographers.

Chapter headings: Collared Pratincole images are copyright free or public domain, from Wikimedia Commons.

Section Dividers: all raptor images are from photographs taken in Nova Scotia by Mark Dennis.

Author photograph by Sandra Dennis.

FICTION BY MARK DENNIS

The Howey Cross Nova Scotia Birder Mysteries

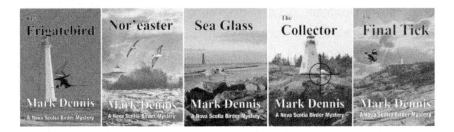

The Frigatebird

When a notorious birder is found dead, a list of suspects is already available on-line, if you know where to look. In the world of the birder, there are two major sins: Stringing and Suppression. But are they major enough to kill for? Well, maybe...

Sergeant Howey Cross juggles his expanding caseload whilst attempting to solve a baffling murder in a community that's all new to him. He even has to learn 'Birder-speak'; otherwise how else will he know what on earth is going on?

Nor'easter

Howey Cross investigates the disappearance of a number of young women from Queens County, even though it is outside his jurisdiction. So, what is his connection? Will he get to the culprits before someone else does?

Complications include his new girlfriend, who he describes as 'nuts', and she cheerfully agrees. Life with her is never dull, but can she settle for being an appropriate partner for a cop?

On top of the crimes and frolics, there's a storm coming, the largest ever recorded. However, the tail might be even more dangerous, it might bring the dreaded Nor'easter.

Sea Glass

Sergeant Howey Cross investigates a cold case, as a favour for his boss, Gordy Cole. It's all a bit on the Q.T., hush-hush, off-the-record, but a police officer was seriously hurt. It needs sorting out and Cole is sure that Cross is just the man to do it.

Life has changed for Howey. He and his 'mad' partner, Moira, now have twin babies, called the 'Terrors' because the responsibility of new fatherhood is truly terrifying. He is torn between pursuing his career in Halifax or heading off at a tangent and taking a job in Kings County. Birds appear, conundrums need to be solved and Howey Cross finds that life is no longer the relatively simple affair it once was.

The Collector

Howey Cross is at something of a crossroads in his life. Two young children, a new home and job, and now his partner, Moira, is seriously ill in hospital. How can he keep his family on an even keel and still manage to make his mark in the Kentville police? Luckily, he has good friends in Darren, Hinzi and the Nova Scotia Birders, who are always ready to help.

There is a sinister undercurrent in the birding world. Rare birds are disappearing from their find sites, more precipitately than might be expected. Then there are the 'Friday Birds', rarities that always seem to disappear before the weekend birders can see them. Is it just a coincidence or is there a Collector operating in the province? And can the projected Wildlife Crime Unit actually be established and get the backup needed to make a difference?

The Final Tick

Hunters die. Are the deaths accidents or something more sinister?

Howey Cross is bored. Kentville is quieter than Halifax but he's not getting any good cases to work on-is that on purpose? His promised promotion has been delayed, maybe indefinitely. Then he gets the hunter death 'cold cases', apparently passed down by the Big Boss. Is this a legitimate inquiry, or is he being set up to fail?

At home, Moira is feeling tied down. This might be the life she had always dreamed of, but has it also turned her from 'weird dingbat' to 'sensible mom'?

The Magowan-Cross household is definitely due a shake-up. The question is, will it be a temporary change or something more profound?

The D.I. Thompson Nottingham Mystery Series

Coldhearted

Laboratories are safe, or so you'd think. Not this one, not for Marie-Eve Legault. Is her death a crime of passion, a revenge attack or has the 'Mafia' come to call?

Far from her Montreal home, alone in a foreign land, Marie-Eve meets a chilly end. Detective Sergeant Dave Thompson is trying to solve the case, but can he unravel the mystery while dealing with events on two continents? Not to mention coping with a nutty boss, a pregnant girlfriend and an overwhelming urge to be an author.

On The Fly

There is more to becoming a Detective Inspector than being a good cop. That's why getting there is such a rocky road.

When Dave Thompson's grouchy old D.I., Jock Charnley, retires. Thompson steps up and finds he has more than enough tidying up to keep him busy. His team squabbles, 'Fiery' Marie Burns, his D.C.I. and probation mentor, keeps him on his toes, and a chance discovery means that transition is less than smooth. Oh, and Charnley won't go away, either.

Then a body is found on a local nature reserve. Solving this is where he'll earn his real D.I.'s spurs.

Spiked

Dave Thompson is feeling the strain. At home he feels cramped, at work he feels put upon, in his head he's struggling to decide what is right and what is wrong in his life - and his workload keeps getting heavier.

When a sports teacher at the private Whitaker School for Boys is found dead, and in rather grizzly circumstances, he gets the case, and it turns out to be a pretty tangled web of lies and intrigue. Things about the case might appear a little complicated, especially the 'Old Boys Network', but, given time, Thompson will get there. Probably.

It might help if his acting-Detective Sergeant stopped saying 'righty-ho' all the time, though – that sort of thing could try anyone's patience.

Wet Bones

Human skulls keep being pulled out of Colwick Lake. Do these wet bones indicate a psychopathic serial killer on the loose? Is there a coven of Witches active in Netherfield, practicing Black Magic rituals on the park at night? Frankly, anything is possible in Netherfield, but it is down to D.I. Thompson and his team to dig out the truth.

Things are not rosy in Thompson's life. His previously happy home is turning sour, and he doesn't really know why. The new 'super' team isn't really gelling, and Superintendent Perkins is getting ever more weird-if that is possible. He really needs his detectives to step up to the mark. Can he trust them all to do so?

Oh, and the Garibaldi-clad heroes are still stuck down in the Championship-sleeping giants, indeed.

Lamb's Tail

Dave Thompson is happy-well, mostly. Admittedly, his team of detectives could be more settled, Superintendent Marie Burns less flaky and the Assistant Chief Constable not quite such an arse, but he's coping with it all. As long as he has Jenny to go home to, everything is good.

That's not to say that Nottingham isn't keeping him busy. There's a trio of nasty deaths to investigate, which will definitely stretch his team. The local crime bosses look to be getting antsy, too, and there seems to be an influx of Eastern Europeans, muddying the waters. Complicated times are coming.

Just don't start singing 'Great Balls of Fire' in his vicinity. Not, that is, if you value your own…

Dystopian Near-Future

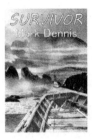

Survivor

The world is changing, and not in a good way.

Climate change is accelerating, sea levels are rising, but people still have their heads lodged firmly in the sand, or worse. Maritime Canada is drowning, civilization is disintegrating, and it is every man for himself.

Can an ordinary man survive the maelstrom? Does he even want to? Being a survivor in this new world order may take more than he is willing to give.

The Harvesters' Galaxy Series

The Harvesters

Kerry Peters lives an ordinary life in Corner Brook, Newfoundland. She likes a beer and, sometimes, the company of her boyfriend Gary, although she is sure that he's not the one.

After a heavy night of drinking, she wakes up in Transit, naked. The staff there tell here they've sorted out her little problems and that she's ready to go on, but 'go on' where, exactly? Kerry didn't know it but she's one of the Harvested and, after that fateful night, nothing is going to be the same. Not for Kerry or for anyone.

The Elementals

Kerry Peters is dead-but you can't keep a Newfie down for long. Although she was cheated out of her fated role as Ruler of the Galaxy, due to the aforementioned 'dead' thing, she is not destined to enjoy her eternal rest. No, Bernice has other plans and needs Kerry's help.

Kerry awakes once again in Transit-it seems strangely familiar. The Harvesters' Galaxy is under threat, an evil force has taken control and whole planets are being destroyed. Someone needs to attract the attention of The Elementals, the beings who set the whole thing up in the first place and get them onside. Who better to do so than a former Ruler of the Galaxy…?

Comic Fantasy

War and Peas

Best described as alternative history, or maybe not, War and Peas tells the tale of the battle for legume supremacy in Eastern England in the early 1970s. It is a complicated tale of love, honour, loyalty and flares. Things were different back then. People knew what to expect from life; a forty-hour week, beer on the weekend, and two weeks in a caravan on the coast and all that might bring. If you were lucky, you would end up in Mablethorpe, Jewel of East Lindsey, with its exotic pubs, endless sands, donkeys and mushy peas-truly, heaven is a place on Earth.

But Heaven is under threat from evildoers from the west. The Men of the Parched are on the march and the Podsters of the Mushy Pea must fight to uphold the supremacy of the one true pea. Life, in Mablethorpe and in England, may never be the same again.

NON-FICTION

Birding Memoirs

Going For Broke

1984 in the UK- 'Big Brother', the Libyan Embassy siege, Band Aid, the launch of the Apple Mac and the start of the Miner's Strike. None of it matters when a birding Big Year is in sight. In the days of no mobile phones, no pagers and no dial-up 'Birdline', all rare bird information has to be obtained by phoning a little café in Norfolk and hoping one of the customers will pick up...

A young birder on a shoestring finds his way the length and breadth of Britain, finding birds and maxxing out the credit card. He really is 'going for broke'.

Twitching Times

Mark Dennis started birding in the UK as a child, but he really started twitching, going for rare birds, in 1981. From then to 2003, when he left the UK and moved to Canada, he birded his local patch, his county (Nottinghamshire), and the UK, going to see rare birds when he could. Here are his birding memories- lifers, memorable birds, occasions and people, and an entertaining swing through the UK birding scene.

Park Life

Colwick Country Park-a haven of peace and tranquility in the midst of the urban sprawl. Well, maybe…

Mark Dennis spent 15 years as a warden at Colwick, the best years of his working life. It was a dream job for an avid birder and naturalist-essentially spending most of his waking hours on his own local patch and being paid to do so. However, there were downsides, the 'members of the public' who also shared the space.

Dog walkers, anglers, boaters, 'twoccers', even a murder…they all made sure that there was never a dull moment for a busy warden. Still, there were also birds. Butterflies, dragonflies to fill the quiet times. Not that it stayed quiet when a national rarity turned up…

The Seven Year Twitch

'Relentless in the pursuit of birds'. That was the lighthearted claim of Mark Dennis on his arrival in Nova Scotia in 2015. To be fair, a new province, alive with birding possibilities, would take some learning, and what better way to learn than through twitching? Living on Cape Sable Island, in the south of the province, birds were found everywhere, and it didn't take long before Nova Scotia, and even Canada, ticks were presenting themselves for appreciation and admiration.

Further afield, twitches were undertaken to the furthest reaches of the province, seeing both new birds and new places. Some were undoubtedly a bit mad, but that was all part of the fun. Seven years on, the fun, and the birding, in the beautiful province of Nova Scotia, still bewitches-and the ticks keep on coming.

Hold My Limpkin

2023-an excellent year of birding in Nova Scotia. It started well with a Common Gull on January 1st, maybe not all that exciting in the general scheme of thing but a Cape Sable Island tick, and they are important. Then it got better and better. 'There's a WHAT?' became a regular cry as Common Ringed Plover, Grey-crowned Rosy-Finch, Brambling, Limpkin, Eared Grebe, Vermilion Flycatcher, Tundra bean Goose and Black-throated Grey Warbler all appeared to delight the twitchers.

What's next, I wonder? HANG ON. WHAT'S THAT?

HERE, HOLD MY LIMPKIN…

Birding Site Guides

Cape Sable Island-a Birding Site Guide

Cape Sable Island juts out into the Atlantic Ocean at the very tip of Nova Scotia. The island is joined to the mainland via a causeway and there the magic begins. For the birder, Cape Island is a must-see place in Canada. Whatever season you choose to visit, there will be birds. During fall migration, there are masses of shorebirds. In winter the wharves are loaded with gulls and alcids haunt sheltered spots. Spring brings the only Canadian American Oystercatchers and summer, the nesting Piping Plovers. Come when you like, and Cape Island's birds will be waiting.

Yarmouth Birding-a Site Guide

The county of Yarmouth offers some of the finest birding in Nova Scotia. Located at the extreme south-west of the province, birds migrating north in spring often make their first land-fall there, while fall birds migrating south can accumulate in considerable numbers at the various birding hotspots found in and around the town of Yarmouth.

This guide is designed to help the visitor find the sites. Finding the birds is a different thing altogether, but if you go to the right places at the right time you stand every chance. If you are planning a quick visit or a leisurely weekend of birding, this guide will prove invaluable in making your birding trip a success.

The Australian Birding Adventure-with Sandra Dennis

Bimbling Round Brisbane

Cruising Round Cairns

Meandering Round Melbourne

Birding Travelogues-with Sandra Dennis

Yucatan-Birding the Land of the Maya

Three Trips to Costa Rica

Cuba - ¿Que Bola?

Panama - Canal to Coast

Down Mexico Way

Ecuador - Andes and Amazon

Isla Margarita-*Venezuela Light*

Northern Belize

Que Giro! - Brazil

Egypt - Ancient and Modern

Another World - Travels in North America

Back in the US of A - Family Travels in North America

Birdin' USA - More Travels in North America

Alberta-Prairies and Mountains

Printed in Great Britain
by Amazon